'Because the company are so pleased with the way the teashops have been doing, not only in London but up and down the whole country, they have hit on the idea to have more posh places in the West End. They will be ever so grand an' they'll be known as Corner Houses. What d'yer think of that?'

'Did it say anything about staff?' Becky queried.

Ella raised her head and prodded Becky, 'Yes, I'm coming t' that. There was a picture of a waitress, dressed in . . . well you know, the usual black dress and white apron only somehow the girl looked different and above the illustration it said, "The perfect Nippy".'

'Why Nippy?'

'I dunno, do I. It also said it was going to advertise on hoardings an' buses in the city with messages like, "Let Nippy take care of you" and "Lunch at Lyons".'

Also by Elizabeth Waite:

Nippy

Elizabeth Waite

WARNER BOOKS

A *Warner* Book

First published in Great Britain in 1997
by Little, Brown and Company
This edition published by Warner Books in 1998
Reprinted 2000

Copyright © Elizabeth Waite 1997

The moral right of the author has been asserted.

Frontispiece 'The Perfect Nippy' reproduced by kind
permission of the Greater London Record Office

A CIP catalogue record for this book
is available from the British Library.

ISBN 0 7515 2047 0

Typeset in Bembo by
Palimpsest Book Production Limited,
Polmont, Stirlingshire
Printed and bound in Great Britain by
Clays Ltd, St Ives plc

Warner Books
A Division of
Little, Brown and Company (UK)
Brettenham House
Lancaster Place
London WC2E 7EN

Acknowledgements

I would like to say thank you to a few people who helped and encouraged me to write this book. Firstly to Alan Samson, from Little, Brown and Darley Anderson, my agent. I hope I have justified their faith in me.

Mr Y.A. Walker, Information Manager for J. Lyons & Company for his information and references about Nippies.

Peter Bird, who so generously sent me copies of articles he had written for *Choice* magazine, entitled 'The Tea Shop Story'.

Elsie Pickering, and her daughter Molly, who took the time and trouble to do some research for me even though they had only met me briefly.

My Yorkshire friends, Peter and Norma Cooke, who never fail to be there when I need them.

My dear friend Audrey Bolton, who shared her nostalgic memories with me. And last but by no means least, Pat Pizzie, Sales Manager for Mills & Boon, who started the ball rolling and gave me a 'crazy' day out in London.

The PERFECT NIPPY

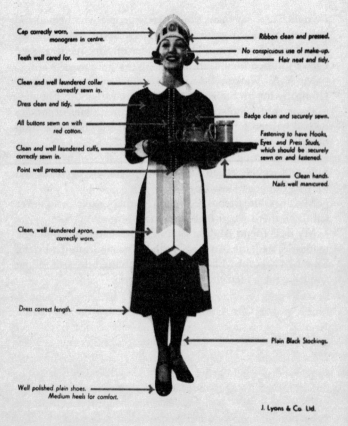

Cap correctly worn, monogram in centre.

Ribbon clean and pressed.

No conspicuous use of make-up.

Teeth well cared for.

Hair neat and tidy.

Clean and well laundered collar correctly sewn in.

Dress clean and tidy.

All buttons sewn on with red cotton.

Badge clean and securely sewn.

Fastening to have Hooks, Eyes and Press Studs, which should be securely sewn on and fastened.

Clean and well laundered cuffs, correctly sewn in.

Point well pressed.

Clean hands.
Nails well manicured.

Clean, well laundered apron, correctly worn.

Dress correct length.

Plain Black Stockings.

Well polished plain shoes.
Medium heels for comfort.

J. Lyons & Co. Ltd.

Chapter One

The Summer of 1920

MISS MACFARLANE, HEADMISTRESS of Malden East girls' school, stood in the playground with the hot tarmac burning her feet as she watched her girls disperse for the long summer holiday.

Her eyes were focused on two girls in particular and there was one thought uppermost in her mind. 'The good ones should always be rewarded, the bad ones get their just deserts.'

If life were really like that then Rebecca Russell and Eleanor James should have a long and happy life.

Miss MacFarlane smiled to herself. Those two were a perfect foil for each other. Rebecca so dark yet with pale, creamy skin, her eyes a rich, deep brown. Eleanor fair with rosy cheeks and deep blue eyes that twinkled in a strong-featured face, her skin turned golden by the sun.

They walked slowly hand in hand which was as it should be, for this was the day that they were leaving school, fourteen years old and about to face the big outside world. As headmistress scores of girls had passed through her school but few had left such a lasting impression on her mind. They were both intelligent quick-witted lasses and their education should not be cut short. If only they had been born in different circumstances they would never have been going to start work. And at the Wellington Laundry of all places! What would their pay be? Seven shillings a week, if they were lucky.

Suddenly Miss MacFarlane laughed out loud, for Rebecca had pulled the two ribbons from her hair and shook her head hard. It was a gesture of defiance. Her dark hair, which had been tied back tightly in two neat bunches, now fell unrestrained, a vibrant mass of thick ringlets reaching well past her shoulders.

'Bye.' Eleanor had turned and seen that Miss MacFarlane was still watching them. Both girls waved and their head-mistress returned the wave. They were of the same height but Miss MacFarlane guessed that Eleanor would love to have the same figure as that of Rebecca. Such a slim dainty girl was Rebecca and her oval face had a gentle look, as though nothing would ever upset her.

Poor Eleanor looked totally different. She was buxom, and that was putting it kindly, although perhaps it was just puppy fat and she would lose it soon enough when she started work in the laundry. It was to be hoped so. Her hair was as fair as ripe corn and today, probably for the last time, it was neatly braided into two long plaits.

Although so unlike in both appearance and temperament they were inseparable. Throughout the infant school and right on up until this important day they had been together. Oh, there had been times when they had squabbled, but such was their friendship that they became known as the daring double.

At this point Miss MacFarlane sighed, turned and went back into her school building. She wished nothing but the best for those two happy, spirited, intelligent girls. Would life give them chances? Treat them kindly? Only time would tell.

Outside the school gates the two friends turned and looked back at the building where they had spent much of their lives for the last ten years. Ella's eyes twinkled. 'Well, Becky, we're finished with all that.'

Becky gazed at her friend, her eyes thoughtful. 'You were

the one who couldn't wait to leave school and get a job. Are you having second thoughts now?'

'No, of course not. Just think of all the things we'll be able to do,' Ella quickly retaliated.

Becky laughed. 'Beside working five and a half days a week, name two.' They were now standing on the kerb waiting to cross busy Burlington Road. An open-topped tram rattled by followed by a delivery boy on his bike whistling 'It's A Long Way To Tipperary'. Further along a group of boys was also waiting to cross the road and one of them yelled out to the delivery boy, 'Oi, don't yer know the War's all over?'

On the opposite pavement two boys were running, bowling huge iron hoops in front of them, and yelling their heads off.

It seemed as if everyone was happy today because the long summer holiday was about to start.

'Well,' said Ella, as if considering the matter, 'we could doll ourselves up and go to the dance that's going to be held in the church hall this Saturday, what d'you think about that for a start?'

Becky giggled. 'Doll ourselves up? Fat chance. Where are we supposed to get dance frocks from?'

'You daft ha'perth,' Ella playfully punched Becky's shoulder. 'It won't be that kind of a dance, it's only being run by the youth club. Here, hold my hand and let's run, now, while there's nothing coming.'

Mrs Turner, who ran the Cosy Café, which was on the corner of George Road, the road in which Eleanor James had been born and bred, heard the girls' lively laughter and came to stand at the open door of the café. Both girls smiled at Mrs Turner, an elderly lady with grey hair swept back into a tidy bun. It was rumoured that Ma Turner had been serving large cups of tea, big breakfasts and even bigger hot dinners in that café since before she was big enough to see over the counter.

'I bet I know why you two are so chirpy. School broken

up for the summer holidays, has it? Have to have eyes out me backside now, won't I? What with all the little horrors roaming the streets and the pair of you living only a stone's throw from me front door.' She laughed loudly, her plump bosom heaving with the effort, and nodded her head towards the now-empty playground on the other side of the road. 'That school ain't ever going to be the same now that you two won't be pupils there any more.'

'We're going to have a week off, then we are both starting work down at the laundry.' Becky made this statement quite flippantly. Her dark ringlets now hanging free and her cheeks flushed with excitement, she explained further, 'And on Saturday we're thinking of going to the local church hall dance.'

Ella, who always did things on impulse, burst out, 'Yes, we really are. Not that there will be a band or anything big like that, just records on a wind-up gramophone, but we'll have a smashing time, won't we Becky?'

'We will if we can sort out what we're going to wear,' Becky answered.

Ma Turner grinned broadly. 'I don't suppose the young lads will give two hoots to what you're wearing. In any case if your mothers are to be believed the pair of you are both very good with yer needles and it is only Wednesday so you've got plenty of time to add a few touches to some of those pretty dresses I've seen you wear.'

'We've got t' go now, bye,' their laughing voices called back to the old lady who raised her eyes expressively and said out loud, 'What's going to happen to those two girls is anybody's guess.'

Ella made to turn down into George Road, saying, 'Call over the fence when you've had yer dinner and we'll decide what we're going to do this afternoon.'

'I will,' Becky said, 'but don't forget we ought to look through what dresses we've got if we are going to go to the church hall on Saturday.'

For answer Ella waved her hand and broke into a run.

Becky had only a few yards to walk on her own for she lived in the very next road at number twenty-four Albert Road, the garden of which backed directly on to the garden of number twenty-four George Road which was where Ella lived.

Her imagination was running away with her as she walked. They hadn't got to go back to school this afternoon, in fact they never had to go back again. A whole new life was opening up for her and her best friend. Together they would be starting work, earning wages, having money of their own. She smiled secretly to herself; suddenly she couldn't wait to tell her mother that she and Ella would like to go to a dance this coming Saturday. What an adventure! Oh, life was going to be so good from now on, she was convinced of that.

Turning into Albert Road, Rebecca decided that living here was like living in another world. Unlike George Road that had a long stretch of terraced houses on both sides of the road, there were only twelve houses on the right-hand side of the road, just the even numbers, and nothing but open fields on the opposite side. The Russell family lived in the last house. Beyond was Harry Horsecroft's farm. The very thought of Harry Horsecroft brought a grin to Becky's face. Her dad said Harry was more of a character than he was a farmer. On the farm he kept chicken, geese and pigs, but added to his living by being a part-time carrier with his horse and cart. Most nights Harry drank in the Tavern which was in Malden Road. Come closing time he just about managed to climb up on to the box seat of the cart and the horse would bring him home. His antics when trying to climb down from the cart provided a great source of amusement to his neighbours.

'Cor, lovely,' Becky exclaimed as she opened the front door and sniffed the smell of their dinner. Then, seeing her dad seated on the bottom of the stairs tugging to get his boots off, she darted forward. 'Here, let me,' she said, dropping down on to her knees.

At the age of forty, Joe Russell was a contented man who had worked for the railways since he was fourteen and had lived all his life in New Malden, Surrey.

At eighteen he had met and married Joyce Wilson, and they had set up home here in Albert Road. Married life had suited them both fine. Jack was born in 1900, Tom in 1901, Fred in 1902 and Rebecca in 1906. Joe hadn't minded a bit that their first three children were all boys but when the last one had been a girl his cup had run over. She was the apple of his eye and he spoiled her as much as he could on his limited wages.

In return Becky adored this big man. He had a ruddy complexion from being out in all weathers and although streaked with grey, his hair was still thick and curly. Her dad was forever laughing, as though inside himself he was always happy. He thrived in company, and had a keen sense of humour. He enjoyed a pint and a game of darts at the local pub with his mates. Her mum had a totally different personality. She was always so serious, preferring to stay close to the house. Whereas her lovely dad was instantly likeable and made friends easily, Mum appeared offhand to strangers.

Boots now off, Becky made to rise. 'Oh, so you ain't got a kiss for your poor old dad that has been at work since four o'clock this morning? Don't matter though, I know plenty of young ladies that will be only too willing to hug an' kiss me.'

Becky stared at him, letting him know she didn't approve of that kind of teasing. He smiled, and put his arms around his daughter's shoulders and squeezed. Becky returned the hug and planted kisses on his cheeks and on his forehead.

'You're an angel, that's what you are, my own very special angel, put on this earth just to make my life a happy one,' her dad was telling her, using a loud and cheery tone of voice.

'Yeah, well, angels still need feeding, you know,' her mother called from the open kitchen door, and Becky thought how tired her mum looked despite the fact that she was smiling.

Going down the passage with her dad she asked, 'Did you know I finished school today, Dad?'

'Of course I did my luv, and already I feel ten years older having me lass going out to work.'

'I'm not starting for a week yet.'

'You'll not be starting at all if you don't sit up and eat this dinner before it gets all spoiled,' her mother retorted.

Becky did as she was told, thinking to herself how lucky she was to have such a loving family. Her big jolly father, her quiet but warm-hearted mother who kept this house as spick and span as a new pin, using what she called good old-fashioned elbow-grease to polish the furniture until you could see your face in it. Then there were her three big brothers so noisy and full of life. She also appreciated the good and plentiful food that was served in this house.

Her best friend Ella wasn't so lucky. Ella's father had been killed in the War, leaving her mother short of money and facing a hard struggle to provide for Ella and her two brothers.

Joyce Russell was thinking along the very same lines as she watched her husband carve the pot-roast. God had certainly been good to them and their four children. She felt a milestone had been reached today. Her baby, Rebecca, named after her own dear mother, was now fourteen years old. Ready to face the world. She couldn't put her feelings into words; she certainly had hoped for better than Becky taking a job in the Wellington Laundry.

She stifled a sigh. There were so many disabled soldiers unable to find employment of any kind. She should count her blessings and be grateful that at least all her boys were working and Becky had at least found a job.

She passed the dish of vegetables down the table and, watching Becky, she grinned. It might not be much of a job but once her daughter got her teeth into something, she wasn't going to give up easily.

They would all have to wait and see how things turned out.

Chapter Two

PUSHING ASIDE HER doubts about starting work in the laundry on Monday, Becky set off to meet Ella, determined to enjoy herself at this youth club dance.

She had accepted her mother's offer to wash and arrange her hair into a neater style. Joyce had brushed the mass of unruly thick ringlets into shining waves tying them back with two lengths of royal blue velvet, allowing soft curls to remain free about her cheeks, thus softening the severity of the style.

Both Becky and Ella had made a peasant-type skirt by cutting the bodice from an old dress and adding strips of velvet at different lengths starting from the hem of the skirt and working upwards. Each skirt was made from different coloured and textured material so there was no question of them wearing identical outfits. Ella was to wear a beige, high-necked blouse given to her by an aunt. Becky's blouse was of fine cotton, embroidered down the front by herself.

Ella's mother Margaret, more often referred to as Peggy, was generous with her praise, coming out to greet Becky with outstretched hands and welcoming smiles. 'My, how lovely you both look, the lads won't be able to take their eyes off you. I hope you both have a good time,' she said, her gaze resting on Becky.

About to say, 'So do we,' Becky remembered her manners and changed the words to, 'Thank you, Mrs James, I'm sure we shall.'

Holding hands the girls walked quickly up the road. What a picture the pair of them made. On this warm summer's evening there was no need for coats, so each girl had a white shawl draped over her arm in case they might need to put them around their shoulders when they were walking home. The church had given out that the social dance would end at ten o'clock and Joe Russell had said that he would be outside the hall to meet them. That made Peggy feel grateful, but it also made her feel sad. Bad enough that she had been widowed at the age of thirty-two.

She would freely admit that despite having three children she still often felt lonely and longed for someone in her life to love her. How much worse for her young daughter. Best of friends with Becky, there must be times her Ella felt envious of the way Becky was loved and protected by her father. They say what you've never had you never missed. It wasn't true. Ella had been just ten years old when the news came through that her Bert had been killed in France, old enough to miss the father that she had barely got to know.

Peggy, a faded ash-blonde who was still slim and quite beautiful, gazed after her plump daughter. The only things that Eleanor seems to have inherited from me are my hair and colouring, she mused. Maybe Ella would slim down a bit as she grew older; meanwhile her mop of gorgeous golden hair was something to appreciate. Tonight she had helped her daughter to pile a few curls on top of her head, leaving tresses to flow freely down past her shoulders. The curls would give her added height and so make her look less chubby.

Margaret James turned to go indoors just as her two sons came through the front door. Jimmy was the next one up to Ella, at fifteen, and thanks to Joe Russell he had a job on the railway. Ronald, her eldest at sixteen, hadn't been so lucky and was threatening to join the Army. Three children in three years. She found herself smiling as she watched them grinning at each other.

'And where are you two off to then?' she asked.

'Just out an' about, Mother, we won't be late,' Ronnie assured her.

'See you're not then,' she called out after them as they swaggered away up the road.

What it is to be young, especially on a Saturday night! She was thinking she'd give a lot to be dressed up and going to a dance herself, but no such luck.

The church hall was ablaze with light and decorated with fresh flowers. Lemonade and orange squash flowed freely for it was included in the entrance price of fourpence.

'Boys, take your partners, please,' Mr Barrett, the local Scout master, instructed, and the boys who'd been lining one wall moved towards the girls lining the wall opposite, most of whom were sniggering and giggling.

Suddenly there was two boys standing in front of Ella and Becky, mumbling the words, 'Would you like to dance?' Both lads' faces were flushed. They clearly found asking a girl to dance acutely embarrassing, which amused them both.

'Thank you,' they replied in unison, each thinking that they had never seen either of these lads before.

'A waltz,' Mr Barrett announced, before bending to the old gramophone on which a record had already been placed. The girls glanced at each other, raising their eyebrows questioningly as they went into the boys' arms, and then they were off, one, two, three, one, two, three, trying to keep in time to the somewhat scratchy music.

Ella was doing well. Her partner was a good dancer, easy to follow, and she relaxed as they circled the floor.

Becky was not so lucky. Her lad was a terrible dancer, stumbling over his own feet and hers. During their last year at school they had been taught ballroom dancing by Miss Patterson and Miss Brown. Learning had come easily because both teachers demonstrated the steps so well. That didn't help if your partner hadn't a clue as to how to keep in time with the music. Halfway through the dance he stepped heavily right on to her foot.

'Sorry,' he muttered.

'Don't worry about it, I shall only be crippled for life,' she answered testily, but immediately wished she hadn't when she saw how her reply had upset him. 'You just need to practise more. We all have to learn. It might help if they hold a few more of these get-togethers,' she added, giving him a smile.

For a brief second he looked into her eyes, then he quickly glanced away, his entire face turning red.

This lad really is shy, Becky thought, which she didn't find unattractive. Most of the boys around where she lived were far too big for their boots, and cocky with it half the time. Someone as shy as this lad was made a pleasant change.

When the record came to the end Mr Barrett told them all to separate into their lines again, then proceeded to describe the Paul Jones. 'This dance will enable each of you to dance with several different partners,' he declared.

Two circles were formed in the centre of the hall, girls on the outside, boys on the inside and to the music they trotted round holding hands. When the music stopped Becky found herself facing Ted Berry who always looked as if a good wash would do him good. She had no choice. Whoever was facing you was your partner. Reluctantly, she went into his arms, praying that before the night was much older her luck might change. After a break and a welcome drink she wondered if the shy lad would ask her to dance again, but he didn't, he asked Ella instead.

Suddenly out of the mass of boys a dark-haired young man appeared and muttered, 'Would you like to dance?'

'Yes please,' she replied, and followed him out on to the floor. God must have heard her prayer!

This boy was tall and he could dance. In fact he was an excellent dancer. Rebecca relaxed; this was more like it. Her wide full skirt swirled as he swung her round, using his elbow to make more room for them on the floor.

'Thank you for the best dance I've had yet,' he said, as the record came to an end, then with what seemed to Becky like reluctance he left her. When later on he asked her if he could fetch her a drink she was more than pleased.

Ella gave a knowing grin in Becky's direction as they watched this dark-haired lad approach them, bringing a mate with him, as the last waltz was announced. As they circled the floor both girls were happy, wondering if and when another dance would be held in this church hall.

Perhaps it was as well that Becky's father was going to be outside waiting to escort them both home.

Their week of freedom had passed all too quickly. The weather had stayed exceptionally warm and the girls had made the most of it by taking themselves off to the river, running through the long grass and scrubby bushes enjoying each sun-filled day.

Soon it was time to start work.

It was just a quarter to eight on the Monday morning when Ella and Becky ran up the outside steps of the Wellington Laundry and pushed open the door that had OFFICE painted on its glass panel in black and gold lettering. Two older girls were working busily at a long table set back against the far wall. One seemed to be adding up columns of figures in a very large book while the other girl was typing on a large upright machine, her fingers flying over the noisy keys. As Ella and Becky entered they both looked up and regarded the pair of them kindly.

'I'm Rebecca Russell and this is Eleanor James, we're supposed to start work here today,' Becky said. 'I think we're a bit early, eight o'clock the manager said.'

The dark-haired girl smiled. 'That's only because you're new. Everyone here, laundry workers and office staff alike, all start work at seven thirty.'

'Oh,' was all that Becky managed to say.

Ten minutes later Ella and Becky stood on the concrete floor inside the main laundry building and they looked at each other in dismay. The rough overall, mobcap and sacking apron they were being asked to put on weren't at all what they had expected, nor were the surroundings.

The heat and the rising steam was frightening, coppers full of boiling water stood everywhere. Becky felt ill as she stared at the women bent over scrubbing boards, their aprons sopping wet. The whole place looked mucky and damp. She offered up a silent prayer that they might not have to work in this department.

'One of you come over here,' called out a deep male voice, 'the other one wait and I'll have someone take you down to the pressing room.'

'Oh hell, suppose it's best if I stay here,' Ella said, doing her best to raise a smile as she crossed the wet floor.

'The pressing is done down the corridor,' a young lad was saying to Becky. She turned to face him and found she was looking into the eyes of the shy lad who had stepped on her feet a week ago at the youth club dance. 'Hello,' she said.

He gave her a startled look, not having been aware of whom he was talking to. 'Oh, hello.'

'Are you going to show me the way?'

'Yes, it's quite a walk, though it is all under cover.'

Becky thought that was a shame. Outside the sun was shining. As she and Ella had walked to the village of New Malden the sun had been bright and warm, giving out a promise of another lovely day and yet here she was shut up in this dreary steamy building with the prospect of spending her working life doing other people's dirty washing.

Oh NO! This wasn't at all what she had in mind when seeking her first job. The likelihood of finding something better might be slim but that would not deter her from trying. Give it a chance, she chided herself. Well of course she would have to do that because at the moment she had no choice.

As they walked, and talked, Becky discovered that he'd only been working in the laundry for a few weeks. He lived in Kingston.

'Whereabouts in Kingston? I've got an aunt an' uncle that live there.'

He hesitated slightly before answering, 'Mill Street.'

She knew Mill Street was in a rough area, quite different from the nice quiet Albert Road where she lived. Mill Street was lower-class, the houses weren't up to much and the lavatory was outside in the back garden. There weren't many men who lived in that area could say they had a decent job and quite a few that wouldn't have a job at all.

'Do you like working here?' she asked.

He shrugged his shoulders. 'It's not that bad once you get used to it. Suppose it takes time.'

Becky felt someone should take this boy under their wing, and suddenly realized that she didn't know his name yet. 'I'm Rebecca Russell, but everyone calls me Becky. What's your name?' she asked.

He gawped at her. 'I've never met a girl called Rebecca before. I'm Tommy Ferguson,' he said, and grinned.

They came to the end of the long corridor. 'Through there is where you've got to go,' he told her, nodding his head towards a large metal door.

She was about to thank him and say goodbye when an idea came to her. 'Do you ever go to the picture show that the Salvation Army put on?' she asked.

He shook his head.

'It's every other Friday night in the congregational hall. I know for a fact they've got two great pictures for this week, *Rin-Tin-Tin* and *Elsie Dies For Love*. We get there about quarter to seven, and it starts at seven. Why don't you come along? You could sit with us, we don't bite, in fact all my friends are very friendly.'

'I don't fancy it. It's not real pictures like you see at the cinema, is it? More like a magic lantern show. No thanks.'

'What do you want for a penny, my lad?' she answered. 'Pity you feel like that. I certainly enjoy my nights there, we even get given free refreshments in the interval. Still, if you've got such a good social life elsewhere good luck to you.'

'Could I bring me mate?' he answered, sounding wary.

''Course you could,' she replied, eyes twinkling mischievously. 'More the merrier, you'll see if you come along and find out.' Moving abruptly, she pushed open the door and let it clang behind her leaving him staring perplexedly after her.

'I'm Mrs Bradford. You are?' It was a short, stout, middle-aged woman who faced Becky. She had a kindly smiling face and her fair hair was set in deep rigid lines of waves very close to her head.

'Becky Russell,' Becky answered in a quiet voice.

'Well Becky, did you choose to be a presser?'

'Not exactly, madam.'

Mrs Bradford studied this new employee; they seemed to get younger every month. 'You don't have to call me madam; Mrs Bradford will do nicely. Have you ever used a flat iron before?'

'Only a small one at home, nothing like the size of the irons those girls are using,' Becky said woefully.

'Or a steam press?'

'Sorry. I've never even seen one of those.'

'Don't worry, you'll get used to them. The size always seems off-putting to new girls. Come along and meet the girls you will be working with.'

Becky followed her down the length of the room, feeling the heat hit her face as she passed young women, all ironing away busily. The steam presses were frightening. At one point they stopped to watch as one girl with bare arms flexed her muscles, rose up on to her toes and with what seemed to Becky a great effort used both hands to grasp the wide handle and bring down the great white pad on to folded articles of linen. The hissing and the burst of steam had Becky jumping backwards out of the way.

The room itself was certainly better than the wash house

where she had left Ella. The light came in from two high windows and the walls were painted yellow. In all Becky decided it was a bright room.

'One moment, girls,' called Mrs Bradford, 'this is Becky Russell.' She introduced all the workers to Becky who quickly became confused, finding it impossible to remember any of the names which were rattled off so quickly.

A table was allocated to Becky and she was instructed on how to heat the gas iron and to use the sleeve boards.

'Try her out on flats first off with just a flat iron,' Mrs Bradford said to the girl working at the next table. 'I'll leave her in your charge for now and I'll be back as soon as I can.'

'Hello Becky, I'm Rose,' the girl said, her smile as merry as her bright blue eyes. She had short brown hair, and looked quite smart in her white overall. At least in this room the employees were not wearing the awful sacking aprons. Becky smiled back, guessing that she was a good few years older than herself.

'Is Becky your real name?'

'No, it's Rebecca, but everybody shortens it to Becky.'

'Well, let's see how you get on. Don't be afraid to ask if you can't manage something, and by the way the girl working opposite to you is Mary.'

They all sounded friendly enough, but Becky was feeling terrified at the thought of having to pick up one of the three huge flat irons that she felt by now must be red-hot. Dear God I wish I was anywhere but here, she sighed to herself.

She and Ella hadn't given much thought to the work that went on in a laundry. All they had been concerned about was the fact that they had been lucky enough to get a job and that they would be earning a regular weekly wage.

Seeing the pile of what seemed to be damask tablecloths that Rose was setting out on her allocated table, Becky groaned.

'These are usually done in the press. Mrs Bradford is being kind to you, starting you off lightly,' declared Rose.

Becky supposed that she should feel grateful, but she didn't and seeing the expression on her face Rose burst out laughing. That made Becky see the funny side of the situation and she also began laughing. But what if she should burn a hole in one of the items? She banished the thought from her head as quickly as it had come.

It was the longest morning of her young life. When at one o'clock the hooter sounded Becky Russell breathed a heavy sigh of relief, spat on to her fingers and gently rubbed two red patches on her forearm which showed signs of having been burnt. At one o'clock the laundry closed down for one hour. Quickly the women turned everything off, snatched up their bags and hurried away in all directions.

Ella looked a sorry sight as she came towards Becky. From head to toe she looked damp. Her lovely fair hair clung to her head as if she had been in a steam bath.

'Come on, luv,' Ella hissed in Becky's ear. 'Shift yerself and let's get out of here.'

The two girls walked through the now-deserted building and down the outside staircase. The warm sun hit them as they reached the street and both girls thankfully turned their faces upwards. They weren't used to spending so long indoors, let alone in a place like that. They ran down Burlington Road until they parted at George Road.

'See you here at a quarter to two,' Ella yelled back over her shoulder.

Hearing Becky enter the house by the back door her mother called out, 'How'd it go, luv?'

Becky forced herself to smile as she opened the kitchen door to greet her mother. Joyce Russell's heart sank as she gazed at her lovely young daughter. Five hours in the Wellington Laundry and already she looked washed out. 'Come and sit up, I've got a full jug of lemonade ready, I made it earlier and when I was squeezing the lemons I knew I wouldn't be wasting my time. You are ready for a cold drink, aren't you?'

'Mum, you're wonderful. I'm parched.'

'Well, it's only salad with a nice bit of cold boiled bacon to go with it, I didn't think you'd fancy anything hot.'

An hour for lunch wasn't long enough by any means.

Ella and Becky were very subdued as they joined the other girls hurrying up the stairs and when they reached the wash house and Ella turned to go in she heard Becky sigh heavily.

Ella stopped in her tracks, turned and patted Becky's arm. 'Stick it out luv, won't be forever.'

Becky nodded her head but as she walked the corridor tears pricked the back of her eyes. 'It certainly won't be,' she promised herself in an agonized whisper and her heart felt lighter as she decided that she was going to make sure that her working life would not be spent in this laundry.

On Friday night at seven o'clock on the dot Tommy Ferguson and his mate Stan Rogers appeared at the door of the congregational hall and handed over their pennies to the smiling lady who was wearing her Salvation Army uniform complete with black and red straw bonnet. Up until the moment they entered, Becky hadn't believed that they would come.

Seeing Tommy look uncertain, Becky dragged Ella over to be introduced. Both lads were well-built with fair hair. Tommy's mate obviously did not work indoors as Tommy did because he had a freckled, weather-beaten look about him and a rugged face which looked as though it had been carved out of granite. Both lads had made an effort; they had polished their shoes and were wearing dark trousers and very clean short-sleeved shirts.

'This is my friend Ella,' Becky told them. 'She knows who you are Tom, from the dance, but we don't know your friend.'

Tommy was too surprised to answer. He simply stared

straight at Becky, thinking how pretty she looked in her pale pink floral dress and her dark ringlets framing her face.

'Come on then,' Ella said, grabbing the other boy's arm. 'You tell me your name.'

Taken aback, but more than willing, he muttered, 'Stan, Stan Rogers.'

'Well, Stan Rogers, the films are gonna start any minute now so we'd better find ourselves a seat.'

Actually, neither Tommy or Stan could have cared less about the films. What had brought Stan along was Tom's description of the girls who had been at the youth club dance.

Becky suddenly realized that Tommy was grinning at her, and she grinned in return. She was ever so pleased he'd come, but it didn't occur to her to ask herself why.

The first film was over. Elsie, the heroine, had been tied to the railway tracks by the wicked villain. The train was fast approaching. Elsie was struggling. Would she die?

The caption came up on the screen: TO BE CONTINUED NEXT WEEK. Becky and Ella rose to their feet, making a beeline for the kitchen. Refreshments were served and when Ella came back to her seat without Becky, Tommy was afraid she had gone home.

Minutes later his face was wreathed in smiles. 'Where have you been?'

Becky laughed, 'Finishing the washing-up.'

Suddenly Tommy was shy again, completely lost for words. Silence fell between them as the lights were dimmed and the next picture began.

'Nine o'clock, time to go home,' Ella was saying to Stan as the film finished.

'Yeah, suppose that's it. We'd better be on our way,' he said, reluctance sounding in his voice.

Ella hadn't minded sitting with Stan. He was quite nice-looking in a rugged thickset sort of way, much more brainy than that clod Tommy, who seemed to have set his cap at Becky. 'Listen,' she said, 'we usually go to Kingston market on a Saturday morning, maybe we'll see you there tomorrow.'

Both Stan and Tommy looked disappointed. 'Couldn't we take you to a café, have a cup of tea and a bit of a natter, get t' know you better like?' Stan boldly suggested.

'No you couldn't!' Becky was first in with her reply. 'Nine o'clock this show finishes an' if we aren't home by twenty past my dad will be up here to know the reason why.'

'I have t' work every other Saturday morning, on the delivery vans,' Tommy quietly whispered to Becky, 'I'm working tomorrow.'

She touched him lightly on the shoulder, sending a shiver through him. 'Well I'm glad you came tonight. Good night then.'

'Good night.'

Becky took Ella's arm as they left the hall. 'Is that Tom tied to his mother's apron strings?' were the first words that Ella came out with as soon as they were out of earshot of the boys.

Becky was more than surprised. 'What on earth made you ask me that? I don't know any more about him than you do.'

'Just curious.'

Becky found this hard to believe. There was more to Ella's question than she was letting on. 'I know he's a bit nervous, didn't you like him?'

'His mate Stan seems all right . . .' Ella dithered, 'but Tommy is a bit simple, isn't he?'

'Ella! You've no right t' talk about the lad that way. We don't really know anything about him.'

'You want to be careful is all I'm saying. I tried to put it nicely, I mean, he's all right, nice really, but no one in their right mind could say he's bright, now could they?'

'What's that got to do with me being kind to him?' Becky asked impatiently.

Ella looked at her friend, her eyes wide with amazement. 'Haven't you cottoned on to the fact that Tom is crazy about you? He doesn't want you t' be kind to him. There's a lot more on that lad's mind than kindness.'

'Oh, Ella! Don't be so daft. We've only just left school, we don't want serious boyfriends for ages yet, do we?'

'We aren't talking about what we want. I'm sorry if you can't see it, but please Becky, luv, be careful, don't lead him on.'

Becky took hold of Ella's hand and squeezed it. 'All right, Ella, I'll treat him with kid gloves when I see him again, but I still think you've got it wrong.'

Joe Russell was waiting at the corner of George Road and he greeted the girls by hugging them both. 'Had a good time, did you?' Releasing Ella but still holding his daughter close to his side, he said, 'We'll stand here till we see you turn into your gate, Ella.'

'Thanks, Mr Russell, I won't be a tick. See you tomorrow, Becky.'

Ella ran, turning at her gateway to give them both a wave. Her face was sad, her thoughts serious. Becky might only be a few weeks younger than she was but she wasn't very worldly. She was such a nice kind girl, someone she was proud to have as her best friend but she had to be mad to see that Tommy Ferguson wasn't the type of boy she should be taking up with. And it wasn't going to happen. Not if she could help it.

Chapter Three

1924

SUNDAY AFTERNOON AND Becky was spending it in the way she loved best. She was sitting on the river wall at Kingston. She loved to watch dear old Father Thames flowing relentlessly on. What a lovely sight, she thought to herself as a saloon steamer came into sight on its way to Henley. Life on the river was never dull, always varied, and today with the sun shining on the old buildings everything seemed to glow.

It wouldn't be like that for much longer. Being the third week in September the pleasure boats would soon be laid up for the winter. Already the trees were beginning to display their bright autumn colours and she found herself wondering where the time had gone. It wasn't only the summer months that passed so quickly; the years themselves were speeding by.

It seemed only recently that she and Ella had been thrilled to be given employment at the Wellington Laundry. She pondered on that thought for a moment then shook her head in disbelief. In actual fact they had been working there now for four years.

'Becky, Becky!'

She looked up and saw that Ella was running along the towpath towards her. 'Hello! What are you doing?' Ella called out and without waiting for a reply she rushed on, 'I must look like a drowned rat.'

Becky reluctantly climbed down from the wall and really looked at her. 'Whatever happened to you?'

Ella's hair clung to her head and her dress was covered in mud splashes. 'It's like always, that daft Tommy tagged on and he's in a right mood because you aren't with me.'

'I didn't know Tom was here. You went off with that new van driver, what's his name? I didn't want to play gooseberry. I knew you'd be back in time to go for some tea.'

Ella held out her hand to her. 'His name is Pete, Pete Tomson, and he's old enough to be our father, but he's ever so nice and I think he's lonely cos he's only moved here when he got the job at the Wellington. You didn't have to stay behind, we were only going for a walk.'

Becky was grinning broadly. 'Ella, you do exaggerate! Pete Tomson can't be much more than thirty years old and that makes him just twelve years older than us. But never mind him, how did you meet up with Tom?'

'Hmm!' Ella sniffed and shrugged her shoulders. 'How do we ever meet up with Tommy Ferguson? He pops up like a bad penny wherever we decide to go at weekends. I told you years ago when you first started to take him under your wing that you were storing up trouble for yourself, but you wouldn't listen, would you?'

'Oh, Ella, he's not that bad.'

'Maybe not. But let's face the truth for once. Tommy is besotted with you. He gets really aggressive if he thinks any man is paying you too much attention. One day he may go over the top and then there'll be trouble.'

'I know,' Becky sighed, 'I can't help feeling sorry for him but I certainly don't encourage him.'

'You may not be responsible,' Ella pointed out, 'but that's not going to stop him feeling the way he does about you.'

'Well, what do you imagine he's going to do about it?'

'I don't know.'

'In that case, Ella, let me tell you. Nothing. Because unless I let him there is nothing he can do even if he wanted to. No, Tommy won't overstep the mark.'

'How do you know?'

'Because I know Tommy.'

'I know him too. In fact I think right from the beginning I've been able to read him like a book. Becky, you're too nice by far. You only see the good in everyone. Well not everyone is as good and kind as you are but I hope in this case you don't live to find that out.'

'What's that supposed to mean?'

Ella sighed. 'Oh nothing. It's just that sometimes Tommy gives me the creeps. Anyway, I'm going to the toilets, see if I can clean myself up a bit and then we'll make our way over the bridge an' have our tea, shall we?'

'Yes, that's fine by me, I'll wait here. By the way, you haven't said how you got yourself into such a state.'

Ella laughed now. 'I started to slip down the bank and daft Tommy, instead of helping, splashed handfuls of water over me.'

'What had you done to upset him?'

'As if you need to ask! I told him I didn't know where you were.'

Becky watched as Ella half ran towards the public toilets. She had grown into a sharp-witted, shrewd young lady with a really nice figure. Becky smiled to herself. She loved Ella dearly, even though she knew her own mind and wasn't afraid to voice her thoughts. That didn't deter her or anyone else from liking her. Oh no! Everyone made an exception for fair-haired blue-eyed Ella, because in the main what she said turned out to be right. A smile returned to Becky's face as Ella came towards her accompanied by Peter Tomson and Tom Ferguson.

Ella rolled her eyes. 'Tommy insists he wants to buy you tea, he said you paid for his drink twice last week in the work-break, so I've invited Pete to join us as well. All right?'

'Of course,' Becky said, falling into step beside Peter. He had been taken on by the Wellington four weeks ago to drive the van.

'How are you getting on?' Becky asked as they walked, more out of politeness than because she was interested.

'Not bad at all,' he smiled, adding quickly, 'but I miss my family.'

'Oh, where did you live before?'

'In the Midlands. I had a nervous breakdown when my mother was killed in a train accident. This job came up and my father thought a change of scenery would be good for me. He's gone to live with my married sister.'

'Uprooting yourself like that was a brave thing to do,' said Becky in amazement.

'Needs must when the devil drives,' he smiled and in that moment Becky decided he was a nice man.

They had their tea and Tommy was all smiles when Becky said he could go home with her on the tram because she had some sewing she wanted to do that evening. Ella shot Becky a grateful smile. It was what she had been longing for, a little while on her own with this new man in her life.

Tommy held on tightly to Becky's hand while the tram took them on the journey home and she was relieved when they came to New Malden village. Tugging to free her hand, she said, 'Ah, next stop's mine. See you at work in the morning, Tom, ta-ta.'

Tommy took a deep breath and said in a rush, 'I'll get off with you. I want to ask you something.'

Becky turned to him in surprise. The look on his face made her realize that their friendship did indeed mean something totally different to him than it did to her. How stupid she had been! She should have been aware of what was happening a long time ago. You've been a right silly fool, Becky Russell! she chided herself. You've had your head buried in the sand.

'I'm sorry Tom, I can't stop and talk tonight,' she replied lamely.

'Why not?'

She knew she had to be honest with him for once, what

else could she do? 'I don't want to, I've a whole lot of things I have to do this evening.'

'Oh!' Tom was fighting to keep himself under control, but if she wasn't careful he was going to let his temper get the better of him.

'I will see you at work in the morning,' she said gently as he moved his knees to allow her to push past him.

She breathed out as soon as her feet touched the pavement and she watched with relief as the tram pulled away from the stop. She could kick herself for having let things get to this pitch. Why hadn't she been aware of it before? She must have been blind. And daft not to have listened to Ella's warnings.

Back home she was relieved to find that her parents and her brothers were all out. With the whole house to herself she could sit down in peace and quiet and sort out her thoughts. Once she had washed her hands and face, she sat down, picked up her sewing and went over the day's events in her head. She knew now that what Ella was saying about Tommy was true. Today's events had proved her right. Why, he had even taken to waylaying her during their tea breaks at work. In fact he got right ruffled if she sat with the girls instead of with him. She was worried, even if she wouldn't admit it to Ella.

Something had to change and if she had her way it would be her job.

Four years earlier she had been delighted to be given a job. Any job would have done just so long as it was honest employment. How quickly she had changed her mind when she had first stepped into that wash house. She had been horrified when faced with the conditions in which they were expected to work.

Eleanor, being the strong-willed tomboy that she was, even at the age of fourteen, had taken the harsh conditions in her stride. If she were to ask her today if she were happy working in the laundry, Becky felt sure that Ella's reply would be, ''Course I am.'

It wasn't like that for herself. From that very first moment she had vowed that she would stay there no longer than was absolutely necessary. So what had gone wrong?

She was eighteen years old, which meant that she had been working at the Wellington for four years now. True, Mrs Bradford had taken pity on her and after just one year had seen that she was transferred to the packing department. Perhaps that was the reason that she hadn't put herself out to find other employment. No it wasn't, not if she was being honest with herself. Truth was she hadn't got the confidence any more. Well, she would jolly well have to find it again. And quick too, before things with Tommy Ferguson got out of hand.

I'll talk to me dad. Yes, that's what I'll do. He'll know the right way for me to go about getting a different kind of work. Her dad was a lovely man. Look how he treated her mum. Like she was his queen.

Sighing softly she packed her sewing away, climbed the stairs and began to lay out her clothes ready for work the next day.

When she finally got into bed, Becky realized that she was mentally exhausted and her last thought before she went to sleep was that she hoped one day she might be lucky enough to find a young man who would love her in the nice kind way that her dad loved her mother.

It wasn't natural, the way Tommy wanted to monopolize her.

Chapter Four

HARDLY HAD HER father stepped inside the house than Becky ran to his side, saying urgently, 'Please Dad, I want to talk to you.'

'All right, my love,' he smiled, 'don't look so worried. What's it about?'

'Can we go out into the garden?'

'No, I need to get this uniform off, else your mother will wonder what's wrong. Come on, we'll go upstairs.' And without waiting for Becky to reply, her father set off up the narrow stairs, his long legs taking the steps two at a time.

Becky followed him quickly, before her mother should start to wonder what was going on. Her mum and dad had the big bedroom with the bay windows that faced the fields opposite and to the side looked out over Harry Horsecroft's farm.

Her dad told her to sit down, then he shut the door and opened the window. The curtains started to flap gently for there was quite a breeze on this autumn evening. Then he seated himself in the other chintz-covered chair, that she had always thought looked so pretty because her mother had also made a frilled skirt for the dressing table out of the same chintz material, and began to unbutton his jacket.

Becky watched and waited.

When her father had hung his railway jacket on a coat hanger and rolled his shirtsleeves up to his elbows, he bent his head until his face was level with Becky's and kissed her soundly before saying, 'Well, my lovely girl? Nothing's ever so bad that we can't get it sorted.'

Suddenly Becky felt tongue-tied. It was going to be so difficult to explain to her father all the reasons why she wanted to leave the Wellington Laundry. 'Dad, I wish I could have a different job.'

'About time you did, if you want my opinion.'

'Dad!' She couldn't believe what she had heard him say. Oh, he was such a wise man. A good man. He understood before she had even said two words. Then it all came pouring out. The laundry was a hateful place. Nothing ever altered there. Monotonous tasks, day after day. Everything stayed the same, nothing to look forward to. Was that all there was to life? Did she have to stick at it? She hated it.

Her dad very nearly laughed but managed to keep a straight face. 'Rebecca,' he said softly, using her full name, 'of course you don't have to work there. You've been trudging backwards and forwards to that place for four years now so no one can say that you haven't given it a good go. Not that it would matter if they did. All your mother and I ever wanted is for you to be happy. Everyone has to work, but seeing as such a great deal of our lives is spent in employment I don't think it is asking too much that we should be happy there.'

Becky's face lit up. 'Oh Dad, I knew you'd understand.'

'Yeah well, one thing is for sure, it won't be that easy to find a different kind of work. Jobs aren't two a penny. Who you know goes a long way rather than what you know.'

He had dashed her hopes and he saw her bottom lip tremble. Quickly he added, 'I'll keep my ear to the ground and now you have actually made the decision to change your job, you'll see, something will turn up.'

Becky felt as if a load had been lifted from her shoulders. She was so lucky to have such wonderful parents; even her brothers were special. And her home was such a happy one. Fresh flowers in earthenware jugs were in evidence most times of the year as were fresh vegetables and salad, all thanks to the hours that her dad spent on his allotment. They were a team, her mum and dad. She couldn't imagine life without either of them, or without her brothers. Jack, her eldest brother, was happily married to Ada. They had a little boy, Ronnie, aged two. He was already a lovable little tinker, into everything but still the apple of his parents' eyes. Tom, the brother that Becky thought took after their father both in looks and personality, was also married. His wife, Joan, had only recently given birth to a baby boy. He was to be christened Joseph, after his grandfather. That left only Fred living at home. Both Jack and Tom had rented flats in Kingston, which made sense because they both worked at Kingston Tannery, but it didn't stop them bringing their families to Sunday afternoon tea, every week without fail.

Fred had a good job with the Co-op bakery. He was tall and quite good-looking, a fact that he took advantage of when it came to the girls. Fred wasn't going to settle down, not yet anyway, he's like me, Becky thought, appreciates his home too much to want to leave it for pastures new.

Joe Russell stared at Becky, wondering what had brought things to a head and a little afraid now to break the silence that had settled between them. With three sons and now two grandsons his only daughter was very special to him, as he knew full well he was to her.

'Rebecca's a Daddy's girl if ever there was one,' his wife was fond of telling folk and he wouldn't argue with that.

Joe didn't want Rebecca to be any different, but there were times when he couldn't help wishing that his darling girl wasn't quite so sensitive. Even as a child, however, Becky had shown signs of individuality, always so impressionable where others were concerned. From an early age, she had always been quite creative, especially when it came to clothes. Her mother raved about what Becky could do with a length of material or indeed with a second-hand frock. Pity she couldn't have found work in that line. But not in the London sweatshops that he'd heard so much about. Oh no! He liked his daughter nearby where he could keep an eye on her. But if she wasn't happy, well, that was a different story.

He smiled at his daughter and she smiled back, but she wasn't surprised when he gently took hold of her hand and said, 'You've only told me half the reason why you want to leave the Wellington. Go on, let's hear the rest of it.'

'Oh Dad! I think you already know, it's Tom Ferguson. He seems to know exactly where I'll be. I keep thinking I'm eighteen and I don't meet anybody else. I don't want to spend my life with someone like him. I think of all the places I read about, places I've never even seen and never shall if I stay in this rut. I scarcely ever remember even going to London.'

'Then go. Go soon.'

'Dad! You know it's not as simple as that.'

'It could be. If you put your mind to it.'

'Perhaps, but I just don't know where to start. Maybe I'm all talk and when it comes to it I won't have the courage.'

'Nonsense. I'll tell you what you're going to do. You are going to have a trip up to London for a start. Yes. I mean it. Next Saturday evening we'll leave our Fred to fend for himself and your mother and I will take you up to sample the bright lights of the city. After that we'll decide what you're gonna do about Tom Ferguson.'

'Do you really mean it, Dad?'

'You bet your life I do,' he said, holding out his hand to her. 'I'm already looking forward to it myself. Come on, let's go down and tell your mother.'

Becky didn't walk down the stairs, she ran. She was going to London with her parents. Not just to see the sights, but to sort things out in her head. She couldn't make up her mind whether she dreaded the day when she might start a new job or whether she was looking forward to it. Then, as she entered the kitchen, came a sobering thought. First she had to find another employer who would look kindly on her.

Her mother stared perplexedly at Becky as she took her seat at the table. One moment her face had been wreathed in smiles and now, seconds later, she was frowning. Now what on earth's got into her? she wondered.

'Youngsters!' she muttered to herself.

You never knew where you were with them.

Her father had kept his word.

Becky still couldn't quite believe that she was standing on the pavement in Oxford Circus. Her eyes were wide with amazement, as were her mother's. Come to think of it her mother looked an entirely different person tonight. She looked beautiful!

She had made her navy-blue outfit herself, its narrow skirt reaching only to her calves. She wore a jade-green cloche hat with her dark hair tucked up tight out of sight. She hadn't had her hair shingled as so many women had recently, her face was powdered, and her lips showed a trace of lipstick.

Becky felt she herself looked a fashionable young woman. She had thought of buying herself a new hat but the only millinery shop in the village of New Malden charged such outrageous prices she had changed her mind. Instead she had retrimmed her straw hat with multi-coloured ribbons to match the floral high-necked blouse she was wearing above her long grey skirt.

Becky now glanced at her father. The word to describe this big man was hard to find. Neat he most certainly was, but not very much in fashion. Quickly she suppressed a giggle. Younger men were wearing wide-legged trousers, navy-blue blazers and straw hats known as boaters. Her dad's plain dark suit, white shirt and modest tie topped by his hard bowler hat suited him well. Wonder of wonders, he had discarded his boots for a pair of well-polished, black laced-up shoes.

'Well, have the pair of you finished yer star gazing? Cos if you have perhaps we could move along.' Joe Russell was feeling really pleased with himself. It had been a bit of a battle, getting his Joyce to dress herself up, but the effort had been well worthwhile and he felt quite proud as they strode off, his wife on one arm and his daughter on the other.

It was grand to see all the different shops, each window-display a show in itself, gleaming with clothes they'd never seen the likes of.

'Oh, Lord,' Joyce muttered. 'Look at that poor man stood in the gutter.' A tray hung round his neck, loaded with boxes of matches. One empty sleeve of his jacket was pinned up, showing that his arm had been amputated. They stopped and Joe put three pennies into his cap which lay on the pavement.

The young man had a card propped against the kerb, on which he had written, I SERVED MY COUNTRY, NOW I NEED HELP TO SUPPORT MY WIFE AND TWO CHILDREN.

'Thank you,' he said as Joe straightened up.

Joe's face reddened and he turned to Joyce. 'There are still so many disabled servicemen, why can't the Government recognize their worth and do something to help the poor blighters?'

Their mood lightened as they looked into some windows which were displaying corsets. Becky looked at her mother and they both had to smother their giggles. The models were male: the corsets were for men!

Now they were in Regent Street. Dickins & Jones, Robinson & Cleaver and then the windows of Liberty's loomed ahead.

'Becky,' her mother said, tugging at her sleeve. 'We'll have to come up to town another time during the day when this shop is open. You'll never believe all the things they sell for people who are interested in sewing.' Becky took two steps backwards and tilted her head in order to read the nameplate above this shop that her mother was drooling over – the Needlewoman.

It was a dream of a shop. 'I've heard it called by several different names,' said Joyce, the nostalgia evident in her voice as she explained further. 'For all brides-to-be a visit to this establishment was a must. Young girls and their intended bridesmaids would be busy sewing for months ahead of the wedding. As indeed would the bride's elderly female relations. A girl was judged on what she had in her bottom drawer.'

Becky laughed, and her mother rebuked her. 'You can laugh young lady, but it is to be hoped that you'll be doing similar work before long.'

'Mum, I didn't mean to laugh but a bottom drawer sounds so funny.'

'Funny it never was,' Joyce snapped. 'A very serious business, believe you me. Tablecloths, napkins, huckerback hand towels, guest towels and pillowcases all had to be hand-embroidered.' She paused as if deep in thought. Smiling softly, she pointed to the skeins of silk laid out so decoratively in wicker baskets. 'I'd like a guinea for every one of those I used when I was filling my bottom drawer. Those extra fine ones my mother used to stitch lazy daisies on the top and bottom of my nightdresses.'

Joe Russell placed his hand on his wife's shoulder. 'And very fetching you looked when you wore them,' he quietly told her.

Becky had to tear herself away from the Needlewoman. What she wouldn't give to be let loose in that store with an unlimited amount of money to spend.

They walked past Hamley's. 'That 'appens to be the most famous toy shop in the world,' her father told her with pride.

A little further on they reached Mappin & Webb. 'THE jewellers and silversmiths to the nobility,' Joe informed them.

'Mine of information tonight, aren't you,' Joyce teased her husband, but there was fondness in her voice.

Down into Piccadilly Circus they went. 'Oh, look!' Becky cried out in sheer amazement.

Her father laughed as he watched the different expressions flit across his daughter's face. For one so young who had rarely in her life visited London, Piccadilly Circus, with its brilliant flashing lights and cascading advertisements, had to be a wonderful sight.

'Mum, all this electricity!'

The babble of conversation that was now taking place between mother and daughter had Joe Russell laughing fit to bust.

'Why do we only have gaslight? Why are our streets still so dim of a night-time cos we've only got those funny old lampposts? Will we ever get lights like these? Why should London be so different from everywhere else?'

'Put a sock in it,' Joe pleaded. 'To answer your last question first, young lady, London is the capital city of England. The powers that be will get around to seeing that the whole country has the benefit of electricity one day. Won't be for a while yet though.' Turning to his wife Joyce, he lowered his voice. ''T'was worth bringing her, wasn't it?'

'Most certainly was. For me an' all. I never knew it was lit up like this.'

'Funny really, with me being in the parcel office most of the time I 'ardly ever put a foot outside of Waterloo Station. True, the platforms have had electric light for some time now though the waiting rooms still have their gaslights an' coal fires. You know, luv, I was talking to one electrician only the other day an' he told me that at the last count two an' a 'alf million light bulbs were being used in London. That's something to think about, eh?'

'Dad,' Becky was tugging at the sleeve of her father's jacket. 'Are we near Trafalgar Square?'

'About a stone's throw away, why? Do you want to go an' see Nelson's Column?'

'Yeah, but mostly I'd like to see all the pigeons and the fountains. May we feed the pigeons?'

Joe shook his head in disbelief. Nelson's Column against pigeons and the pigeons win! Ah well, as long as she's happy. 'Anything you want, my luv. But first I'm gonna buy my two ladies a little present. No gent worth his salt comes to Piccadilly Circus without doing so. Wait there,' Joe ordered as he stepped briskly towards the statue of Eros. The well-known flower seller – an old lady, dressed in black, a heavy shawl around her shoulders and a wide-brimmed hat on her head – sat at the foot of the statue and watched him approach.

'Gonna buy a button 'ole for yer ladies?' she called out.

'Wouldn't miss the chance for the world,' Joe answered as he fished in his pocket for some loose change.

''Ere,' she grinned broadly, showing several of her front teeth were missing. 'A rose for yer missus, an' a sweet bunch of violets for yer young gal.'

Joe handed over a silver shilling and was rewarded by the old lady's jolly remark of: 'Gawd bless yer. You're a gent an' no mistake.'

'Next time we come up we'll tackle the window-shopping from another direction,' her father promised. 'We'll have a look at all the theatres, especially the London Hippodrome, maybe 'ave supper somewhere.'

'That's as maybe,' Joyce quickly butted in, 'but promises are like pie-crust, made to be broken and I'm hungry now. How about you, Becky?'

'Me an' all. I'm starving.'

'Tell me,' Joe said grinning, 'how does fish an' chips sound t' the pair of you?'

'Scrumptious,' Becky cried before her mother had time to answer.

'Well, me money won't run to these London prices, so we'll make Trafalgar Square our last port of call for this trip. Then as soon as we get home you two go indoors, light the oven and put the plates in to warm and I'll trot off for three of the biggest portions of cod an' chips you've ever seen.'

On the homeward journey a tired but happy Rebecca was reminding herself that it was as she had always known, her parents were smashing. The memory of this London excursion would remain with her for a very long time.

During the following weeks a number of things happened which made the future seem a whole lot more rosy to both Becky and to Ella. There was to be a Harvest Supper, followed by a social, in the local church hall and notices were being sent out from the organizers pleading for volunteers to come forward and lend a helping hand.

One afternoon, Becky and Ella were sitting on the outside steps of the laundry during their tea break, discussing this coming event when Ella suddenly said, 'Pete's going to see t' the music.' She glanced quickly at Becky to see what Becky's reaction was, for she knew that Becky wasn't aware of just how often she and Peter had been out together.

Becky smiled to herself before answering. So that was the way the wind was blowing. 'For the Harvest Supper you mean?'

'Yes, and for the entertainment during the evening.'

'That's good, let's hope he comes up with something a bit more lively than the usual rubbish we have to put up with when the village has a do.'

'He will. And by the way, Pete's going to do you a big favour.'

'Me?'

'Yes, you. We were talking about you and Tom Ferguson one evening and I told Pete that you were sick an' tired of the way Tommy always dogged your footsteps.'

'Did you now? And what did your Peter have to say to that?'

Ella's cheeks flushed a bright red. 'Don't be like that, Becky, please. He's not my Peter, it's just that he's lonely an' we seem to get on with each other.'

'Well, well,' murmured Becky, then she relented and stopped her teasing, turned to Ella and said, 'I'm pleased for you both. Honestly I am. I could see from the moment he started at the Wellington that you two suited each other.'

'Aw, thanks, Becky. I've been wanting to tell you. I really do like him and he's not as old as we thought. He's twenty-six. He was in the Army during the War. Saw a bit of service in France, that's probably what aged him. But we're getting away from what I was gonna tell you.'

'Something about him doing me a favour, wasn't it?'

'Yes,' Ella said, a triumphant tone in her voice. 'You remember the Saturday you went up to London with your mum an' dad? Well Pete an' I went to the pictures and Tommy asked if he could tag along. Having said yes, Pete had a brain wave, he invited his landlady's daughter to come as well.'

'And?' Becky asked, her eyes bright with curiosity.

'Her name's Mary, Mary Marsden.'

'Oh, for goodness sake stop yer tantalizing and tell me what happened.'

'Nothing happened. Mary's not the brightest person on God's earth. Seems she's been in service for some time but she was so unhappy her mum persuaded her dad to let her come home. She's not got a job at the moment. She an' Tommy seemed to like each other. Anyway Pete's been busy scheming and singing Tom's praises and the long and short of it is Tom's been asked to Sunday tea at the Marsdens' and Mary's coming to this Harvest do.'

'Are you sure about this?' Becky asked.

'Oh yes, I'm quite sure of it.'

Becky reached out for Ella. She put her arms around her friend's neck and they were laughing loudly. Suddenly Ella, her eyes twinkling, enquired, 'You're not in any way jealous?'

'Jealous! Oh you, Ella, you're mad.'

'Well, I just wondered, he's been your Tommy from the day we started at the laundry. No. I've just remembered from the day he stepped on your foot at that first dance we went to. Own up an' shame the devil, you'll be really annoyed if Tom transfers his attentions to Mary.'

Becky gently slapped Ella's shoulder. She was shaking her head from side to side and still laughing fit to burst.

When their merriment had settled down, Becky muttered, 'Thank God for small mercies. Maybe I'll be able to enjoy the evening without Tommy glaring at me all the time if I so much as speak to another fellow.'

The whistle went, signalling that tea break was over, but Ella couldn't resist having one more jibe at Becky. 'You'd better not start feeling fancy free, thinking you're gonna be the belle of the ball an' have the pick of the field at this barn dance. After all, you weren't there when we went to the pictures. Tommy might have cottoned on to Mary, thinking any port in a storm. When he sees you, arrayed in all your finery, he might just decide there's no one in the world like you, that he can't live without you, you're the love of his life. Then what will you do?'

'I know what I'll do to you right now if . . .' Becky didn't have to finish what she was saying. Ella had fled, her laughter echoing back down the corridor.

Chapter Five

WHAT A WEEK! Everything that could go wrong at the Wellington Laundry had gone wrong. One of the main boilers had packed up, so all the others had to be shut down while plumbers did their best to find the trouble. There had been a fire in the pressing room, albeit only a small fire, but it was a wonder that it hadn't spread. An extra van had been needed to cope with getting the backlog of deliveries out on time. No motor van had been available for hire and as a last resort Harry Horsecroft had been offered the chance of a few days' work.

It had taken more than an hour to load the neat parcels and boxes of freshly-laundered linen on to his cart, because each batch required full details of the route he must take and what roads came first regarding delivery.

'No, there is no need for you to ask for payment from any of the customers,' Mrs Bradford assured a flustered Harry, 'these are all account customers.'

'I doubt whether half of what we've said has got through to that man,' Mrs Bradford whispered to Becky. 'Do you think he's been drinking? Surely not, not this time in the morning, but he is giving me that impression.'

Becky busied herself with the ledger, ticking off each item that had been entrusted to Harry. She made no answer to Mrs Bradford, who had answered her own questions. Probably he's not yet sobered up from last night's session, Becky was thinking to herself.

Why did everybody presume that Harry Horsecroft was dim? Quite the opposite was Becky's opinion. He led a good life doing just what he wanted to. Neither he nor his wife seemed to bother what they looked like or what anybody thought of them come to that. It was as her dad said, 'There's none so daft as those that don't want to know.'

Harry took a reasonably clean handkerchief from his pocket and wiped his sweating brow, tugged his flat cap further down over his forehead and managed to manoeuvre his horse and cart safely out of the yard.

When he pulled his horse to a stop outside the butcher's shop and got down from his seat the horse had bolted before he had time to walk to the back of the cart and take off the box containing the butcher's clean aprons. It seemed that the whole village got to know that Harry Horsecroft's horse and cart were on a runaway expedition and for a while it provided quite a commotion and a great deal of amusement as men and boys tried to grab the reins of the horse.

Such was the situation in the laundry that most of the pressers and packers, including Becky, had been sent to lend a hand in the boiler room once things were on the way to being normal again.

Her back ached, her arms ached, her legs ached, in fact there wasn't a bone in her whole body that didn't ache. The only good thing was, Becky kept reminding herself, today was Friday and at least she had the weekend to look forward to.

She had asked herself a number of times this week how Ella had managed to stand the work in the wash house all these years, and not only stand it but to have got so used to the hard work that she actually liked it. Becky sighed. Why was it that she couldn't be contented? She had never liked her job and never would.

Since her talk with her father she had applied for two new jobs. One was in the local dry-cleaners; she wasn't sorry when she wasn't offered the post because the work hardly differed from what she was doing now. The other position, advertised in the local paper, had been at the cigarette kiosk down on the railway station but it had gone to an older woman. She sometimes despaired that she would ever be able to break away from this place.

'You might feel better if you put a smile on that face of yours.' Ella had come up behind Becky without her hearing.

'Must be looking the way I feel,' Becky answered, and tried to smile. The smile came out as a grimace, and made Ella feel so sorry for her. Becky was different, always wanting the moon, never that which was within her grasp.

'Cheer up for God's sake,' Ella implored, 'there's a heck of a lot t' look forward to in the next couple of weeks. Hope you haven't forgotten the jumble sale tomorrow afternoon. You haven't, have you?'

'No.' Now Becky did smile. 'Ma Turner in the café told my mum that it was gonna be worth going to. Said she'd heard that most of the stuff had come from the big houses.'

'Well, there you are then. Might even find ourselves a decent dress seeing as how the Harvest Supper is the Saturday after.'

'Decent dress! You've got some hopes. Anyway it's supposed to be a sit-down meal with entertainment afterwards. My brother Fred said he's thinking about coming and if he does he's going to offer to do a turn.'

'A turn? What kind of a turn? I would have thought your Fred would make a good comedian, he's always telling jokes.'

'Funny you should say that, Ella. My dad told him the same thing but to remember it would be a family show and not to tell near-the-knuckle jokes nor any about the vicar.'

'Bet that's put him right off coming.'

'Don't suppose he ever had any intentions of coming in the first place. How about your Jimmy? Will he come?'

'Don't know, depends on what shift he's on. He's a damn sight more sociable since our Ronald joined the Army. Ronnie was always jealous because Jimmy had a job and he couldn't get one. Can't say I blamed him, he was the eldest and it must have been awful for him, never having a penny in his pocket except what me mum or Jimmy gave him.'

'Yeah, can't have been easy,' Becky agreed. 'Still your mum told my mum that Ronald was doing well. Said that by all accounts Army life was suiting him.'

'When you've quite finished your little meeting, there is quite a bit of clearing up to be done before the whistle will be sounding.'

Both girls stopped talking and turned to face Mrs Bradford in surprise. 'Sorry,' Ella mumbled, walking hurriedly away.

Once again Becky thanked God it was Friday as she returned to the arduous task of transferring wet linen from one vat to another.

'Gosh, someone important, or at least well-off, must have died.' Becky's voice was quiet and soft, filled with emotion.

Ella, standing next to her, nodded her head. 'I'm sure you're right.'

The two friends grinned and Becky put out her hand and squeezed Ella's arm, saying, 'We've hit the jackpot coming to this jumble sale today, it was worth coming early and queuing outside, wasn't it?'

Ella again nodded her head. 'It certainly was. I've never seen such an array of clothes and most of them are really good quality.'

Rebecca's lovely face lit up with a lop-sided grin as the lady standing behind the long trestle table handed her the black dress, now neatly wrapped in brown paper, that she had just paid ninepence for.

'You'll be able to turn that into something quite dazzling,' Ella beamed at her.

'I'll try,' Becky answered.

'You won't just try, you'll do it.'

'Bully,' Becky teased, pushing the parcel into her almost full shopping bag.

Ella frowned. 'I didn't make you buy it against your will, did I? You do like it?'

'Don't be silly, Ella, I think it's probably the nicest dress I've ever owned, it's . . . well . . . kind of graceful. The material is lovely and I don't want to spoil it. I just think it might be difficult to alter.'

Ella relaxed and laughed. 'Honestly, Becky, you really are an old fusspot. Look at the amount of sewing you do. Loads more than me an' I do my fair share. 'Course it won't be difficult. Not if you put your mind to it. Now, come on, let's see what else we can find, I wouldn't mind a skirt an' a top if we can find one that's halfway decent.'

'Look over there.' Becky's finger was pointing, her eyes twinkling with delight.

'Oh yeah, it's our mums. Did you know they were manning a stall together?'

'No, I never,' Becky protested. 'Wonder why they never said. Let's see if they've got any bargains left.'

Peggy James and Joyce Russell watched, pride evident on their faces, as their daughters came across the hall. Both girls had grown into young ladies worthy of a second glance.

Peggy was asking herself why had she worried for years because her Eleanor was plump. It had only been puppy fat. Today, at eighteen, she still had plenty of flesh on her bones but looked really quite fit and healthy. A real picture. She hadn't lost that country look despite having worked in that laundry for four years. She was still too much of a tomboy but nobody was going to be able to change her. To live for the day seemed to be Eleanor's code of behaviour.

Joyce was also reflecting on how grown-up her Rebecca was – still small-boned and slender, with dark hair that had a sheen all of its own, clear, flawless skin and cheeks that reminded one of a ripe peach. A dainty little miss was how her eldest son Jack had described his sister and today, looking at Rebecca, Joyce had to admit that he hadn't been far wrong.

'They've both hung on to their long hair,' Peggy observed to Joyce.

'Yeah, can't say I'm sorry, can you?'

'Well, in a way I suppose not, though Ella did tell me that they were both considering having it cut in that new style, you know, a short, swinging bob, I think is what it's called.'

Joyce thought for a moment before answering her friend. 'Don't seem only yesterday they each cut their first tooth and we took them down the village for their first trim. Bet it would cost a fortune to have their hair cut now if they wanted that new style. Have to go to an expert, I expect.'

'Wouldn't want to be there, would you? See all that lovely hair falling to the floor. My Ella's so fair an' your Becky, all those gorgeous curls that you used t' do in ringlets, all being chopped off. Don't bear thinking about.'

'Doing your good deed for the church fund, are you?' Ella's loud voice put a stop to all their reminiscences.

'Yes,' Ella's mother smiled, 'and we've got just the thing for two young ladies who are thinking of going out on the town.' With this remark she placed an assortment of beaded handbags on top of the table. 'A lot of work has gone into them but no one seems to want to buy them.'

Becky handled a bag, and murmured, 'They're lovely for evenings, but not much use to us.'

Ella wrinkled her nose. 'You'd have t' be really dressed up to use one of those.'

'What about these?' Joyce Russell was holding aloft two waistcoats, one plain black, the other in pale pastel colours on a grey background. 'We'll let you have these for a couple of coppers each.'

'What would we do with them?' queried Ella. 'They're gents' waistcoats.'

Becky raised her eyes to meet those of her mother and they both smiled. 'I know what you're thinking, Mum. Embroidery down the front of the plain one and it would look gorgeous with a plain black skirt, yes?'

'Exactly,' her mother agreed. 'Set a new fashion. Something out of the ordinary. You can have it for threepence.'

'Done.' A grinning Becky was already fishing in her bag to find the pennies.

'Now, Ella,' Joyce turned to Eleanor, 'you'd knock spots off any other girl if you wore something like this. Better than all the new skinny fashions, especially for the Harvest Supper. Wear something long and flimsy, match up a blouse to one of these colours in this waistcoat, you wouldn't even have to alter it.'

'Better still,' Ella's mother chipped in, 'wear this. I jumped the queue and bought you this long grey skirt, hope you like it.'

Ella gasped as her mother fanned the skirt, displaying the fact that it was very full, the material soft chiffon, fully lined with dark grey silk. Ella took the skirt and held it up against herself. It was calf-length, just right. 'Oh it's gorgeous!' she breathed, letting the chiffon trickle through her fingers.

'Well, any white blouse would go well with the skirt and waistcoat.'

'Yes, I'm sure it would,' Ella said.

Her mother heard doubt in her voice. 'But what?'

'It buttons up on the wrong side.'

Becky looked at her mother, Joyce looked at Peggy and they all three burst out laughing. 'Who's going to notice that?' Becky said, doing her best to control her merriment. 'You can always leave it undone.'

Now it was Ella's turn to laugh. 'Oh, all right. As you say, at least wherever we go nobody else will be wearing the same outfit.'

'True. True,' Becky added. 'You could change the buttons, whatever, we'll look tip-top, you'll see.'

There was no going out for Becky or Ella for the next week.

'You'll have blunted every needle in the house so you will,'

Joyce laughed, using her hip to push open Becky's bedroom door. 'I've brought you each a mug of cocoa, it's time you packed up all this sewing for tonight and you, Ella, ought to be thinking of getting home.' She set the tray holding the mugs down on to the bedside table and stooped to lift some pieces of material from the floor. 'You two certainly got yourselves some good bargains at the church's jumble sale.'

'We sure did,' Ella replied in a frivolous mood. 'We've spent the last half-hour making these velvet bows to tie up our bonny brown hair. Well, Becky's bonny brown hair and in my case, bonny fair hair.'

Joyce grinned. 'There'll be no stopping the pair of you when you step out in all your finery on Saturday, will there?'

'Not unless the fellows are all stone blind,' Ella joked.

Joyce looked at her daughter. 'What's making you so quiet, Becky? Aren't you going to show me what you've done to your dress?'

'No, not tonight, Mum. When I've finished it I'll try it on, see what you think then before I press it.'

'All right, luv, but start clearing up now and don't let your cocoa go cold.' She turned and went out of the room and down the narrow flight of stairs. They're both good girls, she told herself. It said a lot for each of them that the clothes they wore were always nice. It wasn't as if either of them had a lot of money to spend. Come to think of it, hardly ever did they have any new outer garments. Underwear and shoes were about all that they ever bought new. Most of their dresses, yes, and even coats were second-hand, came from the gentry a lot of what they picked up, so I suppose you could say they were lucky. By persevering they managed alterations. If it were a plain dress or skirt often all they did was add a belt, different buttons, or a lace collar. That's where I come in. She smiled to herself and thought, crocheting is the one thing I do well, I can turn out a piece of decorative lace with the best of them. Suppose we've all been gifted in different ways and when it comes to Becky and her friend Ella, well, they are undeniably gifted with their needles.

Harvest Festival time was lovely. It did mean that summer was almost over but there were still the golden evenings. Everyone was out to enjoy themselves, get together, have fun before the dark evenings and short days came to lower their spirits. Although Kingston was in Surrey it did have many large factories and streets of small two-up and two-down houses and the poverty was about equal to that of any South London area. However this time of the year belonged to the country folk. With the harvest safely gathered in, the surrounding fields were yellow with stubble. The river boats were still operating, the dark blue skies still reflected in the dear old Thames and Hampton Court Palace was still attracting lots of visitors.

It was Saturday night and the whole village of New Malden would be socializing, before the long winter closed in on them all. Old and young alike would gather in the congregational hall for this Harvest Supper. Quite a few older members of the community would leave once the supper was over, though others would stay to enjoy the music and to watch the brave ones climb the platform to do a turn.

It had been raining earlier in the afternoon but now Ella and Becky could scarcely believe their good fortune. They couldn't have asked for a more pleasant evening as they set off to walk down to the village, their parents having gone on ahead some time ago.

When the girls arrived at the hall on Saturday evening Peter Tomson was already there waiting for them. As they headed for the cloakroom, with Peter chatting to Ella, Becky thought about how much Ella had mellowed in the past couple of years. This quietly spoken, nicely made-up and elegantly dressed young lady was completely different from the tomboy Ella used to be.

But then she herself was also totally different to what she had been when they had first started to work at the Wellington Laundry. Long-forgotten memories came flooding back to Becky. She recalled the horror she had felt when she saw the sack aprons and the coarse overalls they had been given to wear. She remembered saying to herself, I won't be working here for long.

Whatever had happened to that resolution? The truth was she hadn't made much of an effort. Lately she had fantasized about working in London, maybe in one of the big stores around Regent Street. Talk about going from the ridiculous to the sublime!

Once inside the ladies' room Becky watched as Ella made straight for the mirror. 'It's going to be a marvellous night, I know it is,' Ella was saying, bubbling with excitement. 'And you look smashing in that dress,' she said, admiring Becky from a few feet away. 'It really does suit you.'

Becky smiled. She had worked hard on this dress but it had been worth it. She hadn't altered the length, just the sleeves, which had been too fussy for her liking. Around the bust she had put in quite a few tucks and she had done away with the collar altogether. 'You look a proper treat yourself,' Becky said, 'suppose we had better sally forth before your Peter starts to worry that you've gone off somewhere without him.'

A great deal of time and effort had gone into making the hall look as nice as possible for this Harvest Supper. The backdrop to the stage had a country theme. Sheaves of barley and wheat together with various bunches of tall grass had been woven together and strung from corner to corner and side to side.

Gramophone records were now being played but after the meal there was to be a live band as part of the show.

Becky and Ella's eyes were everywhere, taking it all in, the music, the decorations, the smiling older folk, the young girls in their pretty dresses, the lads decked out in best bib and tucker. Ella spotted Peter and Becky sighed as she saw a smiling Tommy was with him. A few seconds later Peter excused himself, saying he wanted to introduce Ella to some of his mates. Becky was left alone with Tom.

She was speechless. This was the last thing that she had wanted to happen right at the start of the evening. If Tommy was going to monopolize her she would never get to meet anyone else. Then suddenly it came to her that Tommy wasn't the lad she was so used to. Looking directly at him, she was amazed, he looked so different, better than she had ever seen him look before. He'd had his hair cut, he was wearing a navy-blue suit with a white shirt that was open at the neck and for once he didn't have that hangdog look about him.

'Hello, Becky,' he said, smiling broadly. ''Aven't 'ad a chance t' talk to you for a long time. At work I think you've been avoiding me.'

She couldn't have felt worse if he had knocked her for six. 'Don't be silly, Tom, you're just imagining that.'

What had happened to him? Becky asked herself the question, but couldn't answer it. Tommy Ferguson not only looked different, he sounded different.

'Can I get you a drink? There is just about time before we have to sit down.'

'Yes please, that would be nice.'

'Then, Becky, will you do me a favour? Later on in the evening will do.'

'Of course, if I can.'

'I want you t' come and say hello to my friend Mary, I've taken her to see your mum and dad. They liked her. Look, there she is, talking to Ella.' Tommy called out, 'Won't be long, Mary.'

Across the room, Becky saw a plumpish young lady stand up and give a friendly wave. Her round face had a smile on it that spread from ear to ear, but that old-fashioned dress! It was meant for someone years older and as for her hair, shiny and clean but cut short close to her head with a fringe which lay long on her forehead, it was the hairstyle of a young schoolgirl.

Becky thought with satisfaction of the lovely frock she was wearing, and the time that she and Ella had spent in arranging their hair then immediately she chided herself not to be so spiteful.

Tommy was waving back and Becky realized how happy he looked. And that wasn't all. He no longer looked shy or out of place. Without saying a word he went to the bar and returned with a glass of orange squash, which Becky took, murmuring, 'Thank you.'

He answered, 'See you later,' turned on his heel and left her. Before, he had always been all fingers and thumbs. He held himself more upright as he walked, she decided as her eyes followed him across the floor. More than that, he radiated confidence.

That Mary Marsden had done wonders for him concluded Becky as she went to find her parents.

Several women had contributed to the baking of the food and everyone said the pies and the boiled ham were surprisingly good. The meal was complemented with traditional flagons of home-made cider, with fruit juice for the children. Speeches were made, the vicar said how pleased he was to see so many folk there and he gave thanks to God for the bountiful harvest. Then the tables had to be cleared and the hall set up ready for the entertainment to begin.

Becky couldn't believe just how well in with the organizers Peter Tomson seemed to be. It almost looked as if Peter was in charge. It was Peter who asked the band to set up, and who suggested the best place on the stage for them to do so. It was also Peter who organized the acts that had volunteered to be part of the evening's entertainment, and jollied Tommy into helping to line up the chairs for those who'd be watching.

'Marvellous how well Peter has settled in, isn't it?' Ella smiled at Becky. 'I just hope that everything goes off well.'

Becky gave an answering smile and held up crossed fingers for luck. Peter seemed to have become a very important part of Ella's life. Standing next to her friend now, Becky felt a bit neglected. If she sat with her parents it wouldn't seem right; if she sat with Ella and Peter during the concert it might look as if she were playing gooseberry, yet she could hardly sit on her own.

'Becky.' Tommy's eyes met Becky's. 'Will you come and say 'allo t' Mary like you said you would?'

Tom didn't sound quite so sure of himself now, so she gave him a nod of encouragement and said, 'Right now, you lead the way.'

Becky offered up a silent prayer that she might say all the right things to this new friend of Tommy's. It was obviously so important to him. Mary was a short dumpy girl, very intense-looking, and Becky felt hard pushed to guess her age. One thing in her favour was her eyes, big, wide and the deepest blue she had ever seen, Becky decided as she held out her hand. 'Hello, Mary, it's nice to meet you and really nice to know that you and Tom have become friends.'

Mary laughed into her hand.

Becky racked her brain for something else to say.

'D'you like Tommy?' Mary asked abruptly.

'Yes, I do. We've been friends for a long time.'

Mary made a face. 'I've never made many friends because I've been away in domestic service.'

'You'll make a lot now, Mary,' Tom quickly assured her, 'won't she, Becky? You'll help her, won't you?'

Mary laughed and Becky laughed with her. 'Of course I will.'

'D'you mean that?' Mary asked, excitedly raising her voice so that it was overheard by those standing nearby.

Becky took hold of Mary's hand, saying, 'I think it's a smashing idea. Come on, no time like the present, come and meet some of the girls I work with, you'll like them, I know you will.' Still holding hands Becky urged Mary forward.

They took a few steps and then Mary paused, turned and gave Tom a wave of her hand, and he waved back.

Becky took Mary around the hall introducing her to different groups of girls that she knew, all the time smiling and talking, but there was a lump in her throat and a blur before her eyes. She hoped against hope that Mary and Tommy would be good for each other, that life would be kind to them. They seemed well-suited. Two more genuine young folk it would be hard to find.

'The evening has been a great success, and on behalf of us all here I would like to thank the committee for all the hard work that they have put into making it so, and ask that they give some thought as to when the village might next enjoy such a lovely get-together.' Applause instantly broke out and amid great cheering Joe Russell left the platform and rejoined his wife and daughter.

Earlier the vicar had whispered to Joe that Peter Tomson was supposed to be making the closing speech but he couldn't be found and would Joe kindly step into the breach?

'Did you see Ella leaving?' Becky's mother asked as they were helping to pack the chairs away.

Becky shrugged. 'No, I had a drink with her and Peter during the interval, but I haven't seen her since.' They must have cleared off then, Becky told herself, feeling a little put out that they hadn't said they were leaving. Still, it's none of my business what they choose to do.

Chapter Six

MONDAY MORNING. EIGHT weeks since the Harvest Supper and less than a month to go until Christmas.

Peggy James had been downstairs before five o'clock this morning to cook breakfast for her son, Jim, and see him off to work. Slowly she had gone about her daily tasks. Lit the fire, sorted the washing out, putting the whites in to soak. Spread damp tea leaves on to the big rug in the front room to lay the dust before getting down on her knees to sweep it with a stiff hand broom. Through the open window she could see and hear George Road coming to life. Smoke was rising from chimneypots, the lampposts were still alight, relieving the foggy gloom of this November day. The clatter of the horse's hooves drawing the milk cart told her it was half-past six. She listened to the sound of milk bottles clinking on stone doorsteps. Next came the tuneless whistle of the paperboy.

Peggy made another pot of tea, sat and drank a cup, thought about what she was going to say to her daughter and wondered what the hell the outcome would be. 'I'd better go and wake her up, take her up a cup of tea.'

Upstairs she set the cup down and gently shook Ella's shoulder. 'Wake up luv, time t' get up or else you're going to be late for work.'

Ella sat up in bed, smiled at her mother and drank her early morning tea. Peggy gazed at her. Silly, silly girl! She probably hadn't given a thought to the consequences of what she and Peter had been up to. Her head ached, the inside of her mouth was dry, she couldn't put it off any longer. Something had to be said to bring it out into the open. 'You're pregnant,' Peggy stated bluntly.

Ella could only stare at her mother. She hadn't wanted her mum to know, didn't want to talk about it, hoping against all the odds that her period would suddenly appear.

'I'm not sure,' she whispered at last, only because she knew she had to make some answer.

'You've missed two periods,' her mother blurted out. 'I consider that pretty conclusive. Or are you waiting for further proof? Have you been to the doctor's? Told anyone?'

Ella shook her head.

'Well?' asked Peggy. 'Say something, for God's sake. When an' where did it happen?'

'Oh Mum . . . It was the night of the Harvest Supper. Peter an' I came back here early. It was warm an' cosy down in the front room, so we . . . kind of . . . just let ourselves go.'

'God give me strength!' her mother snapped. As she stared down at Ella, her feelings were a combination of love and regret. Such a lovely girl, a good daughter, so kind, outgoing, outgoing was right! It had been her downfall. Where would she go from here?

'Does Peter know?' she asked more gently.

Ella nodded. 'He said when I was absolutely sure we'd get married.'

'Sure! What does he want, the baby to be put into his arms?'

'Don't shout, Mum, they'll hear you next door.'

'Bit late for that luv, people will talk an' you won't be able to stop them, but that can't be helped.'

Ella looked terrified.

A surge of relief went through Peggy. She'd had her doubts about what Peter's reaction would be, but as long as he'd promised they'd be wed, well, the sooner they got it sorted out and a date set the better. She picked up the now-empty teacup and made for the door.

'Get yourself up now and ready for work, we'll talk about

what's going to happen tonight. You'd better get word to Peter to be round here by seven.'

If only she hadn't hidden her head in the sand, she chided herself as she filled the kettle once again. She and Ella must both have been mad. If they'd faced the problem earlier instead of waiting so long they might have been able to explain the baby's early arrival to the neighbours as being premature. Time they got her married now she'd be well on the way. Nobody would need any telling, they'd all be able to see for themselves that her Ella had been well and truly caught.

The local gossips would have a field day, she thought bitterly.

Peter felt really cold as he trudged towards Albert Road. As ye sow so shall ye reap, he was thinking to himself. Ella had been frightened when she had told him she thought she was pregnant and he had made up his mind there and then that he would stand by her. Nevertheless, it hadn't stopped him from berating himself for having been so stupid. When he had left home and come South to look for work he had reckoned on bettering himself. The van driver's job at the laundry was only supposed to be a stop-gap until something better turned up. Wasn't much chance of that now.

Married? He couldn't take it in. He hadn't a penny behind him, only a few bob he'd put away for the railway fare so that he could go to his sister's one weekend, see his father, find out how he was getting on. Right mess he'd made of it all.

The road where Ella lived with her mother was nice enough but the houses seemed to him to have a mournful look. There was nothing about them that spelt prosperity. Two rooms, a scullery and an outside toilet downstairs, a box room at the top of the stairs, five more steps up to another two bedrooms. The few times he had been inside the house he had thought how well-worn everything looked. No carpets, only linoleum and a few rugs, and the furniture and the curtains all

seemed fairly shabby. Back home his mother had kept their
house like a new pin. Perhaps he shouldn't be too hard on
Mrs James, since losing her husband in the War and being left
with two sons and Ella to bring up couldn't have been easy.
It was different for my mum, he mused, Dad was always in
work. As a boy he'd served his apprenticeship as a shoemaker,
well, being born in Northampton, a place famous for the
manufacturing of shoes, it had been inevitable.

Pity he hadn't followed in his father's footsteps. Right
from a lad his dad had taught him how to repair his own
boots and given the tools and the right type of leather he
could still make a jolly good job of it. Time was I thought
I might be lucky enough to get a job with a large firm of
shoe repairers, but no such luck. Damn sight better prospects
if I had! Never going to get anywhere if I stay as a van driver
for the Wellington. He sighed heavily as he turned the corner
into George Road.

I'm twenty-six years old, like a good many more men my
age the years we served in France during the War took their
toll and since then life hasn't been easy. Jobs are scarce and
that's a fact. Still, if I'm to be married and become a father
I'd better start looking around and fast.

Ella opened the door in answer to Peter's knock. He wrapped
his arms about her and drew her close. To him she felt
incredibly small, and he knew she was scared. He made a
vow to do whatever he could to put matters right. He would
take good care of her. As his lips came down gently on to
hers Ella was telling herself that things could have been a
darn sight worse. Peter might have cleared off, leaving her
in the lurch.

When Peter released his hold on her, Ella gave him a tight
smile. 'Come on through,' she said, 'Mum's waiting and my
brother Jim has stayed in.' She stood aside while he closed the
door behind them. He squeezed her arm, a gesture of encouragement, trying not to let on how apprehensive he felt.

The warmth of the kitchen hit Peter and he felt he wanted to turn about and run. Jim fixed Peter with an unblinking stare, nodded his head but didn't speak.

Peter said, 'Hello, Jim,' before turning to face Ella's mother. He wasn't given a chance to say a greeting before her first words came out like a shot from a gun.

'Have you set a date for the wedding?'

Peter looked at her in disbelief. 'There hasn't been time,' he answered frantically.

Peggy rose from her chair, drew herself up to her full height. 'Let me tell you this, Peter, before we go any further. Time is what you and Ella have not got. She is by my reckoning about eight weeks' pregnant. You do admit you're the father, don't you?'

Peter took a step backwards. He hadn't expected to be treated this way.

'Mum!' Ella cried, shocked.

'Ella, just be quiet a minute, let Peter speak for himself,' Peggy commanded.

Ella glanced over at Peter, doing her best to smile. Her mum shouldn't be so nasty to him. 'Jim, you say something,' she wailed.

'Get us all a drink,' Jim instructed his sister, 'and you Peter, sit yerself down, my mother is upset which is only natural but we'll all feel better with a glass of something in our hand and then perhaps we can talk calmly, get things settled.'

Peter breathed a sigh of relief as he took the chair indicated.

Peggy stared at her young son in amazement. It seemed there was a lot more to Jimmy than she'd ever given him credit for.

Ella hurried to get the glasses, 'There's only sherry or whisky,' she told her brother.

'Pour a sherry for Mum an' yerself, I'll see to Peter.'

The whisky bottle was less than half full. It had probably been standing in the cupboard since last Christmas. He poured a good measure into two glasses, holding one out to Peter.

Peter took the drink from Jim and tossed a drop down, paused to catch his breath, then more slowly took another sip. 'Thanks,' he murmured.

Poor sod, Jim was thinking, watching the colour rise in Peter's cheeks. What on earth had he been thinking about? Bad enough to take a girl down but no need to put her in the family way. You'd think a man like him, been in the Army an' all, would have had more sense. There was only one answer of course, Ella had led him on. She's my sister and a damned good girl most of the time but from what he'd heard and seen for himself she'd been no angel. According to his mum, it had happened here in this house.

When Ella had brought him back she must have known the house was empty and if that wasn't asking for it . . . I'd say our Ella set her cap at him good an' proper. Well, one thing was certain, Jim said to himself, our mum is never going to let him get away without marrying our Ella. He'll be a married man before he knows what's hit him.

He looked across to where his mother was now seated, sipping at her sherry, and he found he was grinning to himself. She was scheming. There was no other word for it. She was wearing that look, a look he knew so well. Mind you, he reflected, she's a damn good mother and no one could say any different. Her life hadn't been a bed of roses but she'd done her best for us children. More so when we were kids, gone out cleaning, even scrubbing doorsteps so that we never went short.

He knew roughly what she was about to suggest. It was all that she'd been able to come up with but her plans were hardly likely to please Peter. That's if he agreed to them!

'Any ideas as to where you're going t' live, the pair of you?' Peggy jumped in, once more on the offensive.

Peter blinked, completely taken unawares. 'Sorry, Mrs James, I hadn't thought that far ahead.'

'Then it's about time you did. Don't suppose you've got much cash to throw around, you wouldn't be living in lodgings if you had.'

Peter fancied that he'd heard a softening creep into Peggy's voice, so he took a deep breath and rushed in. 'Mrs James, I'm here to tell you that I want to ask Ella to come with me tomorrow to see the local vicar, make arrangements for us to be married as soon as possible, before Christmas I hope, if I can get a special licence.'

Peggy smiled for the first time since Peter had entered the room. 'I'm glad to hear it. Very glad.'

Jim grinned, raised his glass and winked at Peter. So far, so good.

Peter drained his glass, then said, 'As to funds, I can't promise what I haven't got. The church fees, the wedding ring, and a couple of weeks' rent in advance, if we can find a flat which we can afford that is, and I'll be cleared out. I am sorry. I was unemployed for months before I came South, with no chance to save. My Dad will help out a bit, I'm sure he will, if I ask him.'

'We can do better than that,' Peggy told him, her tone now much quieter. 'You can both live here.'

'Here, Mum?' Ella cried, her eyes wide in disbelief.

'Seems best t' me,' her mother said, 'for the time being anyway, give you both a chance t' get on yer feet.'

'But where, Mum? There's no room,' Ella whispered in embarrassment.

Peggy ignored her and turned to Peter. 'I've talked it over with Jim, he's been pretty good about everything. Reckons he'll give up his bedroom, move into the boxroom and I'll get a bed-settee for the downstairs front room which will do for me. We can fold it up during the day. That will leave the top two rooms all on their own for you two. We could get on t' the gas company, get them t' fix a gas stove out on the landing, and that way you'll have a little flat all on yer own an' neither me nor Jim will bother you.'

Game set and match, thought Jim, as he watched Peter doing his best to take it all in.

Ella was all smiles. 'Oh, Mum! Jim, would you really squeeze into that little room at the top of the stairs?'

Jim rose from his chair, held up the whisky bottle and grinned at Peter. 'Might as well see this drop off,' he said as he poured them both another drink.

Could have been a lot worse, Peter was telling himself. Ella looked as if she was ready to jump for joy as she threw her arms around his neck and smothered his cheeks with kisses. Disentangling himself, Peter crossed the room to stand in front of Peggy. 'Thank you,' he said, his voice tight with emotion. 'I'll do my best for Ella and the baby.'

Peggy opened her arms and they hugged one another, 'I know you will, lad,' she whispered. 'Everything will work out fine, you'll see.'

Later, as Peter walked back to his lodgings, he felt as though he'd been punched in the stomach. Again he was trying to convince himself that things could have been worse. He smiled, but it was a cynical smile. They could have been better an' all. A damn sight better if only he hadn't been such an idiot.

Rebecca was looking forward to Ella's wedding, and the fact that she was to be the only bridesmaid. Shame that it had to be such a rushed affair. After all the girls' talk and plans that she and Ella had made over the years there was to be no white wedding. Such a pity. Between them, with their mums lending a hand, they could have turned out a couple of beautiful dresses in no time at all. Peggy James wouldn't hear of it.

'White weddings are for virgin brides,' she declared. 'How can you possibly think of entering the church decked out in white? The vicar wouldn't know where t' put his face. He knows well enough you'll be along there soon after the wedding making plans for the christening. You, my girl, want to be thankful that the Reverend Davis is such a good man.'

The wedding was to be the day before Christmas Eve. Then would come Christmas and then . . . Rebecca hugged her arms around her chest and squeezed hard. She couldn't wait. It was going to be the best Christmas present her dad could possibly give her.

He kept telling her not to build her hopes up. She couldn't help it. The chances of her getting this new job might be slight but she was going to go for it, give it everything she'd got. The prospects, if she landed it, would be endless.

When Ella had come out with the fact that she was pregnant and that she and Peter were to be married, she had been down in the dumps. More than that, she had been jealous. Not of the fact that Ella was going to have a baby. Oh no, not for that reason. It was that lads, men if you like, looked twice at Ella and asked her out. It had always been that way. True, lads looked at her, but nothing ever seemed to come of it. It was as if in some way she scared them off.

She'd love to get married, one day. Even have a baby, one day. But not yet. Life was suddenly offering her more. Much more, she hoped. When she was ready to settle down and start a family she wanted it all planned out. Where they would live? Somewhere in a big house. In a nice neighbourhood. In the meantime her dad had come up trumps.

She could recite word for word how it had come about. It had been a dirty dark night and her dad had seemed really relieved to be home safely and the first thing he wanted was to get his boots off. Becky had watched as he'd started to unlace them.

'Here, Becky, pull,' he'd said, holding up his foot, and Becky had pulled off the boot. Her dad had groaned with relief, then wriggled his toes. Together they had repeated the process with the other boot.

'Listen pet, how would you feel about being a waitress?' he had asked. Hardly daring to believe that she had heard him right, Becky had raised her head and looked up into his face. Wonderful, her dad was grinning like the Cheshire Cat.

She laughed and gave him a playful punch before saying, 'You pulling my leg, Dad? Where would I get a job as a waitress?'

Her father wiggled his toes and again sighed with relief. 'Oh, it's heaven t' get me boots off.'

'Dad! Stop mucking about. Are you just teasing me?'

Her father grinned. 'You haven't answered my question.'

'Dad, of course I'd like to be a waitress, I'd like to try my hand at anything so long as it meant I could get away from that laundry.'

'Well, you might just get the chance.'

The look she gave him showed how doubtful she was about that.

'Honest, Becky, I'm doing me best for you. One of my regular travellers, a right city gent, was telling me about J. Lyons & Company. You know, they've got teashops all over the place. There's one at Wimbledon Broadway an' another at Tooting Broadway.'

'I know about them, Dad, but knowing doesn't get me a job with the company. It's not as if I have any experience of waiting on table.'

'Becky, luv, don't try jumping fences till you come t' them. Just listen. I told this gent about you and he's written down the address of Lyons' head office, Cadby Hall it's called, you've to write to them with all particulars and maybe you'll get an appointment to go for an interview.'

'You really mean it, don't you, Dad?' Becky's eyes were now gleaming with excitement.

'Yes,' he nodded, feeling pleased with himself. He hoped it would go well for his Rebecca. She was so full of dreams, so full of spirit. He didn't want a lad coming along and spoiling her future. It was bad enough that it had happened to young Ella. Starting married life in two rooms with a baby on the way, with no money and no prospects was no joke. In his experience poverty soon made short work of love. For his daughter he wanted more.

'You won't hear anything until after the Christmas holidays are all over,' he warned.

'I don't care, Dad. I'll write the letter and then we'll see. Oh, you're a dad in a million,' she'd told him as she flung her arms around his neck.

She'd written the letter, time had passed, five days, each one marked off on the calendar. Then it had come. A buff-coloured envelope, franked on the outside with the one word in block capital letters, LYONS. To her disappointment, the large envelope held only a slip of paper. 'Thank you for your enquiry, we shall be in touch at a later date.'

Nothing to do but wait and hope.

She'd drifted ever since she had left school, kidding herself that life would be so different when she got another job. Had she really tried to change her way of life? She'd applied for two jobs. Two, and then only after having stuck at the Wellington for four years. Now, J. Lyons! It was like dangling a carrot in front of a donkey. For goodness sake stop thinking about it. Daydreaming won't make it any more of a possibility. Please God, let the New Year come quickly. Let's get rid of 1924 and see what 1925 has to offer.

First though, she reminded herself, there was Ella's wedding to be got through and then the Christmas festivities.

Becky was ready to go round to George Road. 'I think I've got everything, Mum, you bring the buttonholes, will you?'

'Yes, luv. Stop fussing, get yerself away and help Ella get ready. Dad an' I will follow when it's about time for the carriages to arrive.' Joyce Russell opened the front door and stood aside to let Rebecca out. 'My God, it's cold,' she said, and shivered. 'Wrap that shawl round your shoulders and wear it to the church an' all. You can take it off and leave it in the porch. I shouldn't wonder if there's no heating on in the church today an' we'll all be left standing there freezing.'

Becky pulled up the collar of her coat and stepped out gingerly. The pavement was slippery with a dusting of snow and the dark sky looked full of more to come. She hoped this was going to be a happy day both for Ella and Peter. The whole of George Road would be on the lookout, watching what was going on. Of course the truth had got out. Ella had to get married. Most of the neighbours were kind and generous with their approval, taking the line that it takes two. As always there were the odd few, discontented bitchy women, who whispered that Ella was no better than she should be. Becky kept telling herself that she wished the wedding could have been under different circumstances but Ella seemed happy enough to start off her married life in a couple of rooms in her mother's house. It wouldn't do for me, she muttered to herself. Unlike Ella, she couldn't see herself settling for so little. The man she'd marry would have to provide her with a lot more. A whole lot more, she decided as she knocked on the front door of the James house.

Two hours of confusion, bickering and reminiscences later, bride and bridesmaid were ready.

'Look at you!' Becky cried. 'You look absolutely wonderful! Being pregnant must suit you.'

Ella was wearing a blue two-piece, a spray of tiny white rosebuds pinned to her shoulder. During the night her long fair hair had been twisted tightly up into strips of wet rag. Freed, the hair had been springy enough to wind upwards into a nest of wide curls. The hat she wore, if it could be called a hat, was a tiny cream-coloured straw shrouded with fine veiling.

'You don't look so bad yerself,' Ella retorted. 'In fact you look so grand the men will only have eyes for you,' she joked, her voice crackling with nervous laughter.

Becky's dress was long-sleeved and simple, a deep blue like the colour of Christmas hyacinths thus complementing the paler shade that the bride was wearing. She held out her arms and clasped Ella close, hugging her gently. 'Get away with you, it's your day today,' she grinned, straightening up and slipping her arm through Ella's. Then she glanced fondly around the bedroom. 'Be strange coming round here after today, this will be yours an' Peter's living room.'

The snow was falling softly and gently and the two grey horses whinnied as Ella's eldest brother handed her up into the carriage. Ronald was home on leave from the Army in order to give his sister away.

The village was bright with Christmas decorations and the lights from the church glimmered through the snowflakes. Ella gasped to see so many people. It was bitterly cold as she stepped down and Ronald hurried her towards the protection of the church porch.

A pretty young woman in a shabby coat called out, 'Good luck, luv.'

An older woman tugged her shawl tighter around her shoulders and muttered, 'She'll need it.'

'There's a good omen!' the cry went up from several different voices and Ella turned to stare. She looked at her brother and they both laughed. Near the churchyard, leaning on the lychgate, was a sweep, his long-handled brushes perched on his shoulder. Two grubby, ragged little boys stood by his side. They wore neither coat nor hats, snow clung to their hair, the whiteness emphasizing their dirty faces. Their jerseys and short trousers were in need of repair and the socks they wore had slipped down to the top of their scuffed boots, thus revealing little legs and knobbly knees that were well smeared with soot.

'Chuck us a tanner for luck, guvernor,' the tallest of the two lads yelled. Ronald grinned widely as he fished in his pocket and a great cheer went up as the lad caught the coin.

Peter waited at the altar, his eyes bright with admiration

as Ella came towards him. Ella had never thought to see Peter looking so handsome; dressed in a dark grey suit, white carnation in his buttonhole, he looked inches taller than usual.

When the ceremony was over they came out to be smothered in confetti and roaring cheers from friends and neighbours. As bridesmaid, Becky stood with the bride and groom to have her photograph taken. Snow still swirled mixed with confetti and Becky thought what a lovely scene it all made.

Ma Turner from the Cosy Café had saved the day by offering to not only hold the reception on her premises but to see to all the catering as well. Invitations to the reception had been restricted to family, near friends and just a few neighbours. Peggy had sent an invitation to Peter's father and his sister and her family and was so pleased that they had all accepted.

The food was great. The party that followed went marvellously.

It was getting on for nine o'clock when Peter said he and Ella were about to leave. There had been no question of a honeymoon, but Peter's father had booked them a room at the Fountain public house for the night. Once inside the room, Ella kicked off her shoes and sat down on the side of the big double bed.

'I'll go down to the bar and get us both a drink, shall I?' Peter asked.

'Oh, luv, I don't want any more alcohol, see if they'd let you have a pot of tea for me.'

'Frightened of getting drunk are you?' he teased, then relenting he pulled her up and put his arms around her. 'We'll have a proper honeymoon one day,' he promised.

'Oh, Peter, what does it matter? It's been a lovely day. I didn't know we had so many friends. I couldn't have asked for better.'

Peter sighed. 'Do you really mean it?'

'Yes, I do. Everything has been lovely,' she declared.

'Well,' he smiled broadly now, 'tell me, how does it feel to be Mrs Peter Tomson?'

'Wonderful,' she told him, throwing herself into his arms again.

'We'll get by,' he assured her softly, running his hand through her hair, letting loose the tight curls. 'I'll get another job, we'll find a place of our own before the baby is born.'

And at that moment he meant every word.

'I love you, Peter,' Ella murmured, cuddling him.

'I love you too and that's all that really matters,' he answered softly.

Chapter Seven

THE FOLLOWING SPRING provided a sharp contrast to the bad winter. Although it was now only May the fields and surrounding gardens looked very dry. Up on the allotments, beyond the fields that belonged to Harry Horsecroft, men toiled, the young ones stripped to the waist, the older ones in shirtsleeves, their braces dangling loose, planting young lettuces and the first of the runner beans. On a browning patch of grass, Becky sat watching her father work. Beside her lay Ella, stretched out in an ancient cane chair.

'Sunday afternoon is supposed to be a time to rest,' Becky murmured, 'still I suppose weekends and evenings are the only chance a lot of the men get to come up here.'

Ella didn't open her eyes, just turned her head to the side. 'Yeah, but it's not work t' most of them though, is it? I know my Peter can't wait to come here. We can never thank your dad enough for speaking up for him an' getting him that plot.'

'It wasn't nothing, he was only too pleased to help, an' Dad says Pete's doing marvellous.'

'Becky, even my mum said these plots are like gold dust. Pete's made up with having this patch of allotment. Money's short as you well know and the veg and stuff he brings down from here make a world of difference. It helps me mum out an' all. Besides, coming here an' laying out like this is a treat for me, won't I be glad when this baby is born. I'm sick t' the teeth of waddling along like a deformed duck.'

Becky threw back her head and laughed loudly. 'Bit overweight for a duck, aren't you?'

'Thanks a bunch!' Ella cried. 'You're great for a girl's morale.'

'Sorry, luv, didn't mean it. Anyway, you've only about another month to go and then you'll have your figure back an' as my mum says, all your troubles will be in your arms.'

'Can't wait. It seems as if I've been this huge size forever,' Ella said as she clutched her swollen stomach and pulled a face.

They fell silent. It was very warm, even under the shade of the umbrella that Peter had fixed up for them. Becky closed her eyes. She hoped for Ella's sake the baby would be born on time. She really was huge. Ella and Peter had coped well these past months. It couldn't have been easy. Ella had worked hard on their two rooms. She'd made the big room into a bed-sitting room and it was ever so pretty. Once again, being handy with her needle had helped a great deal. Remnants of chintz had been used to transform second-hand furniture and besides making all those loose covers, Ella had stitched some really beautiful baby clothes. I don't think I would have settled down so well and accepted the little that Peter had been able to provide, Becky was saying to herself when Ella broke into her thoughts. 'You've never heard from Lyons, have you?'

There was a pause. Becky still kept her eyes closed; she would rather Ella hadn't raised that subject. The fact that she hadn't heard any more was a sore point. The hopes she had built up no longer seemed a possibility. The whole episode rankled. 'No I never did,' she eventually answered.

'Shame,' Ella sympathized. 'The reason I brought the subject up was because of something I read in the paper. Our Jim brought the paper home. He often does. People read them and leave them behind in the railway carriages all the time.'

'So what was it you read? Something about Lyons?'

'Yes, it was. When we go back I'll get you the paper, I said to Pete that I'd save it for you t' see.'

'Just tell me what it said,' Becky pleaded.

'Well, it started off by saying that J. Lyons and Company were transferring their tea, coffee and confectionery production out of London, to a site in Greenford, though their main food supplies will still be distributed to their teashops from Cadby Hall.'

'That's where I wrote to, Cadby Hall.'

'Listen to the rest of it,' Ella chided softly. 'Because the company are so pleased with the way the teashops have been doing, not only in London but up and down the whole country, they have hit on the idea to have more posh places in the West End. They will be ever so grand an' they'll be known as Corner Houses. What d'yer think of that?'

'Sounds great, but not much help to me. Did it say anything about staff?' Becky queried.

Ella raised her head and prodded Becky, 'Yes, I'm coming t' that. There was a picture of a waitress, dressed in . . . well you know, the usual black dress and white apron only somehow the girl looked different and above the illustration it said, "The perfect Nippy".'

'Why Nippy?'

'I dunno, do I. It also said it was going to advertise on hoardings an' buses in the city with messages like, "Let Nippy take care of you", and "Lunch at Lyons".'

'Nothing about staff?'

'Why don't you shut up an' listen t' what I'm telling you?'

'Cos you're taking yer time over it, I'm beginning to think you're writing a book.'

'Right.' Ella raised herself up on her elbows, her face suddenly bright with enthusiasm. 'Now I'll tell you the best bit, Becky, it said the company was about to start a recruiting campaign to find suitable young ladies who are willing to go on a training course.'

Becky let out a cry of triumph, 'Please God, let that mean

they'll be in touch with me. Please, please,' she yelled. Then glancing at Ella she felt her conscience prick her. 'Oh, Ella! I'm so sorry. Did I make you jump? I'm right selfish, aren't I?'

''Course you didn't, don't be so daft,' Ella protested gallantly. 'I hope just as much as you do that they write an' offer you a job, you've been at that crummy laundry quite long enough.'

'Oh, bless you Ella. You really have made my day. I'll be up bright an' early every day now, waiting for the postman. Tell you what, you're such a lovely pal, I'm gonna treat you. What d'yer fancy, I'll get us both an ice cream an' one each for me dad and Peter, and shall it be a bottle of cream soda or would you rather have plain lemonade?'

'Just get the ice cream,' Ella said, lumbering to her feet. 'Yer dad brought two flasks of boiling water with him and I've got some tea, milk and a few biscuits. I'm sure we'd all rather have a cuppa, so I'll make it while you've gone over to the shop.'

Becky hesitated, watching Ella walk towards the wooden hut where her father kept all his gardening tools. From the back Ella looked like an old woman and as she reached the doorway she had to clutch at the frame to heave her bulk over the step. Poor Ella. The sooner this pregnancy was over the better.

A whole week went by without any letter arriving for Becky. She was so tensed up that her mother remarked that were she a clock her spring would have busted by now.

'There's always tomorrow,' Becky kept saying as she watched the postman walk by the house each morning. She was no longer sure whether she longed for the day she might hear from Lyons or no longer expected to. There was so much at stake. She had accepted that Lyons were not going to keep their promise and contact her, then Ella had told her about the newspaper article. Hope had been rekindled. The waiting and wondering were driving her mad. Lyons had said they were going to get in touch at a later date. Surely big firms such as Lyons kept their word?

It was Tuesday of the following week when Becky woke early, at seven, to the sound of the postman's rat-a-tat-tat. A crack in the curtains showed the sky was blue and the sun already bright. There was no wind. It was going to be a very warm day.

It felt as if her heart was in her mouth as she shoved her feet into her slippers, pulled on her cotton housecoat and went downstairs. Her mother was in the kitchen and sounds of her preparing breakfast could be clearly heard. If the truth be told Joyce had already been out into the passage, picked up the letter, seen it was from Lyons and addressed to Rebecca Russell and very furtively had laid it back down on the mat.

Becky gasped as she now picked up the letter, hugged it close to her chest and hoped with all her heart that it contained the news she had been longing for. Should she wait until later to open it? Should Mum be there when she did? Supposing it didn't say what she wanted to hear?

Oh for God's sake, she chided herself. Then, not hesitating any longer, she tore at the flap and withdrew the single sheet of paper.

Joyce Russell had been holding her breath for ages, or so it seemed, as she waited in the kitchen, ears alert to every sound. A great whoop of joy, loud enough to wake the dead, split the silence of the house.

'Oh . . .' Joyce let her breath out in one big gasp. 'Thank Heaven for that,' she cried out loud as Becky burst into the kitchen with a smile on her face that spread from one ear to the other.

'Mum, I'm t' go for an interview in London. I can't believe it.'

'When?' her mother laughed.

'Next Monday, oh Mum, how am I ever going t' get by till Monday?'

Joyce set a cup of tea down on to the table and then went back over to the gas cooker to see to the bacon she had in the frying pan. 'You'll live. Besides, these next few days will give you time to think about what you're going to say and also what you'll wear.'

'Mum, I don't even know how to get to Cadby Hall, the address is in Kensington.'

'Never mind about that now, luv, drink yer tea and go and get yerself washed, breakfast is nearly ready. You can talk t' yer dad tonight, he'll know how to get there. Might even go with you if you ask him nicely.'

'Cor, d'yer think he would? I'd dread the journey on my own. Not too much breakfast, Mum, I'm going to leave early, call at Ella's on me way to work. I've just got to tell her that I've heard at last and that I've got an interview.'

As always the main road was busy at this time in the morning. Everyone rushing to get to work on time, Becky thought, as she hurried along Burlington Road and half-ran down George Road. Using the key on the latch string, Becky opened the door and immediately Peggy James popped her head out from the kitchen and yelled a greeting at her. 'By the look on your face you've had some good news,' Peggy said as she came up the passage wiping her wet hands on her apron.

'I have an' all,' Becky grinned.

'Must be the day for it. Ella's up, she'll tell you.'

Becky flew up the stairs and found Ella sitting reading what looked like an official form.

'Hi yer,' Becky greeted her.

'Crumbs, don't need any telling that you've had good tidings.'

Becky nodded, raised her eyebrows and with a big smile said, 'Guess what, it's been a long time coming but I've got my appointment for an interview with Lyons.'

'Oh, Becky, that's great. I'm really pleased for you,' Ella said, with a catch in her voice. Then she stood up, opened her arms wide and with a twinkle in her eyes, she said, 'Come here an' let me give you a hug.'

It was a few minutes before they drew apart. Rebecca was thinking that Ella was someone special, a good friend, the salt of the earth, when suddenly she remembered what Mrs James had said. 'Your mum said you'd had some good news this morning. Sorry, luv, I was so taken up with my own affairs, come on, tell me.'

Now there was a wide grin on her face and a gleam in her eyes, as Ella told her, 'Peter and I have been offered a house to rent. I'm not sure how it's come about. Peter had already left for work when the post came.' Ella giggled. 'It's not in the best of districts, but at least we'll have room to move about and we won't have to keep telling each other to be quiet, you know . . . when we're in bed together,' she giggled again.

Becky joined in her laughter. 'Marvellous, what a day of surprises, eh? I'm going to be late for work if I don't run, I'll come round tonight and we'll have a good natter then.'

'Yeah, if you're late you might get the sack and you don't want to lose yer job.' It took a minute for the fact that Ella was making a joke to register. They grinned at each other.

'D'you know I am late already so I might as well be hung for a sheep as a lamb. I'll think of some excuse. It will be the first time. How about putting the kettle on and making a pot of tea and you can tell me more about this new place you'll be moving to?'

'Peter hasn't seen the forms yet. He won't like the area.' There was something in Ella's tone that made Becky look up.

'Are you saying there's the possibility he may not want to take the house?'

Ella was on her feet, bending over with difficulty, filling the kettle from a jug of water that stood in the corner. 'He will if I have anything to do with it,' she answered with determination. 'I'm sick an' tired of lugging water up the stairs all the time.'

When the tea was made and they were seated opposite each other at the table, Ella asked, 'Are you looking forward to Monday, Becky?'

To tell the truth Becky felt lighthearted with joy, but she played it down by nodding, 'Of course I am but I won't deny that I'm a little bit frightened.'

'Frightened,' Ella repeated.

'Yes, or maybe apprehensive is a better word, but I'm also excited, excited beyond belief if you really want to know. Just think, this time on Monday I shall be on my way to London.'

Ella gave an amused laugh. 'And when you come home you'll know that you're gonna be a Nippy.'

'Bless you, Ella. Wish I was as sure of it as you are. What's worrying me is the fact that they are not looking for girls to work in South London, in their teashops. This is the West End of London we're talking about. The real city of London. Who knows whether my face will fit?'

Ella leant across the table and laid her hand on Becky's arm. 'Don't put yourself down. You'll take it in your stride. Nothing daunts you. I learnt that when we were kids at school.'

Ella's words cheered her on but they also made her feel that she was getting the best of the bargain. Today both she and Ella had been offered a chance that might open up a new chapter in each of their lives. If she were to get this job with J. Lyons it could be a better chapter than any that had gone before. Would it be such a wonderful opportunity for Eleanor? Only time would tell.

Chapter Eight

PETER TOMSON WAS over the moon. Getting this house was a godsend. Never mind that Mill Street was in a rough area of Kingston, it was a house of their own with a front door that they could close on the world and live their lives as it suited them. God knows he'd been almost at the end of his tether, living in those two rooms. As the only water supply was in the downstairs scullery and the lavatory stood out in the back garden it had been a misery. Bad enough for him, creeping down in the middle of the night to have a pee, doing his best not to wake the house up. Poor old Ella, they had resorted to having a pot under the bed for her.

His mother-in-law, Peggy, had come out on top, one of the best, and Jim, his brother-in-law, had turned out to be an absolute diamond. This didn't alter the fact, though, that he felt he was under everyone's feet all the time and when the baby arrived God knows how they would have managed. Still, that worry was behind them now.

He knew who he had to thank for getting him this place to rent. Tommy Ferguson's mother and father had spoken up for him and Ella and he certainly wasn't going to look a gift-horse in the mouth.

He hadn't let the grass grow under his feet. He had hurried round to see the rent collector the same night the form had arrived and he and Ella had viewed the place the next morning. As they had entered the empty house Ella had sighed heavily. There was so much that needed doing. He hadn't been able to get any time off work but Peggy, neighbours and friends had all pitched in and lent a hand.

Now it was Saturday morning, the sun was shining and Harry Horsecroft's largest horse and cart was outside Peggy James's house. So were half the inhabitants of George Road. Harry had done them proud. The cart was clean, and loads of old blankets and sheets had been provided to cover what few bits and pieces they were taking with them.

A nice oak sideboard and a three-piece suite had been discovered in a second-hand shop and for a shilling extra the owner of the shop had been persuaded to deliver these items direct to Mill Street.

'She can't ride up front with me, it'll be too bumpy, she might get hurt,' Harry said quickly, as Ella made for the front of the cart.

'Well, what am I going to do?' Ella moaned.

Peter gave Jim a sideways glance, and they grinned and nodded at each other. 'Ups-a-daisy,' Ella's brother cried as he and Peter lifted her feet up off the ground. Several men rushed forward to help and Ella found herself suddenly sitting in an armchair high above the pavement in the back of the cart, surrounded by her belongings.

Peter held a clean cloth high and shook it open. 'I'll wrap you in tightly with this, don't want you falling out do we?' Peter smiled at her.

'We won't be too long getting there,' Harry assured her, 'but I've got some canvas strips I could tie you in with if you don't feel safe.'

Ella shook her head. 'I'll be fine,' she said bravely.

'Well, if that's the lot then we're ready to go,' Peter called to Harry.

'Thank Gawd for that,' Harry muttered as he climbed up and took the reins.

Jim looked up at his sister and winked knowingly. 'Mum and I will more than likely be there before you, and Becky and her mum must be there by now so between us we'll soon have that place ship-shape.'

'Thanks, Jim,' Becky murmured, her hands gripping the

arms of the chair tightly as Harry indicated he was ready to move off.

Peggy James smiled happily at her son-in-law. She was glad he had been given the offer of this house. Pity it wasn't a little bit nearer, but then you can't have everything in this life. 'You hold on tight to her now, Peter,' she commanded. 'I don't want nothing happening to my first grandchild.'

Peter grinned as he jumped up to sit beside Ella. 'I'll carry the coal in from now on an' I'll chop the wood but she's going t' have to do all the heavy work like scrubbing the floors,' he told her.

Peggy tossed her head in feigned disgust. 'If I thought you meant it, my lad, I'd have your guts for garters.'

Harry flicked the whip and amid cheers from all the onlookers the horse took its first steps.

Ella bit her lip hard to keep back the tears. This wasn't how her life was meant to be. It was wrong, so wrong. Everything had happened so fast. One minute she was young and fancy-free. Then one night of passion, if you could call it that, and she was married with a home made up of odds and ends and a baby due any time now. The constant fear that the baby might not be perfect never left her. Oh, she would be so glad when it was born. Peter was good and kind but this wasn't what he had wanted any more than she had. It was a good thing he was the strong one. He'd certainly paid the price for letting his feelings get the better of him but he never moaned, and was always ready to comfort her. It was silly to keep dwelling on the past; both she and Peter had acted like a pair of idiots, but it was over and done with. There was no going back.

Perhaps now that they had their own place things would be different, though with rent to pay money would be a darn sight tighter.

You know you might be able to find yourself a job, even if it's only a part-time one, once the baby has been born, she comforted herself.

'We'll be there in a few minutes,' Harry said as he turned his head to look back at them. 'Hope one or the other of your 'elpers has got the kettle on.'

That's if they've got a kettle with them, Ella laughed to herself.

As he pulled the horse to a halt, Harry pushed his cap back, scratched his forehead, and gazed down in amazement. 'Gawd 'elp us, the whole bloody street has turned out t' help you. I can see I ain't gonna be wanted here,' he grumbled to Peter. 'I might just as well clear off up to one of the pubs, quench me thirst an' leave you lot to it.'

Peter looked at the folk gathered outside the empty house and wondered what he had done to deserve such good friends. On the pavement was Becky, her mother, and two young women he knew to be the wives of Becky's brothers. One had a little boy holding on to her skirts, the other one had a youngster in her arms. They each called out a greeting, smiling up at them. The large bulky figure of Tommy's mother, Mrs Ferguson, filled the gateway, and through the open door he saw Becky's two elder brothers, Jack and Tom, leaning against the wall. He suddenly remembered that those two not only lived nearby but they worked in the local tannery. Damn good of them to give up their Saturday to come and help, after all they weren't relations but the two families having grown up in houses that backed on to each other he supposed made a difference.

A shuffling of feet could be heard as the women were edged aside and Becky's two brothers went into action lifting Ella down on to the pavement as if she weighed no more than a bag of feathers.

Ella's mum and Jim arrived and between them the men seemed to make light work of bringing in all Ella's and Peter's belongings. Very soon a motor van drew up outside and their sideboard, settee and two armchairs were carried into what was to be the parlour.

Ella stood looking around for a few minutes before saying,

'I just don't know how to say thanks to all of you. This place was so dirty, thick with dust when Peter an' I viewed it.' Looking across at Joyce Russell she added, 'You and Becky must have been here at the crack of dawn to have got this place looking as it does now. Even the windows are sparkling.'

Peter spoke up. 'I'd like to add my thanks to Ella's. It really has been very good of you.'

Joyce smiled at them. 'Becky and my two daughters-in-law here, Ada and Joan, did most of the cleaning.'

'It weren't nothing,' Ada told them.

''Course it wasn't, our pleasure,' Joan added.

Joyce Russell, always a warm-hearted woman who believed that actions spoke louder than words, felt her heart go out to Ella. She was so grateful that it wasn't her Rebecca who had got herself into trouble. Eleanor, so young, talented, so much to look forward to and now what? Landed here in this two-up, two-down little house and a baby due almost any day. Some prospect when you knew that poor Peter barely earned enough to keep himself, let alone three of them.

So far in all their married life, she and Joe had been lucky. Their two eldest boys were both married with wives that she thought the world of, each had given them a lovely grandson and thank God both sons were in work and had a decent home around them. Fred and Becky were both still at home but they were no problem.

She took a deep breath and quietly said, 'If some of us could unpack one of those tea-chests we might find a kettle and then we can see about making a pot of tea.'

'No need for that,' a voice called and a woman came through the front door which was still propped wide open. She was carrying a heavily-loaded tray. Tall and thin, this young woman had a mass of copper-coloured hair hanging down around her shoulders, but the hair on top of her head was rolled up in two lines of curlers. ''Allo, everyone,' she called, 'thought I'd come and introduce meself, I live next door, I'm Martha Tubman. Bet you can all do with a cuppa, it's me big pot I've brought and there's a bag of doughnuts there, fresh this morning they are.'

'Gawd above, save us, another woman!' Tom Russell muttered to Peter. 'What say we men leave 'em to it, clear off and get something a bit stronger than bloody tea?'

'I'm with you,' came the general answer from the blokes, as mob-handed they made for the street door.

'Won't be long, luv,' Peter said as he bent and kissed Ella's cheek. He was the only one who had the grace to tell the women that they were leaving.

Martha Tubman pulled a face. 'Well, they'll be spoilt for choice,' she commented.

'How's that then?' Joyce Russell asked as she took the heavy tray from Martha.

'Didn't ye know, luv, this street alone can boast two pubs, besides 'alf a dozen round about.' Martha was laughing fit to burst as she set the tea things out on to the table. ''Alfway down we've got the Coconut, got a jolly good darts team 'as the Coconut, but if that don't take yer fancy there's always the Swan at the bottom by the little bridge which looks out over the fields. Mind you, the locals don't call it the Swan, the Gobbling Duck is 'ow they see it.'

'Whatever you care t' call it, that's a right nice 'ouse is the Swan,' Dolly Ferguson declared as she pushed her big bosom up higher and glared at Martha. 'Annie Smith runs that place practically on her own and she don't stand fer no nonsense. Fair with it an' all. We always send our Tommy up to her jug an' bottle bar of a Sunday dinnertime, great drop of mild she sells.'

'I was only saying,' Martha smiled at Dolly. She didn't want to fall out with Dolly Ferguson – she had too much sway in the street to make an enemy of her.

'Yeah well,' Dolly was still glaring, 'ole man Smith has too many irons in the fire t' be of much 'elp in the pub. All the veg an' flower stalls on the market are 'is. Up an' away to

Covent Garden before the streets are aired he is. I like 'is missus, I think she gets a raw deal from 'er old man.'

'Don't we all,' Martha muttered under her breath.

Joyce Russell slipped quietly out into the tiny scullery, having unearthed a kettle from amongst Ella's pots and pans. She filled it at the sink, lit a gas jet and placed it on to boil. They were sure to need some more hot water.

Peggy slipped out behind her, wrinkling her nose as she asked her friend, 'Well, Joyce, what d'yer think? Will my Ella take t' these neighbours? Won't be like we've been over the years, will it? We've had our ups an' downs, good times an' bad an' still we're the best of pals. But then we've always known when t' keep ourselves to ourselves. Seems like this lot round here are in an' out of each other's houses as the mood takes them.'

Joyce swilled the sink round and hung a new dishcloth over the tap, and being the peacemaker that she'd always been, she said, 'Maybe that's to the good. Ella's going to need all the help she can get. With us over at New Malden it must be a weight off your mind, Peggy, to know that Ella's got neighbours she can call on.'

'Yeah, suppose you're right . . . it's just . . . well you know, curlers in their hair this time of a day?'

Joyce grinned. 'Perhaps she's going to play darts at the Coconut tonight.'

Suddenly they were both laughing. 'Come on,' Peggy said. 'It's a long time since I had a doughnut.'

The women sat sipping their tea and Becky was feeling comfortable and relaxed, pleased that from now on things might work in Ella's favour. The house, now that they'd all helped to clean it, wasn't half as bad as she'd expected and Ella seemed much more contented. Although she was huge and heavy, Ella's face had a bloom to it that only happy pregnant women seem to acquire. Her blue eyes were clear and bright and her fair hair had lost none of its lovely sheen. Becky couldn't help thinking to herself that if Ella should give birth to a little girl it would be nice if the baby took after Ella in looks. A fair-haired, fresh-complexioned little mite toddling around the place would do wonders for the morale of both Ella and Peter, not to mention everyone else.

Becky finished her tea and stood up. 'If you're ready, Mum, I'd best get going. I've loads I need to be doing. I'll see you,' she called across to Ada and Joan. Then getting down on to her hands and knees to where her two little nephews were playing on the floor she cuddled them each in turn. ''Bye Ronnie,' she said, and tickled baby Joey. 'I'll see you both on Sunday when you come for yer tea with yer Gran. Be good boys.'

Ella got slowly to her feet, 'I'll come to the door with you. Thanks ever so much, both of you, for all your help.' Then, leaning towards Becky, she put her arms around her and it was then that she broke down. 'I'll miss you so much,' she whispered, the tears trickling down her cheeks.

'And I'll miss you, too.'

They hugged one another, each squeezing the other tight. 'Don't be a stranger, will you?' Ella pleaded.

'Don't be daft. Of course I won't be,' Becky hastened to assure her. Then, disentangling herself, she brushed quickly at her own eyes and added, 'The way we're carrying on anyone would think you'd moved a million miles away. I'll be over more often than you think, after all you have promised I can be godmother to your baby.'

'Who else but you? See you soon.' Ella gave her a slight push. ''Bye for now.'

Becky hurried to join her mother, only turning once to wave to Ella who was still standing out on the pavement.

Chapter Nine

THE OPEN-TOP BUS jerked its way through the morning traffic and the crowded, summery streets of London.

Inside Becky sat next to her father. During the train journey up from Raynes Park she had been anxious and unsure of herself. It would be all too easy for her to fluff this interview. She wanted this job with Lyons so badly, she would make every effort to answer questions correctly. But what if she didn't make it? What if the outcome was rejection? To be told that she was unsuitable to be a waitress would be too embarrassing for her to bear.

All the same, as the bus turned into Kensington High Street her spirits lifted. It was a lovely June day, sunny and warm with only puffy cotton-wool clouds in the bright blue sky.

'Nearly there,' her father said, squeezing her hand tightly.

Joe Russell felt a proud man as he saw the look of admiration a fellow passenger was giving his daughter. She deserved it. She was a lovely young nineteen-year-old lass, still small, slim and dainty and today she was dressed up to the nines. Rebecca's shining hair was coiled up at the back of her head, and she wore a dark grey suit with a crisp white cotton blouse. Black shoes and black stockings completed the outfit which made her look sensational: smart, businesslike and intelligent.

'This is our stop,' Joe said, leaping to his feet and holding out his hand to Becky.

The bus ground to a halt, and they stepped down on to the pavement.

Afterwards, Rebecca could never remember which direction they took or how suddenly they were outside, looking up at Cadby Hall. Confronted by such a great building, she began to wonder what she had let herself in for.

'I'll take meself off, have a bit of a look around,' her father said softly as he bent his head and placed a kiss on the side of her face. 'Remember, we're all rooting for you, stay calm an' you'll be fine. Come through with flying colours, I know you will. I'll be around, waiting, when you come out.'

'Thanks, Dad.' Becky hugged him, then quickly turned and climbed the stone steps which led up to the main entrance.

A burly looking man in a braided uniform stepped forward. 'Morning, Miss,' he said, touching the peak of his cap with a forefinger. 'Here for an interview, are you?' he asked. Rebecca nodded and smiled.

'Top of the stairs, can't miss the room, several young ladies waiting,' he told her.

Rebecca wasn't too happy about the several other girls. I only hope there are a good many vacancies to be filled, she was muttering to herself, feeling the relief of actually having made it this far.

The room was crowded, or so it seemed, as she pushed open the door. Heavy leather furniture and wonderful draped curtains hung from the tall windows. Every inch of wall space was taken up by chairs on which were seated young women. 'There's room for you 'ere beside me,' a quiet voice called to Becky.

'Thank you,' she answered as the young lass slid further along the sofa and she squeezed in to sit beside her.

Ten minutes ticked by, but nothing happened. Most of the girls had begun to fidget and Becky was thinking that were they to be seen one at a time she would be here all day. Then the door clicked open and the sound of stiff skirts could be heard as a formidable lady walked to the centre of the room. She clapped her hands together and then such silence settled over the room that one could have heard a pin drop. This was a lady with authority and obviously someone to be obeyed. She wore a wide-skirted black dress so long that it barely showed her ankles. A heavy white lace collar was the only decoration. From beneath the hem of the dress protruded dainty black shoes with three straps, brilliantly polished, and to Becky's way of thinking her feet looked far too small for such a tall lady. But it was the face above the lace collar that stopped Becky's heart from thumping. It was the sweetest, kindest face with a short nose and pale pink cheeks. Her eyes were unusual, soft grey, and although looking into them Becky felt their owner would brook no nonsense, at the same time they gave her the feeling that if you played fair by her then you would be all right. Her thick dark hair had been expertly cut into a fashionable style.

'Good morning, ladies,' the lady said. Without waiting for a reply she went on, 'You will be split into three groups; that way we shall get through the interviews more quickly. Your names will be called in alphabetical order.' She had a musical voice, soft and gentle, and to the surprise of all the girls she smiled and wished them all good luck before leaving the room.

Becky settled herself for what she thought would be a long wait. Clasping her handbag on her lap with both hands she rested her head back against the top of the sofa and closed her eyes. She felt a nudge in her side.

'Shouldn't think we'll 'ave to wait that long.'

Becky opened her eyes and turned to face the girl who had moved along to give her a seat. 'I hope not,' she answered.

'I'm May, May Stevens. What's your name?'

'Rebecca Russell, though most folk an' all my friends call me Becky.'

'Well I'm pleased t' meet you Becky, an' I 'ope you do well.'

'Likewise.' Becky grinned, instantly deciding that she liked this friendly person who had thick straight reddish hair and green eyes.

'Where d'you come from, Becky?'

'You mean where do I live?'

'Yes, not round 'ere that's for sure. Not even in London I'd take a bet.'

'Well, you would be right,' Becky agreed. 'I was born in New Malden, which is near Kingston-upon-Thames, lived there all my life.'

'No wonder you talk so nicely,' May murmured. 'Me, I come from the East End of London. Born and bred on the other side of the river. 'Ere, what did you think of that woman? She seems a bit stuck-up t' me, though I suppose we shouldn't judge a sausage by its skin, wait an' see, eh? Might turn out t' be all right.'

'I shouldn't worry too much,' Becky tried to reassure her new-found friend. 'By the way, not everyone speaks nicely where I come from, a good many originate from London, and as for that woman seeming to be a bit offhand, we'll both think she's the cat's whiskers if she gives us a job.'

May put her hand over her mouth to smother her giggles. 'You're dead right there, Becky.'

The girls had been called three at a time, and from what Becky had been able to gather, outside in the corridor they were sent in three different directions. Not one had returned to this waiting room. She sighed deeply, wishing that her turn would come soon. She longed to get it over and done with, whatever the outcome.

For the umpteenth time the door opened, and this time a young man stood in the open doorway. Tall, slim, fair-haired, dressed in a dark suit, waistcoat buttoned over an immaculate striped shirt, he smiled and called, 'Miss Russell, Miss Smithson and Miss Stevens.'

'That's us,' May muttered. 'Best of luck, Becky.'

'You too, May,' Becky whispered as they followed Miss Smithson out of the room.

May and the other young lady were sent off, while Becky was requested to accompany the slim man who had summoned them. Becky's heart was pounding and, as if he sensed this, the man turned, and looked down at her, smiling.

'I'm Robert Matthews. There's nothing to be afraid of,' he said, 'this interview is all very informal. It serves to sort the wheat from the chaff.'

Well, that statement did nothing to reassure her!

Walking down a corridor, Becky decided this Robert Matthews was not much older than herself. There was something about him that gave her the impression that he was shy. His movements were gentle, his voice soft and kindly as he opened a door and bid her enter.

The first lady they had seen sat behind a square table, flanked on one side by a gentleman whose face had more whiskers than Becky had ever seen and now Robert Matthews, having guided Becky to an armchair, went behind the table and took the empty seat on her other side.

Looking up from a sheaf of papers that lay in front of her, the lady smiled. 'How d'you do, Miss Russell, my name is Florence Nicholls, the gentleman on my left,' she indicated Mr Whiskers, 'is Mr Fairbrother and Mr Matthews, I'm sure, has already introduced himself.'

Becky relaxed. It was going to be all right. She wasn't so sure about 'Whiskers', he frowned a lot, but the other two were friendly.

By the time the clock on the wall had moved on twenty minutes, Rebecca, as they had chosen to call her, had been closely questioned by this extraordinary trio. And finally they seemed satisfied.

'Very well, Rebecca,' Florence Nicholls spoke kindly, 'if you wouldn't mind waiting just a little longer.'

Robert Matthews was on his feet. 'I'll show you where to go, refreshments are being served.'

Becky's skin was crawling with excitement. At least they hadn't rejected her out of hand. They were even going to give her refreshments. The quiet Robert Matthews was holding another door open for her and ushering her into a light and sunny room and then he was gone.

This smaller room was crowded with about a dozen young ladies and bustling with activity. It smelled of mouth-watering food and fresh coffee. May Stevens spied Becky at once, rose to her feet, and came across the room saying, 'Oh Becky, you made it as well, I'm so glad.'

Becky gawped at her. 'Being in here, does that mean we have been given a job?'

'Well I would think so, wouldn't you? I saw some of the girls leaving the building, not everyone got shown into this room. Anyway, let's go and get somethink to eat, it's all free, come on.'

'Cor,' Becky exclaimed as they each took a plate and cast their eyes over the refreshments that were being offered. 'Isn't all this grand?'

Two very young men were serving the coffee. 'Find yourselves a seat at one of the tables and we'll bring your drinks over,' they told the girls. The sandwiches and the hot coffee were delicious. Soon Becky leant back in her chair and glanced around the room. All the girls there were what she would call willowy. In the waiting room earlier there had been a couple of dumpy lasses, even one who could only be described as fat. It didn't look as though they had been selected.

The tables were being cleared and Becky was beginning to wish that someone would come and tell them exactly what was happening. From the snatches of conversation she had heard going on around her most of the young ladies seemed confident that they were going to be waitresses for Lyons. Becky wished that she felt as cocksure.

Finally the door opened and much to Becky's surprise, Mr Fairbrother, or Mr Whiskers, as she had fixed him firmly in her mind, was standing in the centre of the floor.

'Ladies,' he said loudly, and Becky thought how much younger he looked standing up. He was tall and broad with it. 'I am very pleased to be able to announce that each of you has been selected to take part in a training scheme.'

May Stevens leant forward in her chair and winked at Becky while sounds of relief and delight were coming from all corners of the room.

Unhurried, Mr Fairbrother outlined what the course of training would entail and told them it would last for a period of three weeks.

'It will take place here in London and for that period you will stay as guests of Lyons. Your board and lodging will be free. Does that present a problem for any of you?'

There was much shaking of heads.

'Good. At the end of your training, if you all measure up to our expectations, as I feel sure you will, you will be measured for your uniforms. Now, have you any questions you would like to ask me?'

Becky felt there was a hundred and one things she would have liked to ask but like all the other applicants she kept her lips tightly together.

'Very well,' Mr Whiskers' deep voice now sounded a whole lot more kindly. 'You will each receive a letter within the next couple of days which will set out accurately the conditions of employment, when and where you are to report to and for what period of time you will be given this training. At the end of the course a decision will be made as to which Corner House you will be assigned to. So, it only remains for me to wish you every success in your newly-chosen profession and I look forward to meeting you all again in the very near future.'

Becky was finding it hard to believe. She was going on a training course which hopefully would end with her working at a Lyons Corner House in the West End of London.

'Yippee,' May Stevens whispered in Becky ear, 'I'll be looking forward t' seeing you. Can't wait. D' you feel the same?'

'Of course I do,' Becky smiled. 'But right now I'm busting, I need to spend a penny.'

'Gawd luv yer,' May exclaimed. 'Ain't you got eyes in

your head? The ladies is right over there in that corner. It was the first place most of us made for when we got put in 'ere. It was that or pee our knickers.'

Becky was on her feet and making a beeline for the toilet, thinking as she went, there won't be a dull moment on this course if May is around. She certainly calls a spade a spade.

'That's better,' Becky said aloud as she came out of the cubicle. She washed her hands, inspected her face in the mirror above the washbasin, dabbed her powder puff over her nose, faintly outlined her lips with her new pale lipstick and went back to find her new friend.

Outside in the corridor Robert Matthews was talking to Mr Fairbrother. Both men nodded and smiled their goodbyes. Becky was thoughtful as she smiled back. That Robert Matthews was a nice young man, she decided. With his thick mop of fair hair and light blue eyes there was something appealing about his manner and his smile was certainly attractive, though somehow she still had the feeling that he was very shy.

Leaving the building together, May kept up a constant flow of chat. It was just as if she and Becky had known each other for years.

'There's my dad,' Becky called brightly and Joe Russell immediately sent up a prayer of thanks. Just looking at her he knew his little girl had done it and he was so pleased for her. 'Dad, this is May, May Stevens, we are going on a training course together.'

Joe returned the broad grin that May was giving him and surveyed the pair of them. 'So, you've been living it up in there while I've been wearing me boot leather out worrying over you.'

The laughter of the two girls was spontaneous.

'Can I buy you a drink of some kind?' Joe asked May.

'No thanks, Mr Russell, kind of you t' ask but we've been well fed an' watered by Joey Lyons, ain't we Becky? In any case I want to get home, tell me mum all about it. I'll see you soon then,' she said to Becky, 'I'm ever so glad we met up. Nice t' think we'll be training together, ain't it?'

'It certainly is,' Becky quickly agreed, 'I was thrilled to see your friendly face. See you soon.'

Becky and her father watched May depart and then Joe opened his arms. 'Who's a clever girl then?' he teased as he pulled his daughter close to his chest, and disregarding the passers-by he held on to her, tears of joy dimming his vision.

The train snaked its way out of the station, past all the blackened smoke-stained factories and warehouses and over the bridge, giving Becky a delightful view of the dear old Thames. Much busier up here than it is in Kingston, she mused, just look at all the boats. Seems funny that it is the same river, such a distance away, Becky was thinking to herself as she watched her father stand up and place his bowler hat up in the rack above his seat, unfurl his newspaper and settle down to read it in comfort. Soon she would be coming back to London. Learning how to wait on table, leaving home, her parents and her brothers. Suddenly her hopes had become reality.

Would she be happy? You'll be barmy if you're not, she chided herself drowsily as her eyelids closed and the wheels of the train seemed to be saying, soon be home, soon be home.

She wanted to see the smile on her mother's face when she told her all the news.

Chapter Ten

BECKY ARRIVED IN Kingston at just after six on Tuesday evening. She was tired out. She had given a week's notice at the Wellington Laundry first thing yesterday morning. It hadn't been accepted gracefully. It seemed for the short time she was to remain there as an employee she was to be given every hard task that was going. Mrs Bradford had tried to ease the situation, to no avail. With four more days to go she was fed up. Turning into Mill Street she saw that Peter was standing in the small front garden watching her approach.

Becky didn't like Mill Street. It reeked of poverty. Even the men who did have jobs only earned a pittance from the factories hereabout. Jobs on the building sites and on the river were few and far between and the women seemed to be everlastingly pregnant. What future was there for these children? Some lovely countryside lay within easy distance yet the kiddies were always in the street. It was gone six and still ragged snotty-nosed boys played marbles in the gutter while little girls skipped, their ropes stretched across the middle of the road.

The main aim of their fathers appeared to be get home, eat their meal and spend the evening in the pub.

Becky quickened her footsteps and tried not to think too much about what would happen to Ella if she had to live here for any length of time.

'Hello, Becky, you look all in. Come on inside an' see what a lovely surprise we've got for you,' Peter said as he led the way indoors.

Though the outside of the terraced house was nothing

to write home about, it was meticulously neat inside. The curtains were bright and fresh, the fire-range had been recently black-leaded and polished until you could see your face in it. But the furniture was shabby and the rugs showed very much that they weren't new.

Becky had to stifle a sigh. How she wished that things could be so much better, both for Ella and for Peter. They hadn't got off to a very good start in their married life.

She turned to face Peter. He was smiling broadly, looking all bright-eyed and bushy-tailed.

'Something's happened!' Becky exclaimed, her tiredness forgotten.

'It sure has! Ella's had the baby. I'm a father.' His voice brimmed with excitement.

'When? How is Ella? Is the baby all right?' Becky's questions came out in a rush, all jumbled up.

Peter laughed out loud, but his expression changed as he told her, 'Ella's fine now, she's sleeping, she had quite a rough time of it.'

Becky shook her head in dismay. 'Poor Ella. You still haven't told me about the baby, boy or girl?'

Peter smiled, remembering. 'A little girl, so tiny, I held her soon after she was born.'

Becky took hold of his hand and squeezed it tightly. 'Tiny, you say? She is all right, isn't she?'

'Yes, yes, she's perfect. Ella's mum was here, she's only just gone. She said Eleanor was only small when she was born. Shall I make us a cup of tea? You look as if you could do with one, or would you rather go straight up to see Ella?'

'You said she was sleeping, let's leave her for a while. I certainly could use a cuppa, I came straight from work. I'll make it.'

'You certainly won't. I've been home all day, pacing the floor mostly, you set yer bones down in that chair and I won't be a jiffy.'

Becky did as she was told, thinking about all the years that she and Ella had spent growing up together. When they were small they had the whooping cough at the same time. Then the measles, later the mumps. When it was freezing cold they had run like wild deer to school and during the hot summers the riverbank had been their playground. With their frocks tucked in their knickers they had paddled and splashed in the muddy water. Somedays they walked out to the park taking a bottle of homemade lemonade and bread and jam with them. As soon as they got there they rode on the swings. Now Ella was married. Nineteen and a mother already. Don't get maudlin, she chided herself, just remember how great it was to have such a good friend to grow up with.

Peter came in with the tray of tea and Becky poured them each a cup. She drank her own tea scalding hot, gulping it as if she had been dying for a drink.

Putting down her empty cup she grinned, and the sight made Peter ask, 'What's tickling you?'

'The fact that the baby is a girl. Suppose you'd have preferred a boy but a girl is what I was hoping for.'

'No,' Peter was quick to protest. 'I didn't mind boy or girl just so long as Ella was all right.'

'That's good. Me, I've already got two little nephews, it will be great having a little girl around. Can't wait to see her.'

'No sooner were the words out of Becky's mouth than there came a wailing from upstairs.

'There you are, yer see, the baby is demanding that we go up and pay her some attention.' Peter grinned.

This time Becky led the way as they tiptoed up the stairs to Ella's bedroom. Opening the door, Becky smiled in wonder as she said, 'Ella, we thought you were sleeping. How come your sitting up?'

Ella shrugged. 'I have been asleep for ages, now I feel fine.'

Becky crossed the room, sat down on a chair that had been drawn up beside the bed and took Ella's hand in hers.

'You clever old thing, Peter tells me things didn't go so well to start off with though.'

'Well, the midwife took her time getting here, and me mum did most of the delivering. About all old Marie Wilson had to do was clean me an' the bed up.'

Becky felt an absurd lump in her throat hearing Ella tell how she had given birth. A great rush of affection for her friend washed over her.

'Well, where is this little miracle?'

At that point Peter straightened up from bending over the wicker basket and began doing a little dance. 'She smiled at me,' he declared.

'Get on with you,' Ella grinned, 'she's too tiny to smile, it's probably just wind.'

'You, my darling wife, may believe what you like but I know our daughter just smiled and told me she is happy to have us for her parents. So there!'

Ella laughed with delight; her relief at the birth being over and the fact that Peter was acting like a dog with two tails made her feel really happy. She nodded at her husband and he, reading her message, gently lifted the baby out of the basket and placed her in Becky's arms. 'Say hello to your Aunt Rebecca,' he crooned.

Becky looked down into that tiny pink little face and smiled. 'My, look at her tiny fingers, she's beautiful.' Her voice was thick with emotion.

'We're going to call her Margaret after my mum. And we won't let it get shortened to Peggy.' Ella lay back, her face showing exhaustion. 'You promised you would be her godmother, Becky, does that still stand?'

'You bet your sweet life it does,' Becky answered, snuggling the tiny baby up close to her chest.

'I'll go an' get us some fresh tea,' Peter said, feeling he ought to leave the two girls alone for a while.

'Becky? While Peter's not here can I ask you something?'

Becky nodded. 'Of course, anything.'

'If anything ever happens to me, will you watch out for my baby?'

'Ella! Again the answer is yes, of course, but what the hell do you imagine is going to happen to you? You've done so well. Mother and baby doing fine, what more could you ask for?'

'I know all that,' Ella pleaded, 'it's just that Peter isn't in the best of health and, well, times are difficult and I don't want my baby to have to go short of too many things just because we had to get married before we'd even saved a penny.'

'Becky, we've been friends from the day we were born and I promise that if ever the time should come I will see to it that baby Margaret has everything that's in my power to give her, but nothing is going to happen to you. So, stop nattering and start thinking about something more cheerful. Now, sit up again, I can hear Peter coming with your tea.'

The frown vanished from Ella's face and in its place came the sweetest smile. 'Becky, I knew I could rely on you.'

Holding the door open wide for Peter to come in with the tea tray, Becky was hoping she might never live to regret the promise she had just made.

Every day for the past week Becky had come to Kingston. Now she and Ella sat side by side on the windowsill out front in the small front garden staring down at baby Margaret lying in her pram. She was asleep on her stomach, tiny hands balled into fists. As the two girls looked at her, each was filled with love. She was awfully small, which made her mother and her 'Aunt' Becky feel very protective.

Becky put out a finger and stroked the downy head. She had the same fair hair as her mother and the same deep-set blue eyes. To be honest, though she wouldn't admit it aloud, Becky could see nothing of Peter in her. She couldn't wait for her to get just a little bit bigger. She wanted to buy her a pretty dress and maybe a lacy jacket as well. She was thrilled to have a goddaughter.

'Don't look now,' Ella turned her head and whispered, 'but Tommy Ferguson's mother is making a beeline for us.'

Dolly Ferguson heaved her great bosom up with one forearm and with the other hand she patted her thick greying hair, doing her best to fix a flyaway strand behind her ear. Then opening the iron front gate she pushed it so hard it clanged as it hit the low fence.

''Allo you two, enjoying the fine weather? An' how's the baby?' she panted, her breath laboured as if she had walked miles rather than a few yards up the street.

'We're all fine, Mrs Ferguson', Ella answered.

'Well shove up a bit so's I can put me bum on yer windowsill, take the weight off me feet, they're playing merry 'ell wiv me this morning.'

Becky nodded sympathetically and immediately got to her feet, knowing full well it would be a tight squeeze for the three of them to perch side by side.

'Come on Mrs Ferguson, settle yourself alongside Ella and I'll lift baby Margaret out of the pram so's you can have a good look at her.'

'Apart from your feet are you keeping fairly well, Mrs Ferguson?' Ella enquired.

'Yeah, me legs play me up an' all but ain't much good moaning is it? All that apart, it's about time you two girls started calling me Dolly, all this Mrs Ferguson gets on me nerves, so let's 'ave less of it. All right?'

''Course it is, Dolly,' they said in agreement, grinning at each other.

'How's Tom?' Becky asked, thinking it was up to them to make conversation.

''E seems all right an' I've got quite a bit of news t' tell yer. First off 'e's got anuvver job an' that seems to 'ave brought 'im round to getting things settled in 'is mind.'

'Oh, I am pleased,' Becky said, patting Dolly's arm.

'Me too,' Ella agreed, smiling. 'Tell us all about it. Where's he working now then?'

'E's got in at the tannery, I think one of your brothers spoke up fer 'im Becky,' Dolly answered as she took a handkerchief from the pocket of her flowered overall and wiped her nose. 'I'm ever so grateful, wait till I see your brothers, buy 'em a pint I will, that's fer sure. 'Course, I don't know yet what 'e'll be doing there,' Dolly sighed. 'My Tommy's got a good 'ead on 'is shoulders an' 'e's not afraid of 'ard work, though I've got t' admit he's not always quick on the uptake. 'E worked 'ard at the Wellington though. Earned every penny they ever paid 'im. Trouble was, they never appreciated 'im, put on 'im day in day out, an' when this offer came along I sez t' him, you take it lad, about time you got a break in this life.'

Both girls murmured their approval and Becky said, 'I'm sure my brothers were only too pleased to help. Everyone likes your Tommy.' She stopped rocking the pram and added, 'Would you like to hold the baby? Ella won't mind, will you, Ella?'

'Leave the baby be a minute cos there's something that's worrying me a bit an' I'd like you two youngsters t' tell me what yer think about that Mary Marsden.' This last request had been said in a quiet voice, which was most unusual for Dolly.

Ella turned and laid her arm across Dolly's broad shoulders. 'Don't you like Mary? We all thought she and Tom were kinda made for each other.'

Dolly heaved a great sigh. 'Yer right, they are good fer each other but marriage! Well, I don't know about that, an' I'm worried. She's got 'erself a job in the canteen of the tannery an' now it's like they are living in each other's pockets. All I 'ear when my Tommy gets in of an evening is Mary this an' Mary that, can't do no wrong she can't.'

'What's this about marriage?' Ella asked, curiosity getting the better of her.

'Ain't 'e mentioned it t' yer?'

Ella shook her head. 'I only see Tom as he walks past and

then only if I'm in the front room. Baby keeps me busy now. Sorry.'

'What about you, Becky? There was a time when your name was on my Tommy's lips all the time.'

Becky thought hard before answering. 'That's true Dolly. Tom an' I have always been great friends. He helped me out a lot when I first started in the laundry. But your Tom left the Wellington about three weeks ago and I no longer work there now so I don't get t' see him so much and I don't hear all the gossip.'

'What d'yer mean, you left the Wellington an' all?'

'That's right Dolly, I gave a week's notice and I finished there last week.'

'But what yer gonna do, gal? Jobs don't grow on trees.'

'I'll tell you what our Rebecca is going to do,' Ella said, smiling at Dolly. 'She's going to work for Joey Lyons!'

'What, yer mean in the tearooms?' Dolly's eyes were wide with wonder.

'Not exactly,' Becky said in a quiet voice, 'I hope I'm going to be a waitress in one of the Lyons Corner Houses.'

'Gawd above gal, what d'yer mean you 'ope? You ain't given up a good job before yer got another one, 'ave yer?'

Strictly speaking I suppose that is what I have done, Becky was saying to herself. Aloud she said, 'It's like this, Dolly, I've been accepted to go on a three-week training course. It starts in about ten days' time and hopefully at the end of the training I shall be told that I am capable of being a fully fledged waitress.'

'Oh, you will, you will, of course you will,' Ella burst out. 'She went to London for the interview, Dolly, an' they told her ever so much about what she'll be doing.'

'Good luck ter yer, Becky,' Dolly exclaimed, amazement in her voice. ''T'ain't everyone that gets a chance like that.'

'Thanks, Dolly. To get back to Tom and the question of him an' Mary getting married, has he told you that they are seriously considering it?'

Dolly wriggled her bottom and untied the tapes that held her pinafore, then loosening it she let out a big breath. 'That's a bit better. Not in so many words he ain't said so, she's either round my place or he's round her 'ouse every day of the week an' I 'ear bits and pieces of news that they let drop. My Tommy's certainly taken with 'er and I 'eard her telling 'im they'd 'ave t' go to church soon. T' see the vicar an' put up the banns is the only thing I could think of.'

'I shouldn't worry too much,' Becky tried to reassure her. 'Tommy's old enough to take care of himself an' one thing's for sure, he knows his own mind.'

'If that's the case,' Dolly said, sighing, 'why don't he come out in the open an' tell me t' me face that 'e's leaving 'ome an' getting wed? Surely I should be the first t' know.'

Ella was thinking to herself that it was nearly time for her to feed the baby and if she didn't make a move Dolly would have them wasting the whole morning.

'Well, I for one don't think it would be a bad thing if Mary and Tom do decide to get married. After all Dolly, he's been so well looked after by you all his life he must think he's found a good one in Mary or he wouldn't even be considering it. Would he?'

'I agree,' Becky said, 'Mary might well turn out to be the making of Tom. I hope we both get an invite to the wedding.'

Dolly Ferguson slid her backside off the windowsill, flinched as her swollen feet touched the ground, bent low over the pram and made clucking noises at the baby. Then, sighing heavily, she made her way out of Ella's front garden. It was all right for those two lasses to talk about getting married and living happily ever after. She would be left on her own but what would anyone care about that? Mary Marsden would be the one that was getting the best of the bargain. I only hope she doesn't get too possessive towards Tom otherwise I will have to tell her where she gets off. Don't want no uppity miss for me daughter-in-law.

Ella put the finishing touches to the pram, checked that baby Margaret was lying safely on her side and she and Becky were ready to set off on their stroll. As they walked out into the sunshine they were both grinning. Dolly's words were still ringing in their ears.

'You know what it is that's getting Dolly's goat, don't you?' Ella asked, grinning. 'It's the fact that poor Tommy is standing on his own two feet for a change. That mother of his would still be taking him to the lav an' wiping his backside if she had her way.'

Becky gave her a broad smile. 'Don't need no telling, do I? But I like Mary, I was thrilled to bits when your Peter told me about her and Tom getting together, and when I met her I thought how well-suited the pair of them were.'

'Not to mention the fact that she was doing you a favour,' Ella answered, giving Becky a sly lopsided look.

'Yeah, well, there was that,' Becky admitted, 'got him off my back. Still, honestly, you have to agree those two were made for each other.'

Ella raised her eyebrows. 'I'm not disputing that for a moment. As a matter of fact I think that girl is the best thing that could have happened to Tom but I wasn't going spell it out for his mother. You're all right, but I've got to live in the same street as her an' believe you me Dolly Ferguson can make her presence felt.'

This set the pair of them off giggling, much to the amusement of passers-by as they turned into the High Street. Suddenly Becky reached out and covered Ella's hand on the handle of the pram. 'Mary Marsden is coming across the road,' she said softly.

Ella put her other hand on Becky's shoulder and whispered, 'Let's be nice to her.'

'Oh I am so glad to meet up with you two,' Mary said as she smiled shyly and looked into the pram. 'Ain't she tiny, I wish she was awake so's I could see her properly.'

Ella bent and pulled the loose covering back a little, 'She

won't sleep much longer, have you got time for a cup of tea? We were just going to treat ourselves, weren't we Becky?'

'You mean I can come with you? Oh, that would be ever so nice. I'll buy you both a cake if yer like.'

The three of them sat in the café, sipping their tea and nibbling Chelsea buns which Mary had insisted upon. Suddenly the baby yawned and her little fists beat the air.

Ella bent and lifted her from the pram. 'So, you're awake are you, my little precious,' she crooned as she rocked her baby tenderly in her arms. 'Would you like to hold her, Mary?'

Mary's eyes widened. 'Would you trust me? I would be ever so careful.'

'Here.' Ella placed the baby gently into Mary's outstretched arms. 'She won't break,' she assured her.

Ella and Becky exchanged glances as they watched the expression on Mary's face. 'Oh, she's the most beautiful little baby I've ever seen. You want to know something? One day I hope Tom and I will have a baby.' Having made that statement she smiled wanly before quietly adding, 'That's if Tom's mother will ever let him marry me.'

Becky reached out and took Mary's hand in hers. 'If you and Tom love each other I'm sure nothing will stop you from getting married,' she said softly.

'Me and Tom do love each other. We want to be together all the time.' Mary's eyes brimmed with tears.

Becky handed her a handkerchief and Ella said, 'Here, let me take the baby, you can hold her again later.'

Becky patted Mary's shoulder. 'Don't get upset. Have your parents been to see Mrs Ferguson?'

'No. Me mum's a bit afraid of her an' me dad says he wants no rows with her.'

'Maybe if they asked her to your house for tea one day when Tom is coming to see you, that might do the trick. At least that way they'd get to know each other,' Ella spoke up, playing peacemaker.

'Now that is a good idea,' Becky laughed. 'Look at it this way, Tom's mum might be a big woman but even she can get frightened and lonely. She may be thinking that if Tom marries you she'll be all on her own. Never seeing either of you.'

'Crikey, it wouldn't be like that. Honest it wouldn't. I wouldn't expect Tom t' neglect his mum. I'd see he didn't.' Mary sniffed and rubbed her eyes.

Becky winked at Ella before saying. 'Mary, you're a good girl. Why don't you go an' see Tom's mum on your own, tell her what you've just told us and then when the date is set, just make sure you invite us to the wedding.'

Mary put her head to one side and stared at them with a funny look on her face. 'Are you 'aving me on?'

'Of course we're not,' Becky hastened to soothe her. 'Ella and I have both said we've seen the change in Tommy since you an' him have been going out together, everybody has. We think you make a lovely couple, an' if you can't win Mrs Ferguson round to that way of thinking then she must be blind.'

Mary stared at Becky in disbelief. 'I wish I could believe you. I told you the first time I met you, I ain't never made many friends an' now, well . . .'

'Now you've got us,' Ella butted in. 'You do as Becky says, have a talk with Tom's mum and get your parents to do the same, you'll see, you won't have nothing to worry about.'

'Except getting yourself to the church on time,' Becky said quickly.

Mary looked at them each in turn and then she chuckled, 'You're a grand pair an' no mistake. I can't see it happening though . . . Tom's mum ain't 'alf got a paddy on 'er.'

'Aw, come on, Mary, cheer up,' Ella pleaded, 'Mrs Ferguson ain't going to eat you alive. When she gets to know you well she'll probably wonder how her Tommy ever got along without you. You'll see, you'll have her purring like a pussy cat.'

The thought of big buxom Dolly Ferguson purring like a cat was too much. All at once the three of them burst out laughing and it was a minute or two before they settled down again.

Mary took a ten shilling note from her purse, then, as Ella and Becky watched in surprise she walked quickly to the counter and paid for all their teas. Smiling broadly she came back to the table. 'You've been like a dose of salts for me, today. Meeting yer like this. I'm coming round to your house, Ella, the minute Tom an' I get things settled. Will that be all right?'

'More than all right,' Ella grinned, 'I'll come looking for you if you don't.'

'And yer mean it? You'll come to me wedding?'

'We'll be in the front pew,' they promised.

Mary seemed a different girl as she practically skipped away, pausing a few yards up the pavement to stop, turn and shout back at them, 'It's unlucky to break a promise.'

'Gosh I hope things go well for her,' Ella sighed

'Me too,' Becky cried. 'If Dolly Ferguson doesn't take to that lass then she wants her brains seen too.'

'I'm with you there,' Ella said, 'that's one wedding that we'll make sure we go to, eh?'

'Wouldn't miss it for the world.' And Becky knew from the feeling in the pit of her stomach that each of them had done Mary a good turn today and that they ought to make sure they looked her up again, and soon. There was a lot more to Mary Marsden than met the eye and she deserved to have friends that were loyal to her.

Chapter Eleven

BECKY FELT LIKE a schoolgirl as she looked around the room. There were eighteen other girls there beside herself and this morning was to be the first day of their training with J. Lyons.

The weather continued hot. Florence Nicholls climbed up on to the platform fanning herself with a sheaf of papers she carried. Her face was flushed and there were beads of perspiration on her upper lip. Looking down, she counted the heads and looked doubtful.

At that moment the door opened and a flustered-looking May Stevens burst in.

'I'm sorry I'm late.' May directed her apology to Mrs Nicholls who merely nodded and indicated that May should find herself a seat.

'I thought you weren't coming,' Becky chided softly as May sank down on to the chair next to her own.

'I almost didn't, my mum's been taken bad.'

There was no more time for chatter. Suddenly everyone was called to order by a slim lady who had joined Mrs Nicholls. She had brown hair piled neatly on top of her head, a delicate fine-boned face and a body to match. Unlike Mrs Nicholls, who was still dressed in black, she wore a pale coffee-coloured dress, trimmed with narrow lace. The sleeves were full to the elbow then narrowed with rows of pearl buttons down to the cuffs.

'Lovely dress. Very becoming,' Becky whispered to May.

'Cost money!' May answered drily.

Greetings were exchanged and the girls learnt that Miss

Timson, the lady in the beige dress, was to be in charge of their training course.

'The group will work as a whole most of the time, the exception being when you are actually waiting on tables, then you will be split into five groups of four.' Miss Timson had an oval face with pale blue eyes, and her voice, as she continued to instruct the group, was clear and steady, her movements quick and easy.

'There are tables at the back of the room, laid out with exercise books and pencils, if you would like to settle yourselves four to each table, please,' Mrs Nicholls requested, as she came to the fore again. 'I will leave you in the capable hands of Miss Timson.'

Swiftly the girls rose and did as they were bid. Some felt hesitant and unsure as to where they could choose to sit. May was the first to hold out her hand and make the introductions as she and Becky were joined by Joyce Johnson and Maisie Roberts.

After two hours of lectures and taking notes from what was being written on a huge blackboard by several different women and men who came into the room at intervals, each furnishing the group with more information, Becky was dismayed. At one point she felt her throat tighten, and for a moment tears stung behind her eyes. What had she done? Would she ever be able to take in everything that was being said? What if at the end of this course she was told she had failed? She had no job to go back to. She fought back the tears, telling herself sternly that she was not going to be beaten, she would pay attention and she would make herself learn and do well.

Then came the moment when Miss Timson announced that they would take a break. 'I have ordered refreshments,' she said, smiling.

Sighs of relief came from all corners of the room.

They were brought to them by four young men so slim and smart that both May and Becky caught their breath in surprise. They looked every inch top-class waiters dressed in black trousers, short neat black jackets, snowy white shirts with stiff high collars, narrow black ties and a long white apron to finish the outfit.

The young men deftly transferred the cups and saucers and the silver tea and coffeepots and sugar bowls and milk jugs from the heavy silver trays to the snowy white tablecloth that had been spread over the trestle table on the platform. Then they hurried away to return with trays filled with dainty sandwiches and tiered plate-stands laden with small savoury pastries.

'Everything looks delicious,' Becky murmured to May, who was busy filling a plate which had been handed to her by a good-looking lad with sleek black hair.

'Don't it just! I could stand this treatment any day of the week,' May grinned in answer.

During the break May and Becky learnt that Joyce and Maisie knew each other before coming here. They lived near to each other. 'In Chestnut Grove,' Joyce volunteered, 'that's quite near to Balham Station.'

'Oh, that's south London isn't it?' Becky queried.

'That's right, not too far from you. I've been to Kingston once or twice – that's near to New Malden where you live, isn't it?'

Becky agreed it was and the four girls relaxed.

Every one of these girls seem to be Londoners, Becky was thinking to herself. I must be the odd one out. Yet each and every one is friendly, she decided, as they freely chatted and exchanged views on what they had learnt so far. Both Joyce and Maisie seemed to be of the same age as May and herself, all of us coming up to nineteen or twenty, she calculated. These two new friends had short brown hair cut in the same style as May's reddish hair was and she fell to wondering if at some time she would be asked to have her own long hair shortened.

'Girls, I would like to point one thing out to you.' Miss

Timson's voice rose above the chatter and silence fell. 'You may have been too taken up with talking to each other to notice that between each item of china a small doily had been placed. As you proceed with your training this will become second nature to you. It is a practice that Lyons is very proud of and is adhered to at all times, whether you be serving a single cup of tea, a bowl of soup, a cucumber sandwich or a five-course meal. A doily must go between a cup and its saucer, between a soup bowl and the plate it stands on the same applies and food such as sandwiches and pastries must always be laid on a doily, never directly on china.

'That is the first and most important thing for you to learn. One never leaves the still room, kitchen or breakfast bar without first checking that the doilies are in place. It is partly for presentation and partly for practical reasons which you will learn as you go along. Now if you will finish your tea or coffee and return to your places we will proceed.'

'What's wrong with your mum?' Becky asked May as they retook their places.

'She has funny turns sometimes. She'll be all right, her sister is spending the day with her.'

'Quiet, please, I want you to pay attention.' Miss Timson was an easy-going teacher, with the knack of holding her pupils' interest. From that very first day Becky liked her very much and was keen to learn as much as possible. After a few days she began to relax and it seemed to her that she had truly chosen well when she had applied to work for Lyons.

Most days there was little time to think of anything else other than how to wait on table.

During the training period the twenty girls lived in a hostel located behind Cadby Hall and Becky spent what little off-duty time they were given with May Stevens and her mother, a jolly happy-go-lucky woman who, whenever they arrived to visit her, usually had her flat filled with neighbours.

Mrs Stevens certainly made her very welcome though at

times Becky felt she asked so many questions she wanted to know the inside-out of a donkey's hind leg. Another thing was, she was missing her own family and the countryside. The first visit to the district where May's mother lived had been quite an eye-opener for her. The grimy cobbled streets, the tenements so small and cramped without even a small garden, just a concrete back yard that was criss-crossed with washing lines. The dirty industrial buildings which made everywhere look dark and damp. Then there were the pedlars and barrow boys shouting their wares in loud voices, so different from the pleasant village where she had been born and until now lived all her life. When she thought about how she and Ella had everlastingly moaned about the permanent steamy fog in the Wellington Laundry she told herself they hadn't known just how lucky they were.

Near to Cadby Hall she was thrilled by the sight of many fancy carriages as they rattled by; some of the women occupants wore breathtakingly beautiful clothes. To Becky, men and women alike mostly looked as if they had stepped out of a bandbox. And the ladies' hats! Well, never in her life had she seen such creations.

It wasn't like that in the East End of London!

May warned her to be aware of pickpockets and not to upset the painted, gaudily clad women who stood around the street corners near to the tenements that housed her mother. These strange women baffled Becky.

'They're on the game, poor cows,' May told her.

Becky looked mystified.

'Prostitutes, dummy,' May whispered out the side of her mouth. 'Someone's got to earn the money t' put food on the table. Half the men round here haven't worked since the Armistice was declared and the Army slung them out. 'T' ain't their fault.'

Becky sighed. London certainly had many different faces. She was doing her best but there were times when she wondered if she would ever fit in.

*   *   *

The three weeks flew by. Each girl on the course agreed that their feet never stopped aching and others said that their arms had developed muscles due to the heavy trays they had learnt to load and carry. A written examination had been set and now the hour of truth had arrived.

'Young ladies, I am most pleased to tell you that all of you have passed and are being offered employment.' Mrs Nicholls had to pause because the sighs of relief followed by squeals of delight which greeted this statement were extremely noisy.

Some minutes later, Mrs Nicholls looked at their upturned faces and smiled. 'Now, I will read out to what Corner Houses you are to be sent and then we'll go into details of when and where you will receive your uniforms.' May and Becky stood as close together as they could get, fingers crossed behind their backs as the names were read out by Miss Timson.

'Miss Russell and Miss Stevens, to Coventry Street Corner House.' Becky's fingers flew to cover her mouth. Oh, she wasn't to be parted from May. The two of them could remain friends and become workmates, things couldn't have worked out better.

'Cor, I didn't reckon that was on the cards, did you?' May exclaimed happily.

'No, aren't we lucky,' Becky chuckled with glee. 'We're actually going to get our uniforms.'

'No one would ever believe it,' Becky declared in a shocked voice to May as they went through the business of what was what for the umpteenth time that morning.

'Right.' Mrs Morgan, a short thin little body of a woman, and her three seamstresses straightened their pincushions, which they wore on their wrists secured by a velvet strap. 'Let's go through it all once more and remember this.' She stared at the six girls whose uniforms she had been ordered to see to. 'Each morning before you venture out into the hall you will be inspected. From the top of your head to the tip of your toes and that inspection will take into account not only your dress and cap but whether your hands are clean, your nails well manicured and also whether the seams of your plain black stockings are straight.'

'What a palaver!' May grinned. 'Only hope it's all going to be worth it.'

'It will be,' Becky assured her as she looked into the mirror checking that the monogram of JL was in the centre of her cap.

'Take note,' Mrs Morgan said as she bustled to Becky's side, 'that ribbon running through the white part of the cap has to be cleaned and pressed daily, so don't go forgetting it.'

After at least ten attempts May and Becky decided they now knew exactly how the cap should be worn, and Mrs Morgan was able to announce they had got it correct.

Now came the fitting of the dress.

'Jesus wept!' The five other girls, including Becky, roared with laughter as May started to count the two rows of pearl buttons that adorned the front of the neat black dress.

Even Mrs Morgan found herself smiling. 'There are thirty of them,' she enlightened the group of girls, 'and each one has to be sewn on with red cotton.'

'Gawd luv a duck!' Molly, a decent sort of girl who had been on the course, puckered her brow and glared at her friend Elsie. 'I've never been any good at sewing,' she moaned.

Her mate laughed, 'Well, you'll have to learn to cope, won't you.'

'Honest t' God, we'll need to get up at the crack of dawn to get ourselves ready,' May said, looking worried. 'You any good at sewing, Becky?'

Before Becky had a chance to answer Mrs Morgan was droning on about all the other things they would regularly have to check.

'Your white collars will have to be well-laundered and sewn in neatly, and that goes for your cuffs as well; as for the aprons, you will be given three each. They are of the utmost importance, especially the points, pay a lot of attention to the pressing of those points.'

Suddenly Becky laughed out loud. 'At least the years I spent in the laundry won't be wasted,' she said to May.

'Yeah, well, in that case you can lend a hand with mine.'

Becky made no answer to that, thinking it was as well that she had kept the fact that she could sew to herself.

Considering the endless number of things that would be needed to keep her own uniform in good order she'd be kept busy enough without taking on the responsibility of anyone else's.

By the time the correct length of the dress had been decided for each girl and a leaflet passed around informing them to provide their own plain black stockings and black shoes with only medium heels for comfort, the group as a whole felt worn out.

Florence Nicholls followed Miss Timson into the room and saw the girls flopped back in their chairs. They got to their feet quickly, looking embarrassed.

'Don't worry,' Mrs Nicholls smiled, motioning the girls to sit down, 'I come bearing good news. This being Wednesday, you have four days in which to relax, go home and see your families, before you report for duty at ten o'clock on Monday morning.'

The girls, all smiles, now sat up straight as Mrs Nicholls continued. 'To start off with you will be on duty from ten in the morning until six o'clock at night, with a meal break in between. That will enable each of you to travel to and from work at a reasonable hour. Then, shift work will have to be taken into consideration. Will it be too far for some of you to travel back and forth? Especially when a shift is late at night or early in the morning. Discuss this with your parents, heed their advice. The company does have an arrangement with a long-stay hostel here in London, or Miss Timson has names and addresses of homely landladies who have been

thoroughly vetted and approved. Some of you may prefer
to seek lodgings with one of them.'

Becky's heart sank into her boots. She hadn't given a
thought to shift work, although she had learnt that Coventry
Street Corner House had opened an all-night café back in
1923. What would she do? Why hadn't she thought about
the travelling part before now? She comforted herself with
a fact she had gleaned from one of the waiters. Only lads
were expected to be on duty during the night, but that didn't
alter the fact that the Corner Houses catered a lot for the
late evening theatre trade and surely she would eventually
be asked to do late turns.

May Stevens leant forward. 'What's up, Becky? Don't you
want to go home and see yer folks?'

''Course I do,' Becky said as she smiled briefly. 'It's just
that I hadn't given a thought to how I'm going to get to
work when we get put on to shifts.'

'Well, you will live out in the sticks,' May grinned at her.
'Didn't you tell me your dad works on the railway?'

'Yes, that's right an' he does different shifts but I can't see
how that's going to be of any help.'

'Well, you got all the weekend to think about it and then
we're only doing ten till six for a while so why start thinking
about 'ow you're going to cross yer bridges before you've
even come t' them?'

'What a friend you are,' Becky declared.

'And just what d' you mean by that?' May asked, eyebrows raised.

'Down to earth and very sensible, you've given me good
advice,' Becky said, placing her hand on her friend's shoulder.
'I shall miss you, but isn't it great to have these free days before
we start work?'

'Sure is,' May agreed. 'Shan't see you now till next
Monday.' Then grinning and doing her best to speak really
nicely, she added, 'Ten o'clock at Lyons Coventry Street
Corner House.'

They stood up and their arms went round each other, hugging tightly.

'I never thought I'd really make it,' May whispered to Becky. 'You, yes, but me, I had me doubts.'

Becky clutched May's hand as they broke away. 'Thank God we both did. Enjoy your break and I'll be looking forward to seeing you on Monday.'

'Me too,' May answered with emphasis. 'Having found you as a friend is a bonus.'

Later, Becky stood on the pavement and watched May as she took big strides towards her bus stop. From the beginning I decided that lass had a good head on her shoulders and I was right, she told herself, and what's more she's got a good heart as well. I couldn't have asked for a better friend to work with. All the same as she rode the short distance to the railway station her heart was still full of misgivings as to just how her future with Lyons would work out.

Chapter Twelve

IT WAS PAST four when Becky climbed down off the local tram and took a moment to look around. In the warm late summer sunshine New Malden looked a picture. Not much traffic, no big dirty warehouses, not even the posh department stores, just lovely green grass on the verges. Beyond the few houses in Albert Road lay Harry Horsecroft's farm and further over the allotments where her dad spent much of his spare time.

She stopped in her tracks and took a really deep breath. Oh, it was good to be home, so good, it seemed that she had been away for ages. Her footsteps quickened and as she neared her house, the front door was thrown open.

'Mum!' Small, plump, warm, smiling, her mother stood there. Becky threw herself into her mother's outstretched arms. 'Oh, Mum, I've missed you. It's so good to see you.'

'Not half as much as I've missed you, lass.' Joyce Russell sniffed away her happy tears. 'There's only been me against all the males.'

A jumble of excited voices came up the hallway. Then she was surrounded by her three brothers, Jack, Tom and Fred. 'Who's been gadding about up in the Smoke then, leaving me to cope with a miserable mother?' young Fred asked, playfully punching her shoulder.

Then there were her two sisters-in-law, each kissing her with a great deal of enthusiasm. 'Hey, hang on, Ada, and you, Joan,' Becky pleaded, laughing, 'give me a chance to get a kiss from my nephews.'

Bending her knees, she put her arms round the two little

boys, Ronnie and Joey. 'I've brought you each a stick of rock from the Tower of London,' she whispered.

'Don't believe you,' Ronnie retorted as he made a funny face at her. He seemed to have grown a few inches in the short time she'd been away.

'It's true,' she told him, delving into her handbag and fetching out the pink peppermint sticks. 'You'll see when you suck it, it says Tower of London all the way through the rock.'

Suddenly the whole family was pestering her with questions.

'Give her a chance, let her get inside the house, will you?' Her father had, until now, hung back wanting her all to himself.

'Aw Dad!' A lump had come into Becky's throat, threatening to choke her. 'Dad,' she said again, and without so much as a word, Joe Russell, big man that he was, found himself grabbing his slim daughter and holding her close to his chest.

'Didn't reckon on the house being so empty,' he spoke half to himself. 'Are you well, pet?' Holding her now at arm's length, he said, 'God above you've grown up! Quite the sophisticated miss, aren't you? An' you've only been away three weeks.'

At last Joyce managed to get them all seated in the front room. 'I'll away and make the tea,' she said.

Joan put young Joey down on the hearth rug and followed her mother-in-law out to the kitchen. Becky watched the two boys struggle to undo the paper from their stick of rock and she realized just how much she had missed her family. Her two eldest brothers were big and strong, just like her dad, and they were nice with it. She felt a twinge of envy. Her sisters-in-law were lucky. They were happily married with children of their own. A depressing thought came to her. It might be years before I ever get married, let alone have children. You're never satisfied, she chided herself, you wanted a career and now even before you've started out on it you're having regrets.

'Becky, you didn't say how long you're home for,' her mother said, pushing the door open with her hip and guiding in the tea trolley.

'I haven't got to go to work until next Monday and after that I shall be home every night for quite a while.'

Her mother raised her head from the task of pouring out the tea, a question showing in her eyes. 'Quite a while, what's that supposed to mean?'

Becky glanced at her father for help and saw him shake his head at her mother in stealthy reproach. 'Give the girl time to have her tea,' he reprimanded her, 'there'll be plenty of time for us to hear all the news later on.'

'Oh all right,' her mother smiled, 'dinner won't be too long. It's special, Harry Horsecroft let me have two lovely chickens so there's plenty for everyone.'

Their evening meal was jolly. A real family affair with Joyce Russell constantly urging everyone to eat up. 'Especially you, Becky. You're far too thin,' she sternly told her daughter.

All too soon dinner was over; Joan and Ada began to gather together the paraphernalia that was part of travelling with young children.

'Come on Jack, tomorrow's still a work day,' Ada said as she picked up Ronnie's toys. 'You won't be so chirpy when the alarm goes off at five-thirty.'

'Joey, will you stand still an' let me wipe your sticky fingers?' Joan scolded. 'Trust your Aunt Becky to buy you sweets,' she smiled as she took the stick of rock and endeavoured to wrap the paper back around it.

'You eat enough sweets,' Tom told his wife, 'and you don't look so bad on it.'

Joan looked up at her husband, grinning. 'Don't stand there paying me compliments, it won't get you anywhere. You've also got to be up at the crack of dawn, remember.'

When Jack, Tom and their wives and children had left,

Joyce told Becky that Ella was expecting to see her tomorrow. 'I met her down the market, baby's doing ever so well though I thought Ella looked a bit washed out. Still, she was thrilled when I told her you were coming home.'

'Right,' Becky answered thoughtfully. 'First thing after breakfast I'll go round and see her mum, then I'll go to Kingston later.'

It was good to be home, Becky thought, while she listened to her parents fill her in on the lives of her brothers, uncles and aunts, neighbours and friends.

'Joe, come an' have some cocoa and cake before we go to bed. You too Becky, it will help you to sleep well,' her mother called from the kitchen.

'Your room's all ready, Becky, you go on up, I'll pop in and see you're all right in a few minutes,' Joyce said to her daughter, as she cleared the empty cocoa mugs off the table before kissing Becky on her cheek and patting her shoulder.

Then it was her dad's turn. He walked with her to the foot of the stairs and all at once she felt like a little girl again.

'Going to offer to give me a piggyback, Dad?'

'None of yer cheek, young lady,' he grinned, 'it's not so long since I used to run up these stairs with you on my back.'

'Couldn't do it now,' she teased.

He swatted her behind and they walked up the stairs side by side. When they came to her bedroom, he bent to kiss her.

'Good night, Becky, it's great to have you home.'

'Good night, Dad, I do love you.' The words just slipped out naturally. She looked up at him, her eyes bright, and with that he gently put his arms about her again, and she felt safe and loved.

'Good night, pet,' he whispered, gave her a little push and turned to go back downstairs.

Becky opened the door of her old bedroom and gasped. The gas had been lit, casting a shadowy glow around the walls that looked so different. 'Of course they're different,' she exclaimed, 'they've been freshly papered!' What a lovely surprise! The furniture had been rearranged. Even the bed had been moved so that it now faced the window, and her chest of drawers was on the other side of the room. The curtains and the bedspread matched and were all new, a soft floral pattern on a dusty pink background. The material must have cost a lot of money and her mother must have spent hours making them. I must go back downstairs and say thank you to them, she decided.

Her hand was on the door knob, about to turn it, when she heard her parents talking in hushed tones; then her father chuckled. She threw open the door.

'You two are marvellous, even if you are devious with it,' she declared.

'Just so long as you are pleased with it, you are aren't you? Fred did the decorating.'

'Mum, it's lovely, truly lovely!'

'That's all right then.'

More hugs and kisses followed.

She undressed, turned the gaslight out, and climbed into bed, thinking she must be the luckiest girl alive to have such wonderful parents and brothers. Then as she lay in bed she took to wondering how Ella was doing. Had things worked out well between her and Peter? Had baby Margaret brought them closer together or had the added expense of a baby proved a big burden?

Stop worrying, go to sleep, she rebuked herself. You'll see Ella tomorrow and be able to judge for yourself.

Becky was awake before it was light and she lay listening to the rain beat against the windowpane. Gosh, the wind sounds terrific, it hasn't rained for ages but it's certainly making up for it now, she told herself as she got out of bed, pulled her dressing gown on and went downstairs to be thoroughly spoiled by her doting mother.

They say rain before seven will clear before eleven, and

that was exactly what happened, though the gutters were still running with water and the pavements were wet and slippery as Becky left Peggy James's house. At the corner of George Road she turned to give a final wave to Peggy. Her visit had set her thinking again. Peggy's version of Ella's married life hadn't described a bed of roses. Like her own mother, Peggy was of the opinion that Ella was looking tired, not at all well. 'Too much to cope with and not enough money coming in,' was how Ella's mother saw it.

Ella beamed when she opened the door to find Becky on the doorstep.

'Becky! Cor, it's marvellous to see you.' Ella came forward with hands outstretched. 'My, I can't believe how different you look, you're wearing make-up! An' you look so well.'

'Are you going to keep me standing here on the doorstep all day? I'm dying to see baby Margaret,' Becky said, stepping in to the narrow passage. 'Where is she?'

Ella's smile faded and she sighed a little despondently as she led the way through to the kitchen. 'I haven't had time to bath her yet, she had a fretful night and then after her early feed she went off to sleep so I let her lie.'

'That's good,' Becky said eagerly, taking off her jacket as she walked, 'I'd love to help bath her.'

One glance around the room and Becky was appalled.

'I've been trying to earn a few extra shillings,' Ella said quietly, sensing that Becky was embarrassed by the state of the place.

Ella's living room smelt of damp washing and ironing and three string lines had been placed, stretching from wall to wall, each covered with damp articles of linen.

'I'm a bit behind with the ironing,' Ella apologized, 'I was hoping to get it all finished before you arrived. I have to return it all this afternoon.'

'That's no problem,' Becky answered, doing her best to hide her real feelings, 'let me just have a few minutes with the baby. It seems so long since I've seen her. Then we'll both get cracking – be like working together in the laundry again.'

'Hardly that, here it's all slog on me own. It was hard work at the Wellington, right enough, but everyone was pally and we did have mates to have a good laugh with. There's days here when I don't see a soul.'

'Ah, but today you've got me. We'll skip through all the jobs, bath and dress Margaret up fit to kill and then we'll go into Kingston and have a bite to eat out. How does that sound?'

'Wonderful, but I still have to make my deliveries.'

'If we pack it all up after we've done the ironing can't we put it in the pram and deliver it on our way?'

'Yeah, suppose we could.'

'Well, there you are then! Come on, where are you hiding the baby?'

'She's still in her cot, upstairs.'

'All right if I go and fetch her down?' Becky asked, not waiting for an answer but thinking to herself as she climbed the stairs that all these signs of poverty were making her tense. Four years and more she and Ella had put up with the drudgery of working in a laundry and all Ella had swapped it for was this.

Well, it isn't going to happen to me, she vowed. I'll make it to the top, I don't know just how I'll do it but do it I will. I'm never going to live like this.

Margaret, bathed, fed, powdered and dressed had been put in her pram while Ella and Becky together, rotating three flat irons, made short work of the ironing.

Ella seemed much more relaxed, the baby was cooing happily and Becky was sighing inwardly with relief as she pushed the pram towards Kingston.

The next three hours flew by. Laundry was delivered and cash collected. People leant over the pram admiringly with remarks such as, 'What a beautiful baby.' They ate a meat pie and two veg in the market café, and now both girls, feeling a whole lot more contented, made their way towards home.

'What on earth is happening?' Ella cried as they turned the corner into Mill Street.

Women were crowded out on the pavement all up and down the street. Others were leaning out of their upstairs windows.

Just as they drew level with Martha Tubman's gate, her front door flew open and she came running down the path.

'The police are down outside the Swan,' she yelled, 'it's that poor blighter Tommy Ferguson, they think he's interfered with a little girl.'

'What the hell are you saying?' Becky sounded furious. 'There's no harm in Tommy, no harm at all, he wouldn't hurt a fly.'

Martha looked sheepish. 'Well that's what they reckon, come down the road and see for yerself.'

Ella had never liked her next-door neighbour and she avoided her as much as possible, but as she looked at her now she could cheerfully have killed her. 'Tommy's just a bit different, quiet like, but I agree with Becky, he wouldn't harm a child.' Feeling sick to her stomach she took hold of the pram and told Becky, 'I'll take the baby inside and feed her, you pop down and see if there's anything you can do.'

Normally Becky wouldn't have gone within a mile of a noisy crowd but she had to find out what was happening to Tom. It sounded so terrible, this awful accusation, his poor mother must be going out of her mind with worry.

'I'll be back as soon as I know what's going on,' Becky assured Ella, before turning and running after Martha Tubman, all the while telling herself, Tommy might not be the brightest of lads but there was nothing wrong with his heart. Go out of his way to help folk, Tom would. And since he'd been courting Mary Marsden there'd been a marked difference in him. Meeting Mary had been the best thing that ever happened to Tom. No one is ever going to convince me that Tom Ferguson hurt a child.

Becky stood at the edge of the crowd, mainly women, that had gathered outside the Swan public house and clutched her side, giving herself a minute to get her breath back.

'You can't take my boy off just like that, he never did nuffin to no kid, I'd bet me life on that,' Dolly Ferguson implored, her voice an anguished wail as she tried to push past the policeman.

Becky couldn't believe her eyes! By the look of it Tom had been manhandled to the ground and another policeman was standing guard over him.

'Oh, it's you, Becky.' Dolly turned her head and gasped as Becky put her arm around her shoulders. At the same moment Tom looked up, tears were glistening in his eyes and at the sight of her his cheeks turned red with shame.

'Please, Becky, believe me. I've done nothing wrong. I was helping the little girl, truly I was, please believe me,' he begged.

'Come on. On your feet,' the policeman said. 'The van will be here shortly.'

'Let me go,' Tom pleaded as he struggled.

'You ain't going anywhere, me lad, except to the station where you'll be locked up while this matter is sorted out.'

'I don't think so,' a woman's voice yelled from the back of the crowd.

Women began to take sides. 'He's a good lad, do anything for anybody,' was the general cry. Only Martha Tubman and a few of her skinny cronies seemed to want the show to go on.

'Ain't no smoke without fire,' one young mother screamed, hoisting her infant higher on her hip and shoving a dummy into its mouth, 'an' I saw the girl, frightened out of her wits an' covered in mud she was.'

'You'll be asked to make a statement later, Madam,' the policeman said calmly.

'Yeah, well, I'll do that all right,' the woman replied, 'I know what I saw.'

Tom had risen to his feet shakily and was brushing himself down.

'You stay still,' the policeman ordered him as his mother made to take his arm and lead him away.

'I've told you he ain't going nowhere, should be ashamed of yourselves, the bloody lot of yer.' Annie Smith, landlady of the Swan, used her elbows to edge her way to the front of the crowd. 'I saw it all, a damn sight more than that skinny cow reckons she saw, an' I'd 'ave been down 'ere a lot quicker except I was in the bathroom starkers when it 'appened. Good job the bathroom steamed up and I opened the window when I did. Been wedged shut for years an' it weren't easy t' open but I'll say again, damn good job I persevered because that lad's a good 'un, he's no more a child molester than you are, Constable.'

'Gawd luv yer, Annie, I'll be in yer debt for the rest of me life.' A tearful Dolly Ferguson used the corner of her flowered overall to wipe the corner of her eye. 'There's always someone ready to put my Tommy down but they're knocking on my door quick enough when they want some rough work done. Two-faced bloody lot some of 'em are, an' as for these coppers, only too ready to condemn, ain't yer, wouldn't listen to my son's side of the story, oh no, but you'd take 'er word,' Dolly thumbed her hand towards the young mother who reckoned she had seen the child, giving her a look that boded no good. 'Be a damn sight better if she stayed in 'er own 'ome and took care of 'er kids instead of spending 'alf the day on the doorstep gossiping and picking other people to pieces.'

The constable had the grace to look sheepish. 'Only doing me job, Mam.' Then, turning to Annie Smith, he added, 'You'll need to come to the station an' all, give your statement. The little girl in question and her friend have gone ahead in the doctor's car . . .'

He was interrupted by the arrival of the black police van.

'All right, all right, what's going on here?' The voice of authority made himself heard and the women drew back as Sergeant Burton looked suspiciously at everyone.

Annie Smith stepped forward, her face dark with anger. 'You, Sergeant, had better listen to me, never mind none of the others. See that little window up there, the one that's wide open?' She paused and pointed a finger upwards. 'That's where I had me head stuck out when the biggest of the two kids pushed the other one.'

'Madam . . .'

The sergeant didn't get any further. Annie took a step forward.

'Don't "madam" me, Sergeant Burton. A wrong's been done 'ere and I'm the one that can set the record right so the sooner you listen the sooner we can all go about our business.'

'You must come to the station to make a statement,' the police sergeant insisted.

'I'm going nowhere till I've had me say. Not you, Sergeant, nor a team of wild 'orses is going to drag me away. Let these scandalmongers that ain't got nothing better t' do than spread rumours 'ear the truth.'

'Gawd bless yer, Annie,' Dolly put her spoke in yet again.

The sergeant sighed heavily. 'Well, we all know how obstinate you can be, Mrs Smith, so get on with it, if you must,' he pleaded.

'Like I said, the two girls were on the bridge and the older one was kind of daring the little 'un to jump the brook. They got to the edge of the water and the youngster drew back, she was afraid, I could tell that much. They argued for a few seconds then the dark-'aired one, she lost her temper and shoved the little 'un in her back, pushing her forward. What with all the rain we 'ad this morning the bank was slippery like and the kiddie slid down, landing flat on her face in the mud.

'The other little bitch starts screaming at the top of her voice. Tommy was coming across the field, God knows what might 'ave 'appened if he 'adn't been there. Anyways, he broke into a run, waded in an' grabbed the toddler out and was doing his best to clean the mud off her face an' the front of her dress when the crowd gathered and the oldest girl told them it was Tommy that pushed the kid in. Wants her backside whacked if you ask me.'

'Right then you lot, let's see you move off to your own homes,' the sergeant said, stern-faced, 'unless any of you want to contradict this lady's version of what happened.'

Most of the women gave a noncommittal shrug of the shoulders. Annie was not finished, however.

'This matter is over and done with. Tom Ferguson has shown what he's made of today an' anyone that wants t' say different will not only 'ave t' answer to me but to me ole man as well an' you all know how nasty he can get.'

Becky patted Dolly's shoulder, 'I'm off back to Ella's,' she said in a soft voice. 'She'll be wanting to know what's happened and I'm sure Tom will be all right now.'

'Yeah, all right, lass, thanks for your concern,' Dolly answered as she heaved her bosoms higher and watched her son climb into the police van. 'Looks like they're still going to take Tom down the station so I'm going as well. I'll see yer later.'

Becky was smiling to herself as she walked back up Mill Street. She wouldn't mind being a fly on the wall at Kingston police station. What with both Annie Smith and Dolly Ferguson being there stating their case, the next hour should be quite lively.

Over a cup of tea Becky related all the details to Ella.

'Just shows you what mischief kids get up to when they're allowed to run wild in the streets. Could have been real nasty for Tommy,' Ella said thoughtfully. 'I hope Peter has found us somewhere better to live before Margaret is old enough to go to school.'

Becky, too, was having sobering thoughts. That older child must be a right little terror; she knew what trouble she was causing when she accused Tom of having done the pushing. Would baby Margaret grow up to be like that? The responsibility of raising children could weigh heavily, she was thinking to herself, as she pondered on how Peter and Ella were ever going to better themselves when their income was so little.

Peter came in just as Becky was ready to leave.

'Aw, Becky, it's great to see you, don't go on my account,' Peter said, having given her a peck on the cheek.

'No, I'm not,' Becky smiled, 'it's just that me mum will have tea ready and I said I'd be home. Still, I'm glad I caught you. How's things at the laundry?'

'Could be better. A darn sight better if you want the truth. With all this lovely weather we've been having even the big houses don't put out so much laundry. Still, autumn's nearly here and winter won't be far behind, so things will pick up, I'm sure.'

He didn't sound as if he were sure. Neither did he look well, any more than Ella did. They both looked as if they hadn't had a good night's sleep for ages. Becky felt really sorry for them both. But me being sorry for them isn't going to help, she was quietly saying to herself, at the same time feeling irritated because she just couldn't think of any way in which she might be able to help.

Leaving the baby with Peter, Ella saw Becky to the tram.

'I told your mum I'd come over with her on Sunday afternoon,' Becky said, doing her best to keep the conversation cheerful while they waited for the tram. 'I'll get my mum to bake us a cake, come to think of it me mum might come as well.'

'Your mum has all yer family to tea on Sundays, they'll want you to be there,' Ella reminded her.

'Oh yeah, well, never mind I'll make it Saturday afternoon, how's that?'

'Fine,' Ella said, but she didn't sound too keen.

I'll bring plenty of things with me to make a spread, Becky vowed to herself, as she kissed her dear friend goodbye.

Going home, Ella walked faster. It would be so easy for her to be jealous of Becky but come what may she mustn't let that happen. She had made her own mistakes and now she had to live by them. But what a difference there was between Becky and herself now! Look at the skirt Becky was wearing: it was a wool suiting. She'd been ashamed of her own skirt, which had certainly seen better days. Well, things would pick up soon. Peter had promised they would. Meanwhile they had baby Margaret and there wasn't anything in this world that could make her regret having had her. She was a sweet little darling and Peter was good and kind, always doing his best. So what more could she ask for?

Reaching her front gate she didn't bother to search her mind for an answer.

Chapter Thirteen

THE DAY HAD dawned.

If I live to be a hundred I'll never forget the excitement of this first morning, Becky was saying to herself as she listened to the soft but firm voice of Robert Matthews wishing them luck as they prepared to step out and offer their services as waitresses for J. Lyons & Company.

'One last thing you may like to know,' Robert's voice held a hint of amusement as the four new girls turned their heads towards him, 'most of you have probably heard our waitresses referred to as Nippies.' There was a murmur of agreement. 'That came about at one of the big Masonic events attended by female staff for the very first time. An enthusiastic newspaper reporter wrote in his article that the young ladies could not be alluded to as waitresses because they nipped about so quickly. The name, Nippy, was quickly adopted and as such has remained.'

'Don't think we'll be doing much nipping about this lunchtime,' May Stevens commented out of the side of her mouth. 'Don't know about you, Becky, but all that carry-on as to whether or not our uniform was perfect got me down a bit. Talk about grooming a horse! If we don't look the part by now we never will. Surely we won't have to go through all that palaver every blinking morning.'

Becky's only answer was a smile. She thought they looked a treat. A real transformation, she assured herself as she took a last glimpse in the long mirror. Her cap was correct, the badge on her dress securely sewn on. Those cuffs had been a job to sew in and she'd spent a long time pressing the points of her white apron. One last job: fix her order-pad and pencil, which were secured by a bulldog clip and fastened with a fine chain on to the waistband of her dress.

Heart hammering, she threw her shoulders back, took a deep breath and stepped out through the swing doors into the real world.

Today they only had to work the lunch shift. She couldn't believe it! Even in the middle of the day the customers were so glamorous, their clothes so beautiful and as for their scents, men and women alike smelt lovely as she bent over to place the dishes of their choice in front of them.

It was nearly seven o'clock by the time Becky climbed into the railway carriage and thankfully sank into a corner seat. My legs are killing me, and my poor feet are on fire, she moaned softly as she leant back and closed her eyes. What a day!

She, Rebecca Russell, had spent eight hours in the very heart of London's West End. Waiting table at Coventry Street Corner House. God knows how many trips I made to the kitchen and back, she mused. It wasn't only Londoners that ate there – provincial and overseas visitors had helped to keep her busy. In some cases it had been a little difficult to understand their accent. She had constantly reminded herself of a saying that Miss Timson had frequently used during their period of training.

No matter who it is, or where they come from, at Lyons Corner Houses, everyone is served with equal courtesy and consideration.

For everything good in this life there is a price to be paid.

Becky felt that she had got through the first eight weeks of her employment with Lyons reasonably well. The good things, of course, had far outweighed the bad. Now her probation time was over, she needed to make some decisions.

The terms of her employment now meant that she would have to do shift work and travelling home to New Malden in the early hours of the morning was out of the question. It would also prove very difficult, were she to remain living at home with her parents, for her to get into the West End in time to start the early morning shift.

During the test period, all four of the girls had been offered the chance, once the shifts started, to stay at the hostel for a further three months. After that they were on their own. This meant that she had to start searching for somewhere to live without delay. Somewhere she could afford and that would be within easy distance of Coventry Street.

Part of their training had been carried out at Orchard House, Orchard Street, W1, only a stone's throw from the great departmental stores like Selfridges. Becky adored window-shopping in that area but to find accommodation anywhere near that she could afford was out of the question. She had never had to think about money before. Not seriously. There had always been her parents to provide food, warmth and shelter. She had given part of what she earned at the Wellington Laundry to her mother each week and had been allowed to keep the remainder as pocket money. Most of her clothes had been made by her mother until she grew old enough to learn how to make her own. Leaving home meant being responsible for herself. Would she be able to cope? She'd have to, there didn't seem to be much choice.

'Don't be too nervous,' Mr Gower, the short, stocky head waiter, told Becky and May before they started their first late night shift. 'I won't tell either of you not to be nervous at all, because you're bound to be. Serving dinner, especially to the theatre-going customers, is vastly different to serving morning coffees and lunches.'

'I'm too terrified to be nervous,' Becky answered.

'There's really no need,' Mr Gower assured them both. 'I've never had two newly-trained girls in whom I place so much confidence. Each of you is very good at your job, and I'll be on hand should you get into any difficulties.'

Mr Gower was right. Everything was vastly different. The small restaurant to which Mr Gower had assigned them was small and intimate, distinguished by its red plush chairs and sections divided off into convenient corners.

'Talk about a carry-on!' May muttered as she and Becky waited while the commis brought their orders for the hors d'oeuvres.

One of the lads winked at May. 'Seeing how the other half live tonight, aren't you? Plenty of tête-à-têtes going on in those cosy corners, eh?'

'It's what is known as the cosmopolitan atmosphere,' a blond-headed lad said, grinning cheekily. 'You ain't seen nothing yet. Wait till the theatres turn out and the toffs 'ave downed a load of bubbly, that's when things start to get serious.'

'Cosmopolitan ain't what we call it where I come from,' May said, her eyes filled with laughter.

One of the chefs flicked a cloth around the lad's head, gave him a wicked look and said, 'Things will be very serious in this kitchen if you don't move yourself a bit quicker an' allow these young ladies to get on with their job.'

Even the front of the house, as it was referred to, changed its style by night. Colourful window displays encouraged the men to buy presents for their lady companions. Spotlights illuminated exquisite boxes of chocolates of all shapes and sizes resting on carefully ruched satin. Just inside the door orchids and carnations made up as a corsage were displayed on a black velvet board ready for the male escort to purchase and to pin on to the fur coat of his beloved before setting off for the theatre.

The whole building was very much alive, even more so than it was during the day. Customers were shown to a table by black-coated male floor-walkers, always under the stern eye of Mr Gower.

The first sight of the hors d'oeuvres trolley had Becky gasping in admiration. There was a choice of at least eighteen dishes: eggs stuffed with anchovies; tomatoes scalloped and filled with delicious mysteries; sardines, rollmops, Russian salad, red cabbage, asparagus, diced beetroot, fancy-cut colourful radishes, not to mention the various cooked meats, and all offered merely as a start to the main meal!

'God rest their stomachs,' grinned May as they each trundled a trolley through the swing doors.

Becky spent a few seconds thinking how wonderful the friendship with May had turned out. She really liked May and she knew that May felt the same way about her. Some changes had taken place in each of them since they had first met. Becky felt she was less uneasy about things in general and May had settled down very well. She had taken to being a Nippy like a duck to water. She had even altered her speech somewhat. Becky knew without asking what an effort that must have been for May. Nevertheless she had succeeded. She no longer dropped quite so many aitches and she checked herself if the word 'ain't' came out. Becky made sure that she never laughed at May's efforts.

Whatever the diners chose as their main meal it was either served in an individual dish or from a silver salver. Grilled fish served with a creamy rich sauce was Becky's favourite and the Knickerbocker Glory served with a long-handled spoon had her in raptures on the odd occasion when the staff were allowed one for themselves. At such times, May would go off into fits of laughter, watching Becky stand up in order to eat the very last morsel of fruit and ice cream that remained in the glass.

Halfway through the second week of their late shift the police came to the Corner House to inform May that her mother had been taken ill and had been admitted to hospital.

'Of course you must go straight away,' insisted Mr Gower, reaching into his pocket and withdrawing a half-crown. 'Take a taxi, go on, don't bother to change, take off your apron and put your coat on, nobody will notice your uniform.'

'Thanks ever so much, Mr Gower,' May mumbled, the colour slowly draining from her cheeks.

'I hope you find your mother feeling better,' Becky called out as May practically ran from the still room.

It was a long night after that. The compliments the toffs often paid Becky fell on deaf ears and she was truly grateful when Mr Gower signalled that she might leave the floor.

Her room at the hostel felt cold and lonely when she opened the door half an hour after midnight. It was only a short walk from Coventry Street to the hostel and Becky had been glad of the sharp fresh air. May had been in her thoughts the whole evening. May worshipped her old mum. They only had each other. Apparently her father had been killed in the dockyards when May was quite young and her mother had never married again.

Becky was talking to herself as she prepared herself for bed. If it weren't so late and I didn't feel so dog-tired I'd go over to her mum's flat and see if May was back from the hospital yet. At times like these one needed friends or family. For a moment she wished she was at home. Able to open her bedroom door and call down to her mum and dad. They'd come running, I know they would but they aren't here now, are they? She told herself to stop being silly, but it wasn't easy.

It was three days before she saw May again. She turned up at the hostel at nine o'clock one morning. Becky wasn't dressed. She heard May's voice, rough and familiar. Still in her dressing gown she got up and opened the door and held out her arms to her friend. May was trembling, she looked strange, drained of all feeling and Becky didn't need to be told that her mother had died.

'Becky, she wasn't there. I never got to say goodbye. A heart attack they said. She never came home again and that flat is bloody terrible without my mum being there.'

'I know, I know,' Becky soothed. She wanted to cuddle her

again, but didn't dare touch her. May wasn't one for showing emotion.

'Want a cup of coffee?' she asked softly.

'That all you've got? No tea?'

Becky shook her head.

'That'll do.'

They drank their coffee in silence until May gave a deep sigh.

'Want to talk about it?' Becky asked her quietly.

'Nothing I say will bring me mum back, will it? I'm just grateful that I've got a job that will help take my mind off things.'

'Shouldn't you ask for more time off?' Becky suggested.

'I can't stand the flat now, it's so empty, every single sound is like an echo. The neighbours have been wonderful but it's not the same. Time seems to hang so long. And at night I can't get to sleep.' With the words hardly out, May burst into tears.

The next moment Becky was hugging her and murmuring soft words that were meant to be comforting.

'It's funny,' May said as she struggled to pull herself together, 'through all that's happened I've hardly shed a tear and here I am babbling like a baby.'

'And a jolly good job too. That's what friends are for, a shoulder to cry on when it's most needed. As for time on your hands, wait till you get back to work and every moment is occupied with fulfilling other people's needs. You'll be rushed off your feet again with no time to brood and come night-time you'll sleep all right cos you'll be dead exhausted.'

May rubbed her eyes and managed to smile and Becky smiled back at her.

'I just feel so guilty cos I wasn't there when she died.'

'I know,' Becky did her best to console her. 'Let me tell you something, May. One of your mum's neighbours came in to see Mr Fairbrother, to tell him your mum was dying, and I had a word with her. She told me that your mum thought you were the best thing that ever happened to her. She thought the sun and the moon shone out of you. You told me she was always a good mother to you, well, she thought you were a good daughter to her. You haven't got anything to reproach yourself for and there's not many can say that when they lose someone.'

'Thanks, Becky,' May whispered as fresh tears rolled down her cheeks.

Becky waited a few minutes, while May searched in her bag for a clean handkerchief, then she suggested, 'Shall I get dressed and we go to a Lyons for a cup of tea?'

May looked at her in surprise and then laughed. 'Why not. Might as well give ourselves a busman's holiday.'

The laughter reassured Becky. She couldn't begin to imagine what it must have been like for May to lose her mother so suddenly.

At the same time May was deciding that she was very lucky to have made a friend such as Becky.

Before that week was out Becky was given cause to say to herself, It's an ill wind that blows nobody any good.

It was the following Monday week before May returned to work.

'Thanks, Becky, for sending flowers,' May said as they stood ready for inspection, before starting work. 'The funeral went off quite well, I was surprised at how many neighbours turned up.'

'All your mum's neighbours were her friends,' Becky told her. 'It was natural they wanted to pay their respects.'

'Yeah. Becky . . . will you do me a favour?'

'You know I will if I can.'

'Come back with me to the flat when we knock off. Stay the night, will you? Please.'

'Yes . . . of course.' Becky stumbled over the words, wondering what on earth May wanted her to stay the night in that tenement flat for.

'Thanks, I'll explain it all tonight.'

With that, Becky had to be satisfied. Still troubled as to what was on May's mind, she had a word with Mr Gower.

'Don't fret yourself, lass. Miss Timson is going to have a chat with May, during your break. The firm will do all it can to help at a time like this.' Mr Gower patted Becky on the arm. 'You young girls need never fear that just because you have left home you are on your own. Lyons prides itself on being one large family. All employees are treated fairly and with kindness, unless of course they should prove themselves unfit to receive such good treatment. Run along now Rebecca, and just remember there is always a member of staff only to willing to listen, at any time, should you feel the need of help or advice.'

'Thank you Mr Gower,' Becky said, wondering to herself whether he was married and had any children. He'd be a nice kind dad, she smiled to herself, almost as nice as her own father.

It was pitch dark as May and Becky felt their way up the flight of stone stairs to the first-floor flat. May already had the key in her hand and set about opening the front door. At the same moment the door to the kitchen opened, letting out rays from the gaslight. Becky gasped. The faded wallpaper showed clean patches where, until recently, pictures had hung.

'Mind yer shins on the boxes,' May urged as they walked down the short passage. Cardboard boxes were piled high up on one side of the drab lino. What on earth had May found to put into these boxes? Becky wondered.

'Aunt Lil, what are you doing still here? You said you were off home when I left for work.'

Becky took stock of the tiny grey-haired woman who was peering out at them. She looked so neat and tidy in a dark dress more than half covered by a white bibbed apron. Stepping back to let the girls into the kitchen, May's Aunt Lil shrugged.

'Couldn't leave the place, not the state it's in. Better t' get it all over an' done with. Besides I wanted t' know what yer friend said. You must be Becky,' she added, peering hard into Becky's face.

'Move yer body, Aunt Lil, let Becky sit down. You're a crafty old devil, you had no intention of going back to your place.'

Aunt Lil smiled, showing a remarkably good set of teeth for an old lady. 'Like I said, luv, didn't want t' leave you with all this mess to sort out. I've got you a nice bit of supper in the oven. You can wait on yerselves. I'm off t' bed. Good night, May.'

May had to bend her knees to kiss her aunt on the cheek. 'Goodnight, Aunt, thanks for staying,' she said softly. 'See you in the morning.'

'Good night, Becky, afraid there is only the one double bed, I've put a bottle in to warm it up like, you won't mind sharing with May, will you?'

'Of course not,' Becky answered quickly, thinking she was glad she wouldn't be in a room on her own. This place felt strange, perhaps because she had never stayed in a flat before. 'Goodnight . . .' she said hesitantly, not sure how she should address this tiny lady.

Lily Maynard smiled. This young lady was very different to the usual run-of-the-mill girls that May had grown up with. You'll do my sister's girl a power of good, she was thinking to herself, knock the rough edges off our May and maybe she'll end up talking the way you do and that wouldn't be a bad thing. Not bad at all, she decided as she smiled at Becky, saying, 'Lass, I'm Aunt Lil, to any number of young folk, though I was never lucky enough to be blessed with kids of me own, but seeing as 'ow me sister 'as been taken, God rest her soul, I reckon it's a blessing that May's got me. And now, we can't 'ave you feeling left out of things, so 'ow about you calling me Aunt Lil?'

Becky chuckled. What a character! 'Aunt Lil, it would be an honour, thank you.'

'Yeah, well, good night again.' Lily Maynard was well pleased. Reaching the door she turned and added another caution, 'Don't stay up all night chewing the fat,' then giggling to herself she muttered, ''alf the night's gone anyway. Soon be daylight.'

In a short while Becky and May were seated at the table and despite it being the early hours of the morning they enjoyed a tasty supper and felt all the better for it.

May pushed her plate to the side, leant back in her chair and with a smile on her lips, she turned to face Becky. 'How do you fancy renting a room in my Aunt Lil's house? She's offered to have both of us an' she'll be in her element if she has the pair of us under her roof.'

'I'm not sure I know what it is you're suggesting,' Becky said, a puzzled frown wrinkling her forehead.

May sighed. 'About time I told you why I asked you to stay here tonight, Becky. The truth is I've got to get out of 'ere. Council won't transfer the tenancy to me. Rotten lot! They'd let a son take it over, but not an unmarried daughter. They want me out.'

'Good job too, if you ask me,' Aunt Lily cried out scornfully as she poked her head round the door. 'These tenements should 'ave been pulled down years ago.'

'Well nobody's asking you, an' I thought you'd gone up t' bed,' May said sternly.

'I 'ad. I've come down cos I forgot me drink of water. I'll need it in the night.'

'Yeah, I believe you, thousands wouldn't,' May grinned. 'Now you are 'ere, will you tell Becky or shall I?'

'You do yer own telling, and clear that table. Put the plates in the sink, leave 'em for me t' do in the morning.'

'Aunt! Go to bed! Before I do something to you that I'll be sorry for.'

'I'm going,' she said as she turned towards Becky. 'Yer see

what a moody temper our May's got, always wants 'er own way. Yer wanna watch 'er Becky, see 'er bad habits don't rub off on to you,' Lily advised, giving Becky a sly wink as once again she made for the door.

The two girls looked at each other and burst out laughing.

'Aunt Lil loves to know what's going on,' May said with a grin. 'She's got ears as sharp as a bat's, especially when it comes to other folk's conversations. Still, her heart's in the right place. The long an' short of what she's suggesting is that you and I both go and lodge with her. Said we can each have a room of our own.'

'Well,' Becky said, delight and surprise expressed in her wide smile, 'that would solve your and my problem. I can only stay at the hostel for a few weeks more and I am getting desperate, but you haven't told me where your aunt lives. Has she got a big house? Would it be easy for us to get to and from work?'

'Yes, she's got a big house. On three floors it is and it's in South Lambeth Road, only a stone's throw from the Tate Library.'

'I'm not even sure where the Tate Library is,' Becky answered, feeling naïve.

'It's easy to get to, over Vauxhall Bridge and you're practically there. Buses now run through and they stop almost outside Aunt Lil's front door. Besides if we take up her offer, there's a couple of the other waitresses on our shift who live at Stockwell an' we could always share a cab with them when we're on late turn.'

'Sounds too good to be true,' Becky said, doing her best to stifle a yawn. 'Sorry, May', she added quickly, trying to hide her sudden embarrassment.

'It's me that should be saying sorry, keeping you up like this, you must be dead on yer feet. Come on, let's go up to bed. If you like we can take Aunt Lil home in the morning, that way you'll get to see her place and then you can think about it and make your mind up later.'

Becky smiled, colouring up slightly. 'I won't be sorry to get my head down.'

The great big feather mattress was a joy to wriggle into and the stone hot-water bottle was still just hot enough for Becky to put her feet on.

'If things work out as my aunt plans it won't seem so bad, me losing me mum,' May said, snuggling into her pillow. 'Hardest part is getting rid of all Mum's bits an' pieces. Not that any of it is worth much but to Mum an' me it was our home. Aunt Lil reckons the best thing is to give it all to the Salvation Army, we'd only get coppers if we did call the second-hand totters in.'

'You'd know for certain the Sally Army would see it went to a needy family,' Becky replied, her voice sounding very sleepy.

'Yeah, you're right, not a lot else I can do, is there?'

'Except be grateful to your aunt. I expect if you go to live with her you'll be able to take most of your own bits and pieces.'

'Trust you to give out sensible advice,' May said, pulling the bedclothes up higher over her shoulders.

She got no reply this time from Becky. She was fast asleep.

'What's the hurry? Can't I even 'ave another cup of tea?' May asked her aunt, using a tone of voice that was more a wail.

'No you can't. Move yourself, I wanna get 'ome while there's still some daylight left.'

Becky was smiling to herself as she helped to clear away the breakfast things. The relationship between May and her Aunt Lil had to be seen to be believed. There was a bond of understanding, and that it was a bond formed out of love for each other, Becky was in no doubt. They were rough and ready, both of them, but Becky knew that she'd have to go a long way to find better friends.

The sky had darkened, the rain was now falling heavily and Lily Maynard opened up her umbrella as she stepped off the bus on to the pavement. May took hold of Becky's arm, holding her close as they hurried along the few yards from the bus stop to the row of tall terraced houses that had steps leading up to the front doors. 'Number five,' May said, as they practically ran up the steps into the shelter of the wide porch.

When Aunt Lil opened the big front door and Becky stepped into the passageway she breathed a sigh of pleasure. The ceilings were high, the wallpaper bright and the cream-coloured paintwork shone. A half-moon shaped oak table was set against the wall; on it rested a huge copper bowl filled with evergreen plants.

Aunt Lil gave Becky a smile and May put her arm around her shoulders as they went through to the big old-fashioned kitchen.

'The fire's out,' Aunt Lil told them matter-of-factly, as she picked up the poker and rattled the bars of the gleaming black-leaded range. 'Won't take me long to get it going.'

'Aunt Lil,' May began, 'Becky and I have to go to work tonight and we have our uniforms to see to yet. May we just have a look round and then we'll 'ave a cuppa with you before we go?'

Lily smiled. 'I ask yer ter come as me lodgers but what I really wanted to say ter both of yer is, you'd be doing me a favour, I rattle around this place like a pea in a colander. There was a time when I looked after young kiddies while their mothers went out cleaning offices but now they reckon I'm too old ter be trusted with their kids.'

Both girls made sympathetic noises but Lily put her hand up. 'Let me finish. If you do decide to come 'ere, it will be yer home. In every sense of the word, an' I mean that, Becky. May 'as 'ad the run of this place since she could walk an' it would be the same for you. Yer own room. Bring anything yer like with yer and although I know yer get well fed at

Joey Lyons there'll always be a bit of something ready for yer when you finish work an' on yer days off I'll do a roast an' all the trimmings.'

May was shaking her head. 'I don't believe you! Why don't you just let me show Becky around upstairs and then she will be better able to see if she likes the look of the place. Though 'ow she's gonna cope with you an' the way you carry on, Gawd knows.'

'Don't be so cheeky, May! And as it 'appens I ain't finished with Becky yet.'

Becky was laughing. 'I'm listening, Aunt Lil, don't pay her any attention.'

'First thing you got t' do, Becky, luv, is 'ave a talk with your parents. They don't know me from Adam an' they ain't about ter let you move in 'ere without first giving me and the 'ouse the once-over. I wouldn't think much of them if they did.'

May realized she was wasting her time trying to argue with her aunt and she raised her hands in a token of surrender and burst out laughing. 'All right, 'ave you finished what you wanted to say now? Cos if you've no more objections Becky and I will take ourselves upstairs and begin our tour of inspection.'

'And I will light the gas and put the kettle on to boil,' her aunt said, mimicking the posh accent May had just used.

Somebody had been hard at work.

The whole house was spick and span and every room smelt of lavender. On the first floor there were three bedrooms, one large one in the front, two slightly smaller at the back and, heaven-sent, a lavatory on the same landing. The top floor consisted of one huge long room, which ran the width of the house, had three small windows and was charmingly set out.

There was a small gate-legged table folded down in front of one window and an armchair placed on either side. A tall single oak wardrobe stood against one wall with a chest of drawers further along. The walls themselves were wood-panelled halfway up from the floor, the top half decorated with a pretty tiny flower-patterned paper, and the ceiling looked freshly painted. The single bed was covered with a white counterpane the fringe of which reached to the floor and on top of that there lay a patchwork eiderdown.

Wonders would never cease; there was a bathroom. Set at the centre of the wall, the huge white monster of a bath stood on cast-iron claw feet. It had a single brass tap and above it gleamed a copper geyser.

'However much do you have to put in the gas meter to get enough hot water to fill that?' Becky asked May, sheer amazement visible on her face.

'God knows. Whenever I've stayed here I've aways had me bath in a tin bath in front of the kitchen fire,' May laughed.

Becky laughed with her, thinking of her home in New Malden.

'Can I go back into the long room, have another look?' Becky asked.

''Course you can,' May agreed.

Becky crossed the polished linoleum, noticing it was well-worn in places but two pretty rugs had been placed one each side of the bed. She stood looking out of the window.

'What a view, you can see half of London from up here. I bet it would be smashing to lie in bed in this room when the wind is really blustering.'

'You can't hardly see a thing,' May retorted, 'the rain's still lashing down.'

'Use your imagination,' Becky said dreamily.

'Use what you like. I'm going downstairs to have a cup of tea before we think about setting off and getting ready for work. Are you coming?'

'Yes,' Becky answered quickly, her head buzzing with thoughts, 'but tell me, how come your aunt lives in a big house like this all on her own?'

'Well, in a nutshell, she got served the dirty.'

'That's no answer, what happened?'

'If you must know she married a widower, sixteen years

older than she was at the time. He was living in this house with his three young boys and he knew he was on a good thing when he moved my Aunt Lil in.

'She slogged her guts out doing her best to bring those boys up. When Tom died the boys wanted to turn her out of house and home. Nearly succeeded an' all. The landlord was a gentleman, he said the rightful tenant was my aunt. The boys cleared off an' left her, she's not seen hide nor hair of them from that day to this. Been a bit of a struggle for her to pay the rent over the years but one way an' another she's got by. Bless her.'

Becky reached out and patted the back of May's hand. 'What a sad story,' she exclaimed softly as side by side the two girls went back downstairs.

'Yeah, well, that's the way it goes sometimes,' May sighed.

'Well?' Aunt Lil demanded as they sat down at her table, now covered with a snowy white cloth.

'Got the best china out, I see, all in Becky's honour is it?' May chivvied her aunt.

'Good job you're not staying long today my girl, cos if you were I'd end up boxing your ears. Now cut a piece of that gingerbread and pass it to Becky.'

'Gingerbread an' all,' May said as she grinned at Becky. 'You are getting the royal treatment.'

Becky smothered a giggle. 'I love that long room at the top of the house,' she boldly said.

'You mean what I think you mean?' Lily asked softly. 'Cos, if you do, why don't you ask yer mum an' dad to come and see me, then if they think it's all right you can 'ave that room.'

'I'd like that, and I'd be ever so grateful,' Becky replied.

'Good, but you don't 'ave t' go on about being grateful cos the favour will work both ways. So, if your parents agree, that's settled then.'

May touched Becky's arm, gave her a big smile. 'It'll be smashing, you'll see. We'll have a great time.'

'Hang on a minute, Miss.' Lily raised her eyebrows, pretending to glare at her niece. 'I'm not 'aving you out all hours of the day an' night so you can put all those kind of thoughts out of yer 'ead.'

May winked at Becky, ignoring her aunt. 'She won't know whether we're working or not. Get ourselves a coupla those toffs an' we'll be away up West every night.'

'I've got news for you, young lady,' Lily sniffed at May, 'I shall make it my business to find out what shifts you're doing, make no mistake.'

'Aunt Lil, you couldn't be a dragon no matter how hard you tried.' May got to her feet and flung her arms around her aunt's neck, rubbing her face against Lily's cheek. 'I love you,' she whispered in her ear.

'Get off!' Lily wriggled free, winked at Becky and said, 'You'd better get going if you've both so much t' do.'

'Well, it's not bad, is it Becky?' May asked, shivering as they huddled together under an umbrella while they waited for the bus. 'What d'you think?'

'I think I must have landed on my feet the day I met you, May Stevens. Your Aunt Lily's house is beautiful. An absolute credit to her. I thought I'd had my share of good luck when I landed a job with Lyons. The hostel hasn't been so bad but you've no idea how homesick I've been at times. I know my mum an' dad will be over the moon to think that I'll be with you and we'll both have someone to keep an eye on us.'

'Yeah, I'm glad you feel that way. I'll still miss my mum but at least I won't be lost for company.'

'And you'll be able to keep up your running battle of wits against your aunt,' Becky chuckled.

'It's only a game between us,' May said, laughing at her. 'She loves a bit of a skirmish. I've got a feeling this is all going to work out well for all three of us.'

'I'm sure it will,' Becky answered, and there was a note of strong conviction in her voice.

Chapter Fourteen

As the weeks went by Becky couldn't believe how well everything had worked out. She and May were well settled in at Aunt Lil's. Her mother and father had approved whole-heartedly of both the accommodation and Aunt Lil herself. In fact it would be true to say that a good friendship had sprung up between the three of them. Having been made so welcome on the day that they had come up to London in order to see over the house in South Lambeth Road, Joyce and Joe Russell had insisted that Lily must respond with a visit to New Malden.

'Salt of the earth, your parents are, Becky, and that's no exaggeration,' Lily never tired of telling her.

By now Becky had also got to know some of her customers quite well. Morning coffee time had its regulars. The old lady in the hat adorned with glistening cherries probably had more money than she knew what to do with. Time and time again she tried to press a coin into Becky's hand, sometimes as much as a florin. Becky would gently curl the old lady's fingers back over the money, pat her hand, smile softly and point to the large sign which said 'No Gratuities'. Tipping was greatly discouraged by Lyons. Loneliness was that lady's problem.

Then there was a tall striking man, who had probably spent his life in the forces, who barked his order at her, stayed about half an hour then moved into the smoking room to read the paper and enjoy his pipe. At the end of the first month of serving this gentleman he had left a small box, prettily wrapped and tied on top with a tiny bow of ribbon, on the table as he made to depart. Becky was reminding him of the no-tipping policy when Miss Timson had appeared from nowhere.

'In this gentleman's case we waive the rule,' she said so softly that Becky had to strain to hear her.

Aunt Lil had blushed with pleasure when Becky had presented her with the box containing Fuller's handmade chocolates.

'Pity they don't let us take the money instead,' May complained on one occasion when a gent had given her a bottle of lavender water. 'We could end up being real rich if they did.'

Trust May to see the logic in it all.

Lunchtime crowds were the ones Becky liked the best. Young people mostly, always in a hurry, they were sparkling and jolly, living life to the full.

One woman Becky did not take to.

'She frightens the hell out of me,' Becky whispered to May, as she made sure the china and coffeepot were set out right on her tray.

May bent her head towards Becky, her voice a low whisper. 'Word has it that her husband left her for some flighty young girl and she sits out there planning her revenge.'

'Get on with you,' Becky grinned, 'if we believed half the rumours that fly around this place we might well come to the conclusion that every man in London has a mistress on the side.'

'Stick around, Becky,' May called after her, 'you never know, your day may come.'

'Well yours won't if you don't get a move on and do some work for a change.' May's face flushed up as she turned to see Robert Matthews grinning at Becky over the top of her head.

Becky was laughing fit to burst as she made her way back out on to the floor.

Only one thing was bothering her. Miss Timson was forever telling her at morning inspection that her cap did not sit properly on her head.

'And no wonder,' Miss Timson remarked, time and time again, 'it's all that hair you are trying to poke under it.'

Having given in to Miss Timson's insistence and egged on by her workmates Becky had made an appointment for her day off, at a hairdresser's in Stockwell, to have her hair bobbed.

She wasn't looking forward to it a bit.

'Come on,' May urged, staring at Becky. 'By the look on your face anyone one would think you were going to the dentist instead of to the hairdresser's.'

'I half wish I were,' Becky mumbled. 'We're both dressed up, surely we could find something better to do on our half day off.'

May was dressed in a navy-blue suit with a long straight skirt and a kick pleat back and front. Beneath the boxy jacket she wore a high-necked white blouse, the front adorned with a small cameo brooch.

Becky was wearing a pale pink crepe-de-Chine blouse with a soft bow at the throat beneath a loose grey jacket and grey skirt that fitted extremely well over her slender hips, the hem flaring out to reach her ankles. They each wore buttoned black boots.

May was able to wear a stylish close-fitting cloche hat over her short thick reddish hair while Becky, with her long dark thick hair, still clung to the larger boater-shaped felts which she spent a great deal of time retrimming.

The salon was somewhat more elegant than Becky had imagined but the reception she received was most friendly.

Minutes ticked by as the hairdresser, quite obviously a lady of fashion herself, ran Becky's long ringlets through her fingers, lifting the tresses high in the air and letting them fall loosely over the colourful cape that had been draped around her shoulders.

Finally she seemed satisfied. 'Beautiful hair,' she murmured, 'I know exactly what style will suit you to perfection.'

Becky screwed her eyes up in fright as she listened to the snip-snip of the scissors. Parts of her hair were tightly drawn back and dampened, other bunches were piled on top of her head, as a different style started to take shape.

'There you are then,' the stylist said when she finally stepped back and held a mirror at several different angles for Becky to see her whole head. All members of the staff gathered round the chair, assuring her that the new style suited her so well. Reluctantly Becky turned her head this way and that as she gazed into the mirror in front of her. She felt unsure. A different person altogether.

Her hair, still thick and glossy, although tons of it seemed to be lying on the floor around her feet, was now neat, framing her cheeks softly with a soft swirl. She put her hand up to touch the back. It felt good, bouncy, but her neck felt so bare.

May, standing behind her, nodded enthusiastically. 'It's fabulous, you look marvellous.'

'I look so different,' Becky said, voicing her fears.

'Not before time!' May responded with a grin.

At inspection next morning, Miss Timson was on duty.

'Excellent, my dear,' Miss Timson remarked as she gazed at Becky's new look. 'I'm sure you will find it a great deal easier to keep your cap on straight now. And believe me the style certainly suits you. Yes, most flattering.'

Becky flushed with pleasure.

Unseen, standing in the background, Robert Matthews wasn't so sure. From the first moment of setting eyes on Rebecca Russell his imagination had run away with him whenever he had gazed at her oval face framed by those gorgeous thick dark ringlets. No matter how hard she had tried to push her mop of hair beneath her cap some wisps had always escaped. The image of all that hair allowed to hang freely, blow in the breeze, while the slim dainty owner ran through green fields, had been a picture in his mind for some time.

As he made his way to the basement to examine the perishables left from the previous day, all of which would have been listed by the manageress, Robert Matthews was a very thoughtful young man.

Chapter Fifteen

'HOW MUCH HAVE we got to spend?'

'Quite a bit what with us getting paid a bonus as well,' Becky answered May.

They were sitting side by side on the top deck of a bus on their way to Oxford Street to do their Christmas shopping. It was the first week in December and bitterly cold and both girls laughed as they tugged their fur collars more tightly against their cheeks.

Becky hadn't been a bit surprised when her mother had turned up in South Lambeth Road bearing a gift of fur for both herself and for May. Parading up and down in Aunt Lil's warm kitchen the girls had thrown the long strips of fur carelessly over their shoulders, pretending casualness, secretly thrilled.

'How come?' May had been anxious to know.

Becky had already guessed.

'A village jumble sale,' Joyce Russell said triumphantly. 'I asked how much the vicar wanted for the manky old fox fur and he said he'd take half-a-crown. I ended up giving him one an' sixpence.'

'Mum!'

'Well it wasn't worth any more, not the state it was in. Took me ages to clean it and I paid fourpence for a long silk underslip which I used to reline the two parts of the fur which ended up as neck trimmings for you two.'

'Cor, you've shaped them beautifully, we can use them on jackets or on our winter coats,' May enthused as she kissed Mrs Russell on the cheek.

'I got this for you, Lily,' Joyce said, handing over a heavy cardigan knitted in fawn and brown with a cable stitch running up each side of the front.

'Why, it's really lovely,' Lily exclaimed loudly, her face wreathed in smiles. 'Don't tell me you got that at the jumble sale as well.'

'Kind of, but not exactly,' Joyce admitted.

Lily looked at Becky, her face showing bewilderment.

'What my mum means is, yes, she did buy the original at the jumble sale but then she unpicks the garment, washes the wool and reknits the whole thing.'

'Gawd luv us, Joyce, you're a bloody marvel an' no mistake. I ain't got the patience to do anything like that. I promise yer I shall wear this lovely warm cardy till it falls off me back. Thanks ever so much.'

Joyce had beamed with pleasure, her efforts well rewarded by the fact that the receivers of the gifts were so pleased.

Oxford Street was jam-packed.

May laughed and grimaced as they pushed their way to the kerb. 'Let's cross the road and go straight into Selfridges,' she said cheerfully as she tucked her hand through the crook of Becky's arm.

The beauty and cosmetic counter was just inside the door and Becky decided that it was here she would best get a present for her sisters-in-law and also probably something for Ella.

'Ponds cold cream for night care, and vanishing cream as a powder base,' stated the placard above the prettily gift-wrapped boxes.

'I think I'll get one each for Ada and Joan, but I'm not sure that Ella would want that,' Becky said.

'Does she use perfume?' May queried.

'She probably would but I don't think her money would run to it. I'll leave Ella till last, see if I've got enough to buy her something to wear.'

May was having the time of her life. She had pounced on a box of Potter and Moore's soap and lavender powder cream for Aunt Lil.

'Decide for me, Becky please. Shall I buy Evening in Paris, don't you just love the dark blue and silver bottle? Or shall it be Californian Poppy?'

'Depends on the person you're buying it for,' Becky sensibly remarked.

'Don't be daft,' May grinned, 'the perfume is for me.'

'In that case I'm half-inclined to treat myself too,' Becky said, returning the grin. 'What do you think of these tiny pots of solid perfume? Smell that,' she ordered, holding out her arm to May. The very refined lady assistant had just placed a tiny dab of the wax on to Becky's wrist.

'Works wonders for a girl's morale,' intoned the chief saleslady.

May sniffed, raised her head and rolled her eyes heavenward, before saying, 'Go on, be a devil, with a dab of that behind your ears you'll have half the men in London swarming round you.'

'Perhaps you ought to settle for this then,' Becky retorted, her eyes full of devilment, 'between us we'll bewitch all the men.'

Their mood was very lighthearted.

With their packages bought and paid for the two girls moved along.

'Cor, look at that advertisement. "Tangee", funny name for a lipstick,' May remarked, her eyes wide with wonder.

'Strange name and a strange colour,' murmured Becky. 'Whoever would want to use an orange lipstick?'

The actual lipstick was set on a velvet base within a glass box. As Becky made to replace it back down on the counter the smooth box almost slipped from her fingers. Both she and a man standing nearby tried to catch it, and as they grappled their fingers met. Becky looked up into the light blue eyes of Robert Matthews.

The apology she had been about to make died in her throat. She felt her cheeks turn crimson and her hands trembled. He took the box from her, made some comment and replaced it on the counter. She mumbled her thanks, keeping her head down so that he wouldn't see how embarrassed she was. It was a relief when he turned towards May, saying, 'Doing all your Christmas shopping?'

'Trying our best, sir,' May answered with a laugh, not in the least bit daunted by having met one of their bosses on their day off.

'Happy hunting,' he said, smiling at them both, and a moment later he had disappeared into the throng of shoppers.

'Don't know quite what t' make of that bloke,' May said as they stood undecided as to where to make for next. 'He always seems so kind of distant, as if he was lonely all the time. One of the older waitresses told me he's a relation of the Lyons family. Went to public school by all accounts and then Oxford and straight from there into the service of Joey Lyons.'

'What about his parents, or doesn't he have any family?' Becky asked.

'How the hell would I know?' May cried. 'Let's get on with our shopping an' make up our minds that this coming Christmas will be one of the best ever. Agreed?'

'Agreed,' Becky smiled her answer. 'Let's make for the toy department. I've two nephews to buy for not to mention my six-month-old goddaughter, Margaret.'

'How can she be your goddaughter when she hasn't been christened yet?' May was curious to know as they elbowed their way though the shoppers towards the great winding staircase.

'Ah! I've been meaning to tell you. I've had a word with Mr Gower and he sent me to see Miss Nicholls, remember she's over Miss Timson. The long an' short of it is, I'll do extra hours over the run-up to Christmas and then get a few days' leave all together in the New Year.'

'What do you want New Year off for? You're not Scottish.'

'Nobody said I was, dummy. I'm going home for a double celebration. Ella and Peter are having baby Margaret christened, and Tom Ferguson and Mary Marsden are getting married.'

'Is that the Tom you told me nearly got himself locked up when he saved that young kiddy from drowning?'

'Yes, that's the one. I reckon the whole of Kingston will turn out to see those two tie the knot.'

'Ah, that'll be nice,' May said as they joined everyone else hellbent on buying toys for Christmas presents.

Almost unnoticed the weeks slipped by, filled with long hours of hard work and growing proficiency for both May and Becky as Christmas came and went.

May had been able to cope right from the beginning. For Becky it had taken longer. With her slight frame, her huge brown eyes and deceptively gentle voice Becky seemed very vulnerable and many a gentleman tried it on. They had flowers delivered to the Corner House for her with cards offering to take her out to dinner. The bolder ones suggested she might like to visit London's night spots.

Always in the background Mr Gower hovered, ready to protect her should the need ever arise. So far Becky felt she had coped very well. A big factor in helping her to settle into a steady routine was living with Aunt Lil and May in that lovely old house in South Lambeth Road.

Whether it was late at night or during the day when she and May arrived back from a shift she repeatedly told herself how lucky she was to have found such a haven in the heart of London and as for Aunt Lil, that tiny lady never ceased to amaze her.

On the go from morning to night, she never seemed to

tire herself out. Either of the girls had only to leave a soiled blouse or an article of underwear hanging over the back of a chair in their rooms and by the time they returned it would be laid out on their bed freshly washed and ironed.

The only problem was Aunt Lil fed them too well. Appetizing smells met them the minute they set foot in the hall, no matter what the time was. Irresistible puddings were offered and both girls complained that they would end up looking like real ten-ton Tessies.

Pub nights were hilarious. The first time they took Aunt Lil for a drink Becky found it almost unbelievable. Two glasses of port wine and Aunt Lil was standing on a chair singing her heart out to the delight of all the customers. Whether she sang slow sentimental songs or a bawdy ballad her voice held listeners spellbound. Trouble was, all the customers then wanted to treat Aunt Lil to another drink. Once, she had suddenly slipped to the floor and lain full length. So still was she that May and Becky ran to crouch at her side, only to find that she was faking.

'Are you sure you're all right?' May asked.

Aunt Lil merely winked her eye and told them brightly, 'You ain't seen nothing tonight. One day I might surprise you and have a skinful.'

'God forbid,' both girls had cried out.

Ah well, Becky was saying to herself as they led Aunt Lil home that night, there is never a dull moment when this little lady is about.

Christmas wasn't all hard work.

Becky went home for Christmas and Boxing Day. On Christmas Day the whole family gathered in Albert Road and Joyce Russell was in her element with her whole brood to cook for. Two more guests swelled the numbers on Boxing Day when Aunt Lil and May came down from London.

With the midday meal over Aunt Lil sat back in an armchair

and looked at the huge Christmas tree which had already started to shed its needles.

'Well, Joyce and Joe, I never expected anything like this welcome we've had today,' she said quietly. 'All your lads and daughters-in-law pitching in to help, talk about a real family do, it's smashing. Thanks ever so much for inviting us.'

'We're glad you decided to come,' Joyce replied. 'It kind of makes up for the way you look after our Becky. And it's nice the way she and May get on, isn't it?'

Lil nodded and jumped as one of the logs dropped lower in the grate, sending out a shower of sparks, and she was silent as Joe took two more logs from the basket and made up the fire. When he had settled back in his chair Lil spoke again.

'D'yer know what really did me heart good t' see today, Joyce? It were your grandsons' faces when May gave them those little presents. Ronnie's eyes nearly popped out of his head, an' young Joey looked really pleased. We ain't used t' aving young kiddies around, it's a real pleasure just to sit an' watch them.'

Joyce laughed. 'They weren't expecting more presents today. They were thrilled, that motor and the fire engine you an' May bought them are lovely. You ought to be here sometimes, hear the racket they make.'

The afternoon was full of excitement as grown-ups joined in silly games such as pass the parcel, postman's knock and spin the bottle. The kiddies were giggling and uttering shrieks of delight when it was Grandad's turn to kiss their nanna.

Christmas cake and mince pies with cups of tea and fizzy lemonade for the children was followed by trifle well laced with sherry.

All too soon the light faded. Joe put on his overcoat and bowler hat in readiness to escort Lil and May to the railway station. All the women and the men lined up to put their arms around Aunt Lil and plant a kiss on her cheek, while Becky and May stood in the doorway smiling at how popular she had become in such a short time.

Becky watched with her mother as they set off down the road and she heard her father say, 'One each side of me, c'mon, take hold of me arm, pavement's a bit frosty, don't want either of you slipping an' breaking yer neck.'

'Dad likes them, doesn't he, Mum?'

''Course he does, pet, so do all the family. We'll have to make sure that we ask them more often. Perhaps even have Lily down here for a holiday next summer.'

'Thanks, Mum.'

'For what?'

'Oh, you know. For such a lovely Christmas, for making May and her aunt so welcome, for having all me brothers here, the kids as well, for everything, mostly for being my mum.'

Joyce took hold of her hand and said, smiling, 'You're making me feel old. Let's go in, it's getting real cold.'

It was back to work next day for Becky but she left with the sure and certain knowledge that within a week she would be back home to take part in two very different ceremonies, both of which would be very dear to her heart.

Chapter Sixteen

THE FIRST SATURDAY of 1926 dawned bright and clear with a weak sun showing up the heavy frost that had formed during the night. Becky had arrived at Mill Street before nine that morning and was immediately given the task of hemming up the bottom of the pretty dress Ella had made for baby Margaret.

'We won't dress her till the last moment,' Ella said cheerfully to Becky as she stitched. 'With my luck she's sure to be sick.'

'I wish t' God I'd gone to work,' Peter moaned with mock seriousness. 'It seems as if half the blooming street has popped in here this morning on one pretext or another. You'd think it was us getting married instead of just going as guests to Tom's wedding.'

Ella looked a bit guilty as Becky raised her eyebrows in query. 'I made a two-piece for Annie Smith, you know she's landlady of the Swan, well she had this lovely length of material an' she paid me well. She came to collect it.'

'That's only one,' Peter said, laughing loudly. 'You'd have been better off opening a millinery shop the number of ruddy hats you've trimmed.' Turning to Becky he grinned and said, 'Yer know she's always going on about how much she dislikes Martha Tubman, well, she practically remade an old hat for her.'

'Oh, leave it out, Peter, she lives next door and it's far better to hold the candle to the devil, anyway she's been ever so appreciative. But what about you? You've been more hindrance than help this morning. Standing about like a lemon. You're never going to be ready on time. You'd better get down to the cleaners an' pick up your suit,' Ella ordered.

'Are you sure you two can manage without me?' he asked sarcastically.

Ella ruffled his thick hair and kissed him on the cheek. 'Of course we can,' she told him fondly, then quickly added, 'Don't bang the front door as you go out. I'm still hoping the baby won't wake up till we're nearly ready to leave for the church.'

'Are you and Peter coping all right?' Becky gently asked as soon as she and Ella were alone.

'Yes, but . . .' It was difficult to explain, even to herself. 'Peter doesn't talk to me much and some evenings he goes off on his own and I don't see him for hours.'

'Does it matter? He always was a bit on the quiet side.'

'Sometimes it matters. When I'm feeling a bit down. I'm not sure if he's all that well, not that he ever complains. It's just a feeling I get, more so when he has a bad night.'

'What do you mean by a bad night?'

'He cries out, quite loudly, though he doesn't wake up, but he twists and turns and his pyjamas are wringing wet because he sweats so much.'

'Have you suggested he goes to see a doctor?'

Ella turned from the sink, laid down her tea towel and looked Becky full in the face. 'Of course I have,' she said irritably. 'He doesn't want to know. Tells me I imagine it half the time.'

Suddenly the clock on the mantelpiece chimed the hour and both girls were amazed to see it was already eleven o'clock.

'We'll talk later,' Becky said her voice sharp with concern. 'Right now we'd better go upstairs and get our glad rags on and then see to baby Margaret.'

The church looked beautiful; a lot of work had gone into the floral decorations and the sides of the front pews were decked with bows of white ribbon. Most all of the pews were full and people were beginning to fidget and then the bells pealed and the organist began to play 'Here Comes the Bride'.

All heads turned to see Mary walking down the aisle on her father's arm.

Ella nudged Becky. 'What a transformation!' she whispered.

Nobody ever spoke a truer word, Becky thought to herself.

The high-necked white satin dress Mary wore fell to the floor in soft loose folds beneath the gathered bust. It made her look slim and taller. On her straight shiny hair she had a circlet of orange blossom entwined with seed pearls. A long veil was secured by the headdress and hung in folds, framing Mary's chubby face with its lace edging.

As the bride and groom joined hands at the altar half the congregation gave a sigh of joy and Dolly Ferguson, dressed today in a grey silk dress with long loose jacket and wearing a hat that would have done Queen Mary proud, was heard trying to sniff back the tears.

When the ceremony was over, Tom walked, holding himself erect, with his bride on his arm, smiling selfconsciously at all the well-wishers. The photographer continued to gesticulate excitedly until he was sure that no one had been left out of such a momentous occasion. Then everyone went back into the cars and off to the hall for the reception, where great quantities of food were consumed, toasts were drunk and finally glasses were raised to Mr and Mrs Ferguson.

It was Peter who summed up the day. He rose to his feet and in a loud clear voice declared, 'Anyone with half an eye can see that Tom and Mary were made for each other.'

Besides friends and relatives the entire street had turned out for Tom's wedding and they showed their agreement with Tom's statement by much foot-stamping, clapping of hands and very loud cheering.

The dancing started, the first waltz led off by the bride

and groom. Dolly Ferguson, though clearly worried at the thought of losing her son, had borne herself well throughout the proceedings. Then Tom came up to her and asked, 'Mum, will you dance with me?'

Dolly's eyes were watery as she got to her feet and murmured, 'Thanks, son.'

Tom took his mother by the arm and slowly led her on to the floor. 'Everything will turn out all right, you'll see, Mum.' Tom's voice was soft but steady as he did his best to reassure his mother. 'Mary's a good girl and you'll love her when you get t' know her better.'

Dolly took her hand off her son's arm and rubbed her eyes. 'I know, son, I know. An' I promise yer, lad, it won't be for the want of trying on my part.'

The dance ended and Dolly had two fingers crossed as Tom escorted her back to sit with all the other ladies. She was vowing to herself that she wouldn't be so sharp off the mark to voice an opinion in future. I'll keep me thoughts t' meself an' with a bit of luck an' the blessing of God Almighty me daughter-in-law and me might get along quite well. Slowly she unwound her fingers from behind her back. She'd done enough praying for one day. Time I had a few drinks, she mumbled to herself, as she made her way to the bar that had been set up at the back of the hall.

By mid-afternoon the next day the hall, front room and the living room of Ella and Peter's house were crammed with people. The christening of baby Margaret had taken place in the same church as Tom and Mary's wedding and a great number of the people packed into this small house today had been guests at both events.

A group of women was perched on the stairs while kiddies, including Becky's two nephews, were dashing here, there and everywhere, flushed with the excitement of attending two grown-up parties in two days.

The baby looked beautiful in a long christening dress of white lace trimmed with tiny rosebuds. She lay in her grandmother's arms, cooing contentedly, getting lots of ooos and ahhhs as everyone admired her creamy complexion and downy covering of fair hair.

Peggy James sighed as her old friend Joyce Russell planted herself down next to her on the settee. 'What's the matter, luv?' Joyce asked with growing concern. 'I'd have thought you'd be over the moon today.'

Peggy wasn't able to form a reply because Dolly Ferguson pushed her bulky figure through the crowd with a tray of small sandwiches. Handing a plate to Peggy and one to Joyce, she said, ''Ere, take a couple t' be going on with, there's egg an' cress or salmon an' cucumber. Living it up, ain't we? Two days running. Annie Smith's doing the tea an' your Ella's going to cut the cake next. Can't get over 'ow good that baby 'as been. Lawd luv 'er, she's a right precious little mite.'

Joyce watched with amusement as Dolly moved on with her tray. 'Don't she ever pause for breath?' she said to Peggy grinning.

'Don't sound like it, does it?'

Then Joyce raised her eyebrows as she caught sight of a man across the room. 'Who's that, Peg?'

Peggy followed her gaze. 'That's Peter's father. You've met him before, when my Ella got married.'

'Really? I never recognized him. I don't remember he looked so well turned out before.'

'Somehow I don't think he was. Spruced up all right today though, ain't he?'

'Yes, he is an' all. Perhaps he's got a new woman in his life.'

'Wouldn't blame the man if he had,' Peggy said, lifting the baby from the crook of her arm and resting her up against her shoulder. 'Peter told me his dad went to pieces when his mother died so tragically.'

'Has he come all this way just for the christening?' Joyce asked.

'No, I think he's going to stay a couple of nights.'

'Oh, that's all right then. You were about to tell me why you were sighing so heavily when Dolly barged in. Is there anything wrong?'

'No. Not so's you'd notice. It's just that I get this feeling that my Ella's not really happy. She adores the baby, no getting away from that but . . . money's tight . . . it could be that.'

'We still worry about our kids no matter that they're grown-up, don't we? We'll have to talk later, maybe I'll make time an' come round to you tomorrow.' Joyce had to cut the conversation short because a growing number of people were crowding into the room.

'Cake time,' Ella called, adding sweetly. 'Thank you all for the lovely presents you've given us for the baby. Now Becky, her godmother, is going to do the honours and cut her christening cake.'

When the time came to leave Peter gently kissed Becky's cheek, then Ella hugged her.

'I'll see you tomorrow,' Becky said, 'I haven't got to go back to work until Tuesday.'

'Great, I'll have the house a bit more straight by the time you get here. I hope,' Ella ended on a laugh.

'Don't worry about it,' Becky told her, then over Ella's shoulder as she returned the hug, Becky caught sight of Peter's father standing alone at the foot of the stairs, his hands in his pockets, his face frowning. Something was worrying him.

Walking with her mother and her father to where they would catch the tram back to New Malden, Becky felt that she would give a great deal to know just what it was that was worrying Peter's father so much.

Her parents and she were glad when at last the tram rumbled into view. They were all feeling tired and no wonder, it had been a hectic two days. A lot of hard work and preparation had gone into both events. But it had been well worth it.

Oh yes, Becky decided. It had been good to see so many happy people gathered together.

Chapter Seventeen

'GOD ALONE KNOWS what's going on in there this morning,' Martha Tubman called out, tossing her head in the direction of the house next door as Becky came within yards of Ella's house.

'Sorry?' Becky paused, a frown creasing her forehead.

'I've never 'eard the likes of it before, not from in there I ain't.' Martha came down her front path and out on to the pavement to meet Becky. 'After everyone having such a good time over the weekend I can't make it out. The baby's been screaming her head off for the last half-hour and Ella's been yelling at the top of her voice. I've banged on the wall but it ain't made the slightest difference.'

Becky's heart turned a somersault. 'Is Peter in there?' she asked.

'No, he's gone t' work. I know cos I saw him set off when I was getting the milk in just before seven.'

'All right, thanks, Martha,' Becky said.

There certainly was a right hullabaloo coming from inside the house. The front door was ajar and as she pushed her way in Becky felt alarm bells start to ring in her head. The pram was wedged across the foot of the stairs. The baby looked to be in a terrible state and she smelt horrible. Her napkin, into which she had emptied her bowels, had slid down over her little legs leaving her dirty bottom bare. Red in the face, still crying, her tiny fists frantically beating the air, she looked awful.

'There, there my pet,' Becky crooned. 'Whatever have they done t' you? Ssh, ssh, Auntie Becky's here now.'

Wrinkling her nose, Becky coupled the baby's feet together and with one hand lifted her up by her ankles while with her other she removed the soiled napkin to the bottom of the pram. Sliding the undersheet free she used it to wipe the baby's dirty bottom as best she could. Freeing the underblanket from the pram she wrapped it closely around Margaret and took her up into her arms.

'There, there, my little darling,' she hummed, walking up and down all the while rubbing the baby's back with circular movements. 'That's better, isn't it?' The baby's crying grew quieter but as Becky walked down the passage there was sadness in her heart. Whatever had happened that would make Ella leave the baby so long in such an agitated state?

Not knowing what to expect, for she could still hear voices being raised in anger, Becky tapped on the kitchen door and turned the handle. On the table stood the remains of what must have been breakfast and dirty crocks were piled up at one end. No fire burnt in the grate.

Ella jumped to her feet saying, 'Oh, it's you, Becky.'

All Becky could think of was what a sorry sight she looked. She wore a thick skirt and a well-darned jumper. Her long fair hair was parted in the centre, dragged back and tied with a piece of tape. Slumped in a chair, still drawn up to the table, sat Peter's father.

He looked up. 'Hello, Becky,' he mumbled in greeting.

He looked as if he'd spent some time washing and shaving and he wore the same clothes as he had done yesterday even down to the smart jacket, as if he were ready to set off on a journey.

'The baby needs a clean napkin.' Becky spoke the words softly, afraid that the rowing might break out again at any moment.

'Give her to me,' Ella said, making an obvious effort to pull herself together. Taking the baby from Ella, she looked across at her father-in-law. 'I can't believe it,' she said sadly in a voice that was no more than a whisper.

'What can't you believe?' Becky put her arm around Ella, drawing her close.

'That I'm not really married because my Peter is a bigamist.'

'What?' Becky had sensed something was wrong but nothing like this. 'Whoever told you that?'

'His own father.'

Becky saw the tears swimming in Ella's eyes and at that moment she felt she could cheerfully kill the man sitting at the table.

Ella carried on talking, more to herself than to Becky. 'All this time and he's never said a word. Great sense of timing, don't you think?'

'I've tried to explain.' Mr Tomson got up from his chair and came towards Becky. 'I couldn't leave without telling her. Not this time.'

'Why not?' Ella asked.

'I just couldn't,' he said loudly, trying hard to make his voice sound normal.

'I want to know why you've kept silent about this for so long,' Ella insisted.

Peter's dad had the grace to look sheepish. 'My conscience has been troubling me ever since I signed your marriage lines as a witness in the church vestry. That's when I noticed Peter had described himself as a bachelor.'

'Took yer time, didn't you?' Ella accused. Then, shoving the baby back in to Becky's arms, her voice rose to a scream. 'Why tell me now? I have another baby on the way. You've kept quiet all this time, why suddenly tell me now? What I didn't know wasn't hurting me.'

'Stop it,' Becky said firmly. She could see that Ella was exhausted and the baby had begun to cry again. 'Calm down luv, come on, this isn't doing you any good and it's upsetting Margaret. Go and put the kettle on, I'll nurse her while you make her a bottle and then I'll make a fresh pot of tea.'

Slowly Ella shuffled towards the scullery and Becky turned

to Mr Tomson. 'Well? Hadn't you better explain to me just what is going on?'

He pulled a chair up to the table for Becky and when she was settled with the baby on her lap, he seated himself next to her.

'It's true,' he told her and gave a noncommittal shrug of his shoulders.

Becky didn't want to get into a lengthy argument. She couldn't force this man whom she hardly knew to tell her anything because strictly speaking it wasn't anything to do with her, but she couldn't let it go just like that. Besides, who else was here to help Ella?

'Why didn't you say something yesterday? When everyone was here. Surely it would have been better for Ella if you'd spoken up when her mother was here to listen to what you had to say.'

'I thought about it but it didn't seem the right time.'

Becky's eyes flashed. 'No, the right time would have been before Ella and Peter were married.' Suddenly Becky was angry. If it weren't for the fact that she was nursing the baby she would have lashed out at this man who was sitting there so calmly. 'Didn't you even think it would have been better to say what you felt you had to say when your son was present?'

'How can I make you understand?' He shifted uncomfortably in his chair, refusing to look at Becky. 'Anyway all the talking in the world won't alter the facts and I'm going to get ready, it's best if I go home today.'

'God, I don't believe you!' Becky looked astounded. 'Aren't you even going to wait until Peter gets home?'

'No, it's best if I don't. I'll call in and see him at the laundry, I will tell him that I've told Ella.'

Becky sighed heavily, wishing her father was here to deal with all of this. 'At least tell me the truth, has Peter got another wife tucked away somewhere?'

'I don't really know. At least not for sure.'

'What!' Becky hadn't meant to shout at him. Anger was making her reckless and she had made the baby jump.

'It's kind of complicated. Peter did get married in 1916. He met this Vera Brady just before he went off to war. They never really lived together, never had a place of their own like. Though he did come home on leave twice and as far as I can tell you they spent the time at her father's house. He was a widower. By the time the Armistice was declared both she and her father had disappeared.'

'And Peter never tried to trace her?'

'Not to my knowledge he didn't. What you've got to remember is he was only eighteen when he went to France.' Mr Tomson sighed and ran his hand through his hair. 'Came home a sick man, just twenty, but you never would have believed it to look at him. Those lads must have gone through hell in those trenches.'

That's all very well, Becky moaned to herself, everyone had heard the shocking stories of what went on in France during those awful years of the War. That didn't excuse what Peter had done to Ella and certainly his father had a lot to answer for in not speaking up before now.

Ella kicked the scullery door open with her foot. 'I've made the tea and brought clean cups. I'll see to that lot later on,' she apologized, looking at the dirty things which still lay on the table. 'You pour, Becky, and I'll give this bottle to Margaret.'

Peter's father got to his feet. 'If you don't mind, Ella, I'm going to be on my way. I have packed what few things I brought with me and I'm sure there will be a train about lunchtime.'

'Don't you want a cup of tea first?' Ella asked, her expression still downcast.

'No, I won't if you don't mind.'

Becky put baby Margaret on to Ella's lap and looked on as she coped with putting a clean napkin on her in a competent way; it wasn't until the baby was settled in the crook of her arm and contentedly sucking at her bottle that Ella broke the silence.

'So you're not going to wait and see Peter? I think you've acted in a very cowardly way,' Ella said honestly. 'But you know your own business best.'

Her father-in-law, about to leave the room, stopped in his tracks. 'I more than likely would have told you when I first met you, Ella, but just you remember one thing, you were pregnant at the time and my son must have thought he was doing the decent thing by offering to marry you.'

Ella raised her eyes to meet those of her father-in-law and he staggered at the sadness he now saw.

'I'm sorry, truly I am,' he said emotionally looking at Ella so anxiously that for a moment she felt sorry for him, but then she quickly glanced away. She couldn't bring herself to say another word to him.

Becky headed for the door with Mr Tomson close behind her. Stopping in the hallway to pick up his case and put on his macintosh, he put out a hand to Becky, saying, 'She will be all right won't she? I really think I've acted for the best.'

'Ella will cope, Mr Tomson. She'll have to, won't she?' Becky said in a dull voice.

No other words passed between them but Becky stood on the doorstep watching his back until he was out of sight.

When she returned to the room she felt a lump as big as a golf ball rise up in her throat and her heart simply ached at the sight of her dearest friend. The baby was snug in her mother's arms, still contentedly sucking away at her bottle, one tiny fist curled round Ella's forefinger, holding on so tightly. Ella's head was lowered yet Becky had no difficulty in seeing the tears that were trickling down her cheeks.

Becky was plagued with terrible thoughts on her journey home to New Malden. She was only inside the house a few minutes before, very near to tears, she was telling the whole terrible story to her parents.

'Dad, Ella was all on her own when I came home. She looked awful. It was such a shock. What will happen to her now?'

'Don't get yourself worked up so,' Joyce Russell pleaded with her daughter. 'Give yer father a few minutes for it to sink in an' then maybe he'll know what to do.'

'To sort this lot out will need a lot more than a few minutes I'm thinking,' Joe said sternly, doing his best to hide his anger. 'What a man, eh? Opening up that can of worms to a young lass when she's in the house on her own. Good job you went there today, Becky, wish t' God I'd been with you.'

'I've just had a thought,' Joyce cried out in alarm. 'One of us ought to go round and see Peggy.'

''Course you're right,' Joe agreed with his wife. 'There's no man there to deal with this an' the last thing we want is Peggy hearing it second-hand. God knows what it will do to her. I'll put me boots on and go straight away.'

'Peggy is going to feel very bad,' Joyce said thoughtfully.

'And what's that supposed to mean?' Joe asked as he saw the distress clearly showing in Joyce's eyes.

'Well, it was Peggy that practically forced Peter to marry Ella. Oh, it was the right thing to do at the time. Nobody is going to dispute that, not seeing as Ella was already pregnant, but I'd bet my bottom dollar she'll blame herself now.'

'Dad, shall I come with you?' Becky asked.

'No, pet, you stay here with yer mother. I'll bring Peggy back here for the night if she wants to come.'

It was two hours later when Joe Russell came back from George Road. Becky and her mother were sitting close up to a blazing fire, drinking cocoa, each staring into the flames deep in thought.

'Peggy didn't come back with you then?' Joyce asked as her husband sat down and with a sigh started to unlace his boots.

'No, luv. Said she'll be all right, her Jimmy will be home soon.'

'How did she take it, Dad?' Becky asked.

'Stunned at first. Like us she couldn't believe what I was telling her. Anyways I've told her I'll do me best to help. First thing I reckon is for me to have a word with our union bloke, he'll put me on to the legal section, see how we go about tracing missing persons. That's after I've been over and got the facts straight from Peter.'

'You are good, Dad,' Becky exclaimed, jumping to her feet and planting a kiss on his forehead.

'What do you want to know about missing persons for?' Joyce queried.

'Peter's so-called wife. From what Becky's told us nobody has seen hide nor hair of her since 1916 so in my book that makes her a missing person.'

'Oh, I see,' Joyce muttered.

Becky hid a smile. She was not at all sure that her mother did see.

For the first time Becky felt slightly reluctant as she got herself ready to catch the train next morning. It wasn't that she minded going back to work but she did feel awful having to leave without seeing Ella again. It had been such a lovely happy weekend until Peter's father had dropped his bombshell.

She remembered how carefree she and Ella had been when they were growing up. What a pity Peter had come along when he did. If things had turned out differently she and Ella could both have been working for Lyons in the West End of London. As it was she and Ella were treading very different paths.

'You promise to look after Ella, don't you Dad?' Becky needed to be reassured before she stepped on to the train.

'Becky my luv, I've told you, I will do everything I possibly can for Ella, and before you ask me yet again, yes, I will be in touch with you the minute there is anything to tell you.'

Becky went into her father's arms. He hugged her tight

and patted her back as if she were a small child. 'Go on,' he said, giving her a push, 'get yourself back to London and the glamorous life you lead up there.'

Becky laughed. 'You wouldn't say that if you knew how my feet ached some nights when I finish work.'

'Get on with you, lass, you love every minute of that job, you know you do.'

True, she was saying to herself as the train pulled out of the station and she waved a last goodbye to her dad. Even so, for once she wished she had an extra day off to go back to Kingston and see how Ella was.

Chapter Eighteen

IT WAS NINE o'clock in the morning and still there was no sign of Peter. He hadn't been home all night.

Once more Ella opened the front door and stood outside on the doorstep looking up and down the street. Then her whole body sagged and she sighed heavily. She hadn't been to bed. She had found jobs to do, keeping herself busy so as not to brood on the future. Since she and Peter had been married, though of course that was an absolute sham now, she reminded herself, money had been desperately short but they had managed and been reasonably happy. The baby had made all the difference. Even Peter's face would light up whenever he leant over the pram.

'You'll come home, Peter, I know you will,' she whispered, staring down at the corner, willing him to come into view.

Becky had told her that her father-in-law was going to the laundry to see Peter. What on earth had he said that would stop Peter from coming home? She looked up at the grey skies. It was such a miserable cold day for him to be trudging the streets. Perhaps he wasn't, perhaps he had gone into work. But where had he spent the night?

'There's no use standing about out here,' Ella said aloud, pulling her long cardigan tightly round her body. Hearing the baby whimper made her mind up for her. I'll get Margaret ready, put her in the pram and go see for myself if Peter is at the laundry.

Moving quickly now she wrapped a blanket firmly round the baby, settled her in the pram making sure that her bonnet was covering both her ears and laid another thicker cover on top.

'Go to sleep, my pet,' she told her softly.

Twenty minutes later, Ella had washed and changed her clothes. In her long dark grey coat, wide-brimmed felt hat, laced-up boots and woolly gloves she looked neat and tidy.

'What's the hurry, Ella?' Martha Tubman called cheekily as Ella bumped the pram out on to the pavement. 'I didn't see your Peter go off this morning, ain't he well?'

A hot flush came to Ella's face and she wished the earth would open up and swallow her. Either that or Martha Tubman should drop down dead. Nosy cow, she muttered. What she said aloud was, 'Peter left early, he forgot his sandwiches so I'm just taking them to him.'

'Best hurry then, it's gonna pour before long,' Martha said briskly, thinking to herself, there's more going on in that house than meets the eye.

Once again Ella's big blue eyes glittered with tears as she hurried along the main road. Walking alongside Kingston market set her thoughts flying back to the lovely happy Saturday and Sunday she had just spent. Inside that market was the second-hand clothes stall where she had bought a dress three weeks ago. A light navy crepe it was, calf-length, with long sleeves and a V neck that had plunged far too daringly for her to wear it as it was.

I worked hard on that dress, she was thinking to herself. I washed and ironed it so carefully. Sewed a lace inset to the front. All the time I was sewing I dreamed of surprising Peter when I wore it to our first baby's christening.

Well, she had surprised him. And herself more so. Hours she had spent. Not only altering the dress but washing her long hair, curling the ends with the tongs so that it hung softly on her shoulders.

Peter had gasped in admiration when she turned round and faced him in their bedroom. She hadn't meant to tell him about the baby, not yet anyway. It was as he held her

close and her tummy was pressed against him that she had
blurted it out. 'I'm pregnant again.'

'Good gracious!' he had said, and beamed. 'Let's hope
it's a boy.'

Relief had flooded over her. 'I didn't for a moment think
you would be pleased. I worry as to how we will manage,'
she had confessed.

He had declared that he would move heaven and earth to
find himself a better-paid job.

She had hated the next few minutes because she sensed
that he was feeling guilty because he had made her pregnant
for the second time so soon.

Then Tom's wedding had been a lovely affair and the
next day had astonished both Peter and herself. They were
filled with gratitude at the way their friends had lavished
gifts and small sums of money on the baby. It had all been
so unexpected.

As they had climbed the stairs that night it had been Peter
who had more or less summed up the day. 'We may have
had to penny-pinch since we got married,' he said, 'but I am
not the least bit envious of what other people have. I'm just
grateful that our baby daughter is so beautiful and healthy
and all I really want for the future is the chance to be able
to provide for you, and her.'

'And?' She had smiled, patting her stomach.

'Him an' all,' Peter had laughed out loud.

'Don't be so cocksure,' she had chided him. And that night
Peter had made love to her so expertly that she felt from that
day on everything must go well for them as a family. Had all
that happened only two days ago?

At that moment she hated her father-in-law. Why oh why
couldn't he have kept his mouth shut? Why travel down for
the christening knowing that he was going to spoil everything
for them as a family?

As she had told him then, she would have preferred
never to know. Together Peter and she were coping fairly

well, as well if not better than most folk were in these hard times.

'Ella!'

'Wotcher, luv.'

Several voices called out as she pushed the pram into the Wellington's yard. High in the cab of his van Peter sat, lost in thoughts of his home and family. Hearing the excited voices as women ran to see the baby he opened the cab door and quickly closed it again. Oh no! he wasn't ready to face Ella yet.

He wished she had waited until he got home. It was his own fault, Ella turning up here. He hadn't been home all night. He shivered, he couldn't just sit here, he had to get down and face her. His throat almost closed and he found it hard to breathe.

The cab door was opened from the outside.

'You'd better take a bit of time off,' Bill Yates, the other van driver, insisted. 'Your missus is here and she looks all done in.'

But when Peter made to move, Bill laid the palm of his hand on his knee and gently pressed him down again as he said, 'Take yer time, lad, and if I can be of any help you know you only have to say the word.'

'Thanks, mate,' Peter said. 'You saw my dad come here yesterday, didn't you?'

'Yeah, an' a blind man could have seen he wasn't the bearer of good news.'

'You're not wrong,' Peter told him sadly, the frown in his forehead deepening.

'All the same Peter, I'm not prying. Go on, I'll see to your load, take yer missus over t' the market caff an' get her something hot t' drink.'

Ella watched as Peter crossed the yard. He looked utterly wretched. By the time he stood in front of her all her anger had drained away, and nothing but fear and depression remained.

Walking the short distance to the café they barely spoke a word to each other. Peter settled Ella at a table well away from the door and she bent over the pram, loosened the wrappings from around the baby and propped her higher on the pillow. Peter stretched out a hand to stroke baby Margaret's face and was rewarded by a dribbling smile.

'Tea?' he asked Ella. 'Anything to eat?'

Ella shook her head.

'I'll get us a plate of toast,' he muttered, turning and walking to the counter. Minutes later he set two steaming mugs of tea on the table and went back to the counter for two plates and the dish of thickly buttered toast.

'Do you feel really bad?' Peter asked carefully.

'That's a daft question,' Ella retorted quickly.

'I suppose we have to talk about it.' Peter lowered his gaze until it rested on Ella's face, and it hurt him to see her lovely blue eyes were sad and serious.

'I can't see what good it will do. All you have to tell me is whether it is true or not.'

'Don't you want me to try and explain?'

'Not really. It wouldn't do any good. All I need to know is are we married or not?'

Peter smiled. A thin, sad smile that went straight to Ella's heart. 'Condemned without a hearing?' he dared to ask.

The colour had drained from Peter's cheeks and the sorry look he had about him made Ella relent as she said, 'I wish you had told me.'

'You were pregnant. I couldn't bring myself to,' he said regretfully.

'The weekend was so lovely,' Ella said wistfully.

At that moment the baby cried. Peter watched with pride as Ella lifted Margaret out of the pram, pressing her close as she sat down again. Loosening her shawl and taking her bonnet off she fussed over her for a while. There was no doubt that the baby was very special to both of them and it would be her and the coming infant who would hold them together.

'Where did you spend the night?' Ella shot the question without looking up.

'Well, when I first left work I went to see your mum. I felt I owed her that much.'

'Go on,' Ella instructed, thinking to herself, what about me?

'Becky's dad was there.'

'And?'

Peter sighed heavily. 'And that seemed to make it worse. Him telling me that Becky walked in when my dad was telling you. I guessed you wouldn't have liked that.'

'Oh, Peter! For God's sake! What I didn't like was being told that you had another wife tucked away somewhere. Finding out that our baby daughter was actually illegitimate. The fact that my best friend was there to hear the sordid details doesn't seem to me t' matter a tinker's cuss one way or the other.'

Peter was taken back by Ella's sudden burst of outrage and he hurriedly said, 'Mr Russell was ever so understanding. He promised to have a talk with a legal fellow who is attached to the railway union. Said he'd know how to go about finding the records on missing persons.'

'Peter,' Ella cried out in exasperation, 'get to the point. Did you stay all night at my mum's? I can't believe she would have let you without letting me know.'

'No,' he said sheepishly. 'She told me to go home. I couldn't face you. I walked for ages. Spent some time on the railway station. Got meself a wash an' brush up and went to work. I've not been able to stop thinking about you. I just can't find the words to tell you how sorry I am, Ella.'

Silence hung heavy between them for several minutes, until Peter reached across, touched the baby's face with one finger and then took hold of Ella's hand. 'I know it's no excuse but after the War was over I never considered myself a married man. It was wartime. Young folk were rushing to get wed before the fellows went over to France. I hardly knew Vera really.'

Ella decided now was as good a time as any to ask questions. At least here in this warm café they weren't likely to raise their voices and get into a slanging match.

'Your dad said you spent two lots of leave with her.'

'No. Only one. I wrote several letters but she never answered and what made it seem more final, she never registered the marriage with the Army.'

'I don't understand. Should she have done?'

'Oh yes. I filled in forms for her to have the wife's allowance, can't remember how much it was, only a small amount and the Army would have made it up to about thirty-two shillings, seeing as I was only a private. She never put in for it. Never claimed a penny.' He paused, took a deep breath and Ella felt frightened because his face was the colour of chalk.

It was only after he had taken a few sips of tea that he was able to go on. 'I was ill when I was first demobbed, but my mum was alive then and she made enquiries at the Town Hall and every Post Office in Northampton. There were no records of Vera anywhere.'

Ella tried her hardest to smile and transferred the baby from her lap up on to her shoulder. Cautiously, she asked, 'And you've never heard from her from that day to this?'

Peter shook his head. 'Not a word. I promise you, Ella. I took it that she'd gone off with another bloke.'

Ella's face showed signs of relief. 'I'm glad,' she admitted. 'We'll just have to wait an' see what Mr Russell comes up with, won't we?'

The café was beginning to fill up with customers.

'Would you like to have a lunch here?' Peter made the suggestion half-heartedly.

Ella appreciated the offer and any other time might have said yes, but now she thought they had done enough talking and it would be better if they made a move. It would soon be time for the baby to have a bottle and she had come out in such a rush that she hadn't given a thought to that.

'I'd better get home, I didn't make a bottle for the baby,' she told him as she got to her feet and gently lowered Margaret down into the warmth of her pram.

'I'm coming with you,' Peter declared. 'Bill will have put someone else on my round by now. I'll take the rest of the day off.'

It was Peter who pushed the pram.

There was a moment when Ella, walking beside him, almost laughed. Not because of what she had found out but because of the cowardly way her father-in-law had chosen to tell her. And on the very day after they had stood side by side in church and watched as their baby daughter had been sprinkled with holy water and christened in the name of God. The very same church in which she and Peter had made their wedding vows! Laughter turned to tears which she struggled hard to keep back.

'Oh, Peter,' she moaned, taking hold of his arm and hugging him close. 'If we can survive this we'll survive anything.'

Chapter Nineteen

ATHOUGH BECKY AND May worked hard they also played hard. Big Ben had often long since chimed midnight when they let themselves into Aunt Lil's house. The young men who so often escorted them were renowned for their generosity and the majority for their splendid manners.

Becky especially had been excited when she and May had first accepted an offer to join a group that were going to the theatre. That first evening out on the town had opened up for her a world far removed from the world in which she had grown up.

After only a few visits to the theatre Becky managed to square her conscience as to the amount of money these young gentlemen were spending in one night. They were sons of rich people who, if the unions were to be believed, didn't give a damn how they made their money even if it meant grinding the workers down, especially if they happened to be miners.

Nineteen twenty-six was proving to be a very disturbing year for the likes of the poor. The newspapers were full of stories.

'Almost unbelievable,' Mr Gower had declared when reading an article in his morning paper during their mid-morning break.

'What is?' May had saucily enquired.

'Why, the fact that the Samuel Commission has proposed that all employers should lower the wages they pay to the coal-miners.'

Shaking his head and with sadness in his voice he had told

all the staff that were present that his sister's husband worked down the mines.

'Lives in Durham, they have four childen and although my brother-in-law spends two-thirds of his life grovelling in the bowels of the earth he doesn't bring home enough in wages to keep body and soul together. None of them do. And none of those miners will make old bones, their lungs will be shot to pieces before they're forty. Take a cut in their wages? There'll be trouble. Mark my words there will be. They can't live on what they get paid now, never mind accept less.' His voice broke, and sensing that he had let his feelings run away with him he had added lamely, 'We don't always appreciate how lucky we are to work for Lyons.'

Rumours dominated every conversation.

It was the evening of May the first and both May and Becky were run off their feet as they sought to satisfy the customers who on this May Day evening were mostly males. They were working in one of the small upstairs restaurants distinguished by its red plush chairs, Viennese chandeliers and lace curtains.

Five toffs, seated at a circular table, all seemed to be pacified. Becky had served three of them with mutton pie, the traditional London delicacy; the other two had chosen ribs of beef.

'Another chair, if you please, Miss.' Becky frowned in annoyance. A gentleman had stepped in front of her, barring her way. 'I shall join these gentlemen and I too shall have mutton pie.'

She raised her eyebrows at his arrogance and saw a man so tall that she had to tilt her head back to look at him. He had to be well over six feet. He was in evening dress and looked so handsome she gasped. He had thick dark hair and enormous eyes, different to any she had ever seen. They weren't blue, more grey and at that moment they seemed to be laughing at her.

'I'm sorry,' he apologized, 'I wasn't thinking. I'll fetch my own chair.'

'I'll bring your order, sir,' she told him with as much dignity as she could muster, turning away she walked slowly around the table.

'The miners have come out on strike,' she heard the newcomer announce as he drew up a chair and seated himself amongst his friends.

His statement, important as it was, didn't register with Becky for the moment. God, that man was attractive! She was still pondering his good looks as she wrote his order on her pad, admitting to herself that she was fascinated by him and at the same time alarmed. But why him? What was so different about him?

She had no answer to that.

The less she thought about him the better. Determinedly she concentrated on her work, intent on forgetting him. After all he was a customer and at best he would see her as a friendly waitress.

Two days later the Trades Unions Council brought havoc to London, and Mr Gower was proved right.

They called a general strike in support of Britain's coal-miners, two-thirds of whom had been locked out by their employers for refusing to accept the lower wages. The next nine days were a nightmare for everyone and that included the entire staff at each of the Lyons Corner Houses. There were no trains, trams or buses. No newspapers were printed. Iron and steel industries shut down and the docks lay idle.

Many society figures took on the jobs of driving buses and lorries. Listening to the young gentlemen when they came into Coventry Street Lyons for refreshment the Nippies were appalled to hear them laugh and joke about the situation.

It took a while for things to get back to normal, more so because the nine-day general strike had achieved nothing. The miners were still out on strike.

May had taken up with a young gentleman by the name of

Roger Macclesfield and it was Roger who finally introduced Becky to the man that May had teasingly started to refer to as Becky's heart-throb.

Roger had broad shoulders and a real masculine appearance which had attracted May to him in the first place. She had sent Becky off into a fit of giggles when they'd first met.

'He's a joy to behold,' May declared. 'So many men we come across these days are ruddy dandies.'

'You'll like him,' Roger whispered just before he introduced Gerald Palmer to Rebecca Russell.

She did too.

From the moment she had set eyes on him he'd set her heart fluttering. Now his handshake was so strong that it made her wince.

'Will you come to the theatre with me on your first free evening?' Gerald Palmer's voice flowed, so smooth it rolled off his tongue.

I'd go to hell and back just to be near you, is what she was thinking as he held on to her hand, letting his thumb caress her palm.

'I really want you to,' he said huskily, those grey eyes looking down at her twinkling merrily.

'I'd like that very much,' she said, realizing that she was trembling.

He smiled with pleasure. 'I shall count every minute.'

As she walked away, Becky half expected him to reach out and pull her back. But as she took each step away from Gerald Palmer she began to breathe normally again though she had a hard job resisting the impulse to turn and look back at him just to see if he was still watching her.

May was waiting for her as she entered the still room.

'Well, has he asked you out?' May asked, shifting about with impatience.

'Yes,' Becky breathed. 'God that man is . . . well, he just is.'

'Unusual?' May ventured.

'He's that all right,' Becky answered vaguely. 'How old do you think he is, May?'

'Thirtyish, maybe more.' May shrugged.

'Oh don't say that.' Becky looked upset.

'What d' you care? You aren't going to settle down with him for life, you know. We're only going to the London Hippodrome with them.'

'How do you know where we're going?'

'Because Roger already has the tickets an' let me tell you those tickets are like gold-dust.' May paused to grin broadly. 'You may not know it yet but those men have got the money to buy whatever's going, and on Thursday we are going to be treated like real ladies.'

'Is it some special show?' Becky challenged.

'Of course it is,' May retorted as she pointed triumphantly to a poster on the wall. 'It's Jerome Kern's *Sunny* starring Jack Buchanan and Elsie Randolph. All London's fighting to see it and Roger said we're going on to have dinner after the show.'

They both giggled. 'You can be the one to tell Aunt Lil that we won't be home till the early hours of the morning,' Becky spluttered.

'Oh no I won't,' May protested, 'she'll eat me alive. She always thinks it's me that's leading you astray. One of these days I'm going to tell her that it's dainty little you that attracts men like flies. Let her know that they chase after you in droves.'

Becky lashed out at May, slapping her back with the flat of her hand. 'May Stevens, you do exaggerate.'

'That's as maybe, but you'll have to admit you do look so innocent half the time, with your baby face and those great brown eyes. Just for once, though, let me give you a word of warning. Gerald Palmer might be the best-looking man you've ever set eyes on but he's been around. I'd lay money on that.'

Becky was shocked by what May had said. Yet it only took a minute for her to realize that May was probably right. Suddenly in that moment she told herself to act a bit more cautiously.

Then in her mind's eye she pictured Gerald again. He really was so good-looking. She thought of his deep soft voice, his cheeky grin, the way he had looked at her, held her hand for so long. Somehow, through no fault of her own, he had come into her life and the urge to go out with him, to be near him, was more than she could control.

I'll be all right, she thought to herself, he's a lovely man.

May watched Becky's expression, saw the way she smiled. She was so gullible! That one thought made her all the more determined to keep an eye on Becky, and more so on Gerald Palmer.

Chapter Twenty

THE TIME WAS seven o'clock in the morning.

Robert Matthews stood on the opposite side of the road staring at the frontage of Coventry Street Corner House. He was well satisfied.

The white and gold façade looked splendid. And so it should for the appearance of the building was the public face that Lyons was presenting to the world. The paintwork was in good condition and the brass highly polished. It was not widely known that Joseph Lyons, a street trader at the time, who had in 1887 consented to his name being used for the new catering company, was in fact the great-grandfather of Robert Matthews.

Robert had been given a privileged upbringing and had known since he was in his teens that a position within the catering company was his for the asking. While still at school he had rebelled against the idea. It had been his mother who had changed his mind. Gentle, kind and very beautiful she had used no blackmailing pressure, simply took him for meals at different establishments owned by the company, at different times of both day and night.

Interest had come first and finally appreciation.

He would now be the first to admit that he was totally addicted to the art of bulk catering. His working life was as fulfilled as any man had the right to expect. In fact he would go as far as agreeing that he loved his work, although he asked for no favours from anyone.

There wasn't a part of the company with which he was not familiar, from the dozens of items of food for Lyons' very extensive menu which were cooked in large premises at the back of Cadby Hall during the night to the wholesalers who provided the fresh meat carcasses and the fine fish that was filleted by special chefs, right down to the cleaners who saw to the waitresses' dressing rooms and the ladies' lavatories.

Time for me to get myself some breakfast, he decided, crossing the road and letting himself in through the front door. Manageress and waitresses were now in the shop and the ground floor was open to customers.

Robert was of the opinion that Lyons owed the success of its teashops to a meticulous system of supervision. In every premises there were ladies similar to Mrs Nicholls and Miss Timson who at all times had the good of the company at heart. Besides beady-eyed head waiters such as Mr Gower there was another important group, the team of observers.

They acted as normal customers, paid their bills and left. Later they sent a report to head office, with comments on the standard of the service and the food, noting anything at all unseemly.

No ordinary member of staff ever knew who they were.

Having eaten well and signed for his meal the next two hours would be taken up with routine checks throughout the entire building. Robert knew full well that by midday almost every seat in each of the restaurants would be taken. There were often several business parties being held at the same time but the small intimate restaurants situated on the upper floors only functioned at night and the problems involved in coping with these parties simultaneously at lunchtime was very much on his mind this morning. At an extraordinary meeting of shareholders held three weeks ago it had been decided another branch of the company should be formed.

It was to be known as the Outside Catering Department, dealing with private functions, even those held on race-courses, besides banquets, garden parties and many other events.

Selective recruiting of girls considered suitable for special training had already begun. That was the main reason why he was here at Coventry Street this morning.

At three o'clock, the lunchtime rush was over. Becky and May didn't say anything to each other, but their thoughts were troubled. It wasn't a good sign when the manageress told them to report to the main office.

'I hate these lunchtime shifts,' May complained. 'Only good thing about them is we do get our evenings free.'

'Come in,' Florence Nicholls called in answer to the tap on the door. Oh my God! Both girls were astounded to see Robert Matthews, Mrs Nicholls and Miss Timson grouped behind the desk.

'Well, don't just stand there, come and sit yourselves down,' Florence Nicholls said, smiling as she always did.

'Yes, come and hear the new proposal.' Miss Timson, tall, self-assured and dressed today in a grey tailored costume, was a woman who knew what the girls were about to learn would be of great benefit to them and she saw no reason not to enjoy the telling. 'Don't keep them in suspense,' she urged Robert Matthews.

He looked taken aback. He stood there. Tall. Taller than Miss Timson. He murmured, 'Good afternoon.'

'Good afternoon, sir,' May and Becky answered in unison.

He smiled faintly. His light blue eyes were clear, his face thin and brown but Becky was silently smiling to herself because of the waistcoat he was wearing. May would describe it as dandified! Yet it wasn't. The material was a corded silk, the colour blue, darker than the blue of his eyes. Worn with his stiff-collared white shirt and black morning suit it relieved the sombre look no end.

Robert Matthews felt that Rebecca was appraising him and was instantly embarrassed. 'I imagine you are wondering why we have asked you here when obviously you'd much rather be on your way home.' He took out a sheaf of papers from a briefcase that lay on the table and unfolded them. 'The shareholders have decided to branch out, diversify so to speak.' He knew he sounded flustered, but that was because he was flustered. He took a deep breath, letting it out slowly.

Rebecca Russell had that effect on him. She had from the very first meeting. She was so slight. He felt she was vulnerable, and although from having observed her when working on many occasions he knew she was not, he still felt the urge to protect her.

Drawing himself up to his full height he proceeded to outline the programme the company was embarking on. 'Each of you has been selected because of the way you have adapted and performed since becoming employees of Lyons. You have achieved every standard asked of you and you may look upon this new employment as not only promotion but as an award for all your endeavours.'

May was the first to find her voice. 'Sir, do we have to decide now?' she asked, despising herself for sounding so wooden.

Robert Matthews turned to Florence Nicholls, and she, wondering why Robert didn't seem in complete charge of himself this afternoon, quickly got to her feet and took over.

'I know this proposition has been sprung on you,' she began, looking first at Rebecca and then at May. 'Naturally you will be given time to digest all that you have been told. If you decide that you do want to be part of this new enterprise you will be informed of the date the special training will commence and given a few days' leave prior to that date.'

Although Mrs Nicholls was still smiling her tone was dismissive, but May refused to be dismissed just like that.

'Please, ma'am, where would we be sent to do this training?' she asked.

Florence Nicholls' self-assurance flowed out. She considered herself a good judge of character and from the start had seen it as inevitable that these two girls, so totally different in looks and upbringing, would not only be good waitresses but go on to become an asset to the company.

She allowed herself another smile, and went on, 'Orchard House's premises are being enlarged, so more than likely it will take place in Clerkenwell.' Then, almost as an after-thought, she added, 'You will be provided with new uniforms and coronet caps.'

'Thank you,' both girls murmured and were on their feet and outside in the corridor before they realized it.

Becky leant against the wall and closed her eyes. 'What a brilliant oportunity,' she said softly.

May was grinning broadly. 'What a turn up for the book! Think of all the places we'll get t' go to. And all the big-nobs we'll meet.'

'There you go again, May. We shan't exactly be meeting big-nobs as you call them, we shall be waiting on them.'

'Same meat, different gravy,' May laughed loudly. 'Come on, wait till we tell Aunt Lil we'll be living it up. Rubbing shoulders with the upper crust, don't you know.'

Becky followed as May set off on a run. She too was laughing now. May could be a proper comic when she liked. 'Rubbing shoulders with the upper crust!' It was the way it came out. May could impersonate the upper classes to a tee when it suited her.

May and Becky's first visit to the Royal Ascot race meeting had them both gasping in surprised delight.

Without any hesitation, after a long discussion with Aunt Lil, they had both signed up to be employees of the newly-formed Lyons Outside Catering Department. They were due to start their training the first week in July. Since it was now almost a year since they had started to work as Nippies they were granted a whole week's holiday.

'Don't go home to your parents, not straight away,' Gerald Palmer had pleaded. 'Spend a few days with me. At least let me take you to the races. You haven't lived if you've never been on a racecourse.'

The men that frequented Lyons Corner Houses late at night were different. Older, richer and very often married men. Most wanted to shower the Nippies with presents, take them to interesting places on their days off and spend enormous amounts of money on them. What did they want in return? the sensible girls asked themselves. Becky reassured herself time and time again that Gerald was not like that. May, much to her regret, had come to the conclusion that she was wasting her time trying to tell Becky to be careful.

It was a gorgeous day, the sun high in the sky. Becky couldn't believe that she was actually here, at Royal Ascot, her spirits soaring by the minute as she stood on the bright green grass and looked around. The ladies were a picture in brightly-coloured dresses and fluffy hats, large and small. And the men were a sight to behold. Elegant! There was no other word for their grey morning suits and top hats.

Gerald had moved away to stand by the rail, looking sunburned and healthy. Gosh he was tall, Becky thought to herself as across the space their eyes met and held. He had removed his hat and the brilliant sun was showing up signs of grey in his dark hair. She had become accustomed to well-dressed men but she had never met one, or seen one, who looked so at ease no matter what he was wearing.

'Rebecca, there you are,' Roger Macclesfield exclaimed. 'May is getting worried about you. She wants you to come over to where the jockeys are and there are so many people that I would like you to meet.'

Becky looked towards where Gerald had been standing but he was no longer in sight. Disappointed, she turned and went with Roger.

'There you are,' May cried, looking very smart in a cream-coloured suit and a pale yellow hat, excitement making her cheeks looked flushed.

The jockeys came out and stood around the owners of the

horses in little groups. What bright colours the jockeys wore, Becky and May both noted.

Roger was intent on introducing Becky. She felt bewildered by it all: faces she had never seen before, names she would never remember. She felt lost without Gerald being there. Then suddenly his hand was on her shoulder and he turned her round to face him.

'Miss me?' he teased, bending his head and planting a soft lingering kiss on her lips.

He had kissed her! In front of all these people he had kissed her. Her heart was thumping, nineteen to the dozen. From that moment her whole world changed. She swallowed, steadying her breathing. It was love. It had to be. Why else would he kiss her in public for everyone to see? It was an open declaration. There would be no more dithering. She wanted to be with him, every minute of every day.

'Welcome to horse racing,' Gerald said cheerfully, handing Becky a glass of champagne.

The jockeys swung up on to the horses and moved away to go down to the starting gates. Most of the crowds went off to their reserved boxes, others to the stands.

'May, Becky, we're all going to watch from the grass, as near to the rails as we can get,' Roger said as he glanced apologetically at May.

'I don't mind in the least,' May answered quickly. Then in an aside to Becky she whispered, 'If we get half a chance we'll shoot off later, have a peep into some of the boxes cos that's where we'll be working before long.'

Among much laughter and a lot of chatter the four of them set to the studying of race cards. Gerald and Roger insisted that the girls accepted a pound note as their first stake money. With a feeling of foreboding Becky agreed to place a bet of just ten shillings. May, throwing caution to the wind, went the whole hog and staked the full pound.

'Beginner's luck,' Roger cried, waving his hat above his head, allowing his short dark hair to blow free in the wind.

'Ignorance must be bliss,' Gerald declared as he tore his betting slips into shreds.

Both girls were ecstatic. By sheer luck they had backed the winning horse at four to one.

It seemed they were spending countless hours waiting around Tote queues while Gerald and Roger backed their hunches, all the time encouraging them to have a flutter.

'We've both won a packet!' Roger announced, grinning broadly. 'Come on, time we stood you drinks at the bar.'

Gerald was the life and soul of the party and as Becky stood back watching him the thought crossed her mind that he was spending a great deal of money with more good nature than sense.

'Now's our chance,' May whispered, tugging at the sleeve of Becky's pretty floral dress, 'we can sneak off an' get a peep into some of the boxes.'

Gerald had his back to the bar, surrounded by men in grey morning suits and looking remarkably carefree. Becky caught his eye and mouthed, 'We're going to find the ladies.'

He raised his glass in acknowledgement, laughing roguishly, and winked at her. She laughed back and the moment was gone, but for Becky the declaration that he loved her had been made and that was enough for now. Full of contentment and wonder that such a lovely man as Gerald would have time for her she followed May out of the bar.

The boxes were about five yards by four, most of the space being filled with well-dressed men and women. The far end wall was sheer windows looking out over the lovely course, with a glass door opening on to a flight of steps which led down to the viewing balcony.

After they had peered into at least three of the boxes May suddenly murmured, 'I wonder what they'll look like with a dining table?'

'Wonderful I should think,' Becky thoughtfully answered. 'Set up with what, twelve places for lunch? Or do you think there's room for more?'

'I'd say twelve is about right. Just think, Becky, you and me coming to all the races being part an' parcel of all this and getting paid for it!' May was buzzing with enthusiasm.

'It will be great,' Becky said, and meant it, but she had to voice her thoughts, so she went on, 'we won't be coming dressed up as we are today, we shall be on duty, here to work and remember what Mr Matthews said? Some of the dos such as Masonic dinners will be seating as many as a hundred, maybe more. This new venture is all very well but it isn't going to be dead easy so don't kid yourself.'

'Oh, you!' May gave Becky a playful push. 'You can be a proper old wet blanket when you choose. Anyway let's live for today, don't know about you but I'm starving.'

Gerald and Roger did them proud. It was an excellent lunch. For the girls the best part was the fresh strawberries served with thick clotted cream. By the coffee-brandy–cigar stage the restaurant was thinning out as people went dashing out yet again to back their hopes on the next race. There was a good deal of speculation between Roger and Gerald about two horses that apparently they had been given the tip-off for this afternoon.

'Well,' Roger said calmly, 'it's not a bit of good us even thinking of backing the hot favourite, the odds are too short.'

'I agree,' Gerald declared, getting to his feet and taking a tightly rolled bundle of black and white five-pound notes from his pocket. 'Nothing ventured nothing gained.'

The girls followed at a slower pace, each having given Roger one pound to place on the same horse for them.

From where they stood they couldn't see much of the race, only a flashing view as the horses tore up to the winning post. They listened to the announcement of the winner's number. Becky took hold of May's arm and shook it. 'We won, I'm sure we've won.' She was laughing with pleasure, her big brown eyes wide with amazement.

The rest of the afternoon slid away fast.

Becky was both sad and sorry when it was time for the last race.

'No, May, I'm not risking my winnings,' Becky declared, having seen both Gerald and Roger lose on the previous race. Silently she totted up just how much the day had brought her. Forty-four pounds and ten shillings! It was a fortune!

Becky grinned at May. 'I've won quite a bit today. How about you?'

'Enough to frighten Aunt Lil into thinking I'm in danger of becoming a compulsive gambler.'

Becky laughed out loud. 'Your Aunt Lil,' she said, 'knows you a whole lot better than you give her credit for.'

May grinned back at Becky. 'Well, it hasn't been our own money we've been playing with, has it?'

'No, and I felt guilty about that at first. I offered my winnings to Gerald, but he laughed his head off.'

'My conscience doesn't trouble me as much as yours seems to, I only offered Roger his pound stake money back. He told me not to be so daft.'

'Getting to be a crafty pair, aren't we?' Becky whispered.

May nodded her agreement. 'Been a smashing day though, hasn't it? So here goes, last race,' she said, walking towards Roger, holding out two pound notes. 'I'll risk that amount on number five.'

'At least none of us have lost our shirts today,' Roger said as he tucked May's hand through the crook of his arm. Then pulling her close and grinning broadly he added, 'Come on you big spender, come with me, let's see if we can take the bookies for another few pounds.'

'Becky, would you like to go up to the bar for another drink?' Gerald asked as May and Roger left them.

'No, thank you, I've had so much to eat and drink today that I feel I shall burst if I have anything else. But you don't need to stay with me if you'd like a drink.'

'You think I don't want to stay with you?'

The colour rose in her cheeks and before she could form

an answer Gerald said quickly, 'I'd like to spend the rest of my life with you. You have enjoyed today, haven't you?'

'Oh, Gerald! More than I can tell you. It has been a truly lovely day.'

Gerald took one of her hands and held it between both of his. 'Becky,' he said very quietly, 'you are on holiday for the rest of the week. Why don't we make it a truly lovely week? Spend it together. What do you say?'

Becky sighed softly. 'Gerald, I can't. My parents know I have this time off and I must go to see them.'

'You could go for the day. I'll run you down.'

'No Gerald, you don't understand. I haven't been home since New Year, that's six months, they expect me. Besides it's my goddaughter's birthday and her mother, my best friend, is expecting another baby in a few weeks' time and I shan't get another chance to visit them.'

Gerald gave her a dry look. 'Are you a do-gooder?'

Becky looked startled. 'No, I'm not. What an odd thing to ask.'

He made an apologetic gesture. 'Putting everyone else before your own pleasure, I just thought you might be.'

She shook her head. 'My family and friends are very important to me but as to doing good, I wouldn't have the time, even if I had the urge.'

'But what about me? You haven't time for me, is that what you're saying?'

'Gerald, don't twist my words,' she protested as she freed her hand and let it rest on his arm.

He smiled, easing the situation, taking away any seriousness and said, 'When you return to London do you promise that every moment you are not working will be spent with me?'

'Yes, oh yes.' She nuzzled her head against him.

'That's that settled then.' He grinned now, and hugging her closer to him he bent his head and placed his lips on hers in a long lingering kiss that sent tingles right through to her very soul.

Chapter Twenty-one

'OH, SORRY, MAY I change that destination to Kingston?' Becky, having made a sudden decision, asked the young man in the railway ticket office.

The booking clerk raised his head and smiled. If it had been an ordinary housewife he would probably have told her briskly to make up her mind. But this young lady was a dream! So small and dainty that only her head and shoulders were visible above the counter. He leant forward. Her face was lovely, creamy skin and those dark eyes, a man could forget he was married when confronted by someone like her. She looks like she has a rainbow around her head, he thought, looking at the tiny close-fitting hat she had perched on her dark hair. It was all pale shades of pink and blue, pale mauve and cream, the cream matching the loose jacket she was wearing. He shook his head reluctantly.

'Going on further than Raynes Park, are you then?'

'Yes. I'm sorry to have troubled you, I wasn't thinking.'

Becky gave him the sweetest smile as he passed over her ticket and said, 'No trouble at all, platform eight, Miss.'

The train pulled away from the station and Becky leant back in her corner seat of the carriage and relaxed. It was only at the last minute that she had resolved to visit Ella before going home to her mum and dad. With time now to think she was feeling remorseful. She had written regularly to Ella but it wasn't the same as seeing her. If she was honest with herself she felt that she had become too wrapped up in her job, her new social life and indeed her new friends. She sighed. Yes, Gerald Palmer in particular!

If only there were more hours in the day. And what would you do with them if there were? she asked herself. Spend them with Gerald, she freely admitted.

Gerald didn't seem to work. No matter what time of the day or night she finished her shift he was there waiting for her. No one had ever paid her so much attention or tried to lavish so many pretty gifts on her.

As children Ella and she had been inseparable and she loved Ella dearly. Becky bit her lip. Why had her thoughts begun to run along these lines? There was no getting away from it. Where Ella was concerned there was always a small voice inside her head that troubled her. Ella and her problems disturbed her.

Yet it isn't my fault that things are not that rosy for Peter and Ella, she thought. They chose to do what they did. Now that is not strictly true, Becky quickly chided herself. One day they let their emotions get the better of them and they ended up getting married when the truth was they just didn't have enough money to set up a home together. The one good thing to come out of it all was baby Margaret. She was lovely: a real little poppet.

It didn't seem possible that she would be one year old before this month was out. Then there would be another baby! God above, they could have done without another one to feed and clothe.

Becky felt very warm as she walked up Mill Street. She looked around with faint amusement. If ever I doubted I had done the right thing in moving to London to work as a waitress for Lyons, the sight of these ragged kids playing out in the street while some of the mothers had nothing better to do than chat with their neighbours on the doorsteps would convince me, she reassured herself.

In the middle of the road, almost outside Ella's front door, the milkman on his second round of the morning had set down his cart and was surrounded by women, each carrying a jug, and each waiting to be served. Becky recognized Rosie Dawson, a big friendly woman who worked for Annie Smith in the Swan and was reputed to be well-off because she had three sons all working on the river barges.

'Gonna call in and see Ella, are you, luv?' She smiled at Becky, noting her smart dress and jacket, aware that she was employed by Lyons up in London. 'She'll be pleased to see yer. Needs all the friends she can get right now.'

Becky frowned, hesitating for a moment. 'Well, best hurry on in then, eh? I'll be real pleased to see her.'

Becky tapped twice on the door and when there was no reply edged it open, went down the narrow passage and quietly opened the door to the kitchen. And there was Ella . . . heavily pregnant, seated in a wooden armchair, a snow-white shawl wrapped round her shoulders, and her face turned to where Margaret was sitting on a blanket playing with building bricks. Ella's blue eyes were round and intense, staring at the baby with such love that it brought a lump to Becky's throat.

The room was clean and tidy; what furniture there was had been well-polished and there was a small vase of marigolds set down in the centre of the table. What did shock Becky was the pallor of Ella's face. With all the lovely June weather they had had recently surely there should have been some colour in her cheeks. There wasn't. Ella's face was grey, like a piece of dried-up parchment. The skin seemed to be stretched over her cheekbones and her lovely fine fair hair hung lifelessly over her thin shoulders. The very look of Ella frightened Becky so much that she gasped softly, causing Ella to turn around. Her eyes lit up and then filled with tears as she struggled to stand on her feet.

'Becky!' she said in a voice strangled with emotion. 'Oh, Becky, I've missed you so much.'

'And I've missed you.' Rushing into the room, Becky threw her two arms around that bulky figure and hugged her close. They clung to each other and laughed, and Ella cried, letting the tears run down her face on to Becky's shoulder until baby Margaret decided she wanted some of the attention her mother was getting and yelled out in protest.

'Thanks for all your lovely letters,' Ella said through her tears. 'I'm sorry I don't write to you all that often but I do read your letters over and over. Oh, Becky, I've been praying you'd come home soon.'

'Well, I'm here now,' she said warmly. Then, pushing herself up straight, Becky sniffled away her own tears and looked at Ella's face. 'Look at you,' she cried, brushing a limp lock of hair from her friend's forehead.

They gazed at each other quietly for a minute. Soon Ella said in a soft voice, 'I'll put the kettle on, make us some tea, before we settle down to tell each other all our news.'

Becky dropped to her knees, smiling now, her face lit up with pleasure as she took a good look at her goddaughter.

'Who's grown into such a big girl since I saw you last?' Becky crooned, lifting Margaret up into her arms and resting back on her heels. Baby Margaret merely gurgled at her. 'You are so bonny,' Becky went on as she nestled her face into the baby's neck, 'and you smell so sweet, all talcum powder and nice soap. I could bite lumps out of you, yes I could.' She tickled the little mite under her arms and again around her tummy which sent the baby off into peals of laughter and made her wriggle so much that Becky had difficulty in holding on to her.

'Put her into her highchair,' Ella said, coming back into the room carrying a tea tray on which she had set out a dish of homemade cakes, cups and saucers and small plates. Setting the tray down on the table she turned and Becky quickly asked, 'Where are you going now?'

'To fetch the teapot and the milk.'

It was painfully obvious to Becky that every move Ella made was an effort.

'Here, sit yourself down again, I'll go.' She bent low, picked up three brightly coloured bricks from the floor and set them down on the table of the highchair in which she had securely fastened the baby. 'There you are sweetheart, snug as a bug in a rug, Auntie won't be a moment.'

With the tea poured out and the two of them settled one each side of the table and the baby crunching on a Farley's rusk, there was much to talk about.

'You go first,' Becky instructed Ella. 'I told you most of what has happened to me in my letters so hurry up, bring me up to date.'

Ella drained her cup and turned to look Becky full in the face. 'Shall I start with the good news or the bad?'

Wisely Becky didn't comment on that statement. 'Wherever you like, take your time,' she told Ella.

'Well, I'll give you the good news first.' A faint smile came to her lips. 'Thanks to your dad at least Peter and I now know we are legally married.'

Becky's eyes lit up with surprise. 'Ella, that's marvellous. How come?' The thought of Ella being free of at least that worry made Becky cry out, 'Oh, it's wonderful news!'

'Yes,' Ella agreed, sounding very subdued. 'Must say we were relieved. It was bad enough for me, and though at first I didn't realize it for Peter it was ten times worse. Nobody will ever know what he's been through this last six months.'

Becky saw the pain in her eyes and her heart ached for her. 'Tell me what my dad found out,' she urged.

'After a lot of searching, different records – you wouldn't believe how your dad has been an absolute brick – he found out that Peter's wife has been dead for years. Soon after their wedding ceremony apparently. It seems she was killed up in Liverpool, her dad an' all, an Army truck caused the accident, failed brakes. Don't know the details. Accidental death, the records show. That's why she never answered any of Peter's letters. With the War being on and them having just moved up to Liverpool it seems no one down here was notified. Not at the time anyway.'

'Sad news,' Becky said, doing her best to express sympathy,

'but you must have felt as if a great burden had been lifted from your shoulders.'

'Not really,' Ella lied, and her cheeks flushed up.

'Well, how about Peter?'

'Sort of. Nice to know he wasn't a bigamist.'

'So the pair of you should be feeling on top of the world, waiting for the new baby an' all.'

Ella dropped her gaze to the floor and shifted uncomfortably in her chair. Becky was quiet then, sensing that something was wrong. Leaning across the table she stroked Ella's hair and said very softly, 'I'm sorry. You said you had bad news as well as good.' Then, in a lighter tone, 'Don't tell me if you don't want to, you were always telling me I was too nosy.'

'No. It's all right. You are the best friend anyone in this world could wish for and you're bound to find out sooner or later.' She paused, not certain it was fair to burden Becky with more of her troubles. 'Peter's lost his job, he's been out of work nearly two months,' she murmured.

'Two months!' Becky gaped at her in disbelief. 'Why has nobody told me? How the hell have you managed?'

Ella fidgeted, twisting her hands together. 'It isn't for want of trying. Honestly, Becky, Peter has walked miles. He would do anything. Take any job.' Her eyes were brimming with tears and her voice sounded strangely saddened. She sighed, and when she spoke again it was from the heart. 'Sometimes I think God is punishing me and sometimes I feel so ashamed because even though Margaret is such a beautiful child and I love her dearly I wish she had never been born. I can't help it, Becky, you and I made such plans when we were young and you're doing everything you said you would and there's me without a penny to my name.'

Becky had to swallow and take a deep breath before she was able to form an answer. She couldn't blame Ella one bit for feeling as she did. There couldn't be a more terrible time to be unemployed. With so many men in the same boat and things the way they were, thousands were tramping the streets looking for work. It might be ages before Peter got another job. What could she possibly say to Ella? Her normally quick-thinking mind had gone blank.

'Peter will find something soon.' Ella's quiet voice cut in on Becky's thoughts. 'There isn't a day he doesn't go out looking.'

'Where is Peter now?' Becky ventured to ask.

Ella lowered her head, covered her face with her hands and quietly wept. Becky thought it best to give her a minute or two. She lifted the baby from the highchair into her arms and went to stand and stare out of the kitchen window.

At that moment the door to the garden shed opened and Peter appeared, slouching along the garden path. His head was down, his shoulders rounded. One hand was rammed into his trouser pocket and from the other hand he dangled two pairs of old boots. All told he looked thoroughly dejected. Two months with no money coming in, it must seem like an eternity. Becky closed her eyes and prayed. Please God, let him find a job soon. Please! It is bad enough now – whatever will they do when the new baby arrives?

When she opened her eyes Peter was opening the back door, calling out to Ella as he came into the house. 'Ella, you there? I've managed to fix both Ted's boots and mine. Bit of a job though, the leather wasn't up to much. Still, they'll last us a bit longer now.'

As Peter turned to close the door behind him, Becky stepped forward.

'God, it's you, Becky!' he exclaimed as though he were unable to believe what he was seeing. 'You're a sight for sore eyes.'

'I've been here some time,' she said, and smiled. 'Didn't know you were hiding yourself away in that shed.'

'I didn't intend to be so long. I was going to take that little rascal for a walk.' He grinned, stooping to kiss Margaret's cheek. 'But I can see I haven't been missed, cuddling up in your auntie's arms eh?' he whispered to the baby. 'No sooner you're inside the door and you're spoiling my daughter,' he said as he smiled, teasing Becky.

'What were you doing in the shed?' Becky asked, thinking that she already knew the answer.

'Making good use of the skills my father taught me when we lived in Northampton.' He held both pairs of boots up in the air, letting them dangle by their laces. 'Trying to do the impossible really, make good out of bad.'

'Stop your chattering out there,' Ella called, her voice sounding a lot lighter now that Peter had put in an appearance. 'Come on in and I'll make a fresh pot of tea.'

Becky went through the motions, talking too much, playing with the baby, telling them snippets of what she did at work, yet all the time her mind was racing ahead. She asked herself the same question twice over. Will it work? Seeing Peter with those boots, an idea had popped into her mind without her realizing it. An idea she couldn't wait to put to her father.

Putting on her jacket, taking a fond farewell of both Ella and Peter, smothering the baby in kisses, she promised she would be back the very next day.

'You don't have to come traipsing all this way over here,' Ella whispered, giving the baby to Peter to hold. Then looping her hand through Becky's arm she said, 'I'll come to the door with you.'

On the doorstep Becky hugged her dear friend gently.

'Becky, you're to think on what I've said.' Ella was suddenly being very serious. 'You only have a few days so you must spend them with your family.'

'Who's being the bossy one now?' Becky asked, looking Ella straight in the eye. 'Don't tell me what I must do. I shall be back here some time tomorrow. All right?'

A smiling Ella nodded her head.

There was determination in her step as Becky walked towards the tram stop. She wondered whether her father would agree to help her. Someone had to help Peter and Ella and who better than herself? After all, fate had been kind to her, so far. Who knows what would have happened if she had gone along a similar road to that which Ella had taken? She shuddered at the thought.

She didn't ever want to be poor. Being poor was making an old woman out of Ella long before her time, sitting there feeling helpless with Peter out of work. It must be so humiliating for both of them not to be able to pay the rent or feed and clothe their baby properly.

Poor Peter! Walking miles in an old pair of boots that he had cobbled together with a cheap piece of leather. How long would they last, for Christ's sake?

Thank God the weather was good. What if Peter was still unemployed come the winter? If there was no money for food and clothing there certainly wouldn't be any for coal. Then what? With two babies, it didn't bear thinking about.

Ella, sitting deep in thought, worried out of her life. Peter slouching up the garden path, dangling those old boots he had worked on for hours when really all they were fit for was the dustbin. It would be a long time before she could get those pictures out of her mind.

The tram came along and Becky boarded it, still with the one thought uppermost in her mind. She couldn't live like Ella was having to. Scrimping and scraping for every penny. She just couldn't. Like most girls when she had first left school her aim had been to fall in love, get married, and have babies. Now she knew that life wasn't as simple as that.

Her mind was made up. The man she married would have to be in a position to provide her with some of the good things rich people took for granted. Maybe if she had not been lucky enough to land her job with Lyons, she might never have realized that there was a big world out there and it had so much to offer.

But she *had* got the job. She was a trained waitress working in the West End of London. And she was going further.

After more special training she was to be employed by the newly-formed Outside Catering Department and the events she would soon be attending would open up an even wider view of life.

Now she was used to eating really well, visits to the theatre, having money of her own, going places and doing things she had previously never even dreamt of. Not that her wonderful parents had ever kept their children short. But then her dad had been one of the lucky ones. He had always had a good job with a regular pay packet. On the other hand the life they led in Surrey was very limited. It suited them fine, and it had suited her until she had seen how the other half lived.

Becky was thinking hard by now, her eyes staring and her forehead creased in a deep frown. I've seen what it's like to be rich and now I know first-hand what it's like to be poor and one thing's for certain, I know which is best, she said to herself. But was that a selfish attitude to take? She couldn't, or perhaps wouldn't, give herself a truthful answer.

Her thoughts turned to Gerald Palmer. Could he give her the kind of life she now yearned for? I think I am in love with him but when I'm apart from him I'm not really sure what that kind of love really is. I only know that my family mean the world to me, I love each of them with all my heart, but that's a different kind of feeling to the one I have for Gerald. If 'love' meant being happy with someone, longing to see them again, thinking about them day and night, and your whole body tingling whenever that person touched you or even looked at you in that special way, then, yes, she was in love with Gerald.

Did her future lie with him? He was handsome, kind and good, he loved her, so he said, and he had money. Yet he had never mentioned marriage.

As May was always telling her, she would have to tread warily, because there were times when she was apart from Gerald that a warning bell would ring in her head and her instincts told her not to let her heart rule her head.

Suddenly she felt uneasy. It was Ella and her problems that she should be concerned with, not her own. Compared to Ella she didn't have a worry in the world. She was hoping against hope that her dad would go along with the proposition she was going to put to him. Her dad could make it possible. He had to be able to, because if Peter didn't find some way of earning a living soon God alone knew how he and Ella would manage.

'Well, I'll be blowed.' Joe Russell, having listened attentively to every word that his headstrong daughter had uttered, now leant back in his armchair and scratched his greying hair.

Their evening meal over, everything cleared away, there was just Becky, and her mother and father sitting cosily around the table that was now covered with Joyce's best red chenille tablecloth.

'You might not believe this, Becky lass, but I watched Peter getting further and further down in the dumps and I asked myself this question: "What can the lad do that he's been trained for?"' Joe's ruddy face was creased with anxiety. 'The only thing I could come up with was that he was trained to fight for his country.'

'Him and a few thousand more,' his wife scoffed, 'but that don't seem to count with the Government. Breaks yer heart to see the men that are tramping the streets these days.'

'You haven't answered my question, Dad,' Becky pleaded. 'Do you think if we clubbed together and got him all the tools Peter could set up a trade, mending boots in his garden shed?'

'After a while I came up with that same idea, luv, when I found out that his dad had practically taught him the trade. It wouldn't work though.'

'Dad! Just tell me why not?' Becky begged, her tone serious.

'Because the enquiries I made proved that it wasn't practicable. Peter would have to get the landlord's permission for a start.'

'Yeah, and he'd want a share of the profit for himself,' Joyce butted in again. 'He'd say Peter was using his property to run a business.'

'Exactly,' Joe said, 'and that would defeat the object. The repairs Peter would be doing would be for men in the same position as himself and what could they afford to pay? Precious little if you ask me. No, if we are going to set Peter up with a little business it has to be in the town on a busy street where there would be plenty of passing trade. He'd be much better off seeking the kind of person who can afford to pay to have their shoes repaired rather than doing favours for his mates.'

'Oh yes, Joe, and pigs would fly if they had wings,' Joyce mocked, dismissing the idea although like the rest of her family she would do anything to help Peter and Ella. She was almost afraid to go round to see Peggy these days. Peggy was worried sick knowing that each day things were getting worse for her Ella and Peter and with a second baby on the way she was at her wits' end, not knowing how she could help. After all she was on her own with no man behind her.

That woman has done well when you think about it, Joyce was musing to herself, and now her only daughter and her first grandchild are stuck out there in Kingston with Peter out of work and herself not in a position to help much. Joyce shook her head and looked at her own bonny daughter. My, she looked a picture, she'd done well for herself since she'd left home. There wasn't a day that passed that she didn't miss her but there again she thanked God for Lily Maynard. She looked after her niece, May, and Rebecca as if they were her own. Giving them both a damn good home is Lily. Yet Becky never forgot her family and where her real home was. Never a week passed that she didn't write a letter home.

It must break Peggy's heart when she compares the difference in the way our two girls have turned out. I bet she often wonders whether things might not have been different if her man hadn't been killed in the War. Heartbreaking really when you think about it. She sighed softly.

'I could put up a bit of money, about fifty pounds actually,' Becky told her parents, using a very quiet voice, knowing full well they would be surprised that she had such a sum of money.

Both heads spun round to stare at their daughter.

'Fifty pounds!' her mother cried.

'A lot of money that,' her father said drily. 'Care to tell us how you came by it, luv?'

Becky half-closed her eyes. A white lie in a good cause wouldn't hurt, she was saying to herself, aware that if she said she had won most of it at the races her parents would be horror-struck.

'Well it wasn't from gratuities,' she told them sweetly. 'You know we aren't allowed to accept tips. It was two bonus payments. One of twenty pounds six months ago and another twenty pounds when we agreed to join this new training scheme. The rest I've managed to save.'

'Well I never,' her mother said, her eyes wide with amazement. 'Your father's always telling me what a marvellous opening it was for you to go and work at Lyons. I believe him now an' all.'

Becky said a quick prayer. I know it's a lie, but please God, it really is in a good cause.

'Well,' her father said thoughtfully, 'if you're sure you want to part with your savings.' He waited and Becky eagerly nodded her head. 'There's a few of us that will put a little into the pot, one never knows when we ourselves might need a helping hand.'

'That's true,' Joyce said gratefully, 'And what goes round comes round, I always say.'

'I'll start in on it first thing in the morning,' Joe Russell declared. 'Don't worry lass, we'll get Peter sorted out. There must be suitable premises somewhere.'

'Oh, Dad! I knew you wouldn't let me down. If anyone can do it you can.' She jumped to her feet, came round behind his chair and threw both arms around her dad's broad shoulders, leant over and started planting kisses on his forehead.

'Get orf,' he yelled, 'get yerself up to bed. Me saying I'd try and fix Peter up don't make it so. Just you remember that. I'm no miracle worker.'

Becky looked across at her mother and they both burst out laughing. 'No, and you ain't no angel either,' his wife told him, still laughing fit to burst as she held the door open for Becky.

Becky hesitated in the doorway. 'Goodnight, Mum, Goodnight, Dad. You wanna know something? I love you both.'

Joe Russell didn't have to search far. It really was the case that truth is often stranger than fiction, he was telling himself as he strode home two days after listening to Becky plead for help for Peter.

'Where's Becky?' Joe asked his wife the minute he set foot inside the house.

'Round the corner, gone to see Peggy. She went out early this morning to buy little Margaret's birthday present and then went over to Ella's again. Came back in a right depressed state she did.'

'Well, go down the garden and give her a shout over the fence. Tell her to bring Peggy round here with her. What I've got to tell them will put a smile on their faces, I'll be bound.'

Joyce hurried to put her cleaning things back in the cupboard and to set the teacups out ready. Couldn't have a discussion without a cup of tea.

'I have found the ideal place for Peter to run his own business repairing boots and shoes. And best of all it is right in the centre of Tooting Broadway and you can't get a busier place than that.' Joe Russell drew himself up to his full height, puffed out his chest and let his amazing news sink in. He glanced at the three faces in turn, thrilled to bits to see that they were gazing at him as if he were a magician who had just pulled off a fantastic trick.

'You mean it, Dad?'

He nodded.

Joyce stubbornly wanted to know all the details. 'Start from the beginning,' she said briskly.

'I don't know how I'm ever going to be able to repay you,' Peggy James mumbled.

'Don't be so daft,' Joe Russell said quickly. His heart was so full that he had to take a deep breath before he could begin to tell them all his news. 'Almost the first bloke I spoke to yesterday morning put me onto Luke Wyneberg, he works in the railway ticket office at Worcester Park. Seems his uncle has had this cobbler's shop for years. It got too much for him, although he did employ one man, and he's been trying to flog off the lease for ages. He didn't have any luck and because he's over seventy and not in very good health he closed the shop down a month ago. Windows have been boarded up ever since.'

A hush settled over everyone as they gazed at Joe in amazement.

'Oh, Joe, you're a good man.' Joyce stared at her husband and pointing to Becky murmured, 'Look at her face, you've made her day.'

'Women!' Joe exclaimed, laughing loudly, 'you've all jumped to the conclusion that it's all cut an' dried. You might at least let me finish.'

'Go on then, Dad, have your moment of glory,' Becky said, her eyes twinkling with devilment.

'Well, just you listen to this, Miss Clever-Clogs.' Her father said as he grinned broadly. 'This morning I've been to Tooting with Luke. The place really is ideal. The position, as I've already said, couldn't be better and the living accommodation upstairs really surprised me. There's a big living room and a roomy kitchen, two bedrooms and believe it or not a bathroom. The ground floor is just the large front shop with another room at the back which has obviously been used as a workroom.

'With a jolly good clean and a bit of outlay for material Peter could be in business within a very short time.

'The setup is complete. It hasn't been touched. There's a high counter just inside the shop door, and a workbench runs the full length of the far wall and as far as I could tell there was a great many tools of the trade lying about. Out in the back room there was a Singer sewing machine which was worked by means of a foot treadle and another machine whose purpose Luke and I could only guess at. We came up with the idea between us that it might be a finishing machine.'

'Oh, Dad!' Becky couldn't put her feelings into words, so she smiled and squeezed his arm.

'Hang on, lass, I've got the gory details to tell you yet.'

Now comes the crunch, Becky was thinking; the fear that all this was going to cost far more than all Peter's friends could come up with was nagging away at her.

'Don't look like that,' Joe said, directing his voice at Peggy, 'I won't say it was easy cos it weren't but I think I've been able to swing it. It's all down to Luke. He's the only living relative that Mr Wyneberg has. We did quite a bit of bargaining and here's what Luke finally proposed. Fifty pounds key money, Peter can rent the premises at a very low rent for one year. By the end of the year the rent will be increased or, should Peter feel he is doing well, Luke has promised he will be given the option of buying the lease. I've told him I shall go over and lay all the facts before Peter this evening and if he's in agreement we'll contact the solicitor who is acting for Luke and on behalf of Mr Wyneberg tomorrow.' The room was charged with excitement and Joe held up his hand and added, 'Luke has agreed to pay for the premises to be cleaned and to distemper the walls of the shop.'

Joyce and Peggy hugged each other, both near to tears,

then Joyce stood back and looked at her daughter. 'You're a good girl, Becky. A couple of days ago yer dad said he wasn't a miracle-worker. Well, now he's proved he is, but it was you that set the ball rolling.'

Peggy came to stand in front of Becky. 'Thanks, luv,' she said gratefully, 'my Ella's got a damn good friend in you.'

'Sharing troubles is what friends are for,' Becky said kindly, wishing she could be around to see all these preparations get underway. Alas, she had to return to London. She had a new job waiting for her and who knew what else the future might hold?

Chapter Twenty-two

'CAREFUL,' LILY MAYNARD called out anxiously, 'the way you're slamming that iron about your uniform will be ruined.'

Becky stopped ironing and stared at Aunt Lil. 'It's these damn pearl buttons, they're driving me mad,' she replied, frowning.

'Well it's not like you to cuss, and it sounds vulgar and common which is definitely not like you and while I'm about it I might just as well 'ave my say. Something is wrong with both you and May.'

'What?' Becky snapped as she laid the flat iron down on its stand and turned to face Aunt Lil.

'I said things are not right with the pair of you.'

'How d' you make that out?'

Aunt Lil regarded her curiously. 'Becky, luv, I could be blind in one eye an' still see that neither of you two girls are acting normal. One minute you're both as nice as pie, the next you're biting my head off. And you've become so moody. Is there anything you'd like to tell me?'

'No. Nothing.'

'Sorry for asking,' Lil said and turned to walk away.

Becky's mood changed abruptly, and she thrust her arm out. 'I'm sorry, Aunt Lil, I didn't mean to snap at you.'

'That's all right, luv, leave that ironing. I'll finish it for you in a minute, but I've just made a fresh pot of tea so give May a call and we'll all sit down and have a cup together.'

I'm a nervous wreck, Becky thought to herself as she went out into the passage to call up the stairs to May. I just wish I could creep back up to bed, pull the covers right up over my head and stay there in the darkness until my head stops throbbing. But there's no chance of that. Not for hours to come.

Lil had laid out the big breakfast cups and saucers. She poured milk from the bottle into a china jug that had a pattern of roses on each side. She was brooding over what the future held for her two girls when May and Becky came into the room together.

'Here, one of you kneel down on the hearth rug and make the toast.' She held out the long-handled toasting fork, on which she had speared a thick slice of bread, and Becky took it. 'And you, May, can fetch the rashers of bacon from the oven and put them on the table. It'll be your own fault if they're dried up, lying in bed till this time of the day.'

With a full plate in front of each of them and their tea poured out Aunt Lil thought, well, it's now or never. Taking a deep breath she stated, 'It's been all of eight months since you two started this outside catering lark and I can't say that just lately it's been doing you a lot of good.'

May moved her toast around and pretended to study the pattern on her plate. Lil sensed both girls' reluctance to discuss the matter.

'Well, if you won't let on what's gone wrong I'll take a wild guess. You're both doing nicely, as regards funds. You've told me that much and very generous you are to me and I know you, Becky, send money home to yer mum, so it can't be that. A lot of your money comes from bonuses, am I right?'

Becky took a sip of her tea and placed the cup down on the saucer. 'Yes that's quite right, Aunt Lil. When the company or client pay the total bill to Lyons they apparently add a percentage for the staff, and it's given to us once a month as a bonus.'

'So, is the work too much? Is that what's getting you down?'

'Nothing's getting us down,' May snapped.

'Look here young lady,' Lil pointed a finger at her niece, 'you can't kid me, I know you too well. Sitting there looking all gormless. A jolly good night's sleep is what both of you could do with. A quarter to three it was this morning when you two crept up the stairs and don't bother to tell me that you were working t' that hour cos I wasn't born yesterday.'

May and Becky looked at each other and the realization that they were going to have to come up with some explanation was apparent to both of them.

'Oh, Aunt!' May couldn't hide the emotion in her voice as she caught hold of Lily's hand. 'We don't mean to snap at you. We both appreciate everything you do for us. It's just that some of these functions are damned hard work. We do earn nearly twice as much as we did at the Corner House but don't get much free time. Evening social gatherings aren't so bad but some of the daytime functions can carry on over into most of the evening and by then our feet are killing us.'

'That's typical of you, May. Skirt around the truth. Everything you've said about the job I'm sure is dead right. Being on your feet for hours on end can't be a picnic for either of you. But don't take me for a complete fool.'

The colour rose in May's cheeks as she stared at her aunt.

'No men friends, keeping you out all hours of the night?' Lil asked the question, looking at each girl in turn. 'You can't tell me you've got your noses to the grindstone morning, noon and night. What about all these new clothes? Where are you off to when you wear them, eh? All right, tell me I'm a nosy old bitch and what you two choose to do in your free time is none of my business but just remember this, fancy feathers don't make fine birds and the men you're going out with might just have the sense to see that. If they don't then they aren't worth bothering about.'

Lily Maynard sighed heavily and leant back in her chair. She'd had her say. As deeply as she cared for each of these girls there was not much else she could do short of meeting them daily when they finished work and forcibly dragging them home. They weren't children. They were grown-up young ladies and much as it pained her to stand by and watch they had to be allowed to make their own mistakes. She just hoped and prayed if the time came when they really needed her she would still be around to help them pick up the pieces.

Becky had never felt so guilty. May's Aunt Lil had taken her in, treating her as if she were her own daughter and this was how she was repaying her. She looked around the homely living room. Every surface was covered with photograph frames containing happy pictures of Lily and her husband, her sister and her family but no children of her own. Such a tiny grey-haired lady was Lil, yet energy and enthusiasm for life still burst from that small frame. She dressed in a very old-fashioned way, almost always with a shawl draped round her shoulders. She was like a relic from another age but of one thing Becky was certain, Aunt Lil had a big heart and she loved her dearly.

May stood up, eyes downcast, as she apologized to her aunt. 'We'll come straight home this evening, Aunt Lil, promise. All we have on is an afternoon do and as soon as we've cleared up we'll head straight home, nice cosy evening round the fire. How's that sound?'

Lil's eyes were wide and Becky thought she saw a glimmer of amusement in them. 'That go for you too, Becky?' Lil asked. 'Cos if it does I'll have a roast dinner ready.'

'Certainly does, can't wait,' Becky said, and smiled with relief. Aunt Lil was an absolute darling. Both she and May were causing her a lot of worry and when she came to think about it she hadn't played fair with her own family. Two months into 1927 and she hadn't been home since Christmas and then it had only been a flying visit just for the one day. She hadn't even seen Ella. She had left presents for both Ella and Peter with her parents and both girls had been remembered too but it wasn't the same as seeing them and giving the presents in person.

Both girls! It didn't seem possible but it was true. Ella had given birth to her second daughter in July last year. That made just thirteen months between Amy, the new baby, and Margaret. God alone knows how Ella manages, Becky was saying to herself, remembering that if it weren't for her dad she wouldn't get half as much news from home. Sometimes she met her dad on the railway station if their turns fitted in and sometimes he popped into Lil's house in South Lambeth Road. According to him, Peter was holding his own in his business venture. Only just, it seemed, but then again as Aunt Lil was fond of saying, a crust is better than no bread at all.

'You finished daydreaming?' May asked Becky with laughter in her voice, 'because we ought to be making a move.'

'I'll finish off your uniform and pack it in yer case,' Lil told Becky as she ushered them out of the kitchen. 'What about you, May, is your outfit all right?'

'My apron an' cap could do with an iron rubbed over them, please.'

'Hurry up then, fetch them and hand them down over the banisters.'

Lil shook her head as she took the padded iron holder down from where it hung on a hook to the side of the mantelshelf. 'Young girls!' she said aloud. Winding it round the handle she raised the hot iron from the range and spat on the clean surface.

If only she could iron out the girls' difficulties as easily as she could iron their dresses. The pair of them could protest till the cows came home, she hadn't any illusions about what they were getting up to. How could she expect either of them to find a working-class lad, marry him and settle down, after the life they'd become accustomed to? Out on the town with these young toffs. Did they really see their future with that type of man? If they did she was very much afraid that they were in for a rude awakening.

It was bitterly cold, with frost still sparkling on the rooftops, and the pavements were treacherous to walk on even though it was now almost eleven o'clock when May and Becky climbed aboard the tram. The atmosphere inside was damp and steamy. The passengers were mainly women, wrapped up well against the cold, scarves tied over their heads and knotted tightly beneath their chins, clutching empty baskets or shopping bags.

May and Becky each wore a small close-fitting hat, the only adornment being a bow of ribbon which had been chosen to tone in with the grey coat that Becky wore and the plum-coloured coat of May's respectively.

'They're making for Vauxhall Bridge market I suppose,' May remarked as she looked about her.

'Yeah, at least we don't have to wonder where our next meal is coming from, do we?' Becky replied.

'Got a lot t' be grateful for when you work it out,' May sighed.

The afternoon function they had been assigned to was being held on the third floor of the Coventry Street Corner House.

'Long time since we walked through these doors,' Becky stated as she let the big door swing to behind her.

'Good, I'm glad to see some of you are early, there is so much to do.' Miss Paige spoke in a clipped voice full of authority. She was in charge of all the female staff that worked on Outside Catering. She was small and plump and showed signs of having been very beautiful in her younger days. Her complexion was dark, her cheeks well-rouged. Her brown eyes were smiling as she approached May and Rebecca.

'I always know I may rely on you two,' she said, smoothing a hand over the crisp, white damask tablecloth. May had begun to lay out the fine china while Becky was sorting out the heavy silver cutlery.

More girls arrived and cries of greetings were called to May and to Becky. It was good to be back in Coventry Street, to be surrounded by well-remembered things and good friends.

Today's do was a small, intimate ladies' afternoon tea. It would feel different, easy.

'A piece of cake, this do,' May remarked as they unfurled yet another small tablecloth.

When they had to cope with large numbers some of the cloths used could measure as much as twenty-four feet in length and as most of the Nippies would agree, tablecloths of that size were a bugger to lay straight.

'They're all a bit posh like,' Becky remarked as the well-dressed ladies trooped in and took their places at the small round tables which were each set for six. 'Maybe, when we're older, we'll be going to afternoon dos such as this.'

'Yeah, an' maybe we'll be like those women on the tram. Half a dozen kids at home an' us out looking for the cheapest cuts of meat,' came May's quick reply.

Becky shrugged and laughed. 'Not me! I'll make sure of that.'

'Suppose you're banking on Gerald Palmer offering to marry you so's you can live happy ever after.'

'Oh, May, don't tease. Not today, please.'

May straightened her starched apron and twisted the cuffs of her long sleeves. 'Stop lying to yourself, Becky. I know now I didn't pick a winner in Roger Macclesfield but then I never let things get out of hand. Gerald Palmer is . . .' May stopped abruptly, flicking her hand through the air in a gesture that was almost angry. 'For crying out loud, don't look at me like that, Becky. You don't need me to tell you what Gerald's intentions are. I'm beginning to wonder if you have all your marbles straight. You're inclined to believe everything he tells you, no matter how many times he lets you down you go back for more.'

'But . . .' Becky bit her lip. She didn't want to hear this. Not from her best friend. Tears were stinging the back of her eyelids. She blinked hard. Becky might have understood her friend's attitude better if May had told her more about why Roger Macclesfield had suddenly disappeared from sight.

All she really knew was that she had heard May sobbing in the early hours of the morning and had gone along to her bedroom. Just to see the state that May was in had made her heart ache. There hadn't been anything that she could do except climb in beneath the covers and hold her close.

Never ever will I forget the words that May uttered between her sobs. Even remembering them now makes me shudder, Becky was saying quietly to herself, the memory still vivid.

'It's not fair, Becky.' May had raised her tearstained face from the pillow, and whispered the words.

Becky had patted her affectionately. 'No one ever said life was fair.'

'I'm sorry I woke you up, Becky.'

'Don't be daft, May. We're friends, remember.'

May had sniffed hard before replying. 'Just tell me this, Becky. Why is it that both you and I had to attract rotters? Both Gerald and Roger acted like real gents to us at first. We told ourselves what we wanted to believe, that we'd found two good 'uns, but it turned out that I for one hadn't had that sort of luck.'

'It's not your fault, May. It's a shame that Roger went off without a word and I only wish you would tell me the real reason.'

Becky still tried to shut out the sad picture of May sitting up in bed, telling her, 'When it came down to rock bottom I hardly knew anything at all about Roger. Now I want to forget him. Just make sure that Gerald doesn't use you the same way!'

Those last words of May's had given Becky a few sleepless nights and they still rankled as she turned them over in her mind.

'Hark at them!' May had come alongside Becky and broken into her thoughts. 'You'd think to hear these women chattering away that the room was full of magpies.'

Becky laid her tray down on the dumbwaiter and laughed.

'I've just had a word with Miss Paige and she said we can take fifteen minutes, get ourselves a cuppa.'

'Thank God for that,' May said with a grin. 'I hate it when we have to stand around the wall while all the speeches and presentations are being made.'

'Hey, wait for me,' Becky protested as May made a beeline for the still room.

Shoes kicked off and a most welcome cup of tea in her hand, Becky let her mind wander back to Gerald. Here and now she would agree that she ought to heed May's warnings. Right from the start May had distrusted Gerald. Then again May hadn't been so wise when it came to Roger. Poor May, she had been let down badly.

That hadn't altered the way she felt. The moment she saw Gerald her heart would start thumping nineteen to the dozen. Becky sighed heavily. It was all right to be wary and suspicious when she was apart from Gerald, but a different matter when she was with him. His very nearness made her throw caution to the wind. It was his face, his smile, and those eyes! Looking into Gerald's eyes her whole world changed.

He liked her, maybe even loved her, look how he looked at her, the attention he paid her, the presents he offered. Was all that because of true feelings he had for her?

Sometimes she was sure it was. He often did say he loved her. I love him, she breathed. God help me I do. Totally and utterly. He's the man I would like to be with every day and every night for the rest of my life.

Be honest, she chided herself. There had been times when Gerald's desire had got the better of him and when she had put a stop to his wandering hands he had become very ill-tempered. Of one thing she was sure, she wouldn't be able to keep him dangling much longer. If she refused him again, it would be over. All of it. Not just the theatre trips, race meetings and days on the river but also her dreams of a wonderful secure future.

She thought of Ella. Peter was a nice enough fellow but

what had he given Ella? Two lovely daughters, but with hardly a breathing space between the two of them. No means of support until she and her dad had stepped in and even now, by all accounts, they lived a hand-to-mouth existence.

She didn't want to end up like Ella.

A sudden surge of guilt swept over her. Was she really in love with Gerald? Maybe she was in love with his way of life and the good times he provided. Did Gerald love her? May would assure her he didn't. Many's the time she had suspected that May was right.

Gerald wanted her. Oh yes! If she gave in to his demands would he propose marriage? She was tempted to find out. Marriage to Gerald Palmer would mean genuine security. Never having to scrimp and save. Gerald might be her only chance.

A roaring cheer came from the restaurant, and the sound of clapping. May sat up in her chair, reached over and patted Becky's knee. 'Wakey, wakey, luv, all the girls are making a move, so let's be having you. The quicker we see this lot off the quicker we'll be home eating Aunt Lil's roast.'

The prospect made Becky's mouth water. She shook her head to clear it. An evening indoors, sitting around a well banked-up fire with Aunt Lil and May for company, well, she couldn't imagine anything nicer.

Even Gerald Palmer couldn't top that. Not tonight he couldn't.

Chapter Twenty-three

PAUSING BEFORE THE full-length mirror set in the door of her wardrobe, Becky inspected herself from top to toe. She wore a calf-length, sleeveless black dress with a black long-sleeved chiffon jacket. The only adornment was a small silver brooch which she wore high on the left shoulder of the dress. Her hair had been set that afternoon and lay thick and silky in the new shorter style that still suited her so well. The sides curled forward covering her ears and framed her face beautifully.

She looked right, she decided.

Gerald Palmer was taking her for dinner and then on to a show. She reached for her white swagger coat; it wasn't exactly suitable for evening wear but it was the best she had. Being three-quarters in length and with a full swing to the back she could get away with draping it around her shoulders. Taking up her small black evening bag she hurried down the stairs and out into the front garden.

It had been a lovely bright day bringing a promise of spring and with Easter less than three weeks away, Aunt Lil was on her knees setting out a few bedding plants in sheltered spots.

'It's getting chilly out here, Aunt Lil. Shouldn't you pack up for today and go inside?'

'Oh, I've almost finished, dear. Another five minutes and I will go indoors,' she promised cheerfully. 'You have a lovely evening.'

Becky turned as a car drew into the kerb and Gerald called out, 'Good evening, Mrs Maynard.'

Lily just raised her hand in reply.

Becky leant down and kissed Aunt Lil. 'Don't stay out here till you catch a cold, will you?'

'No, truly, I'm almost done. Go on, enjoy yourself.'

Watching Becky walk down the path, get into the car and drive off with Gerald, Lily Maynard was recalling her brief encounter with Gerald Palmer when Becky had first taken up with him. She had disliked him on sight. She had sensed a kind of ruthlessness beneath that charming smile, and she wondered, as she had so many times since, why was it that men with money, men who dressed so well, seemed to have a special attraction for young women. Becky could daydream all she liked but if marriage was what Gerald Palmer had in mind then she'd eat her hat. Toffs like him didn't marry working girls. She had been wrong about Roger Macclesfield. Him she had believed to be a good one.

Oh, May hadn't said anything. Not one word. She hadn't needed to. Just one look at May's face and she could tell how she was suffering. Let down just as sure as Becky would be the way she was going on, but you couldn't tell them. They wouldn't thank you for it and they'd go their own way no matter what advice she dished out. Trouble with Becky was, she was such a trusting little soul.

One day both girls may be lucky and meet a decent man, she was wishing as she gathered up her gardening tools. The words were as much a prayer as a wish.

'Will you be working over Easter?' Gerald asked Becky when they were seated in the lounge bar of the restaurant having coffee and after-dinner liqueurs.

Becky wondered why Gerald had bothered to ask that question. Bank holidays were a time when Gerald disappeared, rarely if ever mentioning where he had been. Up to now she had never set eyes on him during any public holiday. She had always assumed that he spent the time with his parents, not that she knew anything about his mother and father. Gerald shied away from answering any personal questions.

A weary sigh escaped from Becky's lips before she answered. 'Afraid so. Three days on the trot. Huge luncheon with royalty in attendance at the Albert Hall on the Thursday before the holiday.'

'Oh! What's that in aid of?'

'Some charity. Not sure which one. Itinerary we've been given merely states that as soon as coffee is served we are to marshal a line of young children up on to the stage in single file. Apparently each child is presenting a purse of money which has been collected for good causes.'

'Where do the children come from? Are they sons and daughters of diplomats?'

'I wouldn't think so, more like from Guides' and Scouts' organizations would be my guess.'

'You will get a few days off following the holiday?'

Suddenly Becky was uncomfortably aware of Gerald's eyes on her.

'Why don't we go down to Brighton for the rest of the week?' he asked casually. 'I've got a pal who has a nice place the other side of Hove. Don't worry, Becky,' he teased, 'I'm sure he'll find you a single bedroom even if I have to muck in with another chap.'

Gerald noticed that she coloured up and hesitated for a moment before answering. 'I don't think I should expect to stay with your friend. He's never met me.'

'Oh come on, Rebecca,' he pleaded, sounding very formal with the full use of her name. 'My friends drop in on each other all the time. They will love you. Besides you say yourself you are always worn out after waiting on several large gatherings. There's nothing more restful than lying on a chaise-longue and gazing out over the sea. I'll pick you up in the car at ten on Thursday. Find a cosy pub on the way down to have lunch, arrive at John's place about four, stay at least over the weekend and you'll feel so fit and well you won't know yourself. I promise.'

Becky looked at his smiling face. He was as eager as a schoolboy for her to agree. She wavered. 'All right. But . . .' her lip trembled, which only endeared her to him all the more. 'What if your friend doesn't like me? Doesn't want me to stay in his house?'

'That won't happen. It won't be like that. How can I convince you? John Gadsdon and I were at university together. He will make you very welcome.'

The die was cast. There was no going back, not unless she wanted Gerald to walk out of her life forever. Gerald leant forward, took Becky's liqueur glass from her hand and set it down on the table. His eyes were wide and bright, his smile beaming as he took her hands between his own. 'Darling,' he whispered, 'however hard you try you'll never make me happier than you have at this moment. I can't wait to have you all to myself.'

'I'm glad you're pleased,' she told him, her head still buzzing with misgivings.

'Pleased? That's the understatement of the year.'

'What will you be doing over Easter?' she asked, more to dampen his enthusiasm than out of curiosity.

There was a moment of silence before he answered, during which Becky felt that she had asked the wrong thing. 'I have to go to Scotland,' he told Becky. 'My long-suffering parents have given me an ultimatum.'

Good job I'm working then, Becky thought to herself, but had the good sense not to utter the words aloud. A sudden thought struck her. Ultimatum? She'd give a lot to know the exact terms or better still to be a fly on the wall while Gerald was in Scotland. Even a crystal ball would be useful where Gerald was concerned.

'For goodness sake try and look happy,' Gerald rebuked her. 'It's time we were making a move if we are to get to the theatre in time.' Ever the gentleman, Gerald rose to his feet, took her hand and raised it to his lips. Becky couldn't help laughing. 'That's better, that's my darling girl,' he whispered, his lips now brushing softly against her ear.

Becky took a step backwards and smiled up at him at the same time reflecting to herself that it was a good job Gerald wasn't able to read her thoughts.

Brighton weather at this time of the year was glorious: too cold for swimming in the sea, but with the nice warm breezes of perfect spring days. What a beautiful, busy place! Becky was delighted as Gerald drove all along Brighton sea-front, revealing not one pier but two. The wide promenade was colourful with residents and day-trippers taking gentle exercise. Across the wide road lay the great squares with massive, tall, graceful houses on three sides and a centre patch of emerald grass surrounded by ornate railings. To her the whole area was fascinating.

Gerald headed towards Hove, with its even more select gardens and a better class of cafés and taverns. Soon he had left the seafront behind, climbing upwards with the Downs in the distance, taking a route along narrow leafy lanes.

From the road the house had been invisible, protected from nosy-parkers by tall hedges and a long rutted driveway. At first sight Becky had squealed with surprise. It was so old, looking as if it hadn't altered for centuries, gathering over the years a protective covering of ivy and moss. Tiny little windows set deep in the stone walls sparkled a welcome.

The moment of pleasure had gone as soon as Gerald had put the key in the door and with a great smile on his face bid her enter. One look around and she wanted to flee, run away, vanish. Go anywhere other than stay here. She felt trapped. She couldn't look at Gerald. She stood with her hand clenched over her mouth, somehow managing to control her panic.

'You knew no one else would be here,' Becky's accusation came out in a clear, clipped tone.

'Would you have come if I'd told you we would have the place to ourselves?'

'That's not the point,' Becky protested, but before she could say another word Gerald crossed the floor to stand directly in front of her, his face flushed, his eyes stern. Without haste he took hold of her arms and held them in a tight grip.

'You need to grow up, Rebecca. I think I have been very patient with you. You know exactly how I feel about you, you've known from the very beginning. I love you. You drive me wild at times the way you tease and then walk away. A man can only take so much.'

While he had been speaking his grip on her arms had tightened until he was hurting her. She lifted her head and looked at him. 'You really believe I set out to tease you?'

He read the expression on her face and smiled. 'Yes, I do believe it. You accept everything and give nothing in return.'

'What have I got to give you?' she asked cautiously.

'Don't put on your little girl act, Becky,' he said sternly. 'You know damn well I don't mean material things. A few days. A whole week, a lifetime, that's what I want to spend with you, but if the whole idea of being alone with me is so repulsive to you then get back in the car and I will drive you straight back to London.' He released his hold on her and turned to leave the room.

'Why didn't you tell me before?' Becky said at last.

He turned back to face her. 'I was saving it. The thought of us being together in this lovely house. It was something I'd dreamt of. Most of the time when I do get to see you, you're tired out from having been on your feet for hours. This was to be our time. Time for each other and time with each other. Do you not feel the same?'

Tears were stinging the back of her eyes. Oh, he could be such a lovely man at times, so gentle, how could she not love him?

'But ... Gerald, if we stay here won't someone find out?'

Gerald laughed. 'You, my darling, are one of a kind! I promise we will be very discreet.'

She smiled.

'Does that smile mean I can bring our cases in?'

She nodded.

'Right, then I shall give you a grand tour of inspection. After that I shall feed you. See, I have thought of everything, right down to ham, bread, eggs and milk.'

'Gerald, you have been very clever.'

If he thought there was more than one way of taking that statement he had the sense to keep quiet.

Gerald gathered up the suitcases and bags and said, 'Follow me. Bathroom and lavatory facing us, top of the stairs.'

The bath was huge with brass taps and a copper water-heater fixed to the wall. The lavatory was boxed in with a wooden frame and also had a wooden seat. Its long chain had a china handle with a pattern of flowers on it. Further along the passage Gerald put down the things he was carrying and opened another door. The first impression Becky got was of bright sunshine streaming out from the room beyond.

'Go right in, take a look at the view,' he ordered with a grin.

'Unbelievable,' Becky cried, 'I can see the sea.'

'I wasn't lying when I said you could stretch out, rest and look at the sea. In the next room there are french windows which open out on to a balcony and that's where I pictured you.'

'Oh Gerald, everything is so old, these wooden floorboards don't even look safe an' yet everything is so beautiful. Really lovely.'

'Will you stay?' he very quietly asked. 'I do want you to be happy.'

Turning her head away from the window, she answered just as quietly. 'I think we shall both be very happy here.'

In three strides he was beside her. For a moment there was silence as they looked at each other. And then Gerald smiled and said, 'I do love you Rebecca, and I'm never going to let you go.' He opened his arms wide. It was all she needed.

'Oh, Gerald . . .'

Her feet began to slip on the polished wood as she moved. He caught her and swung her up into his arms, twirling her round and round, and their bags and cases lay unheeded out in the passage where Gerald had put them down. He carried her to the big bed, gently laid her down and then stretched himself alongside of her.

There was no one to disturb them. No necessity for them to leave that beautiful room.

Becky's thoughts had run along the lines that when Gerald finally made love to her it would be painful and very embarrassing. Happily, there was no embarrassment. At the first touch of his fingers on her bare flesh she felt Gerald was taking her away from reality. At one point she had cried out the pain was so sharp, like a jagged knife cutting into her. For the main part it was as if Gerald had transported her into a seventh heaven. He was tender, loving, concerned. She would never be able to put into words exactly how she felt.

She must have slept.

'Hello,' he said. He was standing beside the bed, holding a tray of tea, smiling down at her. He was bare-chested and she immediately thought how marvellous he looked. His body was tanned and his shoulders broad.

She struggled to sit up. 'Fancy me falling asleep.'

'They say there is a first time for everything, well let me tell you, young lady, this is the first time that I have brought tea to a lady in bed.' He laughed. 'Must be true that love does funny things to a person.'

Becky raised herself up on her elbows. 'Love?' she queried softly.

He laid the tea tray down on a side table and with one hand he tucked the sheet around her bare shoulders. It was a tender gesture. Then he placed his lips to her forehead. 'I love you very much,' he said huskily.

Becky's eyes lit up with joy. 'Shall I tell you something?'

'What?'

'I love you.'

His expression became serious. 'I hope you do. I'll pour us both out a cup of tea, shall I?'

With Gerald sitting on the side of the bed and Becky propped up by the pillows, they drank their tea in a companionable silence.

'Becky, would you mind if I suggested we didn't go out tonight? I can light a fire downstairs and we could make do with the food we've got here. I don't want to share you with a host of people in a restaurant, not tonight.'

'Oh, Gerald! That's a lovely idea. I don't want to share you either.'

First Gerald showed her the layout of downstairs. The kitchen had a stone-flagged floor, two huge larders and a cooking range the like of which she had never seen before. A door opened out to a neat garden at the end of which lay toolsheds and a wooden hut that was stacked to the rafters with cut logs. 'Hold your arms out,' Gerald insisted, 'we'll each carry an armful of these logs and then the fire will burn all the evening.'

A real log fire and just herself and Gerald. Becky couldn't wait. Surely she couldn't ask for a more romantic setting than that?

Back inside the house Becky marvelled at the splendour of the dining room which to her mind resembled a very posh antique shop.

'We won't bother to eat in here,' Gerald grinned. 'Come and see the sitting room, it's very cosy.'

Cosy was the right word, Becky decided. Warm and

welcoming with soft creamy wallpaper. Two settees covered in a floral chintz and scattered with huge plump cushions were drawn up on each side of the fireplace while smaller chairs and oval side tables were set around the room. The lighting came from two brass lamps, each with a pleated cream silk shade with long fringe and tassels.

'Soon have the fire going,' Gerald told her. 'By the time you've bathed and changed this room will be nice and warm.'

Later, with the curtains drawn and the fire blazing in the open hearth, they ate a simple meal and by the time they both agreed it was time for bed, Becky was positive that it had been one of the nicest evenings she had ever spent.

Next morning Becky made the bed, hung the clothes they had worn the previous day in the wardrobe, put the suitcases out of sight under the bed and went downstairs to find Gerald was laying the table for breakfast.

Gerald looked totally different. He was wearing brown corduroy trousers, a cream coloured polo-necked jumper, and heavy brogue shoes. Casual clothes made him look even more handsome, she concluded.

'You're an old lazybones,' he complained. 'I've been up for ages.'

She threw her arms around his neck. 'Have I told you that I love you?'

'Not today you haven't.'

'Well, I do.'

'And I love you, my darling.'

'Say it again,' she begged.

'I'll say it a hundred times if you want. I love you, Rebecca Russell.'

'You haven't kissed me today.'

'Well, we can soon remedy that.' He kissed her. Many times. Long lingering sweet kisses. Finally he broke the embrace. 'I see I shall have to be more strict with you.' Playfully he slapped her bottom. 'Sit yourself up at the table. I need nourishment to keep up with you.'

Her eyes twinkled. 'Then you'd better eat a hearty breakfast.'

'I fully intend to,' he answered, grinning broadly.

Becky hummed quietly to herself as she washed the breakfast dishes. She had never felt happier. It was as if she and Gerald were already married. The future now looked bright for her. And the good thing about it was that Gerald would be able to provide all the things they would need. There would be no scrimping and hard times such as Ella and Peter had had to endure. Thank you, she prayed silently in her head. I am so lucky to have Gerald.

'Shall I get the car out or shall we walk and explore?' Gerald asked, rising from his chair.

'Let's walk.' Becky smiled in a satisfied way. 'It's such a lovely morning and I'd love to walk by the sea.'

Gerald laughed out loud. 'In that case I shall get the car. Just because you can see the sea from the bedroom window doesn't mean it's nearby. We are high up here, that's the reason for the lovely views.'

Later in the day Gerald parked the car and they scrambled down over a wooden jetty on to the beach. The tide was high and once out in the open the breeze caught Becky's hair and blew it about. 'I wish I had brought a scarf to wear,' she moaned.

Taking a clean white handkerchief from his pocket Gerald tied a knot in each of the four corners. 'Here, try this,' he said, drawing her to him and pulling the handkerchief tightly over her head. Suddenly he roared with laughter and Becky made to snatch the knotted cap from her head.

Gerald grasped her hand. 'No, leave it. Sorry I laughed but you remind me of the picture-postcards which always illustrate men day-trippers to the seaside with big fat bellies, rolled-up trouser legs, braces and a knotted handkerchief on their red balding heads.'

She looked at him in amazement. 'Oh, thanks a lot! You really know how to boost a girl's morale.'

Gerald decided he'd be better off out of Becky's reach. Still laughing fit to burst he sped off along the sand, his heavy shoes leaving deep footprints.

Becky watched. He was a different person tucked away down here in Sussex. More relaxed, easy-going – she was finding it very easy to love this man.

The day was turning out to be one of cloud and sunshine, with the sun popping in and out. She took a big breath and was surprised at the sharpness of the salt breeze. Together they walked, holding hands, until they found a grassy path that led up to a cobbled promenade. They sat on the stone wall and watched the sea come crashing in until the tide was so full that they were getting drenched from the spray.

When they felt hungry Gerald decided that they would return to the car and find themselves a local pub where they could have lunch.

The next two days passed all too quickly. Becky often wondered if she wouldn't wake up to find she was dreaming. They had no contact with the rest of the world. Gerald never even bought a newspaper when he went to the local shops for fruit, milk and bread. Neither of them saw the necessity for regular meals and they had only dined out one evening.

Becky woke on Sunday morning to the sad realization that it was to be their last day. Tomorrow, early in the morning, they would be returning to London. She did her best to close her mind to the prospect, refusing to think about it, and was glad when Gerald suggested they took a flask of coffee and go out for a walk.

Becky sighed softly as she looked around. She had to leave all this stillness behind. It was a lovely morning even though the wind was sharp. Each of them wore heavy sweaters and were sitting side by side high up on the Downs. Somewhere in the distance the grass was being mowed. Becky sniffed. The smell of the fresh-cut grass was wonderful. She leant back on her elbows and watched the wild flowers moving with the breeze, so small and pretty compared with the large floral arrangements that she often had to help display when waiting at functions. She ran her hands through the grass and found a long spiky piece. She pulled at it, tugging it out by the root. She held it up to the light and Gerald laughed. 'What are you going to do with it?' he asked.

'Smell it,' she ordered, pushing it towards his face.

'It's damp and dirty,' he cried, knocking it away and pulling her closer. He put his hand under her chin and lifted her oval face to his, kissed her small nose, marvelled at her big brown eyes and finally placed his lips on hers. Whenever Gerald kissed her, Becky was lost. She would have done anything for him, she decided, as her heart pounded and cheeks grew warm and flushed. Anything at all.

'I love you, Rebecca,' he said, pressing his lips against the top of her head, kissing her thick silky hair. 'I never want you to leave me.'

Suddenly an uneasy thought came to Becky. Gerald's mood had altered. He sounded very serious. She groped for an answer. 'Oh . . . Oh . . . Gerald, is this a proposal then?'

There was a long silence, then Gerald cleared his throat. 'I told you I never want you to leave me . . . but . . .' He hesitated and cleared his throat again, looked down, studied his shoes. When he looked up he fixed his eyes on Becky. 'I don't ever want to leave you but I can never marry you,' he announced, surprising himself and shocking her to the roots of her being. There, it's out at last, he thought. He had finally come out with the truth. Had found the courage to tell her what he should have told her months ago. Guilt surged through him as he sat gazing at Rebecca. Stupefied, totally at a loss for words, she stared back at him, distress and disbelief plainly showing on her face.

'Becky, my darling, believe me, please. We'd get married

tomorrow if it were up to me.' Gerald couldn't stop now, words began to tumble out of him breathlessly and in a great rush. 'My wedding is already arranged, and has been for ages. It is an agreement between our parents. It is not a matter of us loving each other, capital funds and land are the principal reasons.'

Becky's head was buzzing. She had felt the colour drain from her cheeks. She was praying for it not to be true, only hearing him as if from a long way off.

'Becky, say something, anything, just talk to me,' he begged her.

'Oh,' was about the only word she could mutter. She looked ghastly, her face had lost all of its colour, she was shaking and Gerald was truly alarmed as she gazed at him in disbelief.

'Becky, listen to me. I must make you understand.' He took hold of her shoulders and gently turned her face to him. 'As soon as funds are made available to me, real funds I assure you, we will find you a flat. Somewhere nice but discreet. You will be my wife in everything but name. Trust me, Becky. Please.'

There was a dumbfounded look still on Rebecca's face and she appeared to be incapable of moving. Yet in her mind's eye she was torturing herself. Gerald being married. Not to her but to some high society lady. She could actually feel the sense of glamour and excitement there would be at such a wedding.

The reception. Oh, she knew all about those. But only by waiting on the guests. She was good enough for that. In fact if you were to ask her superiors at Lyons they would probably express the opinion that she was excellent. There would be shimmering crystal chandeliers blazing from high up in the ceiling and masses and masses of flowers. Perhaps Nippies to run around with huge silver trays offering champagne from the very finest of glasses. Gerald would be seated at the top table side by side with his bride. Maybe he would request that she be on duty for that occasion. Maybe not. Maybe she should be waiting somewhere, a hotel room perhaps, in case his bride didn't suit his sexual demands. After all he knew now that she suited him just fine. After three days and three nights he could certainly boast that he had had her on approval.

What was it he had said? When 'his funds' were available it was his intention to set her up in a discreet flat, their very own love nest.

A weary sigh came from Gerald and Becky watched as he ran his hands through his hair distractedly. She was conscious of the fact that he was disappointed in her reaction. At this moment his charm and magnetism had deserted him. She still could not fully comprehend what his words had meant. She was however fully aware that she had been used. More than that, he had suggested that if and when he had the money he could go on using her for the rest of her life. Or at least until he tired of her.

Sadly her innermost bitter thought was that she had only herself to blame. She had believed only what she wanted to believe. She had spun her own dream. A dream that the good life and a good marriage could only come if a girl married a man that was well-off.

A peculiar feeling began to flow over her. She wanted to be sick. She was suffocating. She had the urge to get up and run. To run as fast as she could and not stop running until she had put a great distance between herself and Gerald Palmer.

As she struggled to her feet Gerald swung round, guessing what she had in mind. 'Wait, wait, don't be so silly,' he yelled at her.

Becky took no notice. She was up and running downhill as fast as her legs would carry her.

With a rush, Gerald went after her, confident that he could make her see sense if only she would stop and listen to him. With a flying tackle he caught her around the legs and she went down like a nine-pin. The trouble began as he went

down on top of her. 'God Almighty,' he called out at the top
of his voice, doing his damnedest to dig his heels in, find some
kind of a foothold. Nothing helped. He couldn't stop either
of them from rolling and bouncing downhill. It was minutes
before they came to a halt.

Gerald got to his feet and quickly bent to give Becky a
hand. One glance and the look on his face was astonishment,
which quickly changed to one of shock.

She looked a mess. She was lying on her side, not moving.
Blood was trickling down one leg and there was a nasty graze
on her forehead. This can't be happening, Gerald was telling
himself. A marvellous three days couldn't possibly end like
this. He tried to pick her up in his arms and then decided
he might do more harm than good if he moved her.

He could see one solitary man not far away, probably the
person who had been cutting the grass.

He pulled his sweater off, gently covered Becky's legs with
it, straightened up and braced himself, then moving with
speed and judgement he raced across the open ground.

Chapter Twenty-four

BECKY WANTED TO open her eyes, but she couldn't. The effort involved was too much. It felt as if her lashes were glued together.

She couldn't remember where she was. She didn't care much. When she tried to move every bone in her body ached and her head was splitting. She felt rather than saw someone lean over the bed in which she was lying and then a cool wet cloth was wiping her brow, her eyes and round her face. A dry cloth followed, doing exactly the same, being very gentle.

'Miss Russell, now you're awake would you like a cool drink?' It was a woman speaking, her voice calm and quiet.

Becky managed to open her eyes a fraction and saw whiteness everywhere; even the person bending over her was dressed in white.

'Don't struggle, Miss Russell. Have a few sips of water, I've got a feeding cup here for you, then if you still want to sit up I'll put the backrest up and fetch you some more pillows.'

'You're a nurse? I'm in hospital, aren't I?' Oh dear God, she swallowed, forcing herself to forget.

'Yes, you are. We've been taking good care of you, and the doctor was pleased that you had rested well during the night.'

Gerald! Tumbling, bumping, rolling over and over unable to stop or get away from him. No wonder she felt so sore. She had her wits about her now, fully aware of why she had been trying to get away from Gerald.

'Have a few more sips and then I'll leave you in peace

for a little while.' The kindly young nurse held the funny cup which had a spout to Rebecca's lips and very gratefully she drank.

'Thank you,' she said, then winced as she tried to move her arm out from under the bedsheet. She found she was wearing a cotton gown that had no fastenings and no sleeves. Her arm was badly grazed from the elbow down to her wrist.

'Can you lean forward a little, my dear?' the nurse asked. Becky tucked her head down and wriggled her bottom down the bed a little. It took a lot of effort. Nurse tugged at the metal backrest, and the jolt it gave sent sparks flying in Becky's head. Four pillows were plumped up, the door opened and another nurse appeared. 'Oh good,' said the first one that was seeing to the bed. 'You're just in time to help me raise Miss Russell up.'

Each nurse placed a hand under Becky's armpits and with no effort at all lifted her gently into position and she was able to rest her shoulders and head back against the mound of clean cool pillows.

'Does your head still hurt?' the second nurse asked with concern.

Becky forced a half-smile. This nurse was older but much prettier with ginger hair peeping out beneath her cap and a sprinkling of freckles across her nose. 'It feels as if there's a man inside banging away with a hammer,' Becky said in a voice that was little more than a whisper.

'I'll get the doctor to prescribe something for you that will help and then you can have a nice sleep, the doctor will be in to see you again later.'

The first nurse stayed in the room, tidying away what appeared to be washing things.

'How long have I been here?' Becky asked.

'Since midday yesterday,' the girl replied. 'Doctor was afraid you might be suffering from concussion. You were unconscious, that was why I was on duty here with you all night.'

Becky did not answer immediately and when she did it was only to murmur, 'Thank you.'

She made a supreme effort to sit up when the older nurse returned and gave her two tablets to swallow. She managed to drink some more water but was thankful when she felt soft hands pressing her back against the pillows and the blinds were drawn.

She wanted to sleep but her mind was taking her back to those sunny Sussex Downs. One minute she had been the happiest girl alive. Gerald had brought her away. To be on their own. To make love to her. To prove that he loved her, that he never wanted to be apart from her. They would be married, of that she had been certain. What other conclusion was there?

Oh, there had been another one! Another entirely different outcome, according to Gerald. He would make her his mistress. See her whenever he could spare the time away from his wife.

How silly she had been! Head in the clouds. Mrs Gerald Palmer – it had never been on the cards. Gerald Palmer came from a different world. She was Rebecca Russell from New Malden, working in a laundry until she had had the good fortune to get a job with Lyons. She had never been inside a London theatre until Gerald took her.

But she had been a virgin until Gerald took her.

Thinking back, Gerald had never seemed to take her seriously. There had always been that teasing look in his eye, sometimes even mocking. But he was so handsome that just looking at him took her breath away and he could be so charming.

Had been so charming!

She now knew that were she daft enough ever to see him again she could never hope to be anything more to him than just a kept woman. God, what was there for her to do now? She didn't feel as if she was any good to man nor beast. She felt guilty. She certainly felt used, in more ways than one.

She hadn't known a thing for the past twenty-four hours and now the tablets were working and she felt herself drifting back into nothingness. She fought it, but the medicine was too strong for her. Finally she yielded to it, and fell into a deep sleep once more.

The room seemed quite dark when Becky was woken by the door to her room being opened.

'Are you awake?' The redheaded nurse smiled warmly. 'Because you've got a visitor. I'll pull the curtains back while you sit yourself up.'

Oh no, Becky thought, horrified. What if it were Gerald? Relief flooded through her as May put her head around the door and the nurse grinned. 'Another redhead. She'll be able to cheer you up. I'll come back later, bring you both a cup of tea.'

'Hello, Becky, how are you?' May Stevens asked, forcing her tone to be bright and cheerful.

May was shocked. She couldn't miss the look of sadness on Rebecca's pale face and that awful bruise to the side of her forehead. She walked unsteadily across the room, where, with shaking hands, she made a great pretence of unbuttoning her coat before moving a chair up to the side of the bed. Leaning over the bed she softly kissed Becky's cheek, sat down on the chair and folded her hands in her lap. She stared down at them. Gerald Palmer had at least had the grace to come to the house and give her the news that Becky was in hospital. A Brighton hospital of all places. Those few minutes with that man would be fresh in her mind for a long while yet.

Thank God Aunt Lil hadn't been at home. The irony of the situation was that Aunt Lil was down at New Malden, spending a few days with Becky's parents. Both she and Becky had good reason to be grateful for that.

May Stevens smothered a sigh. This hospital room was deathly quiet. She wanted to mention Gerald Palmer, to ask Becky for her version of the events that had resulted in her admission to hospital, but before she could, Becky started to speak, as if it were a great relief to unburden herself. In words that almost choked her she gave May the bare bones of the weekend she had spent with Gerald.

A long silence followed and May felt she shouldn't be the one to break it. Much as her heart ached for Becky, and her hatred of Gerald Palmer festered like a sore within her, she stayed quiet.

A deep sigh escaped Becky's lips, and she said in a quiet sorrowful voice, 'I've been such a silly fool. I really did believe that Gerald loved me, that he wanted to marry me.' Becky's lips had begun to tremble and her eyes were wide and staring in her face that was white as chalk.

May took hold of her hand and peered deeply into her friend's eyes, and said in a tight voice, 'You're not the first to be deceived by a good-looking man and you won't be the last. I know full well that is no consolation to you right now but believe me, Becky, the pain will pass and you will see Gerald for the worthless man he really is.'

Becky was crying softly, the tears running unheeded down her cheeks. 'I'm lying when I say I believed Gerald would ask me to marry him. It was what I wanted, not what he wanted.'

May's green eyes were brimming with tears. 'We all make the same mistakes, Becky, luv,' she said calmly. 'Don't take all the blame on yourself.'

'I think I knew . . . all along . . . deep down inside. From the beginning I think I always knew Gerald had no intentions of marrying me,' she sobbed. 'I just kept hoping. Oh, May, the worst part is I do have to blame myself. You saw through Gerald and so did Aunt May and she only really met him the once.'

May took both of her hands in her own, doing her best to soothe her, to comfort her and the two girls gripped each other hard. But suddenly Becky pulled one hand away, rubbed at her eyes and cried out, 'Oh God, why did I do it? Why did I stay? Why didn't I walk away?'

May Stevens shook her head. Much as she loved Becky she had no answer for her. She had asked herself the same question dozens of times. She hadn't gone as far as letting Roger Macclesfield make love to her but she had believed with all her heart that his intention had been that one day he would propose to her. Everyone had liked Roger. Aunt Lil had gone so far as to say, 'He is a good man.' He had suddenly dropped her like a stone. The memory still hurt badly. They had met since, once in the street. Showing determination she had refused to sidestep. 'Why?' had been the only word she had uttered. How she wished she had never asked.

'Because, my dear, I came to realize that one cannot make a silk purse out of a sow's ear.'

That statement had hurt her more than a blow ever could have. She had never told a soul and it wouldn't help Becky to tell her now.

Becky's quiet sobbing slowly lessened, and finally it stopped. The two girls drew their hands free. May delved into her handbag, brought forth a clean handkerchief and wiped her friend's face.

Becky asked quietly, 'Does Aunt Lil know?'

'No, she doesn't, and neither she nor your parents need to be told. It would have been a different matter if you hadn't come round this morning. That is the way you want it to be, isn't it?'

'Oh May, I'm so lucky to have a friend like you. I couldn't bear it if they were to find out.'

For the first time since entering the room, May Stevens grinned broadly. 'I reckon we're damned lucky to 'ave each other. No other sod seems to want us.'

Becky looked startled and then realizing that what May had said was meant to make her laugh, she too attempted to smile. 'Tell me, how did you get here? How did you wangle the time off?'

'Aah! There yer 'ave a very different story,' May said, deliberately slipping back into her cockney form of speech. 'It were like this 'ere. Someone 'ad t' be told cos I ain't got any intentions of going back to the Smoke till I can take you with me. Miss Paige was my first thought. Then I sez t' meself, no, Mr Gower is a safer bet. Nice man is Mr Gower. Remember 'ow good 'ee were t' me when me mum died.'

Becky wiped her face with the handkerchief. For the moment tears were not needed and with little effort, even though the side of her face was very sore, she found she was laughing. 'Oh May,' she breathed.

Brushing a damp strand of hair back from Becky's forehead, May asked, 'Am I tiring you or shall I go on?'

'Please May, go on. You're the best tonic I could wish for.'

'Well, my luvverly. As usual Mr Gower came up trumps. He's a diamond is that man. Not only did he promise to cover for me and you with Miss Paige until such time as we reappeared, 'ee also found me a knight on a white charger.'

At this point, using her hip to push open the door, the youngest of the two nurses that had been attending to Rebecca came in bearing a wooden tray which held two cups and saucers, a pot of tea, a jug of milk, a plate of thinly cut bread and butter, and a dish on which was set out an assortment of small fancy cakes.

'Here we are then, young ladies, I'll put the tray on your locker, Miss Russell, and perhaps your friend will see to you. I'm sure you don't need me to stay.'

'No, we'll be fine thank you, Nurse.' It was May who answered the nurse, all the while thinking to herself that the only decent thing that Gerald Palmer had done was splash out some cash and make sure that Rebecca had been given a private single room. Not that Becky had queried it and she wasn't about to raise the matter. The toerag hadn't done it out of the goodness of his heart. Guilt was probably the only reason.

Becky run her fingers through her hair. It felt matted and greasy. She looked at her fingers and moaned; they were dirty.

'Don't tell me you're worried about your hair,' May exclaimed and began to laugh. 'We're a right pair, we are.'

Very gingerly Becky sipped at her tea, but she managed to eat two half slices of the thin bread and butter, although her lips felt sore and swollen.

'I've just remembered,' Becky said, 'before our tea arrived you were telling me that Mr Gower had found you a knight on a white charger. How come?'

'Bit of an exaggeration, that was,' May said, establishing a humorous tone for the telling of the remainder of the story. 'My knight was a Lyons van driver and 'is charger was one of the company's Leyland Tiger delivery vehicles. Very distinctive. Just as the name on the outside of all Lyons premises are emblazoned in pure gold leaf to make it too expensive for other firms to copy the same goes for all its vans now, don't yer know. You can see them coming for miles.'

'Really May! Don't tell me that this van driver was given permission by Mr Gower to drive you all the way down to Brighton,' Becky exclaimed, sounding doubtful. 'And I don't believe for one minute that Lyons vans have gold leaf advertisements on the sides.'

'Oh, there's nothing wrong with yer brain box, is there then?' May laughed. 'You're soon back on form. You're 'alf right, but only 'alf. This driver, who incidentally turned out t' be an old mate of mine, had a delivery to make in Horsham an' I was supposed to make me own way from there, but being the bloke that he is, he said what nobody don't know about won't 'urt 'em and we came sailing right through all along the sea-breezy front at Brighton an' on up the 'ill to this 'ospital.'

'That was very kind of your friend and very generous of Mr Gower in the first place.' Becky's eyes clouded and her lips trembled again. 'How much does Mr Gower know?'

'Not much, an' you don't need me to tell you that he is the soul of discretion. But there again Becky, he's not daft, he's known that you an' I 'ave been doing the town with some of the flash toffs so we can't blame 'im if 'ee puts two an' two together an' comes up with four. Can we?'

'No,' Becky sighed. 'Still, I will have to thank him.' Then looking at May carefully she asked, 'What about this old friend who's suddenly appeared on the scene? I didn't know you knew any of our van drivers.'

'Nor did I, until today. It was like being struck by lightning when Stan Riley climbed out of that cab. ''Adn't seen 'im for years. At one time Stan lived in the same tenement as me an' me mum. His dad 'ad a scrap yard in Bermondsey, 'is family were well known in the East End, in fact 'is brother was a right villain. I was scared stiff of Mick Riley when I was a kid, so was half the population of the streets where I grew up.'

'And this Stan Riley is a reformed character?'

'Stan didn't need reforming, he always was a good 'un. Like most of the fellas from the East End they call a spade a spade and live their lives accordingly.'

'Is that why I'm being treated to all this cockney language?' Becky said, doing her best to smother a yawn.

'No, in the first place I was trying to make you laugh, but I suppose talking like that came easy, me 'aving been with Stan. Must say it took me back, listening to him. Sort of reminded me of me roots.'

Becky did smile, but only for a moment. In her mind's eye she was picturing the tenement where May had been brought up. All those narrow streets, grimy walls, stone staircases and gaslight. Dear May, she had tried hard to better herself and she had done so well.

Becky couldn't help herself, she yawned again.

May was on her feet in an instant. 'Oh I'm sorry, Becky. I've tired you out, I didn't mean to stay so long. I'll go now and come back in the morning.'

'Please May, don't be sorry. Seeing you was just what I

needed.' She let her shoulders go back to rest against the pillows and smiled weakly. 'Having an East Ender for a friend doesn't mean you have to forget to speak nicely. Remember what Mr Gower always tells us. Think before we speak.'

May tucked the clothes in gently around Becky and pressed her lips to her forehead. 'Go to sleep again, you'll feel heaps better tomorrow and I'll be in to see you early in the morning.'

'Where are you going to spend the night?' Becky asked, her voice already sounding drowsy.

'Go to sleep and stop worrying, the hospital has already fixed me up with a bed and breakfast.'

Becky was two-thirds asleep as May quietly closed the door. Her mind was in a turmoil. She felt she could have battered Gerald Palmer to a pulp with her bare hands. Yet she was also turning over what Becky had said about Mr Gower. Think before we speak. How often he had said that! Damned pity he hadn't added another warning: think before you act.

Chapter Twenty-five

BECKY WAS STILL being plagued by thoughts of Gerald Palmer. It seemed that almost every time she closed her eyes she could see his handsome face. 'Try as I do I just can't put the thought of that weekend behind me,' she complained to May. 'I remember every thing we did together and every loving word he said.'

There has always been something hypnotic about him, May thought miserably, but she was saved from answering by a sharp rap on the front door. 'I'll go, stay where you are,' she ordered Becky. 'I won't be a moment.' Pleasure and relief showed on May's face as she opened the door to find Mr Gower standing on Aunt Lil's doorstep.

Her breath came out in a gasp. 'How kind of you to come, how did you know Rebecca was home? How did you know we would be here?'

'If you will allow me to come inside I will answer all your questions and put your mind at rest because I am the bearer of some very good news.'

'Come in, come in, believe me, Mr Gower, I have never been more pleased to see anyone in my whole life.'

'Look who's here,' May cried as she pushed open the door to the living room. But seeing the look of fear that came to Becky's face she added quickly, 'It's Mr Gower.'

'I hope I'm not intruding,' he said as he smiled and held out a neat bouquet of sweet-smelling freesias.

Becky stood up and took the flowers, pressing her face to the bright colours of the petals to sniff the heavy perfume. 'They are lovely, thank you, Mr Gower.'

'I am pleased to see you looking so much better than I had feared.' Good old Mr Gower, May muttered to herself, he's saying all the right things to Becky. 'I have brought a letter to show you, Rebecca, to show both of you actually,' Mr Gower said, reaching inside his top coat.

May quickly crossed the room. 'Here, let me take your coat and would you like a cup of tea or coffee?'

'Well, I did not intend to stay but how can I refuse the company of two such clever young ladies? I will have a coffee, May, if you're sure it's no trouble.'

'No trouble at all,' May assured him, 'I'll make some for all of us, but first, tell me please, what have we done that makes you refer to us as being clever?'

'Aah.' His smile was broad, his eyes twinkling. 'You run along and see to the coffee and then I will tell you.'

With only the two of them left in the room, Mr Gower pulled a chair up and sat down so that he was facing Becky, thinking all the while what a pleasant and nicely kept living room this was. He said, 'I bet you think I'm a bit of a crafty monkey getting May out of the room like that.'

Becky looked at him anxiously, wondering what was coming next.

'Rebecca, because I have your interest at heart and because I have known you for a very long time, learnt to respect you, and have a great regard for you in a fatherly way, I feel that gives me licence to speak my mind. To offer you advice and help, not only now but at any time in the future if you feel the need, even if it is only to talk. I shall always be there. That, my dear, is a promise.'

Becky began to cry silently. This was such a good man. Often in the past she had likened him to her father and she hadn't been wrong.

In the two days she had remained in the hospital after the arrival of May, she had made a decision. She had bravely decided that she wouldn't give up and go home to her family with her tail between her legs. No. She would put the past behind her and make a fresh start. It wouldn't be easy but she was certainly a lot wiser now than she had been in the past.

From the pocket of her cardigan she took a handkerchief, wiped her eyes, raised her head and ventured a smile.

'That's better, 'Mr Gower said brightly. 'Now the reason I wanted to talk to you on your own is because this is a matter between you and me only. You do trust me. Don't you?'

Becky nodded.

'I know most of what has happened to you and what I don't know I can surmise. I feel partly to blame. I could have given you more advice, but I wonder whether you would have heeded it. We all have to have our own experiences and very expensive some of them turn out to be. Most parts of London have young men living at the expense of older women, and then there are the greedy ones, waiting for their inheritance to materialize, knowing full well they must marry the partner chosen for them by their parents. They see lovely young girls and some of them try it on, knowing that nothing can come of such relationships.'

Becky said nothing. Her gaze had dropped, she was staring at the carpet.

'One last piece of information to divulge and then this matter need never be spoken of again,' Mr Gower quietly told her, leaning forward to give a reassuring pat to her arm. 'I have it from a friend of mine who is a reporter on one of those glossy society magazines that an announcement is to appear in next month's issue about the forthcoming wedding of Miss Amelia Claremont and Gerald Palmer.'

Becky looked at him, frowning. 'Thank you for telling me,' she said with resignation.

'Better you heard it from me,' Mr Gower began, and then stopped abruptly. Becky's cheeks had reddened. 'Are you all right?' he asked, his voice full of concern.

'I misjudged Gerald so much,' she whispered, feeling that she owed Mr Gower some sort of an explanation. 'I assumed he wanted the same things I did.'

Sympathy kept him from commenting; instead he reflected for a moment, before saying slowly, 'The gossip columnists love Amelia Claremont, although I fail to see the reason why. I suppose the main grounds are that the young lady has very wealthy parents.'

Becky couldn't form a reply. She gave a small smile of thanks, raised her eyebrows and clutched tightly at the hand that Mr Gower was holding out to her.

May, who had been biding her time, listening at the door, deliberately dropped two teaspoons.

Mr Gower grinned to himself and hurried to hold the door open, knowing full well that the clatter had been May's way of warning them she was ready to come back into the room.

'Coffee for everyone, and you can be a devil if you like an' have an enormous sugary jam doughnut,' May told them, her bright smile hiding her true feelings.

'I hope you bought the doughnuts from Lyons?' Mr Gower said, his face deadpan serious.

May put the tray down on to the table and turned to stare at him, not sure that she had heard right. Surprisingly, Becky giggled and then Mr Gower burst out laughing.

'You're 'aving me on, the pair of you are 'aving me on!' May cried, doing her best to stifle her own amusement.

'Took you a long time to realize that fact, Miss Stevens,' Mr Gower said as he grinned. 'And by the bye I think you dropped a couple of aitches on the way and that we cannot have, not from one of our top waitresses.'

May paused, coffeepot in hand ready to pour the hot drink into three of Aunt Lil's best cups. 'What's with the top waitress? First you call us clever and now we're bracketed with the best. Are you buttering us up because you want something?'

'Not at all,' he said quietly. 'Quite the reverse. First let me ask you both a question. Soon after you were transferred to the Outside Catering Unit do you remember being asked to take a written examination?'

'Don't I just!' May exclaimed loudly. 'Please, don't tell me we have to go through all that palaver again.'

Mr Gower shook his head, finding it difficult to hide his amusement. 'And you, Rebecca?'

'Only too well, Mr Gower. There were forty-eight questions, and at first sight I thought the papers set out in front of me had to be handed out along the row. Miss Paige soon put me right. Each participant had eleven pages to go through. Some of the girls hadn't finished when Miss Paige called time.'

'Daft questions most of them were,' May shot back at him, 'such as on which side of each guest do you stand when serving food, clearing dirty plates, placing clean plates and serving coffee. I wouldn't have minded but we'd been doing the job for weeks!'

'I know,' Mr Gower commiserated. 'Miss Paige was instrumental in getting the board to accept that fact and it was then decided that if more than seventy-five per cent of the set questions were answered correctly that was achievement enough.'

'Enough to keep our jobs, apparently,' May boldly stated.

'More than that,' Mr Gower replied. He got to his feet, and looking as pleased as punch walked to where May had laid his coat across the back of a chair, put his hand into one of the pockets and withdrew two small, square dark-blue boxes. Handing one box to each girl, he said, 'Congratulations.'

Becky just sat and stared at her brooch, which had four points. She knew what it was but couldn't get the words out of her mouth to express her delight. The four points of each brooch formed a star. The centre held a small raised disc. This gold disc had been engraved with their names and date of passing the examination.

'It's a gold star!' May cried, her voice full of surprise.

Mr Gower was beaming at both of them. 'The brooch is not the only reward, it has another benefit,' he told them, his tone sounding triumphant. 'A cash bonus goes with it.

To be incremented annually and paid to each person when their holiday leave becomes due. You will be permitted to wear your gold stars on your uniform if you should wish to do so.'

'We'd be proud to do so,' Becky told him, really smiling this time.

May was much more demonstrative. To Mr Gower's discomfort, but secretly to his amusement, May flung her arms around his neck. Softly she whispered, 'You're a brick. You know that, don't you? Coming here, doing what you've done, has worked wonders for Becky. Look at her. Look at her face.'

Mr Gower looked. And what he saw pleased him very much. Becky was sitting up straight in her chair, her eyes were bright and her fingers nimble as she pinned her gold star to the front of the cardigan she was wearing.

'I had better pour this coffee,' May declared, 'before it goes stone cold.'

They sipped their coffee and like three schoolkids they each had a doughnut, licking their fingers between mouthfuls and grinning widely as they wiped the last of the jam up from side plates that were also part of Aunt Lil's best tea service.

'You said you had a letter to show us,' May reminded Mr Gower.

He drained the last of his coffee, smiled at May and said, 'Can't remember when I last ate a doughnut, I'd forgotten how good they taste.' Replacing his cup on the table he took an envelope from his jacket pocket and withdrew a single sheet of headed notepaper.

His tone instantly became businesslike. 'You will be interested to know that the stars entitle you to be sent out to larger venues in future. This matter will be gone into at greater length by Miss Paige at the next staff meeting but tonight I thought I would steal the show and leak the information. After all you are my protégées, been under my wing from the beginning. I feel responsible for you and I am very proud of you both.'

The girls looked at each other. It was May that answered, 'For someone that's probably never seen Ireland you're full of blarney.' She raised her eyes, flashing with merriment, to meet his. You know, Mr Gower, I reckon if anyone ever kissed the Blarney Stone it was you. Still, we'll buy it, go on, tell us where some of these new locations are likely to be.'

Laughing at May's candid humour, he said, 'Olympia in Hammersmith for one and the Mansion House, no less, for another.'

'The Lord Mayor's residence? Opposite the Bank of England?' Becky asked.

'That's right,' Mr Gower confirmed.

'Crikey, we'll have to mind our p's and q's,' May laughed. 'The Mansion House is attached to the police court.'

Becky smiled, sat back in her chair and sipped the last of her coffee. Silently she was thanking God that she still had her job to look forward to. With the varied functions she was called upon to participate in and the variety of people she met surely she should have no bother in putting the episode of Gerald Palmer well out of her mind.

Mr Gower cast a glance in May's direction and having got a nod from her he picked up the coffeepot and poured himself another cup. They are both good girls, he thought. The best. So honest and straightforward. Trouble is they expect to be treated as kindly as they treat others. He looked again at Rebecca. She's such a delicate-looking little thing. There's not a devious bone in her body. Thankfully she now has her eyes open with regard to Gerald Palmer. That young man was heading for trouble and then some. Knowing full well that Rebecca had taken up with that layabout he had felt his hands were tied, utterly helpless. He wished he could have prevented her being hurt. He stifled a sigh, saying to himself, I suppose things could have been a whole lot worse.

His thoughts turned to May. She was a different kettle of

fish. A rough diamond some would say, but he had reason to know that she had a heart of gold. Many a youngster that had started work at Lyons with stars in their eyes would have packed up and left months ago if it hadn't been for May Stevens. He knew a lot more about May and the help she gave to new staff than he would ever let on.

They say that opposites did attract and it was certainly true of these two lasses. From what he knew of Rebecca she had led a sheltered life before coming to work in London. Born and bred in Surrey, the only daughter, three brothers and doting hard-working parents, while May had been born in the East End of London. An only child, her father dead, leaving just her and her mother to cope the best way they could. No wonder she had become a girl who had a bit of toughness in her. She'd learned how to take care of herself and had done remarkably well in smoothing out her own rough edges since gaining employment with Lyons.

Best of friends from the outset, these two, and it would take more than a caddish man such as Gerald Palmer to shatter the bond that now existed between them.

Mr Gower cleared his throat and ventured carefully, 'May I suggest you both pay a visit to Rebecca's parents? Wait until say Friday, have the weekend at home and come back to start work on the late shift Monday.'

May looked at Becky swiftly, then lifted her shoulders in a slight shrug. 'I'd really like that, if you don't think your parents would mind,' she said, adding in an undertone, 'your bruises will be gone by then.'

Becky was thoughtful for a few seconds, and then she murmured in a gentle loving tone, 'I would really love to go and see my mother and father but I wouldn't have gone unless you had agreed to come with me.'

'That's settled then,' Mr Gower said as he caught hold of Becky's arm reassuringly. 'You'll look after each other and your parents will be happy to see you. Now, I think that perhaps I should get off home, my wife will be thinking that I've left her.'

There was a pause, as Becky stared into the caring eyes of this kind man who had shown so much understanding, and the smile she gave him was winsome. 'I will never forget your kindness,' she said softly.

He glanced away, unable, suddenly, to find the words to express his feelings. He made for the door, then paused. 'Don't forget we expect our top waitresses to be punctual.'

He was relieved to hear Rebecca laugh as May accompanied him to the front door.

Chapter Twenty-six

'PENNY FOR YOUR thoughts,' Joyce Russell said as she watched her husband climb into bed beside her.

'You were a long time in the scullery tonight, doing the washing up, I'd give more than a penny to know what you and Becky were talking about behind my back,' Joe exclaimed, but there was a hint of teasing in his voice.

Joyce smiled at him. 'You're worried about our Becky, aren't you?'

'Oh, I don't want to be a wet blanket,' he sighed, 'but don't you think she's looking peaky? No one is more thrilled than I am that she's home for the weekend and more than pleased to have May with her an' all. It's just that . . . there's more t' this visit than meets the eye.'

Joyce was momentarily startled by this statement. She frowned. He was only voicing what she had feared all the evening and Lil Maynard was of the same opinion. Lil had said she felt something must have happened during the time she'd been staying down here in New Malden. She was blaming herself for having left the two girls on their own.

'Don't be so daft,' she had chided Lily. 'Neither of them are kids. You can't be expected t' be behind them all the time.'

The girls were amicable, sociable, and very well turned out. The dresses and coats they were wearing hadn't come from any street market. They were two very smart young ladies. So what were they all getting so upset about?

'You're right Joe,' Joyce said, doing her best not to show too much concern. 'I have to agree that Becky is not exactly bubbling over . . . too quiet, like. Normally when she gets home she doesn't stop talking for the first couple of hours. About the job, funny customers, awkward ones, where she an' May have been, who they've met. There's been none of that tonight.'

Joe leant across and placed his arm around his wife's shoulders, 'Do you think she's finding it hard to cope? She's ambitious, that little girl of ours, perhaps she's pushing herself too hard.'

Joyce gave him a playful dig in the ribs, 'Little girl! I suppose she will always be that to you. Nice as it was to have her as Daddy's girl you've got t' remember Joe, Rebecca is almost twenty-one years old, and we were having children by the time we'd reached that age.'

'I know, I know, but I also know that something is not right. I can't for the life of me put me finger on it, she played cards all right this evening yet I had the weird feeling that May wasn't taking her eyes off our Becky. Here! You don't think she's been extravagant, do yer? Got herself into some kind of a fix over money?'

Joyce smiled. 'If I'm sure of one thing I'm sure it's got nothing to do with money. She was telling me what she's going to buy for our little 'uns and for Ella's girls tomorrow. She'll be spending a pretty penny one way an' other, you'll see.'

Joe nodded, remained silent. He'd been longing to get Becky on his own ever since she had walked into the house. 'Ah well,' he muttered, 'at least she's home until Monday. Better get ourselves to sleep, see what the morning brings. Good night my love,' he said, planting a kiss on Joyce's cheek.

'Good night Joe, try not t' worry so much. If there's anything t' tell then it's to you that Becky will be doing the telling, that's for sure. Sleep well, my luv.'

A lot of heads turned as the five women made their way from stall to stall this Saturday morning in Kingston market. They

certainly seemed to be enjoying themselves, haggling with
the stallholders, laughing a lot. Besides Becky and her mother
there was Ella's mum, Peggy James, Aunt Lil and May. Each
one carried a rapidly filling shopping bag. Tomorrow, being
Sunday, the Russells would be getting a visit from their two
married sons. Jack and his wife Ada would be bringing their
son Ronnie. Becky had found it hard to believe when her
mum reminded her that Ronnie was coming up to seven
years of age. Also there would be her brother Tom, his wife
Joan, and Joey, who was almost five. The youngest of her
three brothers was Fred. Twenty-five and still not married.
He'd got a good job though. He'd been made manager
of the Co-op Bakery where he had worked ever since he
left school.

This Sunday there would also be Ella and Peter and their
two daughters. At least Becky was hoping that they would
come. She and May were going to Tooting this afternoon to
pay a long overdue visit to Ella and Becky had been instructed
to give them a special invitation.

'I think that's the lot,' Joyce Russell said with a sigh of
relief as she placed a large piece of loin of pork onto the top
of the bag that her friend Peggy was carrying.

'You bought Bramleys at the veg stall, were they for the
apple sauce?' Peggy asked Joyce.

'Yes, why, don't you think I got enough?'

'Yes, 'course you did, but I'm just going to go back and
buy some more. Thought if I make two big apple pies this
afternoon that will help towards the pudding seeing as how
there is going to be such a gang of us.'

'Great idea, that'll be a big help, thanks Peggy.'

'And I'll pop over and get some dried fruit,' Lily Maynard
declared. 'If you'll let me have the run of your kitchen, Joyce,
I'll knock up a load of cakes an' make a trifle for tea.'

'That's ever so kind of you, Lil, but you don't have
to.'

'I know I don't have to any more than you have to have

me down here for a holiday. Please, let me do something to help.'

'All right then, but before we get on the tram with this load of shopping I suggest we have a cuppa in the market café.'

Becky looked at May and shook her head. Turning to her mother she said, 'Mum, May and I are going over to Bentalls. I told you I want to do a bit of shopping for the kids. If there's time we'll pop back home but if we don't put in an appearance you'll know we've gone straight to Tooting.'

'What about your dinner?' her mother protested.

Both girls laughed. 'Mum, we don't eat dinner midday. If we're hungry we might get a sandwich but with the breakfast you cooked us this morning it won't matter much if we don't eat anything else all day.'

'How about you, May?' Joyce asked. 'Don't think you've got to starve just because my daughter says you should.'

'Oh, Mrs Russell! Starve is the last thing that will happen to me while I'm staying with you. Just look at what you've bought for tomorrow.'

'You wait,' Joyce Russell laughed loudly, 'when my tribe get their feet under the table it does me a power of good to see them all eat heartily and tomorrow will be extra special because our Becky's home, you and your aunt are here and if Ella and Peter come and bring their girls that will make Peggy's day.'

Very soon after thrusting their way through the crowds of shoppers in the market, Becky and May were pushing through the big doors of Kingston's largest department store, and taking the stairs up to the children's department.

Rebecca was smiling to herself as she thought of Ella's two little girls. Shame really that she didn't see very much of them, or of Ella come to that. At least today she wouldn't visit them empty-handed; she had enough money to buy them some really pretty things. She still worried about Ella and Peter, despite the fact that her dad said they weren't doing too badly. Just about managing was how he put it, well, that could mean anything.

'Spoilt for choice here,' May exclaimed as she held up a pretty white dress trimmed with yellow ribbons. 'I think this would be lovely for the youngest one.'

Becky raised her eyebrows. 'I think it's very sweet but it's a party dress and I don't see Ella trotting her kids off to parties very often.'

Overhearing Becky's remark a saleslady came to her side. 'This area is solely for party dresses, mostly organdie and such like. Shall I show the everyday selection? We have a great choice for both girls and boys.'

'Yes please,' Becky said, grinning widely at May.

A moment later the young lady was taking skirts, blouses, small jumpers adorned with teddy bears and pretty calico dresses from the stands and fanning them out along the counter.

'How old is the child?' she enquired.

'I'm buying for two, both girls, one will be two in June and the other one is just a baby,' Becky explained.

'You make your choice, browse a bit, and then I will see that you have the right sizes.'

Half an hour later the girls were making their way to the toy department each carrying a large shopping bag. Becky had bought one skirt and two tops for each child. May had bought three tiny pairs of white ankle socks for each of Ella's girls because as she said they were so pretty she couldn't resist them and they didn't cost a fortune.

'Now, what do I get for my nephews? Clothes wouldn't interest them.'

'Your mum told me that one boy is seven and the other boy will soon be five, perhaps they would like books.'

They settled for a school satchel for Joey as he would soon be starting school and Becky felt it might make him feel right grown-up. May wasn't to be left out and she insisted on buying him a fire-engine that gave out sparks as you pushed it along.

For Ronnie, Becky purchased a leather football and May bought him a kite that had endless streamers for a tail.

Becky glanced up at the store clock; it was almost half past twelve. 'If we go back home we'll never get to Tooting,' she moaned to May. 'You know what my mum is, she'll want to see everything we've bought and she'll want us to have something to eat.'

May giggled. 'So what's the problem? We don't have to go back, you did say we might not.'

'Right then, we won't,' Becky shot back, grinning. 'Come on, don't dawdle, there's a coffee shop downstairs and we'll grab a snack there.'

As they made their way down the staircase, both girls were aware of the glances cast in their direction. At nearly twenty-one they were both attractive, full of health and vitality. Today May was wearing a dark green cloche hat from beneath which her reddish hair curled over her ears. The fur collar that Becky's mother had made was draped around the shoulders of her long coat. Mostly it was her red hair and green eyes that set her apart. Becky was shorter but just as smart. Her choice of hat was a wide-brimmed felt, sporting a colourful feather in the band. Around the collar of her dark grey coat she had draped a bright red scarf which set off her big brown eyes to a tee.

Arriving at the café, they managed to find an empty table and they both gratefully sat down. Suddenly May said, 'You should wear red more often, Becky. It does something for you, makes your skin glow.'

'Why thank you, May,' she answered, giving her a funny look. 'Can't think why you've suddenly noticed, I often do wear red.'

'Yeah, I know. Perhaps it's because today you seem . . .' She hesitated, not sure if she should speak her mind.

'Go on,' Becky urged, 'today I seem what?'

'Better. Yes, that's it. Today you seem to have pulled your shoulders back, put the past couple of weeks behind you and you're once more showing a smiling face to the world.'

Now it was Becky's turn to dither. Much as she loved May, counted herself fortunate to have her as a friend, she couldn't entirely open her heart to her. It had taken a great deal of effort on her part to be more like her old self today. Last evening she had been a wet blanket. She knew she had and she knew her behaviour had upset her mother and father. Envy was a funny word to use, but the truth was that was how she had felt. Envious.

Her parents had such a loving relationship; even after nearly thirty years they still adored each other. Her brothers had their wives and sons. Ella had Peter and two lovely little girls. Maybe none of them had a great deal of material things but they had each other. No one wanted her. Certainly not Gerald. Except of course as a bit on the side.

An awful expression that. It had kept her awake at night, only because no matter how Gerald had tried to wrap it up she knew it to be the truth. Then, waking up this morning to find her mum standing beside the bed holding out a cup of tea, she knew she was loved. Count your blessings, my girl, she had berated herself. There and then she had decided Gerald Palmer could ruin his own life by marrying someone he didn't love but from now on she wasn't going to let him ruin hers. He wasn't going to be any part of her life. Not even a small part.

She looked across at May, gave her a small smile. 'I'm glad you think I look better. I feel better because I have made a decision. I am not even going to think about Gerald Palmer ever again. At least I am going to try hard not to.'

May grinned at her, her expression one of genuine delight. 'Good on yer Becky, the bugger's not worth it.'

'May!'

May flashed her a lopsided grin. 'Sorry, but swear words are all I can think of to describe that stinker.'

Becky couldn't find words to answer that, so hiding her amusement she beckoned to the waitress who had been hovering a few feet away. 'Please may we have two coffees and two toasted teacakes, if that's all right with you, May?'

'Yes thank you.' May nodded at the waitress, then laughing at Becky she said, 'You an' me both need to mix with a few more normal people, we've been brushing too close to the gentility and they ain't what they're cracked up to be.'

Becky remembered Roger Macclesfield and how upset May had been when he left her high and dry. 'Seems like we've shared a common fate,' she said quietly to May, stretching out her hands and taking both of May's hands between her own. Suddenly they found themselves wrapped in the extraordinary warmth that only true friendship can bring.

Then Becky fell to wondering. Had May, like herself, gone through an agonizing period of sleepless nights, terrified that she might be pregnant? She wasn't even sure that May had slept with Roger.

She only knew that she, herself, had been so besotted with Gerald Palmer that she had been scatty enough to let herself believe her whole future would be entwined with his. How wrong she had been.

The relief of finding out that her ordeal was well and truly over was something she would never forget. When her period had started she had gone down on her knees, there and then in the bathroom, and thanked God. And at that moment she had vowed never again to be so trusting where men were concerned. One thing she was certain of, the experience had left her a whole lot wiser.

They stepped down from the tram at Tooting Broadway and had barely reached the pavement when Becky heard her name being called and turning quickly she saw Mary Marsden waving frantically from the island in the middle of the road. 'Becky, wait, wait a minute!' she yelled above the noise of the traffic.

'Who is that? May asked.

'Mary Marsden. I've told you about her. I went to her and Tom's wedding which reminds me, it's not Mary Marsden, it's Mary Ferguson now.'

Mary reached the pavement safely and threw her arms around Becky's neck. 'Cor, I'm ever so pleased t' see you, Becky. Look at you! Ain't you the lady. No wonder we don't get t' see yer these days, too busy working up in London I suppose.'

'Mary, I'm sorry. I don't get home nearly enough but with the summer coming I promise I'm going to try harder. We're off to see Ella now, why don't you come with us?'

Mary stepped back and took a good look at May and seeing the expression on her face Becky hastened to say, 'Oh I'm sorry Mary, this is my friend May. We met when I first went for an interview with Lyons and we've worked together ever since.'

''Allo May,' Mary beamed at her. 'Becky's always been my friend since I came home from service. I miss her these days.'

May gently touched Mary's arm. 'I'm going to see to it that both she and I visit more often so perhaps you'll be my friend also.'

'Yeah, I will,' Mary said as she smiled enthusiastically.

'Come on then, let's get going to see Ella,' Becky said, tucking her hand into the crook of Mary's arm.

'I can't come with you,' Mary said, and looked crestfallen. 'Me mum an' dad ain't been too well and they've 'ad t' give up their 'ouse an' move into a flat. They live 'ere now, in Tooting, Defoe Road, I'm on me way t' see them now.'

'Oh that is a shame.' Both Becky and May expressed their sympathy.

'Do you still live with Tom's mother?' Becky enquired.

'Yes, but Tommy's 'ad the whole 'ouse altered. Lovely it is. Two separate flats. When Tom's 'ome you must come round t' tea, Becky. You've never been.'

'Never been asked,' Becky said, grinning.

'Well, you're being asked now and you May, you're being asked an' all.'

'Right,' they both agreed. 'Next visit and that's a promise.'

'Bye then Becky, tell Ella I'll see 'er on Thursday.' She planted a kiss on Becky's cheek and then did the same to May. 'Don't work too 'ard, the pair of you.' And waving her hand she trotted off in the opposite direction, looking a bit frumpish in her tweed coat and woolly hat.

'She's got her feet well and truly on the ground,' May commented as they watched her go.

'She certainly has. Doesn't ask for much out of life. Proper down-to-earth is Mary. She and Tom were made for each other.'

'This is it,' Becky declared, staring up at the large plate glass window that bore a notice which stated, 'Heels repaired while you wait'. To the side a young man stood behind a workbench, wearing a leather apron, working away like fury. He made a fascinating sight and Becky and May were not the only two to stop and stare in amazement.

A shoemaker's last was secured to the bench and a boot placed over the foot of the last was being repaired. The young man's mouth was full of tiny rivets and with unvarying speed he spat out one rivet at a time, clasping it between his forefinger and thumb of his left hand. Using his right hand and a small hammer he rhythmically tapped each nail into the new leather sole making a good and speedy job of repairing the boot.

'Wonder he don't swallow one an' choke himself,' a woman remarked, causing a ripple of amusement to run through the watchers.

The shop door opened and Becky looked up to see Peter standing there. At first glance she thought how well he looked; certainly he had put on weight. He too was wearing a leather apron and as he came across the pavement, hand outstretched, she could see his fingers were stained much the same colour as her brothers' always were, caused by them working in the tanning factory.

'Becky, come on in. My God, it's good to see you.'

'It's good to see you too,' Becky told him. 'And this is May, May Stevens, I'm sure you've heard all about her.'

'Yes, I have,' Peter hastened to say. 'Ella tells me your letters are full of what you and May get up to. Come along inside, go upstairs, Ella will be thrilled to see both of you.'

They followed Peter through the shop that smelt strongly of good leather and boot polish out to the back staircase.

'Ella, Becky and her friend are here, take the gate away from the top of the stairs,' Peter called loudly and Ella responded, 'I'm coming, won't be a moment.'

On the top landing Becky fell into Ella's outstretched arms and May stood back silently as the two lifelong friends hugged each other tightly. Within minutes of meeting Ella, May decided she was a charming pleasant young woman. Furthermore she felt at ease with her immediately, not in the least as if she were intruding.

'Told you, didn't I,' Becky whispered to May, 'everyone likes Ella.' All the while she was studying her friend. Ella looked great. She hadn't known they were coming but even so she was neatly dressed in quite the latest fashion. Long hobble black skirt, a cream cotton blouse which had leg-o'-mutton sleeves and a row of pearl buttons leading three inches up from her wrist. A plain black velvet shawl was draped across her shoulders. Her long fair hair, she still hadn't had it cut, was coiled into a tight bun at the nape of her neck.

Sensing that Becky was eyeing her, Ella did a twirl. 'All my own work, takes you back to our rummaging at jumble sales and hours of needlework afterwards. Do you remember?'

'Oh Ella, how could I ever forget? You look fantastic, really you do, but where are the girls? I can't wait to see them.'

'Aah, we've so much room up here that Peter decided they could have a playroom. Gives Peter and me a bit of privacy now an' then,' she said softly, her cheeks flushing slightly.

Both Becky and May smiled.

'Yeah well, come and meet them, they'll probably knock you over before you get inside the door.'

What lovely little girls, was May's first thought, and Becky certainly wouldn't have contradicted her. Margaret was a young replica of Eleanor, with long fair hair, creamy skin and big blue eyes. Amy, the baby, obviously took after Peter. She had the same colour hair and eyes that danced with mischief and chubby cheeks that dimpled as she smiled.

'Amy's already proving to be a tomboy,' Ella laughed, 'she's long and lean and it won't surprise me if she grows taller than Margaret.'

Margaret was across the room in an instant. 'Auntie Becky,' she cried, 'are you going to stay to tea? You've got to, cos we haven't seen you for a long time.'

'Of course I am,' Becky told her, sweeping her up into her arms and holding her close.

'Can I sit next to you?' Margaret asked, her head on one side, looking appealing.

'Of course you may, if Mummy says so, and perhaps Amy might like to sit on my other side.'

Amy wasn't going to be outdone. She wrapped her arms around May's legs and demanded that she too be picked up.

In no time at all a cloth had been spread over the big round table that stood in the centre of the living room and Ella had soon prepared lots of nice things. 'Fruit and jelly,' Margaret cried as May set the two bowls down on the table. 'They're me favourite.'

'Haven't you got a nice mummy?' May smiled. 'She told me she made the jelly after you had gone to bed last night.'

'Yes, but she's Amy's mum too,' Margaret wisely said.

Becky looked at May and they both giggled. These kids were comical.

Margaret put her head on one side and pulled a funny face. 'Auntie Becky,' Margaret whispered, tugging at Becky's skirt, 'we haven't got enough chairs for us all to sit up at the table.'

'Oh ssh, pet,' Ella said, and she sounded embarrassed. 'Margaret, you can sit on my lap and Amy can go in her highchair.'

Amy loudly protested when they tried to put her in her chair and clung to her Auntie Becky.

Ella took a deep breath before murmuring, 'I'm so sorry but if you'll give me a minute . . . I think I can sort something out . . .'

'Can we do anything, luv?' Becky asked.

Ella didn't reply; she was tugging a long plank of wood across the floor. When she had it alongside the table she made a gesture for Becky to follow her. Once inside the little girls' bedroom, Ella said, 'If you clear off that bedside table I'll do the other one and then we can use them for the plank to rest on and so make a form to sit on.'

'Great idea,' Becky replied, lifting a small nightlight and several books and placing them on to the floor. Once she had lifted the cloth it became apparent that the bedside table was a tall wooden orange box upended and covered to serve a very good purpose.

'You're a genius,' Becky laughed.

'Don't know about that, it's more a case of needs must when the devil drives. We haven't any money to spare for more furniture yet. Don't get me wrong, Becky, I'm not complaining, Peter is doing his best, but for the moment any spare cash has to be ploughed back into buying more stock. He can't repair boots if he hasn't got the leather.'

'Oh, Ella, luv, nothing worth having comes easy, we both know that and I think you and Peter have done wonders. The girls are an out and out credit to you both.'

'Thanks, Becky. I hope I haven't offended your friend, May.'

'Don't give it another thought. There's nothing standoffish about May, give yourselves time and I bet you'll have this place well and truly furnished.'

Ella laughed. 'Well I'm glad you know how things are. You must have thought I was putting on airs when I said the girls had a playroom to themselves.' She laughed again, even louder. 'It's only until we can afford to furnish that room and then it will become the parlour, now what d' yer think of that?'

'I think, Mrs Tomson, that you are in danger of getting ideas above your station in life and that it would be a good idea if we took these two boxes back to the living room, set them up and you gave us this wonderful tea the girls have been going on about.'

There was a great deal of laughter as the makeshift form was set in place and everyone was finally settled around the table. When Ella was cutting the Victoria sponge she'd made that morning, Margaret asked if she might say something to her Auntie Becky.

'I'll have to let her, Becky,' said Ella, grinning. 'She'll say it, anyway.'

'Well I just want to tell Auntie that me an' Amy are ever so glad she brought her friend May with her cos we think she's ever so nice.'

'Why, thank you, Margaret, and I have to tell you I'm really glad your auntie did bring me here today because I think you are two very nice little girls.'

Amy giggled.

'You're a pair of little imps,' Ella told her daughters, while doing her best not to smile. 'And you, Margaret, have a smear of jam on the end of your nose.'

Margaret shrieked. Everyone one else roared with laughter. Undeterred by the lack of comfortable chairs to sit on this was proving to be a very happy teatime.

One hour became two and still the three girls sat at the table, talking non-stop. The children had taken themselves off to the playroom.

'Well,' Becky breathed out, 'between us I think May and myself have filled you in on every last detail of how Lyons manage their company. Do you fancy becoming a Nippy, Ella?'

'I've got a job,' Ella said, sounding really proud.

'Oh, good on you,' Becky cried, 'no wonder you look so perky, must be doing you the world of good. Why didn't you tell us before instead of letting us rabbit on about our work?'

'Because you'll probably say it's ridiculous. I don't get paid. Mary Ferguson helps there as well.'

'We won't say any such thing,' Becky hastened to assure her. 'Is it some charity that you work for?'

'You must enjoy doing whatever it is,' May butted in, 'and after all that's what counts the most. Tell us, where is it you work?'

Ella put her cup and saucer to one side and walked over to the big bay window that looked out over the busy Mitcham Road. 'Over there,' she said, pointing her finger. 'Don't have far to travel, do I?' Both girls rushed to stand by her side.

'But that's the Central Hall!' Becky exclaimed, looking at the great building with its mighty flight of stone steps leading up to the entrance and immediately thinking to herself, she hasn't gone all religious, has she? We all need God in our lives but to work for nothing was something that Ella could not afford to do.

May's thoughts were running along the same lines. Being practical she turned to Ella and said, 'Look luv, why don't you tell us all about this job?'

'I will,' Ella quietly said, 'if you don't think I will be boring you. It's a bit of a long story.'

'Well, let's sit down again,' Becky said as she squeezed Ella's hand and added, 'best if you start at the beginning.'

'I got this idea,' Ella began, 'because people round here

are so nice but they're poor. So many men are unemployed and most of the women have an awful job to make ends meet and as for clothing their kiddies, it would break your heart to see some of the poor little mites, especially when it's bitter cold. I thought, why not swap things? Children grow out of their clothes and nobody wants to buy them.' Ella paused and looked Becky straight in the eye, hoping for her approval. She got it.

'I think that was a great idea.'

'So do I,' May added, 'I'm dying to know how it worked.'

'Right from the word go it worked all right,' Ella went on as she smiled at them both. 'It was getting it off the ground that was the hard part. I didn't have any money to rent premises, couldn't even afford a stall in the market.' She paused again and laughed out loud. 'I tried to persuade Peter to let me use a room up here. He went mad. Said business was bad enough without a load of women and tribes of kids traipsing through the place all day long. So I found out who the vicar was at the Central Hall, paid him a visit and both he and his wife were enthusiastic about the idea.

'Big man is Alan Burdett, I was a bit scared of him at first, thought he looked more like a rugby player than a vicar, but he came up trumps. He lets us have the use of the church hall every other Thursday, twelve till four. Mrs Burdett even did some hand-bills for us and saw to it that they were given out to young mothers outside the schools. And to the older women at mothers' meetings, we've had a good response from them.'

'Ella, you say *we* have had good results. Are other women involved besides yourself?' Becky asked sensibly.

'Yeah, I was wondering that,' May chipped in.

'You'd be surprised. I got Mary interested from the start, but as time has gone on we sometimes have more helpers than we need.'

'That's marvellous, Ella, really great, you clever old thing,' Becky told her quickly.

'Tell us more about what you swapped, what kind of people came?' May's interest was genuine.

'The first week was a washout. Nobody came. Mrs Burdett, Mary and myself sat there like dummies. Margaret was disappointed because I had told her she would be able to play with all the kiddies I expected the mothers to bring. Amy slept in her pram the whole afternoon because she was only a baby then, but we've been going nearly a year now.'

'And you've never let on,' Becky cried.

'Sorry, you know I've never been a letter writer and when you did come home there never seemed time to talk about it.'

'Don't go off the subject,' May pleaded, 'I'm all ears.'

'The second Thursday was a day I will never forget,' Ella began, smiling to herself. 'By two o'clock there was such a commotion going on that Alan Burdett came flying up the stairs to see if I was all right. Women had turned out their cupboards and drawers, washed long-forgotten baby clothes, jumpers, school uniforms that were now too small for their sons or daughters, jackets with patches on the elbows, coats that had been given a new set of buttons, you name it, they brought it.

'Now we are far better organized. We have the hall for one hour on a Monday morning, staffed by volunteers. Goods are accepted in advance and a receipt given. Then we sort the goods and different ladies do various tasks. I'm in charge of the baby clothes. I thread new ribbons at the neck and cuffs of matinée coats, iron small dresses and romper suits and generally do any sewing repairs to the garments that may be needed. I look forward to these sessions now. Everyone has a good laugh.'

Ella paused for breath again. 'I don't know about you two but I've talked myself dry. I'll make a fresh pot of tea and then I must see about getting the dinner ready for Peter. Saturday is a long day for him – he started work downstairs before six this morning.'

'I'll make the tea,' Becky volunteered, 'then May an' I will have to be making a move or Mum will be going spare because we're not back in time for dinner.'

'Oh, I thought you would be staying for the evening.' Ella was unable to keep the disappointment out of her voice.

'No, sorry, luv.' But Becky grinned at her and quickly added, 'But we'll be seeing all of you again tomorrow. The whole family, your mum an' all, will be at our house for the day and my mum said if you and Peter don't come and bring the girls she'll be over here first thing Monday morning to know the reason why.'

'That's marvellous.' Ella sounded both delighted and excited as she grabbed hold of Becky and drew her close. 'Gosh Sunday dinner, all together round the one table! It's been so long I shan't sleep tonight, I know I won't. I can't wait. We'll be there. Bright and early. Oh, thank yer mum for me.'

'You can thank her yourself tomorrow, you daft girl.'

At that moment May came into the room with a newly laid tray. 'Actions speak louder than words,' she said grinning to Becky, 'I've made the tea while you two were still nattering nineteen to the dozen. We'll have a quick cup before we set off.'

Ella came downstairs to see them off, carrying Amy in her arms. Margaret, her legs wrapped around Becky's waist and her arms around her neck, was quite content to be made a last-minute fuss of.

The little group stood back, waiting to say goodbye to Peter. A woman with frizzy hair and a very loud voice was complaining to him that she wanted a different-shaped rubber heel put on her shoes. Peter glanced their way. Becky mouthed, 'See you tomorrow.' He raised his eyebrows in question. 'At my mum's for dinner,' she mouthed again. His eyes lit up and he nodded his head.

The tram they wanted was waiting. The driver was leaning against the side of the tram chatting to his conductor and smoking a cigarette. Becky and May climbed aboard, settled themselves on the slatted wooden seat and burst out laughing.

May was the first to recover. 'Talk about how the other half live!'

'No comparison, is there?' Becky asked.

'Not when you compare it with the wealth we see every day. The jewellery some of the women we wait on wear, when you think about it, the cost of one necklace would probably keep an ordinary family for a lifetime.'

'You enjoyed coming here to see Ella though, didn't you, May?'

'You bet yer life I did. I think she's smashing. No wonder you and her have been friends all these years. I mean it, she's great.'

'I'm thrilled to know she's working, even if it's only voluntary work. Really showed a bit of initiative, I'd say. When she was first married it was awful. She went downhill quicker than a sleigh on a slippery slope. She was nothing more than a skivvy. Peter had no money and no prospects. I'd take a bet that life isn't all roses even now for either of them but at least they seem happy and are getting by.'

'Yeah, and their little girls are a credit to them.'

'They are certainly that,' Becky agreed, wriggling her bottom to a more comfortable position as the tram rumbled on its way.

Sunday had been everything that anyone could wish for.

A nice dry day with just enough wind to allow more than half the family to take the children over into the field opposite the house. Watching from an upstairs window Joyce found it hard to decide who was enjoying themselves the most, her sons or her grandsons. The football that the girls had bought for Ronnie was certainly taking a bashing, while young Joey, with the help of his father, had taken charge of the kite, running his little legs off as the colourful toy flew high in the sky.

Now it was ten o'clock at night. The house seemed very quiet, even still, with all the young families having departed for their own homes. May came back down the stairs to where only Rebecca and her mother remained.

'You're ready for bed,' Becky remarked. May had washed and brushed her hair till it shone like burnished copper and she was wearing a pretty cotton housecoat.

Immediately she said, 'I couldn't go to sleep without telling you both how much my aunt and I have appreciated what you've done today.'

'I'm glad you both enjoyed yourselves,' Joyce answered.

'Mrs Russell . . .' May began, her tone very emotional. 'Enjoyed is not perhaps the right word, it's more than that. Our feelings are hard to describe. Aunt Lil has been regretting that she was never blessed with children and watching your close family has made me realize how much I missed when growing up as an only child. We want to thank you and Mr Russell for allowing us to be included.'

'Oh, May, come here an' give me a kiss,' Joyce replied as she got to her feet and held her arms open wide. May went into them and her own arms automatically went round this kindly mother.

'It works both ways, you know, May,' Joyce said gently. 'Your aunt has been a godsend to me, giving our Becky a home and watching over her like she does. Without Lily I would have spent many a sleepless night wondering how my daughter was faring in London. Anyway, time you were in bed, it's back to the grindstone for you both tomorrow. There's one more thing to be said though, May: I want you to regard this as your home, just as much as Becky does. You are welcome here whenever you feel like making the journey. You don't have to wait to be asked. Remember that, won't you?'

'Well, likely I shall take you up on that.' May's face was a picture to behold, she was smiling broadly but her eyes were glistening with tears and as a single tear escaped and rolled down her cheek, Becky gave her a playful push saying, 'Come on dafty, no waterworks, go on up and I'll follow you in just a minute.'

'Mum, you are the absolute tops,' Becky said, her voice no more than a small whisper.

For a moment her mother said nothing, but sat watching her as she drew off her stockings, then she said with resignation, 'Becky, I used to tell myself that I could read you like a book. But not anymore. You've brightened up a lot today, so seeing Eleanor yesterday and again today seems to have worked wonders for you but I am quite sure all hasn't been well with you lately. You could tell me, whatever it is. You know that?'

Becky rolled her stockings into a ball, then she crossed the room to the couch where her mother still sat and, bending low, said, 'Mum, there is nothing for you to worry about. I promise you. I love you and Dad more than I know how to tell you and if I were really in trouble I would come running to you like a shot.'

'If you're sure.' Joyce's voice was low.

Becky forced a smile. 'I'm very sure.' And with that her head came down and snuggled into her mother's breasts.

Joyce drew in a long tight breath. She still wasn't convinced. She closed her eyes tightly as she hugged this only daughter of hers and prayed hard that the Good Lord would watch over her.

Chapter Twenty-seven

IT WAS TWO-THIRDS of the way through 1928 when Becky received a letter from Peter Tomson. She read it through twice before deciding that she wouldn't hurt his pride. The matter had never been mentioned between them and she was pleased that her contribution had helped to open up new horizons. She would accept his offer of repayment and be grateful that things had turned out as well as they had. It was after all a very nice letter.

Dear Becky,

I have only recently found out from your father that you were the main contributor to the fund that set me up in business. I am finding it hard to express my feelings. Just to say thank you seems so inadequate.

I am in a position now to repay your kindness and I have put forward the suggestion that I pay the sum of ten pound each month for the next six months. The ten pound extra being in the way of interest.

Your father has accepted my proposal but not completely. He insists that you will only accept repayment of the original loan.

I have known for a long time that you are a good friend to Eleanor but was not aware of the depth of your kindness towards me.

Recently I allowed an older man to use one of the sheds we have in the back yard in order to repair bicycles. He had walked for miles day in day out searching for employment without success. Not only has he worked up a nice little business he now has a contract with the Post Office to repair the red bikes used by their telegram boys. Now he pays me a weekly rent. So you see, my dear Rebecca, your generosity to me has enabled me to help another. I am truly grateful to you.

Eleanor and the girls send you their love as I do, come home and see us soon, Peter.

Folding the letter and replacing it in the envelope, Becky sighed. Another autumn would soon be upon them and still the employment situation was no better. Educated men were begging in the streets. So many young men had died in the War and many of those who had survived were too sick to work. The fit and able got no sympathy from the Government; it was the same everywhere. So many men chasing so few jobs.

Why? Becky asked herself yet again, as did so many other young women who were fighting to get equal rights for themselves. Why were there no jobs to be had? Had the owners of the manufacturing businesses made their pile during the War? All this poverty was causing a great deal of social unrest.

While standing at the bus stop Becky was still mulling over what Peter had said in his letter. 'There's such a gulf between the working classes and the middle class,' she muttered, more to herself than to May.

'What are you going on about?' The bus had come into view and May grabbed Becky's arm. 'You want to be grateful that we've got a job to go to, you can't take the worries of the world on your shoulders. You should have learnt that by now.'

Seated beside May on the lower deck of the bus, Becky was quietly nodding to herself. She knew that what May was saying made sense. But then these days May was a whole lot more sensible. She and Stan Riley had been seeing quite a bit of each other since he had driven her down to Brighton, over a year ago now. Although very pleased that May had met up with a young man with whom she had grown up there were times now when Becky felt quite lonely.

During the summer months, with the long light evenings, the two of them had walked on Hampstead Heath, taken boat rides on the Serpentine in Hyde Park and generally enjoyed each other's company. Becky had been invited to go along, several times, but she felt she would have been the odd one out.

Aunt Lil thoroughly approved of this young man whose family she had been well acquainted with in her younger days. And why not? He was presentable, of average height, had a good head of brown hair, a nice clean healthy complexion and more to the point he had a good job driving a delivery van for Lyons. What Aunt Lil liked most about him was that Stan Riley didn't talk fancy, his head wasn't full of big ideas.

'I'll tell you this much,' Aunt Lil had called out when watching May get herself ready to go out one evening. 'There's some that would tell you that the Rileys were a family of villains and that the flat they lived in was little more than a mucky-dump. Seventy per cent true, I'd say. Though even in a barrel of rotten apples you can nearly always find one good one and I'd say that you, May, have been lucky enough to come across a good one in Stan.

'D'you know he disappeared from the tenements soon after his father died, cleared off and got himself lodgings? Soon after that the police were around that family so often you'd 'ave thought they were taking up residence. Dolly Riley, Stan's mother, ups sticks an' goes t' live with her sister in Clacton. Can't say as 'ow I blamed her. But it says a lot for Stan the way he's got on with his life.'

'You with us?' May asked grimly, shaking Becky out of her daydreaming. 'You know, before long we'll have the big firms giving their annual dinners, most firms like to get them well out of the way before Christmas.' Without waiting for an answer, May got to her feet and signalled to the conductor that they wanted to get off the bus at the next stop.

Once inside the building the girls quickly changed into their uniform and Becky, ready first, was reading the notices that were pinned up on the notice board.

'Here, come and look at this, May. Funny, it's just what you were remarking on as we got off the bus.'

'Well I never,' May exclaimed as she ran her eye down the printed page.

'Move over or else read it out loud,' said someone. Two or three more waitresses had gathered to see and hear what was going on.

May cleared her throat and began to read from the top of the page. 'The 1928 annual dinner for the construction company Bovis will be held the first week in November. Date and place as yet undecided. In keeping with the spirit of the occasion, the menus will be printed on wood veneer and laid out in the form of a building specification.'

'Good morning, ladies.' All heads turned as the clipped tones of Robert Matthews made them jump. Not one girl had heard him approaching. 'Winter cometh,' he continued, smiling, 'and indoor festivities begin.'

'Company's going to town on that one,' Joyce Johnson, one of the Nippies who had been with Becky and May right from the start, ventured, nodding her head towards the notice board.

'That's right,' Mr Matthews agreed. 'It isn't just the small details that make Lyons such a popular firm and it makes no difference whether we are catering for king or commoner, Lyons will always go to great lengths to make each event special for that particular client. The personal touch always counts.'

'Yes it does,' the merry voice of Florence Nicholls broke in. 'And Mr Matthews, may I remind you that our waitresses are needed on several floors if lunch is ever going to be served today?'

Robert Matthews laughed heartily. 'Don't make out that you're such a dragon, Florence. The girls and myself have good reason to know that you are a soft touch and only grumble now and again to prove that your voice is one of authority.'

Most of the girls giggled but at the same time they moved swiftly to put the finishing touches to their caps and aprons and were soon on their way.

'All right for them to jest among themselves, them being the bosses, but we mere mortals still jump when they're around,' May declared.

Becky looked at her swiftly but made no comment. She was still glancing at Robert Matthews, thinking how wonderful he looked. He had a marvellous tan, his bright blue eyes were brilliant and his hair, always so fair, was now almost white, bleached by the sun. His apparel wasn't dull either. Beneath his black jacket he was wearing a waistcoat, grey silk brocade, no less. 'He looks like a Greek god,' Becky murmured to herself.

May heard and was flabbergasted. Amazement swept across her face as she stared at Becky in disbelief. 'He looks like what?'

A huge smile spread over Becky's face. 'Well, I think he looks great.'

'Are you saying you fancy him?'

Becky stared at her, speechless.

'Well whether you do or not is neither here nor there cos if we don't get a move on we'll both be out of a job and then you will never set eyes on the gorgeous Mr Matthews ever again.'

'Now you're being real daft,' Becky protested. 'Can't I admire a man without you going on?'

'You can if you like but it won't get you anywhere.' With that May sprinted across the floor, held the door open wide and yelled, 'Come on, last one in the still room gets to polish all the cutlery.'

Becky was after her in a flash but she was still wondering where Mr Matthews had been to acquire such a tan and whether or not he had taken a companion with him.

During the week before the Bovis annual dinner, the activity and excitement had grown to such an extent that all the waitresses were affected.

It was a bright but cold day, and both May and Becky had worn not only hats but scarves as well to keep themselves warm on the way to work. Arriving at the back door of the building where the dinner was to take place, May smiled at Becky and said, 'Here we go.' Then she pushed the door open and said, 'Well, it's lovely an' warm in here, so that's one blessing.'

They passed through the great kitchen, walking slowly, taking it all in for this was the first time they had worked in these premises. There were so many white-coated staff and men wearing tall chef's hats that it was difficult to imagine how they could work in such harmony.

'Look,' May said, pointing to the far end of the kitchen, 'there's Mrs Nicholls, she'll tell us where we're to go.'

They dodged past the hot range that had an amazing number of cast-iron pans arrayed along the top and Mrs Nicholls greeted them cheerfully, saying, 'Trust you two to use the wrong entrance. But never mind, come through here, go up those stairs and the first room facing you at the top has been set up as a changing room.'

They followed her directions and halfway up the staircase May remarked, 'Mrs Nicholls doesn't alter, does she?'

'No, except her hair is turning grey, but I know what you mean. She's a very nice lady, very friendly,' Becky replied.

'She is, there's no side to her. We've always got on well with her, haven't we?'

'They say listeners never hear any good of themselves but I don't seem to be doing so badly.'

Both girls turned their heads sharply at the sound of Florence Nicholls' voice.

May was the first to recover. 'You shouldn't wear those soft-soled shoes, though I suppose they're good if you want to creep up behind us girls without being heard.'

'I'll have a little less sauce from you tonight, May Stevens, you should have learned by now I don't need to creep up on you. I have eyes in the back of my head and two sets of ears. There's not much goes on in this company that I don't get to hear about in one form or another.'

Each girl placed a hand to her mouth in order to hide a grin.

They had reached the top of the stairs and Becky held the door open for Mrs Nicholls to enter the staff room first. She did so, laughing loudly as she passed, and Mrs Nicholls' laughter was to set the tone for the whole evening. There were only about sixty waitresses on duty tonight, for compared to some functions this dinner was a small affair.

The sight of the menu was the first item that had the girls giggling. The company had fulfilled its promise. Printed on wood veneer the choice of food was set out exactly in the manner of a builder's specification.

The main course – Brickwork. This consists of roast beef laid in vegetable mortar. Dessert – Joinery. Mort ice anystyle, with a choice of black or white for the finishing.

'Look at the bottom, look at it!' several voices yelled in unison.

'Cor, if that don't take the biscuit I don't know what does,' May laughed sharply.

A request at the bottom of the menu read:

NB: Please don't tip the exca-vaiters.

However the impeccably dressed Nippies were more than pleased when, having taken up their allotted places before serving the first course, the entire ensemble rose to its feet, cheered and waved their serviettes.

★   ★   ★

It was one o'clock in the morning when two tired but happy girls dragged themselves over the step and into the hall to be confronted by Aunt Lil, pink dressing gown tied tightly around her waist, pink furry slippers on her feet and curlers in her hair. She made a welcoming sight.

'Dead beat, are you? Fancy a cuppa or a bowl of broth before you climb the stairs?' she enquired, grinning as she added, 'It ain't all honey is it, being top waitresses in the West End of London?'

May was already seated on the bottom tread of the staircase. 'Oh, my poor feet,' she moaned as she gently eased her black shoes off and began rubbing her toes.

'Aunt Lil, I've said it before and I'll say it again, you are a diamond!' Becky murmured as she wriggled her bottom on to the step next to May. 'I could kill for a cup of tea but I wouldn't have had the strength to make it for myself.'

'Glad to know this old body is still of use to you fair ladies,' was Aunt Lil's comment as she turned to go. Then she changed her mind and threw back over her shoulder, 'Five minutes an' it will be on the table, so if you can't walk you'd better crawl cos I've never yet served tea in me hall and I've no intention of starting now.'

Becky looked at May and merely smiled. May smiled back at her. Turning their heads they could see into the kitchen through the open door. Aunt Lil had already set out cups, plates and food on the table. She had probably spent half the day baking and these last hours of the day sitting in her big wooden armchair set to the side of the fire, resting her feet on the brass fender.

Of course she would never admit it but even if she did go up to her bed they knew she never slept until she heard both of them were safely indoors.

'We're both very lucky,' Becky murmured softly. 'She's like a mother hen where we're concerned.'

'Yes.' May nodded. 'She's a brick, isn't she?' She paused

and sighed, then went on, 'Makes you wonder what will happen if and when we decide to get married.'

Alarm bells went off in Becky's head. We get married? Did May mean herself and Stan Riley? Or did she mean us, herself and me?

She couldn't let her thoughts form an answer because Aunt Lil was standing in the open doorway insisting, 'Come and get this cup of tea right now, I'm not 'aving you fall asleep sitting out there in the cold.'

Becky stared at this tiny woman who was like a second mother to her and thought just how much she had come to love her. Then she got to her feet, pulled May up and said aloud, 'We're keeping our guardian angel from her bed. Let's have our tea and then we'll all go up together.'

Chapter Twenty-eight

BECKY WALKED ALONG the Embankment deep in thought, her hands thrust into the pockets of her coat.

It was a cold, clear night with lots of stars in the sky and there was a bright moon. The wind was blowing up from the Thames and she snuggled her chin deep into her fur collar.

She was very much preoccupied with thoughts that had been troubling her for some time. Somehow she knew that things between May and Stan Riley were a whole lot more serious than May painted them to be.

Not that she blamed May. Oh no. It was May's own business and she would confide in her when the time was right. After all, both she and May were almost twenty-three and that would be a good time to get married. At least for May it would be. Stan was a nice bloke. She liked him a lot. He didn't have any pretensions of grandeur, his feet were firmly planted on the ground and they struck her as being ideally suited to one another. The question was, where would they live when they did decide to tie the knot?

May would never leave her aunt and to be fair-minded there was more than enough room in Aunt Lil's house for them all to live without ever intruding on one another's privacy. What about me? was the woeful thought that seemed to be forever in her mind. I'm sure both Aunt Lil and May would insist that I stay on and have a room as always. I couldn't do that. I would feel I was trespassing. Besides, I would hate to spoil such a friendship as May and I have. I've been so lucky, Becky said to herself. Ever since I came to London I have never been lonely. Never been on my own.

Of course I have missed my family, at times very much so, but what a godsend it was when May and I met on that very first day. Then May's mother died and Aunt Lil stepped in and she's taken care of us both ever since, filling in all those gaps that would have been left. Bless her.

What now? What options do I have? I'm not hard up. I earn good money. I suppose I could rent a flat somewhere but it would have to be on the other side of the river. My income won't stretch to West End prices. Alternatively I could go into lodgings. But do I want to live in a strange house with people I've never set eyes on before?

The very thought made her shudder. She stopped walking, turned and leant her elbows on the parapet, staring down into the deep waters of the Thames. As she stood still she felt rather than saw a tall man leaning over the wall also staring at the water. Since it was too cold to linger she turned away at the same time as the man did and they came face to face.

The man's eyes widened and he leant forward to look into Becky's face then said, 'Rebecca?'

Becky had been frightened for a moment; she seemed unable to speak except to mutter, 'Mr Matthews.'

He was unable to take his eyes off her. She looked entirely different out of uniform. Her long heavy coat emphasized her narrow waist and that close-fitting hat framed a face that in the moonlight looked to be that of a small child.

'What on earth are you doing walking the Embankment on your own at this time of night?' He bellowed the question at her and she drew away, taking two steps backward. 'Oh, I'm sorry. I didn't mean to shout. Are you on your way somewhere?'

Becky recovered, took a deep breath and answered him with a smile. 'No, I didn't want to go home just yet and it isn't much after seven o'clock. The river fascinates me, it's never still. When I first came to London I used to come here quite often.'

'That's as maybe, but I am not leaving you out here on

your own,' he said gently. 'I'd be wondering and worrying about you all night.'

'It's all right,' she quickly replied, 'I am quite grown-up.'

'Well you don't look it,' he said, giving her a quirky grin, 'and I'm now going to take charge of you.' He took a grip on her arm and tucked it through his, and with determination he made sure that they set off at a brisk pace, leaving the Embankment behind them and making their way up the Strand. 'Keep your eyes peeled for a cab,' he ordered.

They reached Trafalgar Square without having spotted one that was for hire. Robert glanced down at Becky. 'Would you like a hot drink? I know I could use one.'

'Yes, please,' she agreed. Then with a wide grin she said, 'Which Lyons would you suggest?'

He laughed back at her, 'Oh no. We're not having a busman's holiday.' Still laughing, he added, 'Instead, Miss Russell, I shall take you slumming.'

Minutes later and Becky couldn't believe it! They were only a short distance from Nelson's Column and here they were, standing in the road, by the side of a brilliantly lit coffee-stall, munching on bread rolls that held a long hot sausage generously smeared with Colman's mustard. And that wasn't all. Perched on the high counter in front of them were two enormous china mugs filled with boiling coffee which the big, fat stallholder had made from a bottle of Camp liquid.

She was a Nippy for Lyons and the man with her, well, she didn't quite know how to describe him even to herself, except to say that he had a top job with the same firm. It would take some believing if she related this to Aunt Lil or even to May. Bringing May to mind brought a smile to Becky's lips. That was one person who certainly wouldn't swallow this story.

Robert Matthews chewed on his roll, all the while looking at Rebecca. She was a dainty person. She had an oval face that was adorable, high cheekbones, a small nose and thick dark hair that he had often admired as it lay against her face when flattened by her waitress cap. Her eyes were large and deep dark brown with thick lashes that curled without any help from that mascara colouring that had become so fashionable.

He picked up his mug and took a sip of his coffee, suddenly wishing it were something stronger. Rebecca Russell unnerved him. She always had from the first moment he had set eyes on her. She also intrigued him, and he longed to know whether some of the stories he'd heard about her were true or just jealous rumours.

He had been an only child; now both his parents were dead and all he had were distant elderly relatives. He had known a few young ladies since he had lived on his own, but he had not experienced the kind of feelings that Rebecca roused in him. There was something about her that tugged at his heartstrings, made him want to watch out for her. He knew that Mr Gower thought the world of her and he was nobody's fool.

'I'm sorry it's only bottled coffee,' Robert said, making an apologetic face. 'Leave it if you don't like it, Rebecca.'

She shook her head. 'It's fine, Mr Matthews, nice and hot and the sausage roll is going down a treat.'

He lowered his head and smiled at her. 'Do you not think we could dispense with the Mr Matthews? My name is Robert.'

'I know full well what your Christian name is but it wouldn't do for me to use it. All you bosses use the girls' Christian names, which is nice, but it would be disrespectful if we did the same.'

'Is that how you see me? One of the bosses?'

'Well, that's exactly what you are, aren't you?'

'That's clever,' he laughed.

'What is?' she challenged.

'Answering a question with a question. I work for my living just the same as you do.'

Oh dear. Becky suddenly wished she was anywhere else but here. Had she upset him? Gone too far, been too cheeky?

Although Becky had no way of knowing it, Robert Matthews was kicking himself for having responded so abruptly. He instantly regretted it. What he really wanted to do was take her in his arms and if they stood here, so close to each other, for much longer he wouldn't be able to resist the urge to kiss her.

So, reluctantly, he placed his coffee mug back on to the counter, and took a deep breath of the cold air, endeavouring to speak calmly. 'It's cold standing here, and it's getting late, I'd better get you home. You stay where you are and I'll go and find a cab.'

'It's all right,' she told him, touching his arm. 'I can get a bus from Trafalgar Square and I'll be home in no time.'

'Miss Russell!' He sounded quite shocked. 'A gentleman doesn't meet a young lady, wine and dine her and then leave her to make her own way home. Whatever can you be thinking of?'

Becky realized that he was teasing her and she chuckled as he hurried away towards the bright lights of the square.

In no time at all he must have found a cab because he was back and as the cab drew into the kerb Robert jumped out, helped Rebecca to get in, telling her to give the address to the cabbie, jumped inside after her, and slammed the door. They sat close to each other, saying nothing as the cab rumbled on its way to South Lambeth Road.

When the cab reached her destination Robert once again jumped out and helped her down on to the pavement. Becky groaned to herself as the front door was thrown open and Aunt Lil stood in the shaft of light that was pouring out of the hallway. At least she is dressed, Becky breathed thankfully, looking really neat and tidy, but did she have to open the door at that very moment?

'Where have you been?' Aunt Lil called out, sounding really worried.

Oh no! Becky gasped in horror. Robert Matthews was asking the cab driver to wait and now, not giving her time to protest, he had gripped her arm and was leading her up the garden path toward the house.

'Are you all right, Becky? I knew May wasn't coming home until late but I was expecting you home about half past six. I haven't known what to do.' By the time Aunt Lil had finished speaking they had reached the foot of the stone steps. Leaning forwards, peering into the darkness Aunt Lil said, 'Thank you for bringing her home, young man. Are you sure she isn't hurt or anything? Don't just stand there the pair of you, come in, come on in.'

Robert turned his gaze away from the tiny lady and looked at Becky. She shrugged her shoulders and they both smiled. 'You'd better do as she says or I shall never hear the end of it. Do you mind coming in for a moment?'

With his voice full of merriment he said, 'Not at all,' and then taking hold of Becky's hand, he climbed the steps with her. Like a couple of naughty schoolchildren, they faced Aunt Lil.

Becky made the introductions and Aunt Lil had to tilt her head back in order to look Robert over from top to toe. 'My, he's a tall one,' she said, ushering him into the living room where a good fire was roaring up the chimney and a pot of bronze chrysanthemums, standing in a copper bowl, had been placed in the centre of the table.

'This is cosy,' Robert exclaimed.

Aunt Lil immediately asked him to take off his overcoat, sit down and have something to eat and drink.

Thankfully Becky listened as he declined. 'The cabbie won't be in the best of moods if I keep him hanging about,' he quickly explained. 'He'll be wanting to get back to the West End, that's where the money is made at this time of night. But you mustn't blame Rebecca for being late home, it was entirely my fault. Will you forgive me?'

Becky couldn't believe it. Aunt Lil was looking all coy. It just went to show what a charmer Robert Matthews could be. Becky went to the front door with him and thanked him for bringing her home. They shook hands and she told herself that she had only imagined that he had held on to her hand for a lot longer than was necessary. All the same she gave a little sigh of relief as she closed the front door and went back to face the questioning she knew was bound to come from Aunt Lil.

Three weeks had gone by and Becky hadn't set eyes on Robert Matthews. Jolly good job too, she repeatedly said to herself, but it was only a half-truth. She had constantly found herself hoping that she would see him again. Only during the course of the day's work, she would chide herself, but again that wasn't entirely true. She often wondered what it would be like to actually be taken out by Robert Matthews.

Sometimes her thoughts were more sensible. At those times she would assure herself the meeting with Robert Matthews was best forgotten. Deep down he was probably no different to Gerald Palmer. Except he did work for his living. That was another thing that preyed on her mind. Robert Matthews seemed to pick and choose what he would do. His job with Lyons seemed to be very flexible. There would be days when he always seemed to be around; she had often felt his eyes watching her as she carried out her duties. Then he would disappear, like now, and nobody would set eyes on him for weeks.

These days when May caught her daydreaming she would give her a good old dressing-down. Having heard from Aunt Lil a very colourful version of the evening Mr Matthews had brought 'our Rebecca' home, May had been like a dog with a bone.

'Keep your head on your shoulders,' was one of May's favourite terms, 'have sense. See through him. Realize he's not one of our kind.'

All a bit daft, Becky wanted to yell back, but she didn't because she knew so well that May only had her good at heart and didn't want her to be hurt again.

Becky was just making up her mind to go to the ladies and make herself tidy before going back on duty when she saw him coming across the floor towards her. She gave a gasp of surprise. She had spent her entire tea break thinking about him and here he was in the flesh.

She hastily got to her feet, almost toppling the chair over, and he quickly straightened it, saying, 'I'm sorry. Did I startle you?'

Becky shook her head in protest; she felt as if she were dreaming.

Robert Matthews stepped away from her and very quietly asked, 'How are you? You look tired. Not working too hard, are you?'

'I'm fine, really. Saturday is always a busy day. I'm just going to change my shoes – pity we aren't able to have a spare pair of feet.'

He did not laugh as she had expected he would. Instead he enquired, 'Are you off tomorrow?'

She didn't answer him immediately, but she had her head tilted back and was looking straight at him when she said, 'Yes, I am.'

'Would you allow me to take you for a drive? I thought we might go as far as Richmond.' She stiffened slightly and Robert Matthews had noticed the reaction. He inclined his head towards Becky. 'If you'd rather not.'

The staff room had gone quiet, the rest of the girls having bustled off to do the remainder of their shift. There would be plenty of people about this afternoon, having done their shopping and in need of afternoon tea. What should she do now? Half of her wanted to yell that she'd love to go with him. The cautious part of her was warning her not to start something she would regret. Remember Gerald! But he was in the past. Was she going to let him ruin her life for ever? Surely she was entitled to one mistake. Blow Gerald and everything about him. She was being given an opportunity to find out if this tall blond man was sincere or not. She made her mind up, she was going to take it. And to hell with the consequences.

'Thank you for extending the invitation.'

He laughed, quite loudly, and Becky, thinking to herself that it was a happy laugh, smiled at him.

'This conversation,' he said, 'is getting very stilted. It's not as if we are complete strangers. Don't forget you have allowed me to buy you dinner before now. Oh yes, and take you home in a cab. So will you or won't you come out with me tomorrow?'

She knew he was teasing her again but she didn't mind one bit. 'I would like to, very much.' Becky's voice was quiet.

'Good,' he grinned, 'that's settled. I know where you live, I'll pick you up at eleven o'clock in the morning. Oh, and you might persuade your aunt that my intentions are honourable.' He turned away, came back and with a mischievous look in his eye, added, 'On second thoughts, don't bother. I shall reassure her myself. Till tomorrow then, Rebecca.'

The last four words were soft and full of feeling. But Becky did not reply to them. She just stood and watched him walking away, every inch a gentleman in a fine grey suit, and his usual waistcoat beneath the jacket. Not until she could no longer see him did she make a move towards the washroom.

Having washed her hands and splashed her face with cold water she now studied herself in the full-length mirror. She looked very smart in her Nippy uniform; she wouldn't be allowed on the restaurant floor if she didn't. Daily inspection of every waitress employed by Lyons wasn't just a matter of routine. It was thorough, never altering in all the time that she had been employed by them. Now, as she had countless times, she renewed her thanks to God Almighty for having been given the privilege of being trained, finally, to become a tip-top London waitress.

All the same, she sighed deeply to herself, life's not easy. Not by any means. She had mistakenly thought that mixing with the well–off toffs would provide the opportunity for her to find a suitable husband. She had seen how the other half lived and she didn't want to be poor.

'You've been very lucky, so far,' she said aloud to her reflection in the mirror, 'you could have fared a lot worse. A whole lot worse! Let's hope you've learnt your lesson.'

She hastened back to the restaurant, for she was late, and the waitress who was sharing her station this afternoon glared at her. She didn't mind. For the next three hours she was run off her feet, while all the time her imagination was running wild. Tomorrow she was being taken out by Robert Matthews.

Chapter Twenty-nine

BECKY WAS READY well in time, standing in the front room looking out of the window ready to make a dash for it as soon as Robert arrived. She was wearing her long grey coat over a navy-blue two-piece suit, a black velvet hat and black kid gloves.

'About what time shall I expect you back?' Aunt Lil asked as she poked her head round the door.

'I really don't know, shouldn't think it will be late, but please, Aunt Lil, don't start worrying about me.'

Aunt Lil came closer and walked around Becky, inspecting her from head to toe. 'I'm glad you've put on your big coat. It's a lovely bright day but not very warm, there's quite a wind blowing.'

Before Becky had a chance to answer her, there was a loud rat-a-tat-tat on the front door.

'I'll go,' Aunt Lil said, leaving the room like a shot.

Becky groaned. The only thing she was thankful for was that she was ready to set off, so there was no reason why they should hang about and give Aunt Lil the chance to question him.

The sight of Aunt Lil re-entering the room caused Becky to smile. She was carrying a bunch of flowers and looking very pleased with herself. Beaming, she said, 'Your Mr Matthews brought these for me. Aren't they nice? And they smell really lovely.'

Becky agreed that they were indeed lovely and turned to face Robert. But he wasn't looking at her, he was smiling at Aunt Lil, saying, 'How are you, Mrs Maynard? I hope you have forgiven me for keeping Rebecca out so late last time we met.'

Becky didn't know quite what to say or do. She was looking at this wonderful man whom she had regarded as her boss for going on four years now, and trying not to take any notice of the look on Aunt Lil's face. She had to press her lips tightly together to stop herself from grinning. Aunt Lil was loving the attention. And Robert Matthews was being an absolute gentleman.

'Thank you again for the flowers,' Aunt Lil was saying.

'Not at all. Not at all. And I promise I shall have Rebecca home here no later than seven o'clock.'

Seven o'clock! She had thought they were only going for a run out, perhaps home in time for tea. Becky warned herself to stay calm. She walked over to her aunt and kissed her on the cheek. They stared at each other for a moment then Becky patted her arm and whispered, 'Don't worry about me, I'll be fine.'

'See that you are, and have a nice time, bless you.'

Becky walked towards the door, while Robert took Lil's hand between his own and said quietly, 'I'll take care of her. We won't be back late. I promise.'

'Thank you,' Aunt Lil answered in a conspiratorial whisper. They were outside the house now and he had his hand on Rebecca's elbow leading her towards a smart Austin motorcar that stood at the kerb. She felt very important as Robert opened the nearside door and handed her into the passenger seat. 'Comfortable?' he asked before closing the door and going round to get into the driver's seat.

The car itself was black but the interior upholstery had Becky gasping in surprise. It was all leather, tan in colour, and the rich smell that comes only from good leather had her sniffing with delight.

'Sunday markets are causing all this traffic,' Robert said. 'But don't worry, we'll soon be out of it.'

'Oh, it doesn't worry me,' she replied with a grin, looking

along Wandsworth High Street that was thick with traders of all sorts. Costermongers had their stalls set out, young lads were pushing barrows and handcarts, and on the pavement at intervals were the shellfish stalls.

'Every Londoner's favourite Sunday tea, cockles, whelks, winkles and shrimps plus the odd stick of celery,' Robert told her with a change in his accent, making the statement into a kind of sing-song.

'Not much different from Kingston market, which is quite near to where I was born and brought up,' Becky laughingly told him. 'And I still regard it as home.'

'And so you should. I think you are extremely lucky not only to have Mrs Maynard to take care of you but still have your parents and brothers back in New Malden.'

Becky turned her head to stare at him. 'You've made it your business to know a lot about me!'

'Please.' He took a hand off of the steering wheel and laid it lightly on her knee just for a second before saying, 'I wasn't prying. I admit I did want to know more about you, though I have known you since the time you first applied for a job with Lyons. Sometimes, such as when you were given promotion, we do update our records. Shall I tell you something, Rebecca? I envy you. I have admired you from the moment I first set eyes on you but when I became aware of the fact that you had a loving family as well as May Stevens for a friend and her aunt as a second mother, I truly did envy you.'

Becky was utterly bewildered. She remained silent, lost in thought. What had Robert Matthews got to be envious about? He had everything. Good job, plenty of money or so it seemed or he wouldn't own such a motorcar as this one she was riding in. There was something else that was niggling away at her. Difficult to pin it down. He had said 'we' update the records. Not the firm. Not the company. But 'we'. Oh, well, she wasn't going to let anything spoil today. This was a rare chance to have a nice day out.

'We're driving through Putney now,' Robert told her, wisely doing his best to change the subject. 'Now the scenery will get better.'

Soon they had left the rows of terraced houses behind and Becky noticed that most properties were now detached with nicely cared-for gardens. She was about to say that they couldn't be too far from her home but decided to let that pass. The signs placed on the walls stated that Richmond was in the county of Surrey. Indeed she was remembering how, as a young girl, she, Ella and all of their brothers had often walked along the towpath and sometimes even been taken on outings as far as Richmond Hill. Not that she could recall such imposing surroundings as those that Robert was driving through at this moment.

The houses were so large! They boasted great big double gates with a smaller gate set in the end of a high solid wall that held a board which stated 'Tradesmen' in large painted letters.

Passing all these obvious signs of wealth Robert suddenly said, 'Here we are. Richmond Park.'

'Oh, Mr Matthews, it is lovely.'

He switched off the engine, turned and smacked her hand gently. 'We are going to spend a lovely day together, have lunch soon and most probably tea before I take you home, so will you please start calling me Robert?'

'I'll try to remember,' she said, her cheeks reddening. 'It just doesn't seem right.'

'Nothing would please me more. Say it now, go on, just say Robert.'

'Robert,' she said quietly.

'There you are, it isn't difficult, is it?'

'No,' she agreed, smiling.

'Shall we walk?' Robert asked, coming round to her side and opening the door.

She stood on the gravel drive looking at the great trees, the shrubs and the wonderful green grass that seemed to

stretch for miles. When he took her hand she didn't feel
shy or awkward, just happy.

They walked on and on, nodding at parents out for a
Sunday stroll with their kiddies, and young men proudly
parading their fiancées.

'We'd better turn back or we shall be late for lunch,'
Robert remarked.

They hadn't gone very far when three small boys came
tearing up to them, 'Mister, would you please help us get
our kite down?' the tallest of the three boys asked politely.

'We can't reach it,' the smallest of the three echoed, which
made both Becky and Robert laugh because this little mite
was very tiny.

'I'll help if I can,' Robert agreed. 'Show me where it has
got caught.'

The kite could be seen quite clearly once all three lads had
pointed a finger in the right direction. The body of the kite
was white, the tail flapping in the wind was bright orange,
mauve, blue, green and yellow and for a moment Becky felt
quite homesick as her mind flew back to the weekend that
she and May had spent in New Malden. Hadn't they bought
such a kite for her nephew and hadn't the whole family gone
over to the field opposite the house in order to fly the kite
while her mum, Ella's mum, and Aunt Lil had prepared the
midday Sunday dinner? It was at times like this that she missed
her family.

'Hold my coat will you please, Rebecca?'

Robert's request brought her back to the present with a
start. They had walked a few yards without her noticing and
were now standing beneath a big oak tree, the branches of
which had tangled the young lads' kite.

As he removed his jacket Becky wanted to do more
than laugh. Robert wasn't wearing one of his usual smart
waistcoats; instead he had on a knitted pullover of an intricate
pattern and she found herself wondering who loved him
enough and also had enough patience to knit him such

a garment. It had to be an older woman, she decided, at the same time coming to the conclusion that the pullover suited Robert. It made him look more carefree, and younger. Up until now she would have set his age at thirty-two or thirty-three, but looking at him now she was sure he wasn't a day over thirty, maybe only twenty-eight.

Robert looked up, then around, and shook his head. 'There isn't anything lying about that is long enough to reach it,' he muttered. 'Oh well, here goes,' and laughing loudly he reached up to grab hold of two thick branches, found himself a foothold on the trunk of the tree and began to climb. The kite wasn't that high and within minutes Robert was untangling the strings that were caught between twigs.

'Oh, that's great!'

'You're super, Mister.'

'Yes, well done, thanks ever so much.'

The cries from the lads, as Robert freed their kite and held it out wide enabling it to float down to the ground, had both Robert and Becky laughing fit to burst.

'Thanks again,' the eldest boy called as the trio raced across the grass, the colourful toy streaming out behind them.

'Come on,' Robert urged, grabbing Becky's hand and starting to run, 'see if we can keep up with them as far as the car.'

Breathing heavily they reached the car and between gasps they were both still laughing as Robert used a handkerchief to brush away at the knees of his trousers. Straightening up he said, 'Does you good to mix with youngsters now and again.'

'I agree,' Becky laughingly replied, 'even if they do leave you feeling your age.'

'Oh, you poor old soul,' Robert taunted her, 'you are out of condition. I see I shall have to take you in hand, bring you out here more often, see that you get more fresh air in your lungs. Meanwhile, young lady, our lunch will be ready and waiting.'

As they got in to the car, Becky was again confused. She had wanted to agree wholeheartedly to his suggestion that they came out together more often but then he had added that their lunch was waiting and she had no idea where or why they were expected for lunch.

'Where are we going?' Becky asked after he had been driving for a few minutes.

'We're almost there,' he replied and seconds later he turned the car into a lane, drove over a hump-backed bridge which straddled a rippling stream and only a few yards further on left the road, turning in between two iron gates that were open as if they were expected, drove a short distance and stopped the car in front of a small but very pretty house.

Becky gazed at the thick covering of ivy that had a hold over most of the wall, it wasn't just green ivy but had shades of deep red entwined. She hadn't time to take in any more details because the front door had opened and a stout woman, in her mid-fifties Becky guessed, with iron grey hair in a knot on top of her head, was smiling them both a welcome.

Becky thought the woman's hairdo was the shape of a cottage loaf but she kept her thoughts to herself.

'Come on, come on,' Robert urged taking Becky's hand and ushering her towards the porch.

'Hello, Caroline,' he called. 'Have we kept you waiting?'

'No, not at all. Bring the young lady in and let's get the introductions over and done with.'

Robert laughed loudly and when they drew near he said, 'This is the young lady I told you about, Caroline. Her name is Rebecca Russell. Rebecca, this is Caroline Louise James.'

The woman took Becky's hand, smiling broadly. 'Oh we are formal this morning, I cannot remember when Robert last called me Caroline. I've been Carrie to him since he learnt to say his first words. Anyway don't you struggle with Caroline, you just call me Carrie and may I say how pleased I was when he told me he was bringing you to lunch. We don't see half as many visitors as we should and sometimes none for weeks on end.'

Becky decided this woman was nice. Very nice. She could easily take to her though at the moment she hadn't any idea who she was or how she fitted into Robert's life, despite the fact that she seemed to have been forewarned that Robert was bringing her here for lunch today.

And that wasn't the only surprise.

Having been led down a narrow passage that led out to a surprisingly spacious hall she was amazed to see a large, portly, white-haired gentleman standing in the doorway of what seemed to be a sitting room. Behind him Becky could see the flames from a log fire lighting up an open fireplace.

'Welcome my dear,' he said, his hand outstretched, his voice loud. Becky took his hand and had to suck in her breath, his grasp was so firm. 'Sit you down young lady, I'm too old to stand,' he added as he sank heavily on to the chair which Robert had pushed forward.

'Rebecca, this is my Uncle Maurice, though now that I am a grown man I'm allowed to drop the "uncle" and use his Christian name.' Robert turned from Rebecca to face his uncle saying, 'Uncle, this is—'

'I know who she is,' Uncle Maurice hastily interrupted. 'You've talked of her often enough. How'd you do, Rebecca. Come and sit beside me, we'll have a glass of Madeira and get to know each other, shall we?'

Robert looked embarrassed as he shrugged his shoulders and pulled a chair closer to the fire for Rebecca.

'Shall I put the finishing touches to the lunch?' Caroline asked practically. 'The table is all set in the dining room and I can be ready to serve in about fifteen minutes.'

'Perfect, Carrie,' Robert said, flashing her a smile that thanked her for saving the day.

Her coat and hat off, a glass of wine in her hand, Becky sat gazing about her. It was a small room, a lot smaller than the front room in Aunt Lil's house and even smaller than the main family room at home in New Malden, but it was cosy and beautifully furnished. Everything from the beams in the ceiling to the pictures on the walls and the actual furniture was old and lovingly cared for. The carpet, lampshades and the draped curtains at the small windows were a maze of autumn colours.

'Lunch is all ready, if you'd like to come through.' Carrie's voice was jolly. 'Sit yourself down, Rebecca, anywhere you like since there are only the four of us, it doesn't really matter.'

Robert held a chair out for Becky and when she was seated he took the chair opposite for himself.

At first glance this dining room had made Becky catch her breath. It was a much larger room than the cosy sitting room they had just left. It had to be the most beautiful room she had ever seen. Again the room was heated by a bright log fire and to each side of the open fireplace a settee had been drawn up. The walls were wood-panelled, the furniture again old, still shining from years of polishing.

Although Carrie sat down to eat with them she seemed to be forever jumping to her feet to see to the next course.

'Is that it now? Have we reached the main course?' Uncle Maurice's voice came from deep down in his throat. 'You've been like a cat on hot bricks ever since you set foot in that kitchen this morning, one would think we were entertaining royalty. Been cooking since the crack of dawn she has,' he finished on a laugh.

Carrie was now placing a heavily-laden tray on a side table, and in a cheery voice said, 'I'd rather prepare a meal for Rebecca any day. Royalty would frighten me to death whereas Rebecca is friendly, she would put anyone at ease.'

A smile spread over Robert's face as he jumped to his feet, saying, 'Let me bring that lot nearer to the table, Carrie, and then we can all help ourselves to the vegetables.'

'Good idea, Robert, perhaps now you'll do as you're told,

Carrie. Come on, sit down and enjoy your own cooking,'
Maurice ordered.

'Bossy pair, aren't they?' Carrie grinned as she retook her
seat next to Becky.

Becky agreed with Carrie. She felt she had known that she
could be friends with this stout cheery lady from the moment
they had shook hands. Yet this house and the three people in
it were a puzzle. So the men were uncle and nephew, but
she had heard Maurice thanking Robert and telling him how
much he was enjoying staying here with Carrie to take care
of him. Where did he live? And to whom did this cottage
belong? And even more to the point, where did Carrie fit
in? She wasn't a maid or even the cook. She was a lot more
than that. Hadn't she admitted that she had known Robert
from the day he was born?

Feeling thoroughly confused Becky decided that she would
wait until such time as Robert thought fit to enlighten her.
Meanwhile she was going to enjoy this plate of lovely roast
lamb that Carrie had set down in front of her.

Throughout the whole of the meal Becky felt at ease. It
was almost as if they were family. She hadn't reckoned on
having lunch with folk that she didn't know but it had turned
out so well. Happy and relaxed she set her spoon down into
her sweet-dish and sat back with a satisfied sigh.

'Would you like some more trifle, Rebecca?'

'Oh no, thank you Carrie. I've had a wonderful lunch.'

'Then I'll fetch the cheese and the coffee.'

'Stay where you are,' came the order from Robert. 'Talk
to Rebecca, I'll fetch the coffee.'

'I don't suppose you are acquainted with the family history?' Carrie spoke softly to Rebecca as Robert left the room
and Maurice moved from the dinner table to seat himself in
a corner of a settee by the fire.

Becky made no reply; she merely smiled.

'The whole framework I'll leave out, that's Robert's
business. I'll just put you in the picture as to where I fit

in. You must be wondering by now, hired help sitting down to eat with the family and guests.'

Becky found the last statement tricky. Of course she had been wondering but she surely couldn't admit as much. She was saved from forming an answer by Carrie throwing back her head and laughing out loud. 'It was naughty of Robert to bring you here without explaining. For want of a better word I used to be nanny to Robert. He grew up, his father died and his mother never had much interest in him after that, or anyone else for that matter. She saw Robert safely settled, persuaded him to join the family business and after that, well, the truth is she never wanted to live. She and her husband were everything to one another, never known two people so in love as those two were. With her husband gone she willed herself to go too. No matter what the doctors had to say at the time that is the simple truth.'

Becky felt it was such a sad story yet she couldn't resist asking one question. 'Have you looked after Robert ever since?'

She got no answer.

'Poor Rebecca.' Robert had entered the room and having set down the tray he was carrying he looked sheepishly at Rebecca. 'If I had told you I intended to bring you to lunch with Caroline and my Uncle Maurice I was afraid you might have shied away, so instead I have let Carrie bear the brunt of my cowardliness. What are you thinking now?' he asked, handing her a cup of coffee.

Becky looked into his eyes. They were full of sadness and she felt unable to hide her own feelings. 'I was thinking that this is a beautiful house and that I have been very privileged to be invited here for lunch today. I shouldn't have asked questions of Carrie, I'm sorry.'

The sadness in his eyes intensified. 'I've done this all wrong,' he muttered, more to himself than to her. 'Rebecca, when you've had your coffee I would like to show you the grounds and tell you the history of this house. Will you come with me?'

Rebecca nodded her head and Robert smiled at her. It was a gentle smile as if he were trying to thank her for something.

Their coffee finished, he now got to his feet and, standing in front of Rebecca, he said, 'We'll go into the garden now while it's still light. It won't take long, there's not a great deal to see.'

At the end of the hall he pushed open a heavy door and they were in the kitchen. It was a large square room, the main feature being the huge kitchen range which had an open grate and an oven to each side of it. Most of the floor space was taken up by a white wood-topped table.

'This way.' Robert pointed to the large window that had a white painted door to the side. 'This door leads out to the herb garden and on through to the main lawn. It shouldn't be muddy today but there are boots in the shed if you would like to change your shoes.'

'No, it's all right,' Becky assured him, thankful that she wasn't wearing high heels.

As he had said, there wasn't too much garden but what there was was well-planned. 'Easy to set out and easy to maintain,' Robert explained. 'Carrie can't do too much.' He paused and laughed and Becky knew that he meant she was too fat. 'A gardener comes once a week now and twice a week during the summer months. I love this house, I come here as often as I can, it's a place to unwind in peaceful surroundings.'

Questions were still nagging away inside Becky's brain. If only he would get round to telling her what she was doing here.

'We won't go down beyond the lawn, as least not today, but there is a pond and a marshy piece of land which has become a sanctuary for countless birds and wildfowl. Lovely sight when the weather is warmer. Come, we'll sit in the summerhouse for a while and then we'll go back into the house.'

The summerhouse was quaint, almost like a doll's house. It had a white wrought-iron table and chairs with red padded cushions. Three sides of the house were all windows, giving a complete view of the garden and also of the house.

Becky sat down and laid her head back against the top of the chair. She was silent for once. When Robert had held open the door of this summerhouse she had squeezed past him, her hand had accidentally brushed against his and she had almost jumped out of her skin. Touching his fingers had been like an electric shock and she had pulled her hand away quickly. That hadn't been what she wanted to do. Grab hold of him and hold on tightly was what she had really felt like doing.

'I expect you are wondering about Carrie,' Robert said, startling her.

She took a deep breath and admitted, 'Yes, to be honest I am. Does she live here on her own?'

'Mostly she does. It suits her fine, she does have friends in the village and she always knows where I am and how she can get in touch with me. Carrie has been part of my life from the day I was born.'

'I gathered that much from what she told me.'

'Did she tell you this was my grandmother's house when she was alive?'

'Oh no, nothing about your family, only that both your parents are dead.'

'Didn't you want to ask her?' Robert had the grace to smile. 'I thought all females were blessed with a deal of curiosity.'

'That's as maybe,' Becky answered him quietly. 'You don't ask questions when you first meet someone.'

Robert Matthews was having a funny effect on her, making her aware of emotions that were sending her off-balance. There wasn't much room in this summerhouse and he was sitting so close to her. Their knees were almost touching. As if reading her thoughts, Robert said, 'You arouse the curiosity in me.' His voice was low and husky.

'But you know everything there is to know about me,'

she said, sounding quite indignant. 'You've only to check the records.'

Robert moved his chair slightly, sat back, draped one arm over it, and gave her a long, very meaningful look. 'Well then, perhaps it is about time I evened up the score. I won't start at the beginning, not yet, we'll settle the matter of Carrie first. As a young woman she was employed by my parents to be nanny to me. I was an only child and when my father died and my mother became ill Carrie was always there even though my grandmother came to live in our house. It was, and still is, a family-owned house in Hampstead and that is where Uncle Maurice, my father's elder brother, lives at present. When my mother also died matters continued much as they had been for a long time with Carrie and my grandmother being there for me.'

All the while Robert had been talking he had not taken his eyes away from Becky and under his close scrutiny she felt the colour rise in her cheeks. As if to reassure her, Robert took hold of her hand and held it as he continued, 'This small house belonged to my grandmother and when she died she left it to me. It has always seemed right that Carrie should live here for as long as she wished to. She has never married.'

In the silence that followed Becky closed her eyes. Piecing together the half that Carrie had told her and now what Robert had added, it was in some ways a very sad story. For Carrie a happy ending? Maybe. For Robert a lonely life? She had no way of telling, but it did explain why he had said he was envious of her having parents and three brothers.

Robert touched her arm lightly. 'I feel I should go the whole hog and tell you about my position with Lyons. That's if I am not boring you.'

'No, no,' she cut in, giving him a small, almost shy smile, 'I would like you to tell me. I would have to be very dim-witted not to have realized that you are more than just an employee of the company.'

'I never lied to you,' he hastened to say. 'You assumed

what you wanted to from the first, and given that you only saw part of my duties, no one could blame you. The truth is my great-grandfather was one of the founders of Lyons. Truly Rebecca, I have never tried to hide that fact from you.'

She was unconvinced, but she tried to smile.

She had already been led up the garden path by Gerald Palmer. Was Robert of the same mind? Did he see her as just one of the waitresses employed in the family firm? He must be as well-off financially as Gerald, probably a great deal more so. That being the case, then why was he bothering with her? As well as this beautiful house he had admitted there was a house in Hampstead and apart from that God knows what else. He could have any young lady he chose, one from a wealthy background such as his own, she thought bitterly. Again she asked herself, why is he bothering with me? She bit her lip, blinking rapidly to keep the angry tears back. Casual affairs were probably part of his life since he never seemed to be in the same place for any length of time but if he thought he was going to add her to his list then he was greatly mistaken. Once bitten was enough.

She got to her feet and made to push by him, seething inside because she had let herself believe that this time she had found a decent young man who worked for his living. She couldn't deny that she was attracted to him, what girl wouldn't be? He had boyish good looks and a kind of mesmerizing charm. Of course she had known that he was well up in his job with Lyons, had been aware of that from the beginning, but to find out that he owned part of that great company! Well, it puts me well out of his league, she muttered under her breath.

Her problem now was how to get home. She didn't have much choice; she would just have to keep quiet during the journey and let Robert drive and in order to do that she knew she would have to keep a grip on her feelings.

Robert was wondering how things could so suddenly have gone wrong between them. He placed a restraining hand on her arm. 'Don't go, Rebecca, not like this, please, sit down again and let's talk.'

Becky slumped down onto the chair again, instinctively feeling she should at least give him a chance.

Robert remained standing. 'Rebecca.' He tried to put a hand on her shoulder but she wriggled away. 'I wish to God I had made my position clear to you when we first met. It is unfortunate that I didn't because even then I was attracted to you. You had such charming appeal, not in the least worldly, you not only looked different, you acted differently to most of the young girls I had come into contact with. Even then I wanted to ask you out but you seemed so young and I was away out of London so often I thought I would wait. See if you liked the work, if you were going to stay with the company. Maybe I was wrong to bide my time, but I don't think so.'

Even feeling as angry as she did Rebecca still could not ignore the note of sincerity there was in his voice. 'But why? Just answer me that one question. Why would you, a man who owns part of a vast company, be interested in a girl who worked for him as a waitress?'

'If you want to put it like that what causes any man from any walk of life to be attracted to a particular female? And vice versa, come to that. I don't know the answer, do you?'

Becky was finding that just sitting here looking at him was tormenting her and she mumbled, 'I come from a working-class family.'

'Oh!' Robert laughed loudly, and Becky felt she could have hit him, but as she raised her hand to do so he caught it and said, 'Now you will listen to me. The man who consented to his name being used when the company was being formed was a Joseph Lyons. He earned his living as street trader but he also had some exhibition know-how. He spoke well, was of a presentable appearance and like me he had a persuasive manner. His style appealed to the men who were putting up the money, an agreement was drawn up on a single sheet of paper and as I have always been given to understand signed by all the men concerned on a train journey between London and Manchester. That Joseph Lyons was my great-grandfather. Now you tell me, does that make me a better person than you?'

'You still only work from choice,' Becky mumbled defiantly.

'You are wrong. Totally wrong. I have to work as does every male member of the board. We carry no dead wood. We need to work, it would be soul-destroying not to. Besides which it is mainly the involvement of the directors, at every level, that has helped make Lyons the great company it is today.' Robert took a deep breath and leant towards her. 'You can be very maddening, do you know that?'

Even Becky had to grin as he said those words.

The sight of her grinning prompted him to keep going, and he took another deep breath and plunged in. 'It was always expected that I would join the company. I never wanted to. My father, whom I hero-worshipped, and my mother simply adored, had died so suddenly of a heart attack and I was supposed to take his place. My mother, a wonderful loving lady whom no one could ever replace, was very persuasive and I have lived to be thankful that she was. There is hardly a job within the company that I haven't been taught to tackle. From waiter to van driver I have done it all with the exception of training to be a chef.'

He sat back, looked across the small table at Rebecca. She had a face that was positively lovely but at the same time she looked so innocent. He had heard rumours that she had been out and about with what were to him the wrong kind of men. Even news of one in particular, Gerald Palmer, had reached his ears but he didn't care. He understood that coming to London and seeing how the other half lived, she naturally wanted as much out of life as possible. It was bad luck that she had been attracted to an unreliable man.

He had sown a few wild oats of his own in the past

but this was serious. Rebecca Russell was to him without equal.

'I would like to get to know you really well, Rebecca,' he said, 'and I want you to know me, too, but that will never happen if you insist that I come from a different class of people from your own. I don't care what your background is and you shouldn't care about mine. We both work for our living. I have thought about you often, from the first day that we met, and as I've already said I would like to get to know you better, and, as far as I am concerned, that is all that matters.'

'Robert,' Becky began sheepishly, 'I have to tell you, recently I was mixed up with a young man . . . I went away with him . . . for the weekend.'

There was a slight pause as he levelled his eyes to hers. Then, speaking very slowly, he asked, 'Is it over and done with?'

'Yes,' she answered at once, giving him a direct straightforward look. 'But . . .'

'No buts, you have said it is over and that is good enough for me. Promise me you won't dwell on it, or let it come between us, put it from your mind and we shall never mention it again. Will you promise?'

'All right, if you say so.'

He stared hard at her, reached out and took her hand. She was trembling. He was so overcome by his feelings for her that he could not speak; he didn't want to frighten her off. For the moment things between them were very much up in the air, although he did feel he had made a little headway against her preconceived notion that all bosses were beyond the reach of their employees.

Eventually he said, 'My turn to tell you that there have been women in my life, I won't deny that, but I can say, hand on heart, there has never been anyone special.'

How badly he wanted to add, none that could compare with you. Should he use this opportunity and tell her exactly how he felt about her? How when he was miles away from her he wasn't able to concentrate on any business matters because his mind was full of her? Even sleeping the picture of her lovely gentle face and those big brown eyes crept into his dreams.

He made a sudden decision and threw caution to the wind. 'I love you, Rebecca. I think I have from the moment I first set eyes on you. Please, don't back away from me,' he pleaded. 'I will never ask you to be anything but what you are. I don't want to change even the smallest thing about you. I love you, I love *you*.'

Her face told him nothing. She didn't look pleased, she didn't smile, but she did hold out her hand which he quickly took hold of and raising it to his lips he kissed each finger in turn.

'Don't fret Rebecca, I won't hurry you in any way. We shall take things slowly, become firm friends. Please, just say you'll agree to that for the time being.'

This time she did smile, though her thoughts were in a turmoil. Her heart never told her the same thing two days running. He is sincere, it said most times they met, then when she didn't see him it became uncertain. No matter what he said his life was very different from hers. He lives in another world. I don't hanker after what he has, I only want him to be the lovely man that I am halfway sure he is.

Robert put a stop to her daydreaming. He pulled her close, hugged her tight before saying, 'Carrie will be wondering why I've kept you out in the cold for so long, shall we call a truce for now and go and have some tea?'

Becky closed the door of the summerhouse firmly behind her and took the hand that Robert was holding out to her, sighing softly under her breath as she did so. Me, Rebecca Russell, meaning that much to Robert Matthews! Whichever way she looked at it he was still a major shareholder of a great company such as Lyons.

Could there be any future for the two of them together? Only time would tell.

It was almost six o'clock when Robert finally said he had better see about getting her home.

'I hope we get to see you again soon,' Carrie said, hugging Rebecca goodbye.

'Keep in touch, a bit more often,' Maurice bellowed at Robert.

Becky got into the passenger seat and Robert closed the door. She leant out of the window. 'Thank you, Carrie, for everything,' she called, and Robert drove off with her still waving her arm.

'Have you ever regretted your decision to become a Nippy?' Robert half-laughed, breaking the silence.

'No, never. Not for one moment,' she replied.

'Achieved all your ambitions then, have you?'

Becky thought for a moment before saying, 'Not quite. I still have one.'

'And that is?'

Without hesitation she said, 'To serve at a function in the Mansion House.'

'Really?'

'Yes, really.'

'What in heaven's name is so special about the Mansion House?'

'Icing on top of the cake,' she laughed. 'The official residence of the Lord Mayor of London.'

They had driven quite a distance in complete silence and Robert was feeling pleased with himself for having broken the ice. 'You sound like Dick Whittington,' he said with a grin.

'Well then, all I need is a fairy godmother to grant my wish.'

'How about a demon-king?' They looked at each other and burst out laughing.

Then, looking very thoughtful, Robert said, 'It is not beyond the realms of possibility. In 1925, which is the year I think you joined the company, we did one of our biggest functions ever.'

'What, at the Mansion House?'

'No. The event was much larger than that. It was a banquet for the Freemasons, held at Olympia. As I remember, about eight thousand guests sat down and were served by more than a thousand waitresses, probably nearer thirteen hundred.'

Becky frowned. 'But surely that was before the Outside Catering Unit was formed.'

'Officially, yes. But as far back as 1921 the company was taking on such functions. Waitresses were drawn from Lyons tearooms up and down the country. Then demand became so great that it was decided to make outside catering a special entity. Young ladies were chosen.' He paused, took his eyes off the road for a second and smiled at Rebecca. 'You and your friend May Stevens were among the first to be given special training and from then on that branch of Lyons has existed independently.'

'Well I never! Kind of pioneers in the field of catering, would you say?'

'Yes, Miss Big Head! That is exactly what I would say.'

'Why, thank you Mr Matthews.'

When they had both stopped laughing, Robert was about to bring up the subject of when they would meet again but they had run into a patch of fog and he had to give his full attention to the main road.

'This is rather sudden,' he said gloomily.

Becky sat back in her seat and remained silent. The traffic was only crawling along and their headlamps, unable to pierce the fog, merely lighting up the blanket so that seeing through it was even more impossible.

Crossing Wandsworth Bridge was a bit dicey. The fog was worse, rising thickly and swirling up and around from the

Thames. When finally Robert drew the car in to the kerb in South Lambeth Road he breathed a sigh of relief.

'Are you coming in?' Becky asked quietly.

'No, I won't, thank you. I don't like this peasouper, I think it will get even worse before the night is out. I have to be in Manchester early tomorrow and I'm just wondering if it wouldn't be better if I got a train up tonight.'

Ever the gentleman, he got out of the car, came round and held the door open for Becky. She hesitated for just a moment and when he made no move she very quietly said, 'Thank you for a lovely day. I enjoyed it very much and I learnt a lot.' Giving him no time to answer she turned on her heel, opened the gate and walked up the path towards the house.

'Take care!' he called and before she had her key in the lock she heard the car drive off.

So that was it. It was over before it had even got started. Slowly she took off her hat and coat, walked down the long hallway and into the kitchen. The light was on, the fire well banked up and a note from Aunt Lil lay on the table. May was out for the evening with Stan Riley and Aunt Lil had gone along the road to play cards in a neighbour's house. She felt lonely. With only herself in the house, everything seemed terribly quiet.

Chapter Thirty

It was Wednesday, Becky's day off. Having decided that she would spend the day with her parents she had been up since seven o'clock. After a night of heavy rain the early part of the morning had been dull and dark, but now the sun had finally struggled through the murky clouds.

Becky stood at the window. The passing traffic was heavy and she couldn't decide whether to set off for the railway station now or to wait until the peak hour had passed. You've only got the one day, so there is no time to waste, she sensibly said to herself as she went back upstairs to put on her hat and coat.

Preoccupied with all that she was going to tell her family she hurried down the front path. She was surprised by the unexpected brightness of the sunshine reflected in the still-wet pavements, the glittering colours of the few leaves that were left on the trees in the street, and the funny damp smell. It was kind of a wet woolly smell, such as when Aunt Lil was drying jumpers indoors. It's coming on winter she reminded herself, thinking that autumn had soon come and gone.

Buttoning up the top button on her coat and pulling on her gloves, she drew herself up straight and was about to step out for Victoria Station when a familiar black car drew slowly into the kerb alongside her.

'Would the lady like a lift?' Robert Matthews had wound down the window and was smiling broadly at her.

Becky's heart gave a lurch. She was thrilled to see him. It was seventeen days since he had driven off in the fog, she knew because she had kept count, and never a word had she heard from him in all that time.

By the time she had calmed herself enough to at least say, 'Good morning,' he was out of the car and standing on the pavement in front of her.

'Rebecca, how are you?' He was wearing cord trousers, a thick Arran jersey and a three-quarter length car coat, and when he put out a hand and touched her cheek she could scarcely believe it. She even wondered whether she was dreaming.

He drew back from her. He still felt she was very special. Her sweet face, glowing with health, her eyes, such big dark brown eyes. 'You're looking very smart, are you going somewhere important?'

'I'm on my way to the station because I'm going to spend the day with my parents, but what are you doing here this time in the morning?'

He took her by the elbow, steered her towards the car and opened the passenger door, before saying, 'Get in, I'll run you to the station.' Given no time to protest she sank down into the leather seat and within seconds Robert was seated beside her and the car was moving.

She glanced at him. He looked tired, his blond hair wasn't as neat as usual, in fact it looked if he needed to visit a barber's shop and there was a night's stubble on his chin. All the same, just looking at him had her glowing inside. She had thought never to see him again, except at work and that would have been terrible, so near and yet so far. Not now. Here she was in his car, she could put out a hand and actually touch him. Instead she reminded him, 'You never answered my question.'

'And what question was that?'

'How come you were in South Lambeth Road at this time in the morning?'

'I wanted to see you.'

'Oh,' was all she muttered and he laughed loudly.

'Don't sound so surprised. I only got back to London early this morning and I have to confess I looked up the rota for today and discovered you were not on duty. So I came to find you.'

'But why so early?'

'I had a feeling you wouldn't waste a day, that you would be off out and about, so I took a chance hoping to catch you before you left. Good job I learnt early in life that the early bird catches the worm.'

Becky grinned. 'Oh, so I'm a worm am I?' Then before he had time to answer she called out sharply, 'We're at Stockwell, you've come the wrong way.'

'I know what I'm doing,' Robert told her, sounding just a little ill-at-ease. 'I couldn't let you get on the train, I would have only seen you for about a quarter of an hour.'

'But . . .' she protested strongly. 'I must go home, I sent a postcard to my mum, she'll be expecting me. Please Robert, take me back to the station.'

He turned his head and beamed at her with a grin as wide as the Cheshire Cat's. 'How long do you think it will take me to get you to New Malden?'

'You mean you're coming with me?' Becky twisted her hands, mentally hugging herself with anticipation. A whole day with him! Then almost immediately her thoughts changed. What would she do with him? Could she take him home? Would he want to spend a day with her family?

As if he had read her thoughts he said, 'I don't have to come to the house if you'd rather I didn't. I know I'm showing signs of travel weariness so I could go off somewhere, get myself a shave and a bite to eat and pick you up this evening when you're ready to leave.'

Becky felt awful! He had taken her to visit his lovely house in Richmond, she had eaten with Carrie and his Uncle Maurice and now she was acting as if she was ashamed to let him see where she lived, ashamed for him to meet her parents.

'I'm sorry,' she said quietly. 'You took me by surprise. You most certainly won't go off somewhere. My parents would love to meet you and I'm sure they will make you most welcome.'

Through Balham and Tooting down into South Wimbledon, Robert was whistling as he drove. On through Merton Park, up over Carter's Bridge and suddenly he said, 'From here on in I'm lost.'

Becky laughed. ''Course you are, you're a townie.' Then as if the thought had just come to her she exclaimed, 'D'you know I haven't any idea where you do live. Proper deep dark horse, aren't you?'

'Most of the time it seems as if I live in hotel rooms. I do have a flat in Chelsea, just off Cheyne Walk, very near the river. Lovely spot in the summer.'

It wasn't a nice life, she decided, pretty lonely being all over the place never having relatives to visit and chew over everyday happenings with. But there again he took part in all the glamour. Had this lovely car, ate the best food, stayed in the best hotels. Which side of the coin was best? Hard question to answer!

'Turn right up there,' Becky said, pointing to Burlington Road. 'We are now in New Malden and Albert Road is the first turning on the left.'

'I hope your parents won't mind me coming,' Robert said, not feeling so sure of himself now. 'Will your mother like me?'

'My mother likes everybody.'

Robert turned to face her and gave her a smile that was rather woeful. 'I hope so.'

With Robert by her side Becky looked at Albert Road through different eyes. Just the line of twelve terraced houses, with her home the last of the row. Each had its own little front garden with a short path that led up to the porch. Suddenly she smiled to herself, wondering what Robert would make of the fact that the house had no electricity. Wondered if he had ever had to put a match to a gas mantle when entering a room in the dark. What if he should ask to use the bathroom? She knew what her father would say: 'Sorry mate, we ain't got one.' They were the proud owners of a flush toilet, her mother's pride and joy, but it was positioned just outside the kitchen door.

Living here in New Malden did have its compensations and if Robert couldn't see them then he was a fool. There was no traffic rushing up and down Albert Road. Not even fumes from buses in Burlington Road. Only trams that ran on tracks. Facing their upstairs bedroom windows were green fields golden with gorse most of the year and at the end of the road there was Harry Horsecroft's farm with fresh eggs and plump chickens for the asking. The thought of Harry had Becky giggling as she wondered if he still liked to drink down at the Fountain pub. Did the locals still lift him up into his flat cart? And more to the point did his old horse still manage the short journey to bring him home?

Here in the country, not that far from London, everyday life was entirely different to the life that Robert apparently led. And that's a fact! Becky grinned to herself as Robert turned the car into the road where she had been born and brought up. It was as if it had all been planned.

Her father was walking down the street, wearing his railwayman's uniform, swinging his empty lunch box, his morning paper sticking out from his jacket pocket, just coming home from having done an early shift. Becky watched him; he was still a big, thickset man. She saw he still took long strides. Her mother was waiting at the gate, looking as always a quiet, respectable lady dressed in dark colours, her dress covered by a floral apron.

Becky had to swallow hard to get rid of the sudden lump in her throat as she watched her parents kiss and her father pat her mother's back as if to say everything is all right, I'm home safe and sound.

Becky was out of the car almost before the wheels had stopped turning. 'Hello, Mum, Dad.'

Her dad's arms were round her tight. 'Gosh I've missed you,' he crooned, lowering his head, kissing her.

'Rebecca,' her mother said, tears shining in her eyes as she pulled her daughter close to her chest.

The three of them were so absorbed in each other that Robert just stood quietly by and watched. Then Joyce Russell quite suddenly became aware of Robert standing there. She nodded her head towards him and raised her eyebrows to her husband. Robert was only a few yards away. But at once, realizing that this young man was with his daughter, he covered the short distance, held out his hand and said, 'I'm Rebecca's father, Joe Russell, pleased t' meet you, son.'

'I'm Robert Matthews, a workmate of your daughter's and I'm very pleased to meet you, sir.'

'Robert, this is my mother,' Becky said, wishing that her voice sounded more firm.

He held out his hand to Joyce. 'Now I know where Rebecca gets her colouring and good looks from.'

'Starting off with flattery, are we?' Becky whispered to him as her mother led the way into the house. 'And don't call my father sir.'

He nearly smiled at that but he was still feeling nervous. 'Well, don't you dare start on about me being one of your bosses,' he warned, stern-faced.

'I don't think either of us want to pursue that line of questioning,' she grinned.

'Take off yer coat, lad,' Joe Russell ordered, 'I'll not be long getting out of me uniform. I'll bet you a tanner mother has the kettle on an' the tea will be nicely brewed by the time I come downstairs again.'

Joyce was feeling slightly intimidated by this tall blond young man but she was determined not to show it. Becky followed her through to the scullery and as her mother bent over to lift the kettle, she whispered, 'You didn't mind me bringing Robert home, did you, Mum?'

'Of course not, luv. For my money you could bring who you like with you just so long as you come home yourself.' But to herself she was thinking what a nice solid, dignified young man this Robert Matthews seemed. Wide-shouldered and long-legged. Only one thing was worrying her. If he worked for Lyons teashops, he must have a very good position. That car that was standing outside their house hadn't come cheap. She just hoped that Rebecca knew what she was doing!

'Mum, the day will never dawn when I stay away too long. Shall I take the tray through?'

They drank their tea out of Joyce's large everyday cups. Had she known that Becky was bringing a young man with her she would have got the best china out of the cupboard and washed it. Through the kitchen window could be seen two lines of washing flapping high in the brisk morning breeze. And further down in the garden that backed on to theirs, Peggy James had also taken advantage of the weather and hung out snowy white sheets and pillowcases.

There was a tap on the kitchen door and it opened at the same time. 'You there Mrs Rus . . .' Tommy Ferguson, his head halfway round the door, looked stunned. ''Allo Becky,' he said, a smile full of pleasure lighting up his rugged features. 'I didn't know you was going t' be 'ome.'

'We didn't know ourselves, till yesterday,' Joyce hastened to tell him.

Becky got to her feet. She couldn't believe the difference in this old friend of hers. He always used to look so shabby, his clothes old, even threadbare. Today he was wearing a smart tweed coat and he had a scrubbed, clean look about him. Marriage clearly suited him. 'Hello, Tom,' she said, tilting her face up for him to kiss her. 'How are you an' how's Mary?'

'Mary's the reason I'm 'ere,' he said, turning to look at Joyce. 'She's into this bring and swap thing with Ella, you

know, over at the Central 'all in Tooting an' she said you'd
got a parcel of things for 'er an' would I pick it up this morning
seeing as 'ow I don't start me shift till two o'clock.'

Joyce gave him a big smile as he stopped talking and
caught his breath. 'I'll pop upstairs and get the parcel for
you, it's all ready. Pour Tom a cup of tea, Becky, I won't
be a moment.'

Becky and her father both remembered their manners and
each started to speak at the same time.

'Sit yerself down, Tom. This is . . .'

'Tom, I would like you to meet Robert Matthews, he's a
friend of mine.'

Robert smiled at Tom, stood up and held out his hand.
'Nice to meet you, Tom.'

Tom shook Robert's hand, his eyes never leaving Robert's
face. 'Becky an' I 'ave known each other since when we
were kids,' he declared, sounding as if he were jealous of
her new-found friend.

'Here, take your tea,' Becky said to Tom as he seated
himself down next to her father, 'I'll see if Mum's got any
biscuits in the barrel.'

'No, 'onest Becky, I don't want anything to eat, this tea is
fine. Mary will 'ave me dinner ready and I'll 'ave t' be going
cos I clock on at two.'

Joyce came back into the room, watched as Tom drained
his cup and then held out a large brown paper carrier bag.
'It's only a few bits and pieces I made, thought some little
kiddy might be glad of them, but there are some things in
there that Ella's mother has run up. She got the material
given to her so she said will you tell Ella they didn't cost
her anything.'

'Will do, Mrs Russell, thanks, 'ope t' see yer soon. You
too, Mr Russell. 'Bye Becky, luv.'

Tom was halfway to the door, carrier bag clutched under
one arm, when he stopped in his tracks, turned and looked at
Robert. 'You're a lucky bloke, mate. I 'ope you realize that.'

I do. Very much so, Robert said quietly to himself.

Robert's protests fell on deaf ears.

'There is more than enough to go round,' Joyce assured him as she spread a red-and-white checked tablecloth over the big table and placed a bowl of apples and bananas to one side. There were no more interruptions as the four of them sat down to what seemed to Robert an enormous shepherd's pie flanked by three dishes of vegetables. When he thought he had eaten his fill Joyce came back with a deep apple pie and a jug of custard. When they had finished, Becky made coffee and bringing in the tray she was happy to hear her father and Robert discussing the rights and wrongs of the railways. Presently Becky asked, 'Would you like to go for a walk, Robert? I'll show you the school I went to.'

It was her mother that answered, 'Good idea, and I'll have tea ready by the time you get back.'

Becky looked at Robert and they both groaned. 'Mother, we have to leave soon. Robert didn't get much sleep last night, he was working late and I have a six o'clock start in the morning.'

'But you must have some tea before you set off.'

Even Becky's dad laughed at that. 'Joyce, do you think they starve these young people up in London?'

''Course not.'

'Mum, we've eaten enough to last us at least until suppertime. We'll have a short walk and then we'll come back and have just a cup of tea before we set off. All right?'

When Robert and Becky had left them, Joe leant his elbows on the table and asked, 'Well what d'yer think, Mother?'

'He talks as if he went to a posh school, but really I couldn't help liking him. What d'you think?'

'Young days yet,' her husband warned her. 'Must say our Becky looks a darn sight better than she did a while back. Never did make head nor tail of that visit. Very nice having her and May here for nearly a week but I still say t' this day there was more went on afore they came down than either of them ever let on.'

'When will you be back?' her mother asked Becky as they stood in a group on the doorstep.

'Just as soon as I can manage it.'

'We'll be here,' her father told her, unnecessarily.

'You'd better be,' Becky laughed.

'I wish you didn't have to go,' her mother said feebly. 'A day isn't long enough.'

'Goodbye, Mr Russell, thanks for making me so welcome.'

''Bye Robert. Anytime. Be glad t' see you.'

'Thank you for my lunch, Mrs Russell, it was delicious. Just the job.'

'I'm glad you enjoyed it, Robert.' Joyce smiled broadly, reaching up her hand to pat his arm. 'Thank you for driving our daughter down; we appreciate it.'

Both her father and mother stayed on the doorstep watching the car drive away, until the taillight went out of sight as it turned the corner. They went back into the house, closed the door, and both were hoping for the same thing.

'If it's t' be, Mother, it will be,' Joe said optimistically. 'Things have a way of turning out for the best if left alone.'

Chapter Thirty-one

CHRISTMAS WASN'T VERY far off. Another two weeks and it would be here. Robert had offered to take Rebecca down to Richmond for both Christmas Day and Boxing Day. She wasn't clear as to whether that meant she was invited to spend a night there but in any case she wouldn't be able to accept the invitation. Her own family saw little enough of her as it was and she knew darn well that for her mother and her father Christmas wouldn't be Christmas unless they had their complete family with them.

All three sons and Becky herself knew that anyone they cared to bring along with them would be welcome to join in the festivities. There would be a few spare presents laid beneath the tree solely for that purpose.

Ella's last letter had been bursting with news of Margaret and baby Amy and what they were hoping for from Father Christmas. Peter was closing the shop at five o'clock on Christmas Eve and travelling down to Ella's mum. As a family they were staying with Peggy in George Road for the four days of the holiday. Shame really that Peggy's two sons, both married, had moved up to the Midlands and their mother only saw them once or twice during the summer months. Must be true what they say: a daughter's a daughter all your life, a son's a son till he takes a wife.

But that wasn't so with Joyce and Joe Russell. With Christmas dinner over everybody would gather for their tea and the giving and opening of presents in Albert Road. And that included Peggy James, Ella, Peter and their two little girls. Becky grinned to herself. What a crowd. Once again her mother would be in her glory. Both Jack and Tom, with their wives and their small sons, would be there. Their lives wouldn't be worth living if they refused to come. Even Fred, Becky's youngest brother, was bringing a young lady to tea with them this year. According to Ella's letter she had seen Fred in Tooting with a girl she knew by sight.

'Her name is Molly Cousins and she is a cashier in Tooting Co-op,' wrote Ella. 'Peter said that's probably how they met, seeing as how your Fred is manager of the Co-op Bakery, not that the bakery is actually in Tooting. Your Fred did introduce me to her and she seemed ever so nice, friendly like, wonder if they'll be getting married? Be lovely, wouldn't it? We haven't had a wedding since Tom and Mary's.'

Becky sighed. They were so busy at Lyons with functions right up to the Christmas and beyond. She would miss Robert, of course she would. Everybody gathered in my parents' house will have a partner except me, she thought dolefully.

This year not only were Aunt Lil and May coming down for Christmas, Stan Riley would be coming with them. Still, Christmas was a time for families, and Aunt Lil and May had become as much a part of the Russell family as had Ella and her mum over the years.

Her own mother seemed to have taken it for granted that she and Robert were going steady, as she put it, when she urged her daughter to invite him to join them. That wasn't exactly true. It wasn't like that at all. There would be days on end when she wouldn't see hide nor hair of Robert. Oh, he was very attentive when he was in London, Becky reminded herself hastily, but there were times when she was sure he was only offering her his friendship. There was never any question of romance. Robert did pay her compliments, bought her chocolates and flowers, had even taken her to see *Broadway Melody*, which was the first-ever musical film to have a sound track. It had been an amazing experience.

Yet he had never taken her dancing. And he certainly

never kissed her. Mostly when he appeared out of the blue she got an exciting, bubbly kind of feeling and more often than not she was tempted to make the first move. Throw caution to the wind and sling her arms around his neck and cry out loud, Robert, I've missed you. But she never did.

'You're mad, you know that, Becky. He's probably just as much afraid of making the first approach as you are and if you keep it up much longer we'll be pushing you down the aisle in a Bath chair,' May had laughingly warned her, when Becky had told her how she felt about Robert.

Becky felt it had been a lovely Christmas, as always. A truly family affair. Church early on Christmas morning with just her mum and dad for company and then home to sweat and slave helping her mum in the kitchen, preparing enough food to last an army for a week.

Christmas Day teatime!

'Leave the front door open till everyone has arrived,' Joe Russell had yelled up the passage. 'I'm sick an' tired of getting up to open it.' Then came the real chaos. Nothing short of bedlam.

'This is for you, Grandma.'

'No it isn't, that's Grandad's present.'

'Cor, look what I've got!'

'No need to look. Just cover your ears,' Becky said to May as young Joey began to beat the life out of his new drum and Ella's two girls were having a competition to see who could blow the longest blast on their tin whistles.

The floor was covered in wrapping paper, amidst screams crackers were being pulled and there were tears from Amy because her balloon had gone off bang. Fred and his girlfriend Molly Cousins, a slim, very pretty friendly girl with bouncing dark hair that reached to her shoulders, had made the day by announcing that come Whitsun they were getting wed.

'Told you so!' Ella laughed at Becky, as they huddled together with a hot mince pie and a glass of sherry in the far corner of the room. 'Get your needlework box out and start sewing, I expect Molly will want my two as her bridesmaids and we'll be expected to make the dresses.'

'Hasn't she got any family of her own?' Becky found herself asking.

'Only an elderly aunt she lives with.'

Becky looked hard at Ella. 'How come you know so much about her when me an' most of the family have only met her for the first time today?'

'Running a swap shop in Tooting you get all sorts coming along. Young mums with kids. Old people looking for a warm coat, even men who are out of work are glad to swap a garden tool or such-like for a thick pullover or a stout pair of boots. I don't need to buy the *Wandsworth Borough Herald* no more, I get all the news, good and bad, first-hand.'

Becky chuckled several times as she relived that Christmas teatime. That had been five days ago though. As for Robert, she hadn't seen him since the first week in December, he hadn't been in London once in all that time. Well, not to her knowledge anyway. Robert was, however, on duty for the New Year's Eve gathering that Becky and May had been allocated to. In comparison to some such functions this New Year's party was small. It was held on a private estate in Banstead, which wasn't far from Epsom; the house was old and very grand, standing alone within acres of parkland. The catering and service ordered from Lyons was for three hundred.

'Surprised to see your Robert Matthews in attendance for a do on such a small scale,' May whispered out the corner of her mouth to Becky as they prepared to serve the first course in what to ordinary people was still a vast dining hall.

'He is not my Robert Matthews,' Becky muttered under her breath.

'Oh no? Well you could have fooled me. My guess is he wangled himself in here tonight simply because he knew you would be waiting table.'

Becky half-believed her. Maybe that is what you want to believe, she chided herself many times during the course of the evening as she and the other Nippies served delicious hot food, including thick slices from whole sirloins of beef and great roast turkeys, not to mention the mouth-watering sweets that had all been prepared by Lyons chefs in the customer's own kitchens on the actual premises. As the evening wore on it was more wine than food that the waitresses were offering the guests.

It was quite late when the sound of a band playing could be heard coming from another part of the house and the host rose to his feet to suggest that his guests might like to adjourn to the ballroom, promising them that drinks would still be available and that champagne would be served five minutes before midnight in order that they might toast in the coming New Year of 1929.

May and Rebecca were just folding the last of the tablecloths when Robert Matthews walked in on them. 'All silverware is checked and packed,' he told them, 'glassware also with the exception of the crystal champagne glasses which half a dozen of the girls are now setting out. I think it's time you two got yourselves something to eat. Come along, Miss Timson or Miss Paige will show you where to go, leave that, our drivers will come in to carry the linen out to our vans.'

May smiled her thanks and moved off and Becky would instantly have followed but for the restraining hand that Robert put on her arm. 'Come hell or high water, Rebecca, I want to be near you when twelve o'clock strikes. I am going to make a New Year's resolution, one that I intend to keep, and I very much want you to hear it.'

Becky was finding it difficult to match the soft caring voice Robert had just used to the loud voice that had barked firm orders to all and sundry during the course of the evening.

The New Year was at least half an hour old before Becky caught sight of Robert again. She had been kept busy serving her share of the champagne and right now she felt she would have sold her soul just to be able to drop down on a bed and sleep for days on end.

'You look tired,' Robert said softly as at last he had her to himself. 'And no wonder. It was a very busy evening, and every one of you girls sailed through it with flying colours.'

'Shall I tell you something in return, Robert? I'm not the only one; you look deadbeat yourself.'

'I know,' he sighed, 'I haven't been to sleep for thirty-six hours and it is just beginning to hit me. But I was determined to be wherever you were this evening. Getting to see you is getting harder for me than performing a miracle.'

Becky found herself smiling in spite of the sadness in his tone.

He took her by the shoulders. 'Listen carefully: I, Robert Matthews, am determined to travel to far-flung stations no more. I have served my time and served it well. In future I shall be London-based and my free time will coincide with yours or I will know the reason why.' Then, for the first time ever, he kissed her. Gently, full on the lips.

As she gasped, half from surprise and half from sheer delight, he drew back and looked deep into her eyes. With great tenderness, he took her in his arms, lowered his head and placed his lips on hers and kissed her again. Very firmly this time.

Her first reaction, as he loosened his hold, was to shout out his name at the top of her voice but she didn't give way to that pleasure.

'Happy New Year, Rebecca.' Even his voice sounded like a gentle caress.

With her heart thumping against her ribs she smiled. 'I'm glad you're going to ease up a little,' she told him. 'Have time to do some of the things you enjoy.'

'Some of the things we both enjoy,' he said, returning her smile. 'Now hurry up, the coach will be waiting for you and,' he paused and his smile changed to a wide grin, 'if I'm not mistaken I can see Miss May Stevens peering out from behind that pillar. I wish you both a very, very happy New Year. Good night, Rebecca.'

'Good night, Robert, I wish you all the best for the New Year.' Then because her heart was still thumping away like mad and she couldn't think of anything else to say she walked away from him to where an excited May was eagerly waiting for her.

'Now tell me he is not your Robert Matthews,' May whispered, and as Becky laughed May added, 'You're not the only one who has seen the New Year in with a kiss, I didn't even know Stan was one of the van drivers tonight until he crept up behind me.'

'Oh May, isn't that lovely. I am pleased for you.'

'And me for you,' May assured her as she held out Becky's winter coat for her to put on.

Then with their arms linked they went out to get on one of the coaches that would drop each and every Nippy off within yards of her own front door. Lyons were very particular when it came to providing transport for their special waitresses who had been out on late-night assignments.

Chapter Thirty-two

FOUR MONTHS OF 1929 had gone by before Becky's ultimate ambition was to become a reality. Even then she couldn't quite believe it.

'There couldn't be much more of a palaver if this do was taking place at Buckingham Palace instead of at the Mansion House,' May grumbled to Becky as they listened to yet another set of instructions.

'Have to say I agree with you,' Becky whispered. 'If it were an Army officer planning a military operation he couldn't do so with more precision than this lot.'

'A system of signals has been designed to instruct not only the kitchen staff but also you girls who are part of the waiting staff.' Efficient was how Miss Paige sounded this morning, and she also looked the part.

'Been on a diet I shouldn't wonder,' May muttered as they wrote in their notebooks.

'No, I don't think so, it's more the suit she's wearing, a straight skirt makes all the difference. It not only slims her hips down, it makes her look a bit taller.'

'If your conversation is so interesting perhaps one of you should come to the front of the room and let us all hear what it is you have to say.' Both May and Becky found themselves feeling flustered as they raised their heads to see Miss Paige standing within a few feet of where they were sitting.

'Sorry, Miss Paige,' they uttered in unison.

'Very well, with your permission I shall continue.' Silence hung heavy over the entire room. There wasn't a girl that would have dared to even smile. Small Miss Paige might be, friendly and kind, but when she was in charge of any business matter she let it be known she would brook no interference. 'On this occasion,' Miss Paige began, her voice loud and clear, 'the banquet area will be set out in seven sections, each one to be designated by a different colour. You girls coming originally from Coventry Street Corner House will be banded within the yellow section.'

Pencils could be heard scratching the pages as the colour yellow was recorded. God help the girl who forgot on the day.

'Very well, ladies, that will be all for this morning. I shall pin a notice on the board when I have further information, giving you the time and date of our next meeting.'

In the noise of chairs being scraped back and everyone talking at once, May grinned at Becky. 'On the warpath today, wasn't she? And it was our scalps that we nearly lost.'

'It's not too late to lose them yet, you shouldn't be so cocksure, Miss Stevens, even walls have ears at times.'

May turned her head quickly and let out a gasp of relief. 'Oh, it's you Mr Gower, where did you spring from?'

'Never you mind, I suppose it's not your fault if your tongue runs away with you at times. What I am here for is to offer both of you an invitation, though the Lord above knows whether you deserve it or not.'

Becky turned her most beguiling smile on and softly said, 'Get on with you, Mr Gower, you know full well we're your two favourite waitresses in all of London.'

'Well!' Mr Gower's look was stern, but only for a second, then he smiled broadly. 'There's not much to choose between either of you, is there? What I've come to tell you is that in three days' time I shall be going to the Mansion House to iron out the last few details. As a special favour, not that I think you deserve it,' he paused and smiled, 'you may both come with me and if we're lucky we shall be taken on a tour of the Mansion House. At worst you will be able to have a thoroughly good look at the Egyptian Hall which is where the banquet is to be held.'

May and Becky looked at each other in disbelief.

'D'you really mean it or are you having us on?' May asked.

Becky in her usual quiet way merely mumbled her thanks.

'You don't have to thank me, it's Mr Matthews who has done the arranging. He said the Lord Mayor's residence had always held an attraction for you, so here's your chance. I would appreciate it if you didn't make our visit widely known although we really shall be going on official business.'

'You will, don't know about us,' May answered cheekily.

'Yes, well. Best bib an' tucker and all that and best behaviour especially you, May. No telling the footmen or whatever that you like his knickerbockers.'

All three of them showed signs of amusement as they went their separate ways.

Rebecca saw him before he saw her.

He stood with his back to her, but then he moved his head slightly and she caught a glimpse of his face and her heart missed a beat. Oh Robert, she sighed to herself. He looked so at home in these regal surroundings of the Mansion House, so well turned out and yes, so handsome. Even more amazing was the fact that he was actually talking to the Lord Mayor of London.

Mr Gower hovered a few feet away. She and May were standing next to an enormous potted palm, one of the many exotic plants used to enhance the entrance hall of this beautiful building. Becky stepped back further behind the plant so that she was partially hidden from view herself but able to observe the two men quite clearly. She felt afraid. Out of her depth. She could never hope to meet Robert's standards. His life belonged in an entirely different league to her own. Becky, May and Mr Gower had arrived at the Mansion House about three-quarters of an hour ago, and, after having been greeted by a female member of staff, Mr Gower had left them to be taken on a tour of the premises while he climbed the main staircase to the first-floor office in order to settle the business that was the reason for him being here.

Much to the amusement of Miss Jackson, their prim, neatly-dressed, very businesslike guide, Becky and May were gasping in surprise at almost regular intervals as they made their way through the building.

'Underground cells!' May exclaimed in sheer amazement.

'Oh yes,' Miss Jackson quickly assured her. 'The Lord Mayor is also the chief magistrate of the City, and at times the Mansion House serves as a police court, though as you can see the comfort of the cells is dubious.'

'How many cells are there?' Becky enquired, her eyes roving over the heavy wire grid that covered the door of each cell.

'Eleven in all, ten for men and one for women,' Miss Jackson told them.

That statement had both Becky and May giggling, and when May laughingly stated, 'Well, we all know men are the worse villains,' even Miss Jackson tittered.

It was, however, the great tapestries and the enormous Waterford glass chandelier that hung in the Egyptian Hall that brought forth the biggest gasp of admiration from each of the girls.

'When your company has set up this room in readiness for the coming banquet it will take on an entirely different atmosphere,' Miss Jackson guaranteed as she shook hands with them each in turn before taking her leave.

'Fancy spending your working life in a building such as this,' Becky mumbled more to herself than to May as she watched the trim young lady walk between the magnificent tall gold pillars which rose to the domed ceiling of the Egyptian Room.

'Yeah,' May said cheekily to Becky, 'especially if she lives in a tenement block in the East End and has to go home to that every night!'

The two girls had to quickly smother their mirth as Mr Gower appeared to escort them back to Coventry Street and the reality of working for their living.

Becky hadn't seen Robert leaving and apparently he wasn't going to put in an appearance on the night of the Mansion House banquet. Ah well. So much for his New Year's resolution! On average she had seen him once a month this year and there had been nothing exciting about any of those meetings. Robert had, at all times, seemed preoccupied though Becky had felt a little disappointed to see him looking so fit and pleased with himself. At least he had given her an explanation of sorts.

'Arrangements take time,' he had said, 'especially if they are to have a lasting effect. Believe me, Rebecca, I am getting the situation sorted out.' With that she had to be content. Even more frustrating was the fact that when she did see him all he greeted her with was an affectionate kiss on the cheek. I get more from my brothers, she reminded herself ruefully, at least they give me a hug as well.

The night of the actual banquet had finally arrived, and Miss Jackson was proved right! The Mansion House was a blaze of light and the Egyptian Room had been truly transformed. The whole setting was inspiring, the guests elegant.

The men wore evening dress, their ties black. The women were clothed in glamorous gowns, their jewels sparkling beyond description. It was an extremely dignified gathering with the cream of London society.

There was no time for reflecting on who or what was what. Even with one Nippy placed behind every other chair the waitresses had their work cut out to serve each and every varied course that was on the menu.

The colour coding of the staff worked well. Each area of

the great dining hall was served by its own chefs, superintendents and other staff all the way down the line.

It was an experience not to be missed, was the unanimous verdict of every waitress on duty that night as they prepared to serve the final champagne for the Loyal Toast.

What a contrast! Becky thought as she read her mother's letter for the third time. What a funny affair this coming wedding of her brother Fred and Molly Cousins was turning out to be. Perhaps funny wasn't the right word, she chided herself. It wasn't Fred's fault any more than it was Molly's fault that it kept being put off because they just didn't have the money to buy furniture, bedding and whatever else it took to set up home together. Never mind paying for a wedding reception.

Upper-class folk never gave a thought to such details. They called in a catering firm and the strain was taken from them. All they had to do was pay the account at the end of the day.

There was two ways of looking at the problem, Becky kept telling herself. On the one hand you had all this hunger and poverty with thousands of unemployed up and down the country and on the other hand perhaps she ought to be a whole lot more grateful. If it weren't for the upper classes Lyons wouldn't be so successful. The ordinary Lyons teashops which could be found in every high street from one end of the country to the other did bring catering to the masses, so to speak. Even the poor lashed out now and again and had a cup of tea and perhaps a toasted bun.

But it was the rich that held the private parties. And the great thriving businesses, of which there were far too few, that held banquets and suchlike purely for professional reasons. Entertaining clients was a way of selling their merchandise and without their custom you'd soon be out of a job. Becky nodded her head, knowing her thoughts were all too true, but that didn't help Fred and Molly with their plans.

Neither did King George or Queen Mary and the way they rode around London in their open carriage! Becky threw back her head and laughed loudly as that reflection came to mind. It had been last week; she and May had been trying to cross the main road into Hyde Park when the police had held pedestrians back. As the carriage passed they'd had a clear sighting of the King dressed in full ceremonial uniform, the Queen in her fur-collared coat, laid open to reveal all her jewellery and as always wearing an elegant veiled hat. They certainly were a regal couple but the sight of them was a sharp contrast to the demonstrations and the hunger marches which were being organized up and down the country.

Molly and Fred's wedding was to have been at Whitsun but as that was now only three weeks away and no plans had been settled it seemed unlikely. In any case the weather during April and on into the first few days of May had been ghastly. Day after day the rain lashed down. It was supposed to be spring yet both May and Becky, and a good many more people, hurried to work bunched up in macintoshes and scarves and their hats pulled well down over their ears.

Aunt Lil was forever yelling for them to hurry up and close that front door because when it was open gusts of cold air swept down the passage causing smoke to billow out from the kitchen range.

Both May and Becky were longing for a cup of hot tea as they got off the bus feeling grateful that at least, for the moment, it had stopped raining. Becky stretched her arms above her head and yawned as May put her key in the door and let them into the house. Straight away they heard voices and May automatically looked at her watch. 'It's just on half past six, sounds as if Aunt Lil has visitors. Any ideas?' May asked as she hung her outdoor clothes on the hall stand.

'Only one way to find out,' Becky replied, leading the way down to the kitchen.

'Good God!' She couldn't have been more taken aback if

there had been a trio of angels sitting there. 'What on earth are you doing here?' she asked, looking first at her father and then at her mother, hoping for good news but fearing she'd hear bad.

'London isn't that far away from New Malden,' her father chided as he rose to his feet. 'We don't exactly live in the back of beyond.'

Becky allowed herself to be kissed, all the while looking over her father's shoulder at her mother's smiling face and the rather amused look on Robert Matthews' countenance.

'I felt I wanted to see you,' Robert said by way of explanation as he too got to his feet. 'I thought I'd miss you if I came to the Corner House, so I came straight here. Your aunt kindly invited me in.'

Rebecca was touched. 'I'm glad she did,' she said, doing her best to reassure him. 'Were you already here, Mum?'

'Yes love. We wanted to discuss your brother's wedding with you, and with Lily and May. We've had a family pow-wow an' yer dad thought it best if we found out what you think of the outcome.'

'An' it being me day off . . .' her father added.

'I'll leave you all to it.' Robert placed the cup and saucer he had been holding back on to the table and took a step towards the door.

'Robert, you'll do no such thing,' Joe Russell declared.

Robert stopped and looked back. 'Sit down, lad,' Aunt Lil said encouragingly. 'If you're gonna get an invitation t' this wedding I'd say it concerns you almost as much as the rest of us.'

May spluttered, pulling her handkerchief down from her sleeve and covering her mouth. Oh, it was so funny to hear Robert Matthews being told to sit down in her aunt's kitchen.

Becky's heart leapt with gratitude. She could have hugged Aunt Lil. Robert had done exactly as he was told, whereas he could have been out of the front door and halfway up the street by now and God knows when she would get to see him again. Oh God bless you, Aunt Lil. Though what the hell her father was thinking of she couldn't fathom! Robert invited to her brother's wedding! Well she'd lay ten to one he'd shy away from that.

Robert was watching the different reactions flick across Rebecca's face and as their eyes met he grinned and he mouthed the words, 'I've missed you.'

'Any tea in that pot?' May asked.

'I'm just about to make a fresh pot an' get us all something to eat. You can come and help me,' Aunt Lil replied, nodding her head in the direction of the scullery.

I get the message, good luck, said the silent wink May gave Becky as she slid by her.

Becky went to sit down next to Robert before she eyed her parents. 'So, you came up to London in order to tell me what you've all decided to do about our Fred getting married. Is that right?'

Joe Russell made an exasperated face. 'Give me an' yer mother a chance to set the facts out before you get uppity, young lady.'

Robert smiled at them all, took Becky's hand in his. 'Your parents are going to do the wedding from their house, the catering as well, seems as if everyone has agreed to pitch in and help, even me,' Robert told her, as though it were the most natural thing in the world for him to be involved in their family plans for her brother's wedding.

Becky was dumbfounded. She couldn't find words to say. She leant back in her chair, closed her eyes, counted to ten and then opened them again. Her parents and Robert were waiting for her to comment.

'We wanted to tell you before we went ahead so you an' May can make sure you put in for the time off. What d'you think?' her mother asked.

'I think,' she told them, 'that you are all being very kind, acting with the best of motives, but have you given the idea enough thought?'

'Enough thought?' Joe Russell exclaimed crossly. 'Here we've all been, trying to work out ways an' means ever since Christmas. It's bad enough for yer brother but it's even worse for his lass. We all feel right sorry for Molly, don't we, Mother?'

'Yes we do,' Joyce agreed. 'I went t' see that aunt of hers, didn't get me anywhere.'

Becky felt duly chastized. 'Why, what's wrong with Molly?'

'There's not a thing wrong with Molly,' her mother said quickly. 'It's that selfish old aunt of hers. She took Molly in when she were a child but that girl has repaid her ten times over an' now because she wants to get married the aunt is playing up something rotten.'

'Leave it out, Joyce,' Joe Russell pleaded. 'I said I'd get it sorted out and I have.' Turning full face to Becky he said, 'They live in Derrington Road, Tooting and by rights the council could put the aunt into a one-bedroom flat once Molly leaves home. Instead they're going to let a friend move in with her, a lady about the same age as herself, so that solves that problem though she still refuses to have anything at all to do with the wedding, won't even come to the church, so she says.'

Becky smiled to herself, a little bit grateful that she hadn't been living at home while all this wrangling had been going on. Robert saw her smile and decided it was time to be practical. 'Why don't you tell Rebecca what you have in mind for the reception?'

That was right up Joyce's street. She was going to relish having the whole family come to her house for this wedding.

'Well, if they set the date for the second Saturday in June, hopefully the weather will have settled down and we can have the wedding breakfast in the garden.'

'And if it rains?'

'Yer dad has been promised a loan of two very big tents an' all the neighbours have come in with the offer of chairs an' tables. Ella's mum, Ada an' Joan, that's me two daughters-in-law,' she said by way of explanation to Robert, 'and meself will manage the food very well. It won't be the first time we've had a gathering in Albert Road.'

'But Mum . . .'

Becky was allowed to get no further with her protest; her dad thought it was about time he was allowed a say. 'I've already knocked part of the fence down between Peggy's garden and ours, been meaning to do it for years an' never got round to it.'

Robert was laughing outright but Becky was astonished. 'How the hell does knocking the fence down come into all this?'

'A gate, if you'll listen an' let me finish,' her dad said, undoing the buttons of his jacket and loosening his tie. 'Peggy has come up trumps, as usual, not only going t' help with the food but agreed that your brothers can set up a bar in her garden an' she's promised t' sleep some of the guests. Can't see many of you going home on the night of the wedding, though there'll be a few that will have to kip down on the floor.'

Becky had begun to give up hope that she would ever be able to make head or tail of her family's plans. They'll be telling me next that Robert is going to sleep in one of the tents alongside all me brothers!

Aunt Lil saved the day by coming back into the room bearing a tray set out with teacups and two piled-up plates of bread and butter. 'Do you like fish an' chips?' she asked Robert and when he grinned and nodded his head, she said, 'Thank God for that. I've got the plates in the oven and May's gone up the road to fetch some for all of us. Joyce, give us a hand to clear and lay this table, will you?'

Becky didn't know where to look. This was a nightmare.

First off her parents had invited Robert Matthews to Fred's wedding. A wedding that was going to be done on a shoestring because nobody could really afford a big splash. He had admitted he was going to be involved, in what way she didn't yet know and was too scared to ask. Now, to top the lot, Aunt Lil had calmly asked if he liked fish and chips! Not would you like to stay and eat with us, which would at least have given him the opportunity to excuse himself, but put in a way that took it for granted that he would. The way things are going, she muttered beneath her breath, you shouldn't be surprised if May comes back with six individual parcels and Aunt Lil hands them round still wrapped in newspaper!

It wasn't like that at all. In fact as Becky looked round the smiling faces of those seated around this big kitchen table and watched as May passed the vinegar bottle to Robert the contents of which he vigorously shook over his meal, she felt relaxed and happy.

Aunt Lil had done them proud. Cod and chips, crisp and golden, served on her best dinner plates with the red and gold band round the edge. Bread and butter on side plates that were part of the same dinner service, hot strong tea in cups that also matched and fish knives and forks that only saw the light of day on high days and holidays. It was a meal good enough for a king and by the look on Robert's face as he tucked into his plateful he was really enjoying it.

The only pleasure that was denied Becky that night was saying good night to Robert while on their own. She had felt frustrated when he had insisted that he drive her parents to the railway station, adding that it wasn't out of his way at all.

The three women stood in the lighted doorway and watched as Robert settled Becky's mum and dad into the car. Then with a final wave from him the car was quickly out of sight.

'Well, well, well!' May couldn't resist the teasing. 'Staff room memo tomorrow I think. Mr Matthews, top executive, dines with waitress in South London on fish an' chips.'

'I'll kill you if you so much as breathe a word,' Becky cried, doing her best to sound serious but not quite succeeding.

'You just let me know if she opens her mouth even a crack and I'll do the job for you,' Aunt Lil declared as the three of them set to to do the washing-up.

Nevertheless it was two happy girls, arms around each other's shoulders, who later went thoughtfully up the stairs to bed.

Straightening her cap, checking her stocking seams, Rebecca was heading for the morning inspection, her mind full of last night, Robert and fish and chips, when standing in the corridor she noticed Mr Gower, beckoning to her in a manner that could only be described as secretive.

'You are early,' he told her in a low whisper, 'come into my office, it won't take a minute.' Ushering her before him, he quietly closed the door and when she raised her eyebrows in question, he smiled at her. 'Rebecca, last night I was given a piece of news that I think will be of great interest to you.'

Oh yeah. An awful lot seemed to have taken place yesterday, she was saying to herself as she sat down in the chair he offered her.

'Mr Gerald Palmer now lives in Delhi! How's that for good news?'

'Delhi?' Her mind was a blank.

'Delhi as in India. Headquarters of the Indian Government.'

'Oh!' Becky suddenly realized what he was talking about.

'Yes, he's out of the country. Out of your hair. I just thought I would let you know.'

'Thanks, Mr Gower, you really are a guardian angel of mine, and I do appreciate it. Do you have any details?'

'Yes, if you're sure you want to hear them.'

'Make it more positive if I know he has really gone.'

'Oh, he's really gone all right. Got a job in the Embassy out there. Don't suppose the fact that Amelia Claremont, now Gerald's wife, and her parents can boast friendship with people in high places has anything to do with the appointment,' Mr Gower told her, not even trying to keep the sarcasm from his voice.

'I don't care if the devil himself got him the job,' Rebecca laughed. 'Do you know, Mr Gower, it has been my one dread that Gerald would turn up some time, mainly late at night, pleading his cause and still wanting me for his bit on the side.'

Mr Gower looked shocked. He hadn't realized that Rebecca could sound so bitter. 'You shouldn't talk about yourself like that, young lady. It isn't nice and what happened was not your fault.'

She smiled, a lovely gentle smile that showed the real affection she felt for this older man who had, over the years, become her friend.

'In many ways it was my own fault, Mr Gower. I have a friend, we've known each other since we were children, she got pregnant and married in haste. Love soon departs when poverty comes in the door. Both she and her husband found that out. I didn't want that to happen to me. I was going to marry a rich man. Gerald Palmer singled me out, and I was daft enough to think I loved him and that he was the answer to all my prayers. I couldn't have been more wrong, could I?'

'Never mind all that now. It's in the past and I just had to tell you that the man was no longer around for you to worry about.'

'Thank you again, Mr Gower, I'd better get a move on, mustn't be late.'

'I'll come with you, my presence will ward off any questions but, Rebecca, as we walk, please, tell me what happened to your friend?'

'Her name's Eleanor, she is still very much my friend. Her husband's name is Peter. They have weathered most of their storms and he now works for himself repairing boots and shoes. They have two lovely little daughters, Margaret and Amy, and I am godmother to both of them.'

'What a lovely happy ending to your story,' Mr Gower said, putting out his hand and laying it on her shoulder. 'And just you remember, the future is what counts and it is going to turn out just as good for you as it has for your friend Eleanor.'

'Yes, I'll remember,' she answered him, a smile lighting up her lovely big brown eyes.

Chapter Thirty-three

'WE DON'T WANT to go to school,' Ronnie, the eldest of Becky's two nephews, declared. 'If Uncle Fred is getting married tomorrow an' you all say you've so much to do why can't Joey an' me stay off and help?'

Ada Russell looked at her mother-in-law and moaned. 'Joan and I were going to wait and take them to school before coming here but we thought it best to get an early start.'

'You did right, and they've been good boys,' their grandmother told them placidly, 'but you do have to go to school. Now, finish up your toast and get yourselves ready.'

Ronnie gave up, lapsing into silence. Joey drank the last of his milk. It was nice here in his grandmother's house with so many aunts all getting lots of food ready for this wedding. Much better than going to school. He decided he might as well have a try. 'Grandma, it's Friday and we don't do much at school on a Friday. I could carry things for you, I'm six now, and Ronnie could help Grandad put up the other tent cos he's only got one up so far.'

Joyce reached across the table and rumpled his curly hair. 'Yes, I know you would both be a big help, but you have to go to school. And anyway your Grandad will meet you both this afternoon and bring you back here. There will still be plenty of jobs for each of you to do.'

Both little boys sighed deeply.

Becky looked at her mother and then at the faces of her brothers' wives, then turning her gaze on to her two nephews she smiled at them lovingly. Her thoughts were confused. While in London she was happy enough in her job. She counted herself lucky to be part of the everyday hurly-burly of London. Now, though, she watched enviously as Ada and Joan rubbed a flannel around their sons' faces and ran a comb through their hair. She saw the expression in Ada's eyes as she said, 'Auntie Joan is going to take you but I'll be here when Grandad brings you back this afternoon.'

Ronnie held up his face for his mother to kiss him, then came to where Becky was standing. ''Bye Auntie Becky, I can't wait for t'morrow t' come, can you?'

Becky squeezed his hand, kissed his cheek. 'It will be a grand day, well worth waiting for, you'll see.'

It was late in the afternoon and all the women were beginning to feel it was time that they stopped, made a pot of tea and put their feet up if only for half an hour. The front door was propped open. What with the kitchen range banked high because the oven was in constant use and the oven and all burners on the gas stove in the scullery going full pelt, the house was hot and airless. June was living up to its name, flaming June, and while that was great for eating outside and probably for those who would end up sleeping in the tents tomorrow night it didn't go far towards helping today.

'Good God!' Joyce Russell lifted the corner of her apron and wiped the sweat from her forehead. 'There's a Lyons delivery van drawn up outside the house,' she called to the cluster of women, who having taken chairs outside were sitting near the back door escaping from the heat of the kitchen.

May looked across to where Becky sat. 'Are you expecting a van?'

'There's a black car drawn up behind it now,' Becky's mother called before Becky had time to answer May. 'You two better come an' see what's going on.'

Raising her eyebrows in question Becky got to her feet, wishing that she had time to take off the apron her mother had insisted she wore, followed by May, who had on an enormous wraparound flowered overall. They went through the house and out into the street.

Stan Riley was busy taking boxes from the back of the van and stacking them on to the pavement. Robert Matthews was having a hard job trying to manoeuvre out from the back seat of his car a large square white box. Both men saw the girls, stopped what they were doing, looked at each other and burst out laughing.

'Oh, very funny,' May said, looking directly at Stan. 'So we look a sight and so would you if you'd been slaving away all day as we have.'

Robert did say, over the top of the white box he had managed to extract from his car, 'Hello girls, glad to see you've been making yourselves useful,' but he said it in an absent sort of way as he crossed the pavement and walked straight up the garden path towards the house. Becky watched as Stan kissed and hugged May. Not knowing what else to do she turned and followed Robert.

The big kitchen table had been pushed right back against the wall and was already more than half-covered with meat platters, plates, dishes and bowls of every shape and size. Joyce rushed to clear a space so that Robert could dump his box.

'That's just the bottom tier,' he told Joyce. 'There is another smaller one and I have a silver stand and the knife in the car. I'll fetch them.'

Robert left the room and Becky stared at her mother. 'You didn't tell me he was bringing the wedding cake!'

'He asked me not to.'

'Did he?' was all she could think of to say. 'I'll give him a hand to carry the rest in.'

'Stan will probably need some help.' Joyce flung wide a white tablecloth, spreading it out to cover more than half of the dishes on the table.

'Mother!' Becky was obviously exasperated. 'I didn't think they were coming down until tomorrow but you aren't a bit surprised to see them, are you?'

'No.' Joyce pushed a strand of hair off her face, and heard both of her daughters-in-law laugh. But it was Peggy James who came to the rescue, by saying, 'Calm down, Becky, what you didn't know you couldn't worry about and they're here now so let's be grateful. From what your mum tells me that Robert of yours has been very generous.'

'Oh.' Becky was lost for words. She was beginning to get flustered, and no wonder. Not only was her boss coming to her brother's wedding, it seemed he was providing the wedding cake and God alone knows what else. A Lyons van outside their front door, would you believe, and Stan Riley delivering goods! She breathed a sigh of relief as Robert came back into the room accompanied by her father.

'Finished now till Tuesday afternoon,' Joe Russell said cheerfully as he greeted the room full of women. 'Seems I'm just in time. I found these two townies outside and Jack and Tom aren't far behind. They've stopped at the paper shop for some cigarettes.'

Joyce bent over the kitchen range and lifted the lid of a huge black saucepan, picked a long-handled spoon from the hook where it hung beside the fireplace and stirred the contents. 'Good job I got up early and put this pot of braising beef on, with a load of vegetables and some dumplings it should be enough to feed us all. So busy seeing about things for tomorrow we nearly forgot you'd all be coming in starving.'

Becky watched her mother with admiration. She saw her as a small warm-hearted lady who asked nothing more out of life than to have her family around her and to know that each and every one of them was healthy and happy. She would go to great lengths to see that they were.

Robert had come to stand beside Becky. She still felt self-conscious about him being here. 'I'm sorry it's like this, all the chaos, we seemed to be doing all right and then somehow it's got disorganized, but it will all turn out all right in the end.'

'You bet yer life it will,' her father broke in. 'While your mother is getting the veg ready, you girls see about setting the table up in the front room and me and the lads will get that other tent up. First one went up with no bother last night.'

The men trooped out making for Peggy's back garden. 'I've still a few things to fetch from the car,' Robert whispered to Becky. 'Come and help me, please.'

'What do you think of that?' Robert asked her, stepping away from his car and holding out a reel of wide white satin ribbon. 'It's to decorate the two cars your brothers have hired for tomorrow and for my own because your father has said I may have the honour of driving him and the bride to the church. It's nice that he's giving the bride away, isn't it?'

'You seem to have become very much involved in all this.' Inwardly Becky was furious, especially so with her father. Now he'd got Robert acting as chauffeur! 'I haven't been told anything, you turn up with the wedding cake and all plans set out nicely, how do you think it makes me feel? The fact that my father has been using you.'

'Oh no.' Robert sounded shocked. 'I offered, I very much wanted to help, believe me, Rebecca, to be caught up in all this excitement is a real pleasure for me. I think I must have led a very dull life before I met you and your family.'

'But my father never said a word to me.'

'That wasn't his fault. I asked him not to.'

'And Stan Riley? How does he come into it? What on earth is he doing with a delivery van?'

'Rebecca, it is no great deal. Stan isn't staying the night, he's just dropping off a few items of food and some trestle tables. He'll be getting an early train down in the morning.'

'Are you staying the night?' Becky steeled herself for his answer.

'Well, the wedding is at ten o'clock, have to be up early, lots to be done at the last minute and your friend's mother, Peggy, has offered me a room for the night. Be childish to refuse, don't you think?'

Becky nodded. It was wonderful to have him here, but suddenly she felt a little shy. 'I'm sure we're all very grateful to you and I'm flattered that you even accepted my parents' invitation. The only thing is . . . well . . .'

'You're going to tell me that the sleeping arrangements won't be what I'm used to?'

'Now you're reading my mind. But, yes, that is what I'm doing my best to point out.'

'Rebecca, have you ever stayed in a hotel bedroom on your own? It can be the loneliest place on earth. Soulless. Occupied only by strangers. A room that no one leaves a mark on. No one speaks to you, except to pass the time of day. I know what goes on in that head of yours. You think I am wealthy. Far better-off than you are and when you're with me you act as if you are treading on eggs. Afraid to say what you really feel.'

The dejected look in Robert's eyes was too much for Becky. She wanted to throw herself at him, comfort him, but he wasn't finished with her yet. 'It is you that are so much better-off than I. Both parents still alive, loving you, protecting you. A great big family of relations and friends. Somewhere to go when you have time off. Birthdays and events to look forward to. Let me tell you now, when your father shakes my hand and in parting says to me, "Take care now, son, come and see us soon," I feel part and parcel of his family and I go away believing that he cares, that he would be pleased to see me again. And that, Rebecca, is a feeling that no amount of money on earth can buy.'

'Oh Robert, I'd no idea.'

Robert smiled. 'Confession time over, come on, I'd better go and give your brothers a hand.'

By eight o'clock everybody had been fed, Stan Riley had taken his leave and everything else had come to a stop. Because it was such a lovely warm evening everybody had gathered in the garden. Jack had hung a dartboard onto the wall of the shed and amidst much ragging and suggestions that Fred should get to bed early because he'd need all his strength tomorrow when he became a married man, a serious game was in progress.

Joe Russell was partnering Robert against his two sons; the game now on was the decider in a match of three games. It was a very close call with Jack and Tom having won the first set and Robert and Joe taking the second.

'Sixteen you need for the game, Robert,' Fred, who was doing the marking, called out.

'G'on my son, show them what you're made of,' Joe Russell cheered him on.

Robert poised his dart, double eight he needed, he aimed, missed by a whisker scoring only eight. He flexed his muscles, took a deep breath and his second dart found its mark. Double four. 'Yes,' Joe Russell yelled and his sons patted Robert on the back.

'That's only for starters,' Tom told him, 'we'll show you what's what tomorrow.'

Robert's eyes lighted on Rebecca. Although she was smiling she looked bewildered. If he could have read her thoughts at that moment he would have laughed. Once again he had her confused. Darts were very much a public-house game. She wouldn't have put Robert down as a darts player. She was learning more about this man with every minute that passed.

May Stevens' thoughts were running along the same lines. She'd bet a week's wages that there wasn't one person at Cadby Hall who had ever seen Robert Matthews throw a dart. God, but he was a dark horse! Out of the top drawer, no mistake about that. She hoped to God he wasn't dilly-dallying with Becky, seeing how the other half lived, so to speak. She didn't think so. The look in his eyes as he watched Becky move about had to be seen to be believed. Either he adored her or he was a damn good actor.

'I thought I might go for a short walk before going

to bed.' Robert was standing in front of her, his eyes twinkling.

Becky brightened. 'Oh, do you want company?'

'I hadn't counted on going on my own.'

Five minutes previously she had been thinking if she didn't get to bed soon she would fall down. Now she couldn't wait to get out of the house.

It was a lovely evening, very still and warm. They went out the front way and crossed over the road to the fields that lay beyond. They had walked quite a distance without any conversation.

'Are you all right?' were the first words that Robert spoke.

'Yes.'

'You are a ninny. You worry over the slightest thing. You never wanted me to come to your brother's wedding, did you?'

'No.' She felt she had to tell him the truth. 'Somehow I just couldn't see you fitting in. Please, don't get me wrong, I love my family but all three of my brothers are rough diamonds.'

'Oh Becky! There are times when I feel like giving you a good shaking. I wouldn't be here if I didn't want to be. I was really pleased when your parents invited me.' He sighed and shook his head. 'How many times must I spell it out for you? I think you have a wonderful family. I envy you. And more to the point I love you.'

Suddenly she was in his arms, his mouth gently covering hers and she had such a feeling of pleasure as his tender kisses gradually became more long and lingering. Robert was here. She was in his arms and once more he had declared that he loved her.

Her feelings had changed. All her fears and doubts had been swept away. Robert wanted her and she wanted him. It no longer mattered that they had been born into different backgrounds, they were a young man and a young woman who loved each other. This feeling of wellbeing had happened so suddenly, so naturally, that she kept her eyes closed wanting it to last for ever.

All too soon he took his arms from around her and stood back. Rebecca shook her head slowly from side to side as though disbelieving what had actually happened.

'Now tell me you don't want me here,' he said in a voice that was little more than a whisper.

'Oh Robert,' she gently sighed, 'I want you here, of course I do.'

'Rebecca, will you tell me you love me?'

She took a step forward, standing on tiptoe to kiss him. Robert pressed his face to hers. 'Say it Rebecca, please, go on, say it out loud.'

'I love you. I love you, you know full well I do.'

'That'll do for me,' he laughed. 'Now we had better turn back before I forget myself and let my feelings run away with me.'

Hand in hand they walked, not saying a word, but neither of them could hide the smile that was on their lips nor mask the sparkle that shone from their eyes.

Chapter Thirty-four

'MORNING, MAY.' BECKY raised herself up on her elbows, screwing her eyes up against the sunshine that was pouring in through the open curtain. 'Doesn't seem as if we've been in this bed for more than a couple of hours.'

'I know what you mean,' May mumbled. 'Yesterday was a long day.'

'I was going down to make us some tea but I changed my mind.'

'Why?'

'Just lift your head off that pillow an' you'll know why.'

May half sat up. 'What on earth is all the fuss and commotion about?'

'I can't imagine and I'm not yet in a fit enough state to go and find out.' Becky reached for the glass of water that had stood by the bed all night and had a little drink. She set down her glass and shook May's shoulder. 'You'd better move yourself. I'm sure I heard Stan's voice coming from downstairs.'

'Oh blast,' May grumbled, 'that's all I need for him to see me before I'm properly awake. But Becky, I would like you to know that I'm ever so grateful to your mum an' dad for inviting Stan to your Fred's wedding.'

'Hoping it will give him ideas, are you?'

'Well, I could ask the same question of you, Becky. You really like Robert, don't you?'

Becky grinned. 'He seems so different when he's away from London, not dealing with the company.'

'He looks different, if that's what you mean, not such a

stuffed shirt. Real handsome I thought when he arrived yesterday, grey flannels, no jacket, short-sleeved shirt open at the neck showing golden hairs on his chest. I'll tell you what, if he was to walk about like that in the Corner House you'd have to fight the girls off. They'd be forming a queue to get at him.'

Becky looked amazed. 'I've never thought of him like that, he always seems kind of shy.'

'Maybe with him it's a case of once bitten, twice shy. It isn't only us girls that get taken for a ride, you know. Men like him are considered a jolly good catch, and you never know, someone might have put out the bait. But what are we going on about? As you said, we'd better move ourselves and you, Becky Russell, ought to be thanking your lucky stars that whatever befell Robert before you met him he had the sense to wriggle free.'

Deep in thought Becky crossed the room to the marble-topped washstand, poured water out of the enormous jug into the bowl, took off her nightdress and began to wash herself. When she had finished she wrung out her facecloth, placed a dry towel ready for May and said, 'Now you get out of bed and come and wash. There's a hell of a lot still to do before we set off for the church.'

Already the front room had been stripped of furniture and against the two main walls long trestle tables had been set up and were already spread with appetizing joints of meat and ham, savoury pies, bowls of salad and delicious-looking sweet flans and trifles. Away in one corner of the room a square table had been covered with a white linen cloth the drapes of which reached to the floor. Dead centre stood one of Lyons' silver bases, such as were used in very highbrow functions, and on it had been placed the two-tiered wedding cake. To one side lay the long silver-handled knife.

'Thank goodness we don't have a wedding in the family every day of the week,' Joyce Russell said to her daughter as she hurried into the room, her arms full of serviettes. She set half of the pile down at one end of the long table and then the other half at the other end.

'Mum, I'm sorry we're so late coming down, I meant to wake up early.'

'Never mind, lass, take May and the pair of you go an' get some breakfast. It's all laid out on the kitchen table, sorry there's nothing hot but you can make yourselves some toast an' boil eggs if you like.'

'But Aunt Joyce, you've all done so much already,' May protested. 'You're making us feel guilty.'

'Don't worry,' said Joyce. 'Go on, do as I say and then you can see to the flowers and buttonholes and perhaps you can go through to Peggy an' see if she needs a hand with the beds or whatever. Or perhaps yer brothers need a hand setting out the drinks. By the way May, your aunt is in the scullery, she's baking fresh rolls, so don't go banging any doors.'

May and Becky looked at each other and together they scurried to the door. Once out of her mother's sight Becky burst out laughing and May did the same. Becky was the first to quieten down. 'What did my mother say when the question of Fred an' Molly getting married was first discussed? "Seeing as how they haven't got much money we'll put on a bit of a do for them." Makes you wonder what would have happened if they had decided to give them a posh wedding, don't it?'

'Oh, Becky, I know we can't help laughing but they're all doing their best, working like slaves if you ask me. Time they come back from the church everyone will be so worn out they won't want to eat or drink.'

'Don't you believe it, May, if the world were coming to an end and there was still food about my brothers would stay behind to see it off. What makes me laugh is the difference between getting this reception ready and when we're doing one for Joey Lyons.'

'Yeah, all order an' precision and we get paid for doing it.'

*   *   *

Peter and Ella arrived with their two little girls just as Becky and May were on their way upstairs to change. They came in a small van that belonged to a man who had a greengrocery stall in Tooting market. Margaret and Amy, together with cases that held the dresses, petticoats, shoes and bonnets they would later wear to the wedding, plus cloth-covered dishes of food that were Ella's contribution to the feast and pretty posies of flowers for the girls to carry as they were to be bridesmaids, were packed in so tightly at the back that it took some time to get them out.

When that had been achieved safely, Becky led them through to the garden and told them to play in one of the tents until it was time for them to get ready. Their grandmother James, seeing them from her kitchen window, flew out to greet them.

'Come upstairs with us,' May said to Ella. We haven't got that long, it's turned half past eight already. We can all get dressed in your room, can't we Becky?'

'Of course we can,' Becky agreed.

May sat at the dressing table, wrapped in an old dressing gown that belonged to Becky's mum, and brushed her copper-coloured hair. What to wear had been no problem for her: she had bought her outfit. Unlike Becky, Ella and both of their mothers, neither she nor her Aunt Lil were clever with their needle. When she had finished doing her hair, and applied a little make-up, she squirted herself with the toilet water that Becky had bought for her birthday. Then she stepped into the long silk skirt that had all the colours of a peacock's fan in it, put on the plain blouse that picked up the predominant shade and added a wide belt.

'I love it,' Ella declared.

'Yes, that was a good buy,' Becky agreed. 'It makes you look so tall and slim.'

'You both look good too,' May said, settling herself on the edge of the bed and gratefully accepting one of the glasses of sherry that Ella had poured out for each of them. 'You two work wonders with a length of material.'

'Old habits die hard,' Ella told her, 'it was a case of needs must when we were young, weren't it, Becky?'

'Certainly was, luv,' Becky quickly agreed, 'but I've never regretted those days, stood us in good stead. By the way, when I popped downstairs for that bottle both your mum an mine were almost in tears.'

'What?'

'Oh don't worry, nothing has gone wrong. It's just that all the kids are dressed in their finery and the sight of them, even the boys, looking like little angels was all too much for their emotions.'

'What did you think of Margaret and Amy's dresses?' Ella asked.

Becky took a sip of her sherry and laughed. 'Fishing for compliments, are we?'

'Well, you had seen the dresses half-finished but the bonnets you made for each of them did the trick. Even Peter was bowled over when they had a dress rehearsal. I'd swear he had tears in his eyes. They did look so sweet, it was enough to choke you. You'll know what I mean when you have kids of your own.'

Becky looked at May. 'Best get on downstairs,' she said practically.

Everyone was waiting nervously, the women in the front room, the men lining the passage. Fred put his head round the door. 'Mum, how long since Dad left?'

'Oh do stop worrying, son. Yer dad went down to Mrs Dywer's before eight o'clock just t' make sure that Molly was all right, and it's only about ten minutes since he left ready to go.'

'Nice of your neighbour to let Molly stay the night in her house,' Aunt Lil commented.

'The cars are ready,' Ada called, making a grab for her Ronnie.

'The first car is for you, Ella, and the bridesmaids,' Joan shouted, making sure she had hold of her Joey's hand.

'Come on Mum, you can get in the back with us, we'll put the girls on our laps and Peter can sit up front with Jack.' Ella was issuing instructions left right and centre.

'For goodness sake get in the car,' Tom pleaded, 'I'm driving the second car so I'll bring me mum and Aunt Lil. May and Becky can ride in the back.'

'What about me?' Fred sounded right doleful and everyone burst out laughing.

'No one's likely to forget the groom, yer silly sod. Let's just get all this lot settled in the pews and then I'll come back for you seeing as how I'm your best man. The bride won't be on time, I'll stake me life on that.'

The room had emptied when Tom came running back into the house. 'Hey little brother,' he yelled, 'I haven't got a buttonhole and Gawd Almighty neither have you. I'll take mine with me, get yours fixed on quick an' by the way you're entitled to one drink t' steady yer nerves but don't go hitting the bottle hard while you're waiting, remember you've got vows to make.'

'Jesus, is it worth it!' Fred sighed as he made for the sideboard and reached for the bottle of whisky.

'What's keeping the bride I wonder?' May said, turning her head to look back to the open door of the church.

People were rustling in their seats; the church was very full. Becky had her eyes to the front. Her two brothers, Tom and Fred, were moving about nervously, each with his hands clasped behind his back.

There was a commotion in the porch and organ music filled the church, then Molly came slowly up the aisle on Joe Russell's arm. She looked absolutely lovely. Just as a bride should look. A floating figure draped in pure white, with Margaret and Amy in the palest of pink, their bonnets trimmed with the same fresh summer blooms as those in the posies they carried, treading carefully behind.

Becky glanced to where Ella and Peter sat. They were

holding hands, their eyes were fixed on their two daughters and anyone would have to be blind not to see how proud they were. Those two had endured some hard times yet over the years they had found the meaning of true love.

How could she ever have thought that what she had felt for Gerald Palmer had been love? It had been an obsession. Nothing more.

As the bride drew level with her, Becky smiled at what was to be her new sister-in-law and Molly smiled back. A smile full of joy, Becky thought enviously. And then Molly looked ahead to where her husband-to-be stood and her eyes lit up. Fred, looking so much like a younger edition of his father, though not so tall, his dark hair slicked down, his new grey suit immaculate, his eyes seeing no one but Molly.

The moment the bride reached the altar rail, Robert slid into the pew alongside Becky, took her hand in his and squeezed it. While they waited for the sound of the organ to die away Becky looked at Robert. 'Doesn't Molly look happy? You can feel she and Fred are right for each other.'

Robert nodded. He felt pretty happy himself, right now. This family he had come to know had a kind of permanency about them. You could feel the happiness the minute you walked through their front door. There was a companionship about them that he had never known in his life.

Fred's voice was loud and clear. 'To have and to hold from this day forth, in sickness and in health, till death us do part.' He gave the words their full meaning and more.

Becky glanced up at Robert, catching him unawares. He was looking down at her with such an expression in his eyes that it was all she could do to sit still. She knew, at that moment, if you loved a person it didn't matter whether he were king or commoner. There were no rights or wrongs to loving someone. You just did. She knew it now. Full well. She wanted to belong to Robert, to spend her whole lifetime with him, to make him happy.

The ceremony was over. The organ swelled its music out

again as the newly-weds came down the aisle. Molly's face was wreathed in smiles. Becky leant forward, looking to where May and Stan were sitting. May was wiping tears from her eyes but even so Stan had his arm around her shoulders. The tears May was shedding were tears of joy.

Outside the church the sun shone down from a cloudless blue sky and chaos had returned again to the Russell family. The mood of the wedding guests was now bent on enjoyment. The air was filled with laughter and excited screams from the children as the folk with Brownie cameras endeavoured to get them to stand still long enough to have their photographs taken. On the grass and pathways friends and neighbours were milling about but there were two couples who were oblivious to all that was going on around them.

Robert drew back, then changed his mind and placed his lips against Rebecca's once more. It was a kiss that needed no explaining. It said all that was in his heart. Every ounce of feeling that he could drag up from his body was there to be passed from his lips to hers.

'From today, no more buts, no more long partings, you are my sweetheart, my love for the rest of my life.'

The words were said in little more than a whisper but Rebecca heard every word. Her only answer was to breathe, 'I love you, Robert.'

Robert gently took her hand between both of his and then lifting her fingers to his lips he held them there for a long moment before saying, 'Rebecca, will you marry me?'

Only yards away Stan Riley was making the same request to May Stevens.

Ella, her own mother, Becky's mother and May's Aunt Lil stood in a group and the same happy smile was on each of their faces.

'If I 'adn't seen it with me own eyes I never would have believed it. Look at them, happy as two pairs of larks,' Aunt

Lil declared. 'When it all boils down it's feelings what count in the end. Just goes to show, don't it?'

Ella laughed out loud as arm in arm, across the grass, came Rebecca and Robert, followed closely by May and Stan.

Turning back to face the three women, a broad grin still on her face, Ella said, 'I'm going to predict that before this year is out Lyons are going to lose two Nippies and Robert and Stan are each going to gain a wife.'

Thank God the sun was shining, Becky was thinking to herself. They never would have got this host of friends and relatives inside the house.

'Went off extremely well I thought,' Robert said. 'I have to tell you yet again, Rebecca, you are so lucky, you have a truly wonderful family.' Side by side they gazed down the garden to where Becky's mum and dad were surrounded by grandchildren, each looking as pleased as punch.

Suddenly Dolly Ferguson's voice rang out. 'Would yer look at that!' she yelled, her big bosom heaving as she pointed her finger to where young Joey was feeding Amy with pieces of chocolate. 'Talk about starting young!'

'Going to take after all the Russell men, eh Dad,' Tom, Joey's father, commented. 'We've all had an eye for the ladies.'

The whole garden echoed with laughter.

Mary and Tom came to where Rebecca and Robert were standing. 'Me mum's still got a mouth on her, ain't she, Becky?' said Tom.

Before Becky had a chance to form a reply, Mary said, 'Yeah but I've lived t' know she's got a heart of gold to go with it.'

'How about that,' Becky exclaimed. 'I think it's wonderful the way things have turned out for you two. You both get on well with Dolly now, don't you?'

'Yeah, you get t' learn in this life it takes all sorts,' Mary wisely answered. 'Smashing day though, great t' all be together like this. Come on Tommy, you can get me a drink.'

Becky turned to Robert. 'If ever there were two youngsters who started out with everything set against them it was Tommy Ferguson and Mary Marsden and look at them today. They live for each other.'

Becky felt Robert's arm go round her shoulders, and placing his lips close to her ear he whispered, 'The sooner you set a date for us to be married the sooner we'll be able to give your parents another grandchild.'

Becky's heart missed a beat as she pictured herself holding their own baby. Again she looked across at her parents. Years ago they had found the formula for happiness and contentment. She turned her eyes to look up at Robert and she knew she, too, had found the man who could give her just that.

Within six months the forecast Eleanor had made outside the church had come true.